Red Tales

Red Tales

In The Beginning

Kirsten Tautfest

Copyright © 2008 by Kirsten Tautfest.

Library of Congress Control Number: 2007908515
ISBN: Hardcover   978-1-4257-9819-2
           Softcover   978-1-4257-9811-6

All rights reserved. No part of this book may be reproduced or transmitted in any form or by any means, electronic or mechanical, including photocopying, recording, or by any information storage and retrieval system, without permission in writing from the copyright owner.

This is a work of fiction. Names, characters, places and incidents either are the product of the author's imagination or are used fictitiously, and any resemblance to any actual persons, living or dead, events, or locales is entirely coincidental.

This book was printed in the United States of America.

To order additional copies of this book, contact:
Xlibris Corporation
1-888-795-4274
www.Xlibris.com
Orders@Xlibris.com
44388

To Section 8
"If you can't be an athlete, be an athletic supporter."
Principal McGee, "Grease" (1978).

Chapter I

Saturday, April 4, 1998: Molly Karver arrived at Soldier Field for the debut of the Chicago Stampede. The sun shone warmly on her face. Unfortunately, she was not a ticket holder. She smiled and looked over her charges. It was her job to make sure the spectators were seated properly, among other duties.

She pushed her loose chestnut hair behind her ears and began her spiel to her ushers. She could tell that her crew couldn't give a rat's ass about soccer. They were all into the big three American sports: football (the bastard child of rugby), baseball and basketball. Oh well, as long as they did their jobs, she did not care what they liked. Just as long as they kept those other sports' ball caps off their heads. Per company policy, only the company cap or the Stampede cap was allowed.

There were other things on her mind. Her long-term relationship was starting to fall apart. Molly had walked in on tattooed guitar stud Jack getting groped by a large-breasted groupie. The look on his face said it all. Molly just was not "good enough" for him anymore. Fine, whatever. Molly threw her hands in the air. Better classy than trashy.

Her friend Renata walked by. "How is everything?" she asked.

"Still thinking about Jack."

"What do you mean?" Renata cocked her head.

"I'm not so much still shocked as just pissed off," replied Molly. They descended the stairs to field level.

"Oh, just dump his ass, Molly."

"I know. I really should. But he's the type that would try to cling to me if I did that. I don't need a clinger in my life. I've done that before. The FBI had to instruct him to stop trying to contact me."

"Oh yeah, I remember you telling me about that asshole Todd." They reached the area called the track in between the field and the stands. "Have you gotten a chance to see any pictures of our team? There's a young single hunk playing."

"Like I have a shot in hell at that."

"No, no, think about it. You start seeing someone else. That would piss Jack off to no end. He would dump you, Molly. That's the way you want it, right?" Renata always over animated.

"Yeah, but not with number whatever. There's no way." Molly shook her head.

7

Renata looked over the field as a few Stampede players were coming out for pre-game warm-ups. "That's him coming out now, number 14, Ian Harris. They call him Tigger because of his ability to win headers."

As he emerged, Molly's eyes fell on him. She almost sensed that he was looking at her. Ian stood 5'10", with strong well-developed legs. "Renata, he's probably got a girlfriend. Any man who looks that good probably has a trophy girlfriend stashed somewhere."

"Why can't it be you?"

"Are you kidding? Me? A trophy wife? No way. I don't look that good. I'm only 5'4", a B-cup & have an ass." She patted her own rear end.

Renata laughed. "I don't mean be his bimbo. I mean be *his*."

"Well, if it happens, it happens, okay. Don't you dare do anything stupid. You know how anal this company is about talking to the celebrities, be they sports or whatever."

Renata shrugged. "Fine, whatever, but I see that you can't take your eyes off him."

The lot at Soldier Field was not too full. Kick off for the inaugural match was still about three hours away. Most of the cars, though, seemed to belong to museum patrons. At least the party Jacqueline Harris was in search of was on the far end of most of the museum folks. She parked her car as close to the tailgate area as she could. She grabbed her wallet and her supporters group ID. She had registered with the group two weeks ago via the Internet. She was number 35, at least it said so on her laminate.

Performing one last check in the rear view mirror, she pulled a few strands of long hair away from her face and tucked them neatly behind her ears.

In the distance she spotted a pair of redheaded blokes in kilts. Beer in hand, they chatted with other fans on the edge of the tailgate area. Jacqueline was drawn to them. She recalled seeing them in the bar at one of the preseason parties, but never talked to them. Of course, they were not clad in kilts then.

"Hey, guys," she began casually. "I saw you last weekend at the bar, but didn't get a chance to introduce myself." Deep breath, so far so good.

The shorter and younger one spoke first. "Hi, I'm Matt. This is my brother Colin."

"I'm Jackie."

Matt bent over and reached inside a cooler. "Would you like a beer?"

"Yes, thank you," she said. Matt twisted off the cap and tossed it inside the cooler. The act of not littering impressed her. Most guys tossed their garbage wherever they felt like. She took a long swig of cold brew. "So where are you sitting?"

"We're all in section 12 with the supporters group. You?"

"Same. I was able to get seats on the first row."

"Season tickets?"

"Of course!" She lifted her bottle for a toast.

Colin asked, "So, how long have you been a soccer fan?" He had the more masculine face, but with baby softness. His legs were much more developed than his brother Matt's. His close-cropped, conservative hair was a sandy blonde with red highlights that glinted in the sunlight. Metal framed his eyes. But as handsome as Colin was, Jackie felt more pull toward Matt. Maybe it was his boyish charm. Her intuition told her that Colin was probably spoken for anyway: a man who looked that good had to be.

"I played a little as a kid, then things got too rough in junior high so I just became a fan," Jackie replied.

Matt said, "I played in high school, got a college scholarship for soccer. Then late in my senior-year season, I broke my foot."

"Ouch," said Jackie cringing.

"Yeah," Colin put in, "I told him to stay off that motorcycle." As he lifted the beer bottle with his left hand to his lips, Jackie saw a gold wedding band glint in the sunlight. Bummer, she thought.

"No, it happened in a match. Just one of those freak things," said Matt.

"That sucks. So what happened with the scholarship?"

"The college was nice enough to let me keep it. I guess they liked my grades, too. They tried to talk me into getting into coaching, but that's just not me." Matt's eyes met Jackie's. She felt a little spark, but did not put a whole lot of stock into it. She flirted with men often enough to know it usually meant nothing. It was just an innocent way to get her kicks. "So, Jackie, what did you mean by too rough? You look like a tough girl." He looked her up and down, eyes following her every sturdy curve.

"I mean the competition. I wasn't as good as some of the other girls and found myself on the bench a lot. Besides, I started getting more involved in stuff like quiz bowl, academic stuff."

Matt listened intensely. He found himself attracted to her but he wanted to take things slow. There was no reason to hurry. He would see her all season.

Ian Harris came out of the locker room. His girlfriend awaited him. Deanna was an aspiring actress and model, so she looked good enough, and could look him in the eye. But something was missing. She had argued bitterly with him about moving to Chicago. He had been in Los Angeles playing for the LA Stars. She was happy there, but not Chicago. Deanna had taken time off to help him get settled and promised to stay for the first home match, but after that it was back to LA. Ian could sense the end of the relationship drawing near.

Ian gave Deanna a quick peck on the lips. "Go on up to the skybox, honey. I've got to warm up."

She nodded. "Good luck."

He could see in her eyes that it was over. Another quick, but mechanical kiss, he turned to head to the playing field. He could not worry about Deanna right now. He needed to focus on the game.

As he emerged from the tunnel, his day suddenly grew brighter. In the distance, he saw two ladies standing and chatting on the track. He felt the eyes of one on him.

Yes, he would play this match for these strange, yet compelling women, not Deanna. Mental focus problem solved.

As kickoff approached certain groups of supporters entered the stadium: the banner crew, the drummers, those who just needed to use the john. Jackie, Matt and Colin stayed behind to help pick up the tailgate area. Just as the FIFA anthem began to play, the clean-up crew entered and found places in Section 12.

Colin handed Jackie a brew in a plastic cup. She thanked him and took a drink. She tried not to make a face when the Budweiser hit her palate. She preferred imports and microbrews.

The national anthem was sung. About halfway through, Section 12's voices were heard throughout the stadium. The main drummer started a build up as the song approached end. A small African-American man hopped up on the concrete ledge in front of Section 12. He balanced himself with one foot braced on a seat back in the front row. He began a chant to help motivate the team during kickoff. Many referred to song sheets that the leader had passed out at the top of the steps as the fans entered the section. The chants and songs were simple for the most part, based on nursery rhymes and other familiar tunes.

Jackie had heard many while watching English Premiership matches on Fox Sports World. All one had to do was change a team name, city name or player name. She noticed that Matt was just as familiar; he did not refer to the crib sheet either.

Across the south end of the stadium, in Section 9, was an equally, if not more boisterous group of fans. Polish flags flanked a banner that read "Chicago Ultras". At kickoff, a smoke bomb was let off. A lime green horde descended upon them. The group of fans scattered like roaches when the lights are turned on. Jackie craned her neck to see what was going on.

Matt cracked, "I suppose I shouldn't let off my smoke bomb after we score."

Jackie smiled and turned her attention to the action on the pitch.

At halftime, the score was 2-0 Stampede over the New York Mad Cabbies. Ian had an assist on the first goal and made a spectacular defensive move that sparked the second. Things were going well.

He headed toward the northeast corner of the field to go to the locker room. There she was, working in some type of security position, backing up the usher standing sentinel on the stairs leading from the stands to the track. He flashed her a big smile. Blushing slightly, She gave him a thumbs-up.

Yes, he thought, I must get to know this woman.

Just before halftime, Molly took a back up position on the stairs between sections 24 and 26. Groups of kids had started to gather there to try to get autographs from the players. The poor usher was struggling to keep them back. Molly kept one eye on the crowd and one eye on the field action. Several kids screamed out players' names to try to get them to come over and sign various items: "Novotny! Come here! Hey, number five! Can we get your autograph? Cristobal!" And so on until three or four girls' soccer teams screamed in unison at a deafening level: "Tigger! Tigger!"

Molly turned both eyes to the field gate and saw Ian Harris coming off. He smiled. She gave him a thumbs-up. Her eyes followed him into the tunnel until she could not see him anymore.

About midway through the second half, Molly spied Renata. "Hey, I think you might be right."

"About what?" Renata replied. She took off her hair elastic so she could redo her ponytail.

"Ian, number 14."

"See, I told you. So what happened?" She blinked in anticipation.

"He gave me a huge smile—the flirty kind, not just a friendly one." She watched the action on the field. Ian had the ball and was blowing by the New York midfielders as he headed for the goal. He passed it to number 12, O'Connor. It was a perfect leading pass and O'Connor was barely onside. O'Connor dribbled around his defender and passed it back to Ian who was struggling to stay out of an offside position. As soon as the pass was released, Ian flew past the Cabbie and with a high right foot drove the ball into the net. The keeper lunged, but to no avail. Ian had scored his first goal for the Stampede.

Renata and Molly jumped up and down with the rest of the fans. "Oh my god!" Molly exclaimed, "That was beautiful!"

"That's your man," Renata grinned broadly.

"Don't even go there, girl. It's probably never going to happen."

At the 88th minute, Molly grabbed some ushers and stationed them in key spots on the stairs. She stood on the track and kept an eye on the gaggle of boys and girls leaning precariously over the cement wall.

The final whistle sounded. The score would go down in history as 4 to 0. The Cabbies exited the field via the northwest corner field gate. They hung their heads, as they should—their performance was abysmal.

The press circled like vultures waiting for the players to come off via the field gate near Molly. The Spanish-language television station caught Ian Harris. They asked him questions about the match. Molly strained to listen. She knew *un poco español.* To her surprise, Ian answered in perfect Spanish.

Several players stopped to sign a few autographs. Most signed 5 or 6, and then hustled into the locker room for a well-deserved shower. Striker number 9, Brendan "Iceman" Glazier, signed until Molly thought his hand was going to fall off. The platinum blonde forward was a favorite with the young starry-eyed girls. Several had brought his Nike poster for him to sign. He obliged with a broad smile.

Ian soon joined him. By this time, Molly had moved around to watch their backs. She continually scolded the kids who tossed down shirts and balls and other items. Still, she assured that everything down was autographed before it went back up.

Kid by kid, Ian and Brendan worked their way along the wall. Molly floated nearby and provided general assistance.

Brendan spoke, "I'm going to head on in." He turned and half-walked, half-jogged down the tunnel.

Ian finished signing the last one. He turned around and looked Molly straight in the eyes. "Thanks for watching my back."

Still in very professional work mode, but internally struggling to stay there, she replied, "You're welcome."

Ian looked down at her work ID. "You're Molly?"

She swallowed and nodded.

"I'm Ian, nice to meet you." He extended his hand. She shook it, still sweaty. His fingers lingered on hers for a moment. A surge of electricity coursed through her body.

"Nice to meet you. You played a great match."

He smiled. "You don't have to make with the standard niceties." He ran his hand through his hair. "Would you like my autograph?" he asked with a wink.

"I can't. It's against the rules."

"You're not asking. I'm giving." He scanned the ground; he picked up a ticket stub. "Let me use your Sharpie."

Without saying a word, she handed it to him. He signed the ticket and handed it to her. "See you soon, Molly."

She watched his form disappear down the tunnel. Only then did she look at the ticket stub. He signed it: *Molly, Call me. 312-555-9090. Ian Harris, #14*

After the match, a group of fans gathered at The Filling Station, a nearby pub, to celebrate the team's victory.

Jackie was one of the first to arrive for the after party. She secured a table, a waitress, and a drink. In waves, a sea of red began to fill the small sports bar.

A flashy character sat down next to Jackie. He wore a red cape trimmed in rainbow and gold. The number on the kit he wore under the cape was 14. Jackie had seen him before, at the tailgate and during the match.

"Oh my god, what a game," he said.

"If only we could be sure the rest of the season would go as well," said Jackie.

"You have your doubts?" He leaned forward and rested his chin on his right fist.

"You have to admit that we have some stiff competition, last year's champions for one, the DC Eagles. They had a strong game this afternoon against the San Francisco Fog Dogs."

The man nodded. "I hate to admit it, but you're probably right." The waitress stopped by. He ordered a diet cola. "By the way, I'm Lawrence."

"Nice to meet you. I'm Jackie."

Meanwhile, Matt, still clad in kilt, came in and sat on Jackie's other side. "Hey, I just heard a rumor that we might be getting Sin Brazos for our open foreign acquisition," Matt announced. The waitress set a Jack & Coke down in front of him. He thanked her and pressed a tip in her hand.

"Sin Brazos? Doesn't that mean 'without arms'?" Jackie came back.

"Yeah, Sin Brazos is from Mexico. He's the kid who's been rising up through the youth leagues south of the border. I'm surprised you haven't heard the story," Matt said in between long sips of his drink.

Lawrence said, "I'm surprised you even follow Mexican fútbol, Matt."

"I usually don't, but the Fútbol League America has been shopping a lot down there. Remember the Campos disaster?"

Jackie nodded. "Yeah, he's god down there. Wanted the money up here, got sent to a team that he didn't want to go to and promptly started to act like a baby. But who's Sin Brazos?"

"Okay," Matt paused to take another drink. He gestured with drink in hand, pinky extended. "Sin Brazos is the offensive midfielder who lost his arms in a freak accident when he was 15. Before that he potentially would have been one of the best goalkeepers in the world. The Mexican men's coach was looking at him hard to join the team for the 1994 World Cup. Just before his trial date with the team, the accident happened. He lost the left arm above the elbow and the other just below. To make a long story short, his uncle worked with him and coached him back onto the field. Turns out, he's a helluva midfielder and a great striker. He worked his way back onto the national level, but was left off the U-23 squad. No Mexican league team wants him right now either. Which makes no fucking sense to me whatsoever. Anyway, he's secured an American agent and has been talking to the FLA."

"And we might get him?" Jackie asked.

"I think it's still in negotiation. But everyone is trying to keep it all under wraps. There's even a rumor going around that he's married a US citizen and is going for his green card, which then, of course, he wouldn't be classified as an FA anymore."

"He really is missing his arms?" Jackie just looked at him in disbelief.

Matt maintained a perfectly straight face. He looked into her eyes. Jackie felt like she was falling into him. She quickly averted her eyes. "Jackie, he really is. I'll email you a photo, if you give me your email address."

"Do you have a pen?" She reached for a cocktail napkin. He handed her a pen. She scribbled the info.

"Thanks. I'll send it tomorrow when I get to work." He slid the napkin into his sporran.

Just outside Soldier Field, Molly nervously dialed the number that Ian gave to her. It rang three times.

"Hello." There was loud music in the background.

"Ian? It's Molly," she shouted.

"Yeah, I was hoping you'd call."

"Where are you?"

"I'm at Axis. Come by, if you're up to it."

"Sure, I'm up to it."

"Do you know where it's at?"

"Yeah, I'll be there in about 10 to 15 minutes."

"I'll meet you outside so you won't have to pay the ridiculous cover charge."

"Thanks, Ian, see you soon."

Molly ran to her car and sped out of the lot inside the north end of Soldier Field.

Ian smiled. Tonight, he would get to know someone new. Deanna had already headed back to the apartment. They argued about him going to the post-match team party. She left with a huff.

By far the ugliest player on the team and one of the oldest, number 2 defenseman Tomás Lozowski asked in thickly Polish-accented English, "Was that Deanna?"

"No, it's a girl who was working in the stands."

Tomás raised his eyebrows. "Isn't Deanna coming?"

"No, she's mad at me. She didn't want to move to Chicago. She's going back to LA in the morning."

"So, this is the end? I'm going to miss looking at her." Tomás pouted.

"Oh, shut up, old man. You have a wife back in Poland. I'm going out front to meet her."

"I'm coming with you." Tomás got up. "I want to see who she is."

The pair walked to the entrance. Ian talked to the door security. Outside Tomás pulled out a tobacco pouch and began rolling a cigarette. "So, where is she, Ian?"

"She'll be here." A thought struck him. He pulled out his cell phone and clicked to bring up her cellular number. "Molly, just come pull up and use the valet," he said when she answered.

"I can't afford that." She was circling the block for the third time, hoping for a free space to open up. "I'm just a lowly usher supervisor."

"I'll pay for it. Don't worry."

Molly pulled up and tossed her keys to the valet. She spotted Ian standing next to a weathered Polish man. Ah, she thought to herself, that must be Lozowski. Oddly, she was not nervous, as she approached them. Everything seemed perfectly natural. She had always been comfortable hanging out with celebrities, per se. She partied with road bands all the time. Why should a soccer team be any different than a band?

Ian spoke, "Hi, Molly." He embraced her and kissed her cheek. How European. "Glad you could make it out."

Tomás smiled at her, then winked at Ian.

Ian introduced Molly to Tomás. He kissed the back of her hand in a very gentlemanly manner. They entered the club and met up with the rest of the team.

The Axis was a discothèque. The lights were low and flashing continually. Bodies gyrated. A few of the team members were fixated on two girls dirty dancing with each other.

Ian grabbed the waitress; he ordered a round for the table. Then he turned his full attention to Molly. He took her hands in his. "I'm really glad you came," he repeated. "I don't know. Call me crazy, but when I came out for warm-ups and saw you, I just knew that it was going to be a good game."

Molly rolled her eyes.

"I'm sorry. That sounded so corny. But seriously that's how I felt."

"My friend pointed you out to me, said something like I should get to know you, or whatever," Molly said.

"You should listen to her." The waitress returned with two bus boys in tow to help her carry all the drinks. Ian grabbed two Newcastle ales and handed one to Molly. "Cheers!"

She was still a bit skeptical about all this attention. "Aren't you seeing someone?" Tomás leaned a little closer to hear Ian's answer to this one.

"It's pretty much over. She's a model living in LA. We met when I played for the Stars. She's too wrapped up in herself."

Tomás could not resist. "What did you expect when you started dating a model?" With his index finger extended, he raised his glass of vodka neat.

"Shut up, old man," Ian shot back.

Tomás shrugged and turned back to other conversations at the table.

"Molly, what's your situation?" Ian asked.

"I recently caught my boyfriend cheating on me."

"I'm sorry."

"Oh, it's not your fault."

The loud music made a real conversation difficult, so Ian proposed, "Would you like to dance?"

"You have the energy after playing for 90 minutes?" She raised her eyebrows.

"I do. I get a rush from playing."

"Especially after your goal." She smiled.

He leaned over and said in her ear, "You are my goal."

Chapter II

SUNDAY, APRIL 5, 1998: Jackie checked her e-mail. There was a message from Matt.

"I enjoyed talking to you last night. Maybe we could get together sometime, just us. Let me know if you're interested. By the way, here's the picture I promised you of Sin Brazos.—Matt M."

Jackie clicked on the jpeg attachment. It was a photo of Sin Brazos playing. The photo was clearly not retouched. Matt was telling the truth. The caption was in Spanish, but Jackie knew enough to translate it: "Sin Brazos beats Juan Garcia in U-21 match."

"Wow," she said. She set the photo as wallpaper.

Deanna said nothing to Ian as he drove her to O'Hare. He could tell that she was really mad at him for not coming home until almost 2 a.m.

The silence was growing unbearable. They pulled up to the departures unloading at Terminal One. Finally, Ian broke the iciness. "Do you want me to park and see you to the gate?"

"No, that's fine," she replied as she flagged down a United skycap.

"So where do we stand?" He stared at the asphalt. He couldn't bear to look at her anymore.

"It's best that we let this go. Your life is here now. Mine is in LA. I think everything has run its course with us."

He nodded but still did not look at her. "You're right. It's best to end it here and now."

She stuck her perfectly manicured hand under his chin and lifted his head. "I still am very fond of you. I know you'll be in LA later this season. Call me if you want to." She kissed him on the cheek, leaving behind a smudge of wine-colored lipstick.

Ian watched her until she disappeared inside the hustle and bustle of the terminal. He got in the car and rested his forehead on the steering wheel. A tear oozed out of the corner of his left eye.

A police officer tapped on the glass. "Hey, buddy, you okay?"

Ian wiped the tear away and nodded.

"You need to get moving."

Ian started the engine and headed toward the expressway.

Renata rang Molly in the afternoon. "Where did you run off to last night? I saw you break out in a dead sprint to your car."

"I went to Axis."

"Why did you go there?" She crinkled her nose. "And why in such a hurry?"

"Ian invited me," Molly said smiling broadly. She was still on a high from last night.

Renata's jaw dropped. She did not think any of her suggestions would actually be able to come to fruition. It was all meant as joking good fun. "Ian Harris?"

"Yeah, I couldn't believe it either, but he's really interested in me."

"What about Jack?" Renata said, trying to be realistic.

"Fuck Jack. I think he's been staying at that slut's apartment."

"You know, girl, he doesn't deserve you."

"Give him time. He'll start acting all apologetic and shit, begging, possessive. You've seen him at the clubs when he's drunk and guys have flirted with me."

"So, it'll be fun to have Ian on your arm when he does," Renata suggested.

"Well, I haven't even gone out technically with Ian yet."

"Will you?"

"Without a doubt," Molly replied enthusiastically. "But I want to take this one slow. We'd both be coming out of relationships."

"What's his situation?"

"His model girlfriend didn't want to move to Chicago. They had a big falling out or something right after the game because he wanted to go to Axis with the rest of the team."

"You partied with the whole team last night?"

"Yeah, so Ian and I never really had anytime alone. It seems that he and Tomás, the Polish defender, have gotten to be good buddies. Anyway, I'm going to wait for his call. I plan to play this one kind of girly, if you know what I mean, at least in the beginning."

"Right on, girlfriend, by *The Rules*, but don't wait too long and let him slip through your fingers."

"Agreed."

Chapter III

MONDAY, APRIL 6, 1998: Chicago Stampede owner and general manager Carl Costello paced around the large oval, oak conference table. He removed his suit jacket and hung it on the back of the head chair.

A young bespectacled mousy woman poked her head in the room. "Everyone's here."

"Send them in," he replied. He greeted each participant with a firm handshake. "Lance, Michael, good to see you again. Mirek."

Sports agent Michael Quigley introduced his client. "This is Carlos Cortez." He had his hand on the shoulder of a handsome Mexican teenager. "Carlos, meet Carl Costello."

Carl extended his right hand and gripped the latex-covered artificial hand of Carlos. The shake was meant as a symbol that Carl did not think that the lad was to be treated any differently than the rest of his team.

Sin Brazos was tall for a Mexican kid. His jet-black hair was cropped close. The desire to play burned in his eyes. Everything about him screamed, Let's make this happen. He wore a prosthetic on his right arm, but not his left. The right arm was amputated just below the elbow, while the left was removed halfway up the upper arm. The Mexican doctors left heavy scars on both stumps.

Quigley was a squat portly character. He pushed his glasses up on his nose and said, "Now, let me get this straight. The Stampede wants to sign my boy for two years with a third year option. You're offering $70,000 the first year, with $10,000 increases over the next two years based on performance. I'm wondering, though, what your criteria is for performance?"

Coach Mirek Koneki, a lanky man in his forties with a weather-beaten face, said, "I'll field this one." He ran his long fingers through his thick blonde hair. "I think Sin Brazos would work nicely in our system. I've followed his career, even before the accident. In Europe, as a national team coach, I was scared we might have to play against him. As a goalkeeper, Sin Brazos let very little past him. Frankly, I'm not concerned about his performance. However, the reason we would like the clause in the contract is if, God forbid, Brazos was seriously injured."

Carlos shuddered, but said nothing. He knew enough English to understand that last comment without Quigley's translation.

Costello, a trim man with sharp Italian features and exceedingly thick, close-cropped chestnut hair, spoke up. "The performance clause is one thing we will not budge on."

Quigley translated for his client. Carlos spoke for himself in halting, but understandable English. "I understand that it is necessary. Business is the same way. It is okay." Brazos smiled broadly. "I want to play in Chicago."

Merton, the only one in the room in a suit and tie, asked, "Tell me again his legal status."

Quigley said, "He has secured his work permit."

"Without marrying a *gringa*," the teen joked with a toothy grin.

"We have a contract drawn up on those terms," Merton said. He pushed a pen across the table. "You have a copy, Quigley."

Carlos reached for the pen. Quigley held his client's right arm back. "Not yet. *Necesita una casa, mio.*"

He nodded.

"There is no housing allowance for the first year of the contract." Quigley tapped the paper. "Or any provisions for transportation."

Costello dug in his front pants pocket. He tossed a set of car keys at Quigley. "*Feliz Navidad.*"

Quigley caught them and looked at the logo on the fob: BMW.

"It's a red ZR3, convertible. We have a mechanic on standby to rig it up however Brazos would like so he can drive it," said Carl.

Carlos wanted to touch the keys. Quigley would not let him.

Merton pushed another pen toward the prospect.

Quigley intercepted and flicked it back across the table. "He can't live in his car. ¿*Casa?*"

Costello reached in his other front pants pocket and produced another set of keys. "A Bucktown loft, one year's lease. The bills will be sent to the Stampede office. That's enough to settle Brazos in. We can talk later about the next two years."

"Can we have that in writing?" Quigley pushed a legal pad and pen across the table.

Costello nodded with a glance at Lance Merton who had a look of 'yeah, let's hurry this along.' The Italian-American scribbled out everything he had just said. He signed it, pushed it toward Merton who glanced over it and signed, then across to Quigley and Carlos. They looked it over. Quigley signed and then helped Carlos position the pen in his synthetic fingers.

The air was heavy with anticipation and tension. Quigley then had Brazos sign the contract: *Carlos Cortez*

Coach Koneki presented Sin Brazos with his first red Chicago Stampede kit. He was to be lucky number 7.

Lance and Mirek stayed behind with Carl to clear up some details. Carl ran both hands through his short, thick chestnut hair. He lowered his head and let out a heavy sigh. "How do we keep Cortez from becoming a novelty?"

Lance shook his head. "I don't know. It was your idea to bring him here."

"No, I blame you, Coach," said Carl, glowering at Mirek.

"Hey, the kid has mad foot skills. I think he'll be fine," said Mirek. "I'm happy to have him here. I would not want him on any other team."

"But we really didn't need another forward player," said Carl. "Yeesh, how did I let you talk me into this?"

Mirek, with his weather-beaten face, looked at Carl as a father would. He laid a hand on Carl's arm. "Because, my son, you know it's the right thing to do."

Lance spoke, "You're new at this, Carl. I admire what you've done so far. Now quit second-guessing yourself and set up a press conference. It's imperative that you invite the local Telemundo and Univision reporters as well as our amigos at *La Raza*. There's still time for the weekly to do a nice article on Cortez." Lance stood. "You know the Mexican community here will eat this up."

Carl and Mirek rose. Carl said, "You're right. I guess I do still need some handholding from time to time."

"I'm here for you anytime," Mirek offered with a smile. He walked with his boss.

The hallway was lined with memorabilia from Chicago's soccer past, especially the Sting of the long defunct N.A.S.L. The carpet was the same deep scarlet tone as the Stampede kits.

Carl entered his office, or as he like to call it, his haven. Here, he purposefully put in cell phone signal dampening material in the walls and window treatments. He had one phone line with the ringer turned off, most of the time. He preferred email. All phone calls were routed through his secretary, Carrie. His door was nearly always closed.

Mirek trailed the six-foot-four frame and shut the door. "Carl, I'm worried about you."

Carl turned and looked at the team's head coach. "What do you mean?"

"I think you are taking on too much and not having fun anymore." Mirek sat on a brown leather sofa. "You shut yourself in here to get work done, which you're doing a fine job of by the way, especially taking on the ownership of two teams. But who do you hang out with for fun? Hell, I'll even have a drink with you during the week if you want, but you never ask. I haven't heard you mention anything about family or a woman for that matter."

Carl seated himself on the opposite end of the couch. As much as he did not wish to discuss his life, he welcomed the concerned intervention. "I'm sorry. There's not much to talk about. I have no family and no girlfriend."

Mirek cleared his throat. "Is there a boyfriend?"

Carl crinkled his nose in a face of disgust. "Oh god no! How dare you even think that."

"Sorry, just trying to help."

Carl leaned backwards and cast a gaze to the beamed ceiling. "Jesus H. Christ, Mirek, go back to your office and start working on game plans with Carlos in them. I want him to start on Saturday." Carl grabbed for a sharp pinching pain originating behind his eyes.

"But."

"I'm fine. Just go." Carl thrust a finger toward the door. When he heard it click shut, he reached toward an end table for a bottle of Excedrin brand painkillers and Evian water.

Chapter IV

TUESDAY, APRIL 7, 1998: Ian stared at his cell phone for at least 24 hours after Deanna left. Granted, he slept, but he wanted to call Molly. He just did not want to do it too soon. Tuesday, he finally broke down and dialed the woman of his desire.

Molly's voice rang in his ears like a carillon. "Hello."

"It's Ian. How are you?"

"I'm fine." Her day began to shine a little brighter. "How are you?"

"Much better if you would be so kind as to be my escort tonight," he asked in a formal tone.

Molly paused to digest the question. Then said, "Yes, but don't you have practice today?"

"Not at night, silly."

"Oh, yeah, right." She giggled. "What time?"

"I'll pick you up at seven. That's time for dinner and whatever," Ian said. "Where do you live?"

On a bit of a high, Ian arrived at practice. He spotted Tomás warming up. Ian started stretching next to his friend.

Tomás sensed something different about Ian. He gave his young comrade a knowing, yet fatherly look.

"Molly?" Tomás said, as he carefully stretched his hamstrings.

Ian nodded. "Yeah, Deanna and I broke everything off. Molly and I are going out later tonight." Ian began with some yoga positions, each movement slow, deliberate, but very limbering. An old college girlfriend had introduced him to the healthful art. He found it to be the best way to stretch out before workouts and matches.

"It's just as well. Deanna wasn't right for you. Nice to look at, but not for anything else." There was a glint in Tomás' eye as he remembered what Deanna's body. "Now, Molly, I sense, is a good woman. Strong, independent, but not all flashy and wrapped up in herself."

"Yeah, I picked up on that too." He switched positions. "Well, the first date is always the most awkward."

"I don't think you will have any problems. You two looked like one body on the dance floor. You and Deanna never had that kind of chemistry."

"Really? You think so?"

Tomás nodded. "I think you may have found a winner."

Mirek strode onto the pitch. Sin Brazos was at his side.

"Holy crap, would you look at that," Tomás exclaimed to Ian.

Ian looked up. "I can't believe they pulled it off. The Stars were hot and heavy for him, too. Must have been the salary cap."

Tomás put in, "Or Mirek's insistence."

Mirek clapped his hands twice. "Attention everyone, we are pleased to introduce a new team member, Carlos Cortez, or as most of you already know, Sin Brazos."

Most of the players knew whom Carlos Cortez was and how he became to be known as Sin Brazos. Only the backup goalkeeper, Virgil Amat, stared as a child would.

"*Hola*," said Carlos.

The team responded in unison, "Hello."

Coach Koneki continued, "We're going to need someone to help him with his English. Ian, I think you are sufficiently bilingual. Do you have time?"

"*Sí*, coach."

"Today, we're going to run some plays with Carlos here, in various positions. He's used to being a forward or a striking mid, but that may not work best in our usual 3-5-2. Alright, boys, let's get to work." Mirek made a weeping motion with his hands; the whole team jumped to their feet.

Later that evening, Ian pulled up to Molly's Lakeview apartment building in a red Jaguar XJ convertible. As she sat on the car's plush leather seat, Molly tried to hide her astonishment at his ride.

Ian leaned over and gave her a peck on the cheek, while handing her a single red rose. "It's good to see you again, Molly."

She drank in its scent. She blushed. "Same here, Ian. I've been looking forward to this all day."

"You've been on my mind, too." He started the engine and pulled out onto the street.

"So where are we going?"

"I made reservations at Mike Ditka's for dinner. Then, we'll see from there."

"Sounds good." She ran her hands through her hair to keep it out of her face as they made their way down Lake Shore Drive.

Ian popped in a CD, Frank Sinatra.

"Oh, I love Frank," Molly cooed. She settled back in her seat. Ian's free hand slid over on top of hers. Both felt a rush of excitement that neither had experienced in a long time.

Over dinner, Ian told Molly about working out with Sin Brazos. She told him about some of the other places she had worked security at. As the level of liquid in the Burgundy wine bottle dropped, the conversation shifted to more personal things. Ian asked, "You never said much about the status of your situation with your boyfriend."

"There's not much to tell, really." She finished her glass of wine. "Jack is a metal guitarist who thinks he's a rock star. I dropped in on an out-of-town gig his band was playing and walked in on him getting sucked off by some bimbo."

Ian was slightly shocked by her choice of words, but could sense that she was still bitter about the incident. He refilled her wine with the last of the bottle and signaled the garçon for two glasses of sherry.

She continued, "Since then, Jack hasn't been staying with me. He never had his own apartment, always crashing with friends or girlfriends. Anyway, that night, it was clear that I wasn't good enough for him anymore. He's just not worth fighting for, so I turned around and left."

"So, is it officially over?"

"As far as I'm concerned, yeah." She lowered her head but maintained a flirting eye contact with her handsome date. "That's why I'm out with you. I think I made a wise decision." The garçon arrived with the order. She swirled hers thoughtfully. "What about your girlfriend?"

"What girlfriend?" Ian smiled. "No, seriously, we broke it off at the airport the morning after the match. But it was over, I think, the minute my agent and I inked the deal for me to come help kick off this expansion team."

"Do you still love her?" She took a sip.

He nodded. "It's still too fresh. I mean, I was ring shopping before I was transferred to Chicago." He took his first sip of the sherry. "And you?"

"Yes and no. I don't know. Yeah, for me, too, things are still too raw. And we never had an official breaking up." She squeezed her eyes together and rubbed her temples.

Ian nodded. "I understand. We're both rebounding. That's the most dangerous type of relationship. I think we both know that. So we'll take everything slow and see what happens." He had reached out and touched her forearm tenderly, squeezing gently.

"What do you say that we just call it a night? I don't feel so well right now."

Ian understood. He could sense that something was seriously wrong. Actually, both of them were damaged goods. "That's fine. I'll take you home. But I think you need to talk to someone, okay? You call your friend when you get home. Promise?"

She nodded. "I'll be right back." She excused herself to go to the ladies' room. Once there, she turned on the cold water and splashed some on her face, as she stared at herself in the mirror. "Oh god, I can't do this. What the fuck am I doing? Jack, you fat bastard, why the fuck did you have to do this to me?" She punched the mirror, shattering it, slashing her knuckles. Staring at the blood running and pooling on the counter and floor, she sank to the floor.

The bathroom attendant rushed over. "Oh my god, honey, what's wrong?" The sturdy African-American woman grabbed hand towels and wrapped Molly's hand to stop the bleeding.

Molly remained silent and let the matronly woman take care of her.

A waitress on a quick break came in. "Hey, doll, go grab one of the busboys to clean up this here glass. Tell him it's okay, there's no one else in here right now."

The waitress nodded and left to fetch help.

The matron attended to Molly's wounds. "I think you might need stitches. Who made you that mad, dearie? It's okay, you can tell Big Mama."

Molly uttered, "Jack," in a barely audible voice.

"Is he the one you're here with tonight?"

Molly shook her head.

"Who are you here with tonight? Can they help?"

"Ian," she whispered. "He's not Jack. I hate Jack."

"Tell me, what did Jack do to make you so mad that you had to go and break my mirror, now?"

Tears started to pool in her eyes and trickle down her face. "He . . . he . . . ch . . . ch . . . cheated."

"Oh, my poor, poor girl. Everything will be okay." Big Mama guided Molly's head to rest on her large bosom. With her free hand, she stroked Molly hair soothingly.

Meanwhile, Ian had paid the check and waited in the lobby for Molly to appear. He noted some hustle and bustle around the ladies' room, but did not pay much attention to it. Probably an overflowing toilet or something else mundane like that, he thought.

A sharp-eyed waitress—the same waitress who fetched the busboy who was on his way with a broom and dustpan—spotted Ian in the lobby. "Sir, I think you should come with me."

Ian raised his eyebrows, but followed her tug. "What's wrong?"

"It's your date."

His left hand flew to his mouth. "Oh my god, what's happened to Molly?"

"I don't know. But you need to take care of her. Big Mama is taking care of her now."

Ian entered the forbidden domain of the ladies' room. He saw Molly and Big Mama on the floor surrounded by mirrored shards and drops of blood. "Molly, Molly, what's wrong?"

Big Mama looked him up and down. "I hope you're not Jack."

"No, I'm Ian, her date." Molly raised her head. Her makeup was streaked from crying. Ian bent to help her to her feet. "I'm here for you, Molly. We'll get you patched up."

Slowly the two women rose. Molly leaned into Ian. He held her close. Big Mama said, "You take care of her, now, you hear? Or you'll have to deal with me."

"Yes, ma'am."

"Keep pressure on those cuts until you get her to the emergency room."

"Yes, ma'am." Ian reached in his pocket for his wallet. He handed Big Mama a fifty-dollar bill and a business card. "Have the manager call me in the morning and we'll talk about the damage in here."

"I will, sir. Thank you."

"No, thank you for being here."

Ian bundled Molly outside and into the Jag. He drove over to Northwestern Memorial Hospital's emergency room. As he waited for her to be stitched up, he sighed loudly and shook his head. This Jack must have really messed with her head for her to suddenly react like that. Oh god, what the hell have I gotten myself into?

Chapter V

THURSDAY, APRIL 9, 1998: Jackie looked at the clock on her mantle, 4:17 PM. The USA men's friendly was scheduled to kick off in less than three hours. Thank god, she thought, I need a break.

Ever since last Saturday, she had been preparing taxes for clients. Tax day was six days away. She spent hours on the computer entering data in between meeting with them in person and calling them to ask questions that arose.

She hated her job, but it was good money. Her first three years out of college, she worked in her father's CPA firm. Once she had a client base established, she decided to go her own way. She needed the space.

Her loft was comfortable. She chose the building because of the conference room facilities, which she frequently met clients in. Her balcony overlooked the Chicago River in the rapidly developing River North neighborhood. Plus, she was finally able to justify having a car, since the loft unit came with a parking space.

She stood and stretched. Her hands and wrists started to cramp. She shook them as she walked to her bathroom.

She gazed at the reflection in the mirror. "Oh, gawd, girl, you look like hell," she said aloud. The stress of deadlines and chasing down clients for information was taking a toll. Since she had not met in person with anyone since Tuesday morning, she had not showered in as many days. It was now Thursday.

"Fuck it. I'm going early."

She cranked up her stereo. Madonna's poppy voice filled every corner of the loft and probably disturbed her neighbor below, but she did not care. He often kept her up at night when he had loud bawdy encounters with call girls.

Sueños del Fútbol was an Irish pub with a Mexican-born owner, Jose O'Shea. The Stampede supporters club selected the place to watch away matches and national team games. Jose welcomed all soccer fans with open arms.

Jackie entered and spotted Matt, sans kilt, sitting at the bar. His eyes were transfixed to the television. A replay of a recent English Premier League match danced across the screen. Jackie deposited herself on a stool next to him.

"Hey, Jackie," he greeted. His eyes barely left the screen. "Sorry, I haven't had a chance to email you. I've been busy."

"Oh, that's okay. I've barely had a chance to breathe myself."

"Buy you a drink?"

"Sure, thanks." She ordered a Newcastle draught from the bartender, Jose's cousin from Ireland.

Matt looked at her fully for the first time since she entered the bar. "Your usual poison, I see." He smiled.

Wow, he noticed, she thought to herself. "Yeah." She returned the smile. Their eyes met. A spark flew between them.

Joe O'Shea set the brews before them. Jackie lifted hers. "Thanks." She took a long swallow. The pint glass was half empty when she set it back down. "So, Matt, what do you do for a living?"

"I'm a systems analyst. What about you?"

"CPA," she replied.

"That explains it," he thought out loud.

She looked at him puzzled, then chuckled lightly when he gestured at her glass. She added, "I really shouldn't be in here, but I desperately needed a break."

"This is your busy season, then?"

She nodded, running her hand through her hair. "I've been fried all week. You?"

"I had a big project due earlier today. That's why I didn't have a chance to get back to you on a more personal level."

"Don't worry about it. We'll be seeing each other all summer." She smiled flirtatiously.

They stared at the remainder of the Premiership match in silence, except for an occasional analytic comment, until more supporters' group members filtered into the bar. Jackie and Matt impressed each other with their respective knowledge of the beautiful game. Sometimes, their thighs touched, filling Jackie with sexual urgency. Just before the kickoff of the national team match, she stood. The sexual tension was becoming too great. She had to go to the ladies' room to splash some cold water on her face and bring her mind back to reality.

Lawrence came in and usurped Jackie's vacated bar stool. "Hey, Matt, how's it going?"

"Good, good."

"So I hear we signed Carlos Cortez."

"Yeah, Sin Brazos will fit in well with our team. Coach Koneki knows what he's doing."

"I can't believe the closed-minded criticism of some of the other people on the list," commented Lawrence.

Matt shook his head. "I know, man, I think they'll change their minds when they see him play."

Joe set Lawrence up with his usual diet cola with a lime. He paid and tipped generously, winking. Turning back to Matt, he asked, "Do you think he'll start tomorrow?"

"I think he will. The kid is so versatile and hungry. Actually, I took a long lunch earlier this week and picnicked at Halas Hall. They were running full drills with him. Carlos and Ian fit together on the midfield perfectly."

"But if he's so good, why didn't any Mexican league coach want him?" chimed in a third person.

"Sean," replied Matt in a slow condescending tone, "because they're all *idiotas*. That's why. We've hashed this out all week on and off the damn list. You'll change your tune when you see him score a hat trick Saturday."

Lawrence leaned back with an 'I'm-staying-out-of-this-one' look. Sean looked Matt squarely in the eye. "I'll bet you a hundred bucks that he won't." Sean slapped a big Ben on the bar.

"You're on." Matt stuck out his hand. The two opposing forces sealed the bet. Matt added his own c-note to the pot. "Hey, Lawrence, do us a favor and hold this until after Saturday's match."

With a heavy sigh, Lawrence put the $200 in his pocket. "I don't like this one bit."

"It's okay. It's just a friendly bet," Matt assured.

"We're not going to kill each other." Sean grinned. "At least, not yet."

Sean was a young Irish-American fellow. His strawberry blonde hair was cropped short. Round wire-rimmed glasses complemented his soft features. His six-foot frame was fit and lean from playing varsity soccer. And despite his age, a mere seventeen, he could spout historic facts and tactical analyses as good as or better than most of the oldest and most dedicated of supporters. Matt knew this and that annoyed the piss out of him.

Sean drifted off to find a table in the back room. Jackie came out of the ladies' room and literally ran into the lad. "Hi, I'm so sorry," she spouted clumsily.

Sean replied, "It's okay." He looked down at her. His blue-green eyes met hers. "Are you headed to the back?"

She shrugged. "Sure, why not? Matt was starting to annoy me anyway," she lied.

Sean rolled his eyes. "You, too, huh? He and Lawrence seemed to be enjoying each others' company," he smirked.

Jackie smiled. "Oh yeah, cool. I think Lawrence has a crush on him."

Sean laughed. "Probably, better Matt than me."

"The TV's bigger back here anyway," she added.

Together, they found an open table and sat. He turned to her and said, "I don't think we've met formally. I'm Sean Murphy."

"Jacqueline Harris, no relation to Ian. At least that I'm aware of." She beamed. "I've seen your posts on the list. You're very sharp-witted."

"Thank you. What's your nickname on the lists?"

"Razor Girl."

"You don't post much, but when you do, oh man, look out." Sean grinned broadly at her, making every effort to meet her eyes. "No wonder you call yourself Razor." Both turned their attention to the big screen for a moment. The US—Greece friendly had started. "So, Jackie, where do you stand on the whole Sin Brazos issue? You haven't posted anything one way or another on it."

"I'm reserving judgment until after the match."

"Matt just loves the kid. For the life of me, I can't figure out why. The idiot thinks Carlos is going to score a hat trick tomorrow."

Jackie raised her eyebrows. "Really? That's a bit of a stretch."

"Yeah, I wouldn't believe it. So I made him put his money where his mouth is. I bet him $100 that Carlos wouldn't score a hat trick."

"I think that's a wise bet. It'll be an easy $100 for you."

"That's what I thought, too." Sean smiled broadly at her.

At halftime, Colin and Matt wandered into the back room. "Hey," Matt said, "we wondered where you went, Jackie." He shot Sean a territorial look.

Matt sat across from Sean. Colin shook his head. He put his hand on Jackie's shoulder. He whispered in her ear, "Come with me. We need to talk about Matt."

Jackie rose. "Okay."

"Matt, Sean, you two play nice," Colin warned.

Both sneered at him.

Jackie followed Colin out the back door. Colin pushed a rock in place so the door would not close and lock on its own.

"Jackie," began Colin, "as you know Matt likes you a lot, but he's afraid of you."

She looked at him quizzically.

"Sean seems to have taken a liking to you, too, but he's just a pup."

"Well, don't worry about him. Nothing is going to happen there."

"Thank you. We don't need another Paulie in our group." Colin paused to take a drink and push his glasses up. "I'm afraid you are going to hurt my brother. He doesn't need that pain again."

"Again?"

"He was terribly hurt by a woman a couple of years ago. She was a strong woman just like you are, but she left him for another man."

Jackie's hand flew over her mouth. "Oh, I didn't know."

"I'm not telling you to stay away. I'm just warning you. Don't hurt my brother."

Colin went back inside. Jackie was left to gather her thoughts. Strong woman? Well, she had been called that before. She had scared men away in the past by coming on too strong. Perhaps, she should not pursue Matt so hard, and just let him come to her. It might be fun to play hard to get for a change.

She went back inside. Sean and Matt were in a heated argument about how well the US men would do in the World Cup. Before rejoining the table, she fetched two pints from Joe.

As she sat down at the table, she said bluntly, "We suck. Sampson is an idiot. We won't make it out of the group play round. I just hold out hope that we can at least beat Iran."

Both men blinked at her.

"Now shut up and watch the game." She gestured at the big screen with her glass. The second half had begun.

Chapter VI

SATURDAY, APRIL 11, 1998: On a warm afternoon in the underbelly of Soldier Field, Molly pulled her work polo shirt on carefully. Her hand throbbed. It would be at least another three days before the stitches could come out.

Renata entered the ladies' locker room in the usher room. She saw her friend's bandaged hand. "What the hell happened?"

Molly shook her head. "I'm still not for sure. I had a few glasses of wine, on a date with Ian, and well, I end up putting my hand in a mirror at a nice steak joint."

Renata looked at her friend. She recognized the expression. "Jack?"

Molly sat down on the narrow bench to attempt to tie her shoes one-handed. She sighed heavily. "Yeah, the bastard's got a strangle hold on my mind. I don't know. The rage about the whole situation just came to the surface." She threw her hands in the air. "I can't even tie my fucking shoes. Damn it! Why do I do this shit to myself?"

Renata stooped and tied her friend's shoes. "I wish you would have called me. You know, I'm here for you, if you ever want to talk seriously about it."

"Thanks, I know."

"My quick advice is to forget all about Jack and focus wholly on Ian."

Molly nodded. "Yeah, I know. I will. I just wish it were that easy. After all, Ian was very sweet to me that night."

Carlos pulled on his kit, then took off his prosthetics and placed them in his locker. A trainer assisted him with securing his shin guards and boots. Carlos never liked receiving this assistance but he had come to accept it. He had tried many times to perfect putting on his own shin guards, but never got them adjusted right. He kept practicing at home in hopes that someday he wouldn't have to rely on anyone.

He was shocked when Coach Koneki said that he was going to start. He did not expect to make his FLA debut this soon.

Ian approached Carlos once the trainer had left. "Are you nervous?"

Carlos gave him a confused look, so Ian asked the same question in Spanish.

"Oh, *sí, sí*," replied Carlos.

Ian said, "Don't worry. Everything will be just fine."

Jackie circulated at the tailgate. She felt Sean's eyes on her. He busied himself with grilling. Charcoal smoke swirled around his head. He held a Koozie-wrapped beer in one hand and a spatula in the other.

All the chatter around the area focused mostly on the announced starting lineup. Sin Brazos was going to start as a striker. Word of the bet between Sean and Matt got out, with a large consensus believing that Matt was a fool.

All this conversation about Carlos Cortez was getting rather tiresome, so she decided to head on into the stadium. It was still 45 minutes before kick off, a bit early to go in, but she needed to take a piss from all the beers she had slammed. The supporters had not gathered enough bargaining power to get the park district to set up portable toilets for the matches yet.

Both teams were on the field warming up. So she descended the stairs between sections 16 and 18 to get a closer took at Carlos Cortez, suited up in a red kit, sporting #7 proudly. Jackie watched Carlos take some practice shots at the keeper, "Captain" Danzig.

Even this early in the season, Captain Dan seemed destined to be the FLA Goalkeeper of the Year, but even as instinctive as Capt. Dan was, Carlos kept slotting them past him. Then, Ian and Carlos passed the ball back and forth to each other—one touch and in, one touch and in, every pass with extreme precision and beauty. It seemed like Ian and Carlos had been playing with each other all their lives. Jackie began to think that maybe Matt might be right.

Molly felt relaxed as she paced back and forth the east half of the stadium. She helped with seating whenever her ushers became backed up. Everything was running like a well-oiled machine. She descended the stairs to the track and watched Ian warm up.

Ian spotted her and jogged to the sideline. Like a gazelle, he leaped over the boards and hopped the chain-link security fence. "Hey, sweetie." He gave Molly a hug and a kiss.

"Hi," she replied just as enthusiastically. "You're going to hurt yourself one day doing that."

"Oh, hurdling? Nah, I was a hurdler in the off-season for my high school years." He lifted her bandaged hand and tenderly kissed it. "How's this feeling?"

"It throbs a little, but otherwise, it's fine. I feel so guilty about what happened." She felt lost when she looked into his eyes.

"I wish you didn't have to work today."

"I'll still be able to see the match. Don't worry. My ushers today, so far, seem to know what they're doing," she assured him.

"Well, we'll get together after the match, okay?" They kissed each other lightly on the lips again. "The team wants to take Carlos out for a big welcome home—or something like that—party. Probably Axis again, but I think we might have access to a private party room. I'm not sure. Carl's putting it together."

"I'll be there, honey. Don't worry. Just connect with dear Carlos for lots of goals, okay?"

"Will do, my dear."

Both Stampede and the San Francisco Fog Dogs started jogging back to the locker rooms.

"I have to go."

She nodded. "I know." They kissed again. "*Buena suerte.*"

"*Gracias, mi bonita,*" Ian replied with a broad smile.

Michael Quigley paced nervously in the owner's box.

Carl Costello arrived. "Michael, good to see you."

The two men shook hands. "Oh my god, I'm so worried about Carlos tonight."

"Oh, you sound like a father," Carl joked. "Have a beer and relax. Carlos will be fine tonight."

Just before kickoff, Jackie filtered into section 12.

Sean, reeking like a barbeque pit, sidled up to Jackie. "You left early."

She shrugged. "I was bored. Besides, I was able to see Sin Brazos warm up. There might be something to Matt's prediction."

"No way is Carlos going to get a hat trick. That hundred bucks is mine. Besides, the Fog Dog defense is one of the best in the league right now. They only allowed two goals out of normally high-scoring DC."

Jackie nodded. She saw fire in the lad's eyes. He was a handsome fellow. She could see herself going out with Sean, despite the age difference, at least for fun.

Both teams entered the sacred battleground of Soldier Field. The Fog Dogs' line up was introduced. Then the Stampede's starting eleven:

> "Number 18, Goalkeeper, Daniel 'Captain' Danzig.
> Defender, #2, Tomás Lozowski.
> Defender, #3, Vladimir Starkov.
> Defender, #6, Patrick Mathison.
> Midfielder, #5, Paul Novotny.
> Midfielder, #10, Heinrich Baumgartner.
> Midfielder, #9, Brendan 'Iceman' Glazier.
> Midfielder, #12, John O'Connor.
> Midfielder, #8, Juan Cristobal.
> Forward, #7, Carlos 'Sin Brazos' Cortez.
> Forward, #14, Ian Harris.

And your coach of the Chicago Stampede, Mirek Koneki."

All the Stampede players brought large cheers, but none as much as Sin Brazos. Signing Carlos had attracted a large Mexican contingent to the stands. Carlos, in response to the cheers, raised both upper limbs. The crowd roared even more enthusiastically.

Ian turned to his new teammate and repeated the question he asked in the locker room. "Are you nervous?"

In his native tongue, Carlos replied, "No, not anymore."

Novotny heard the exchange and said to Carlos. "*Už jsme doma.* Now we are home."

Carlos repeated with a broad grin. "Home."

In the twelfth minute, Starkov made a diving header save after Capt Dan missed the opportunity. The ball rebounded off the loins of a Fog Dog. Mathison gained control and passed it forward to Novotny, who blew past Dogs down the left side of the field. Novotny then slotted the ball to Ian who scooped it cleanly toward Carlos who sent a right-footed one-touch rocket past the keeper. Stampede 1, Fog Dogs, 0.

The stadium erupted!

Sin Brazos ran around, doing a front flip in orgasmic celebration. Ian and Novotny came over and leaped with joyous hugs with Carlos.

Carlos said, "*Už jsme doma.*"

Novotny's eyes nearly popped out of this head as those words fell on his ears. All he could say in reply was, "Yes! *Už jsme doma!*"

In the owner's box, Quigley's ale went flying. The dark brown bottle shattered as it hit the wall. The agent jumped around screaming and shouting.

Carl just grinned. "See, nothing to worry about."

"We shouldn't be up here. We should be down there." Quigley pointed across the pitch to section 12, whose cement front was draped with a long banner: 12th Man: Stampede Supporters Section.

"You're right." Carl grabbed two fresh pints and a pair of drumsticks. "Let's go."

In section 12, Matt cornered Sean and stated, "One down, two to go." Then continued celebrating.

Carl, drumsticks poking precariously out of his back pocket, made his way down to the front of section 12. The drum line was partly in the first row of that section and spilled over into the front row of the mostly tarped-over section 10.

The lanky leader of the Stampede pulled out the pair of Vater drumsticks and gestured toward the kit. The drummer obliged the request. Carl slid behind the set up of a floor tom, snare and cowbell.

The cheering for the first goal had wound down, as the teams on the pitch settled back into play. A new chant was in order. The little man who called himself the Minister of Merriment bellowed in a voice that carried across the stadium, "CHI-CA-GO, CHI-CA-GO!"

The section joined him. A large single bass drum beat followed each "GO". Carl joined by hitting the floor tom hard and loud.

After that went of for a full minute, Carl decided to launch into a rapid fire, surf beat. Da-da-da, da da; Da-da-da, da da; Da-da-da, da da . . . "GO CHICAGO!"

Sean leaned over to Jackie. "I think that's Carl Costello, the owner and general manager of the Stampede." He gestured toward the man.

"I always figured he was cool," Jackie replied. She found herself looking at Carl. The man had rhythm, just one of the little things she looked for in a man. She could easily picture him fitting the rest of her mental checklist.

On the pitch, the heads up passing among the Stampede continued. They danced circles around the helpless Fog Dogs. Granted, the San Francisco goalkeeper made some spectacular saves over the next fifteen minutes, then . . .

Tomás intercepted a long goal kick and played if off his chest. He drove down the east side of the pitch. Past midfield, he back heeled it to Carlos who made a spectacular between the defender's legs move to be able to cleanly dump it off to Baumgartner who took the shot.

A powerful kick, clocked at 62 mph, which the keeper simply could not handle. Goal! 2-0.

Sean and Jackie leaped together. They embraced in a celebratory hug. Sean drank in her scent, tempted to kiss her.

A large Chicago flag was unrolled and held aloft by section 12. Quigley found himself underneath it. Arms aloft, he enjoyed the revelry.

Carl continued to beat the skins.

During stoppage time, Ian fed the ball off a header to Carlos who launched a bicycle kick toward the back to the net. 3-0. Halftime.

Sean's eyes nearly popped out of his head at what he just saw. He stared in disbelief at Sin Brazos. "Jackie, did I just see what I think I saw?"

Jackie shook his shoulders. "Yes! A perfect bicycle kick goal!"

"Sin Brazos?"

"Yes! By Sin Brazos. I'm starting to think you might lose your bet."

Sean nodded numbly. Then he smiled. "I was stupid for doubting Carl's and Mirek's judgment. Excuse me a minute, I'm going to talk to Carl."

"Sure, I'm going for some overpriced beer."

"Beers of the World stand?"

"Yeah, I'll bring you one." She ascended the stairs.

Sean made his way over to Carl Costello. Carl was pocketing his drumsticks. Sean spoke, "Thank you for signing Carlos Cortez."

"You're welcome," replied Carl. The two men met at eye level.

"I have to be honest with you. I had my doubts."

Carl nodded. "Yes, I saw your venomous posts on the list. But you've changed your mind now?"

"Oh, absolutely. The way he fits in with Mirek's 3-5-2 is like hand in glove. I've never seen such clean and precise passing in this league before, much less what I've been able to stomach of the Mexican league."

"You rarely see it consistently anywhere," Carl concurred. "By the way, I hear you have a bet going."

"I'm worried that I might lose $100. But I'd still be happy for the team, and for Carlos, too, for that matter. A hat trick in a major or first division debut is almost unheard of."

"Good. Well, I need to check on things with Mirek."

"Will you be back here for the second half?"

"Are you kidding? This is where it's at! That damn box is so boring."

Meanwhile, Molly continued to patrol the yellow seats. She found it heard not to get caught up in the excitement. But if she jumped around too much, her hand throbbed.

She was glad that she was recording this match at home.

Fans continued to arrive late. They were mainly Latinos, who seemed to never buy tickets in advance. Almost everyone coming in now was walk-up traffic. She had a feeling that, as long as Sin Brazos was on the team, the Stampede would thrive on this breed of ticket buyer.

Molly looked at the game clock. It was nearly halftime. She headed toward section 26 and prepared to back up her usher there.

On the track, she leaned on the fence and watched Ian run up and down the field. He was unlike Jack in almost every way. Ian was strong. Jack was so lazy he paid his buddies in beer to schlep his equipment. Ian's interests were broad. All Jack ever talked about was his heavy metal music. Ian was clean cut and articulate. Jack's hair was long and scraggly; he denied that it was thinning, too. Jack mumbled a lot, which grew worse whenever he was drunk or stoned, which, lately, seemed to be almost all the time.

In stoppage time, Molly watched Ian feed the ball off a header to Carlos who launched a bicycle kick toward the back to the net. At the whistle, Molly stood at the base of the stairs at section 26.

Ian spotted Molly on his way off the field. She watched the small gaggle of kids, some leaning dangerously over the concrete barrier. The usher, a strong, smart ox of a young man, had things under control. Ian bounced up behind her and grabbed her around the waist.

Startled, she spun around. "You scared me."

He chided, "You should always watch your back."

"You've had a great game so far. And that new kid plays awesome."

"Yeah, next half, I'll get a goal. Can't let the new kid hog the spotlight." He grinned broadly and pulled Molly into a long lip lock. Some of the older boys in the crowd whistled and shouted at the public display of affection.

Molly melted in his arms. She knew it was unprofessional, but she did not care. It felt too good. Even the nagging pain in her hand stopped for a moment. As they pulled back from each other, Ian took her injured hand gently again in his. "How do you feel?"

"It still throbs a little, but otherwise, okay."

"Good." He kissed her hand. "Sweetie, I need to head in. Mirek will be expecting me."

"I'll see you after the match, like we talked about."

They kissed briefly and he turned to go inside the locker room.

Mirek Koneki looked around at his players. The first eleven, minus Ian, were drying off sweat. The substitute pool began stretching, in anticipation of the honor of being called to duty. There was not much to say. His team was playing perfect so far. He would probably make two substitutions at some point in the second half, but whom? And where was Ian?

"Where's Ian?" barked the coach.

Everyone looked around and collectively shrugged, except Tomás. "I saw him with Molly."

"Who's Molly?"

"That's his new woman."

Mirek raised an eyebrow. "What happened to Deanna?"

"They broke up. She dumped him to go back to LA."

"Well, he needs to get his arse in here, if he wants to play in the second half."

Just then, Ian came in, followed closely by Carl Costello. "Hey, coach, sorry I was delayed," said Ian.

"Glad you could join us, Ian." Mirek smirked. "You know you're needed in here to translate."

"Yes, coach." Ian hung his head.

Baumgartner raised his hand. "Who are you looking at for subs?"

Mirek scratched his head. "I don't know. Maybe this is a good day to play Manny Larsen and try the 4-4-2. Does anyone not want to play the second half?"

Ian quickly translated for Carlos, who then burst out laughing.

"Something funny, Carlos?" Mirek asked, as a strict father would.

"No, no, señor," Carlos said. "*Quiero a jugar. Queramos a jugar.*"

Mirek smiled. He knew that he'd get a smart aleck response to that question. He just did not expect it from Carlos.

Carl added in a stern voice, "Don't anyone dare think they can slack off now. I want you to run up the score. There will be none of this fall back and just play defense crap. You hear me?"

Ian quickly translated for Carlos. The whole team looked stunned. General managers, much less owners, normally did not set foot inside locker rooms during halftime. Somewhat in unison, the Stampede replied, "Yes, sir."

Carl, pleased, turned and left to grab more beer from the owner's box before heading back to Section 12. His Vaters still protruded prominently from his back pocket.

Tomás commented, "It looks like he's been hanging out in Section 12."

Novotny nodded. "That's one of the things that makes him such a great manager. He loves the sport as a fan."

Mirek interrupted them. "Okay, you heard the boss. No dropping back just to play defense. If Carl wants more goals, we're going to give him more goals. Okay, on *tres*."

"*Uno, dos, tres,* Stampede!" the team roared in unison.

Matt spotted Jackie in line at the Beers of the World stand. "Hey there! So, what do you think of Sin Brazos now?"

"He's a brilliant player. Sharp, crisp passer, can read the pitch and the game like he's psychic. But, let's see how he does over the next few weeks. This game could just be a fluke."

Matt reached in his sporran to show his ID to the security guard standing next to the vendor. "It's not a fluke. I got hold of some video of him from Mexico. He's always like that."

Jackie flashed her driver's license and paid for her beer. Together, the two stood off to the side for a moment. "Matt, do you think Mirek will sub Carlos out before he gets his hat trick?"

"He'd better not," spat the Scotsman. "On a different note, how come you're hanging out with Sean?"

She shrugged. "I don't know. I like to make the rounds." She took a long swig of beer. She was parched from cheering and singing.

"He's too young for you," said Matt.

"Is that all you can say? He's an adult and so am I. What if I want a boy toy for a while," she shot back. She was baiting Matt. The kilted one had given her so many mixed signals. She wanted to see how he'd react.

"Sean's got issues. A woman like you in his life would just complicate matters for him. And seriously, he is too young for you."

Jackie looked at Matt. The reply puzzled her. This almost sounded like he cared about Sean like a little brother. On the other hand, it sounded like one of competition. "We can talk about all this later. I'm here to enjoy the match." She spun on her heel and returned to her seat.

"Just don't lead him on, Jacqueline," Matt warned. She bristled at hearing her true first name.

Meanwhile, Madeline and Lawrence watched the exchange from the upper concourse. Madeline, a spunky blonde all of five feet tall, asked Lawrence, "What do you think of Matt?"

"I think he's delicious," he replied with a brief lick of his lips. "It's the kilt that really does it."

"I think he's got his eye on Jackie, but I'm not for sure. They look comfortable with each other."

Lawrence nodded. "Do you know if he might swing my way?"

Madeline shrugged, "I don't know."

"Sometimes, I think he flirts with me, but I don't know. I suppose I could ask. What's the worst he could say? No?"

The whistle sounded signaling the beginning of the second half. Madeline and Lawrence ended the conversation and dashed to their seats. Neither wanted to miss a second of the action. It was clear that most of Section 12 was still stuck in the beer lines. Regardless, the chanting arose like a thunderous roar that challenged the rest of the stadium. The referee's whistle could barely be heard over the din.

The Stampede started the second half with a full bore attack. The Fog Dogs backpedaled trying to keep up. Carlos made a run up the field with *la pelota*. Dog defender Jack "Nasty" McDuffy targeted the lad. Cleats bared like a mad dog's teeth, he made a hard tackle from behind. Carlos crumpled in a heap from the blow to his left knee. The referee could not whip the yellow card out fast enough, holding it up to Nasty's face. Cursing, Nasty spat at the ref. The ref pulled out the red card, which, of course, sent Nasty into a tantrum. Nasty shoved the ref down then stomped off the field. Field security swarmed to make sure McDuffy left the pitch without further incident. A Dog and Ian both extended a hand to help the ref to his feet. Both players, nearly in unison, complimented the ref on the call.

Meanwhile, two trainers rushed onto the field to attend to a Carlos in agony. Blood oozed from Carlos' upper calf where metal cleats had ripped through the sock and tore his flesh. He held his knee. One trainer pulled the can of 'magic spray' from a holster. He sprayed the back of Carlos' knee. They assisted the boy wonder to his feet. He limped, blood trickling down, off the field, with a trainer on either side.

Play resumed shortly, with both teams down a man.

Sean strode confidently over to Matt. "Well, looks like our Sin Brazos won't be getting a hat trick today."

Matt opined, "They haven't subbed him out yet."

Mirek surveyed the incoming wounded. The bench cleared to begin warm-ups and to give Carlos some room for evaluation. One gash, the trainer said, would require stitches. Mirek looked at it as Carlos lie face down on the bench.

The Coach hollered for Manny Larsen. "You're going in for Carlos. Have the Iceman move his bleached blonde ass up to striker so we'll be shifting to a 4-4-2. When the rest of the team sees you come on, it should be clear."

Manny nodded. "Sure thing, coach." Together, they went to notify the fourth official. At an opportune moment, the board was held aloft. #7 in red lights, #17 in green.

Matt cried out, "Goddammit!"

Sean hollered, "Yeah!"

Lawrence, standing nearby, reached inside his cape and pulled out the $200. He handed it to Sean. "Now, can we just watch the rest of the match in peace?"

Both man-children nodded: one with a broad smile, the other with a defeated look.

At the end of the 7-0 match, the Dogs left the field with their tales tucked between their legs, literally. The four second-half goals were divided between Iceman and Cristobal.

Carlos had insisted on lying on the bench for the rest of the match. The team doctor had to come out and stitch his calf up right there. It was just five quick whips, but Doc Gina hated that it was not the most sterile of environments. She also examined Carlos' knee and just said to keep ice on it for now to keep any swelling down.

"*Quiero a ir a la fiesta,*" Carlos said to her.

"*Sí, sí, mi jugadorito.* You can go. But no dancing," she said with a motherly tone.

The supporters headed for their usual post-match locale for a few more drinks and merriment. Jackie gave Sean a ride. Matt watched them walk out of the stadium and shook his head. Lawrence and Madeline a bit further back, watched Matt stare at Jackie. Madeline said, "I think Matt really likes Jackie, but doesn't know how to express it."

Lawrence just nodded. After a thoughtful pause, he added, "It doesn't help that Matt and Sean are sparring partners, so to speak."

"Yeah, definitely."

Quigley headed for the Stampede locker room after the match. His enjoyment level of the game dropped as his concern for his "adopted son" grew. Quigley was a natural worrywart.

He was somewhat relieved when Sin Brazos limped across the field to exit at the southwest corner. Channels 44 and 66, the Spanish language radio station that carried the matches live, and reporters from *Exito* and *La Raza* all awaited Carlos. However, before Carlos even acknowledged their presence, he asked Ian to get his prosthetic designed for writing from his locker. Ian jogged back. Shouts of "Tigger" rang in his ears. He'd be back. He was not about to disappoint the fans.

Quigley stood back and watched in amazement at how well young Carlos handled the press. Granted Quigley spoke fluent Spanish, but even he had trouble with the rapid-fire exchanges between the reporters and Carlos. However, when Ian returned from the locker room with the requested item, Carlos cut them off. Ian had thoughtfully attached a Sharpie marker to the specialized writing prosthetic, which his teammate donned.

Amid flashbulbs, Carlos walked over to the horde of kids pressing against each other, trying to be the first one in Chicago to get Sin Brazos' autograph. Molly automatically knew what to do to help Carlos. One by one, she gathered all manner of T-shirts, jerseys, ticket stubs, programs, and balls. She held each one up for Carlos to sign, then handed it back to its owner.

Ian came up by her side. He kissed her cheek. "Hi, sweetie."

Molly started handing signed items to Ian for him to sign. Then Ian tossed them back up. "You both looked great out there."

"Gracias," said Carlos. *"Ian, ¿es ella tu novia?"*

"Sí, sí, su nombre es Molly."

"Ella es muy bonita."

Molly blushed. "*Gracias,* Carlos."

The three worked their way down the concrete wall. Ian spoke, "You're coming with us tonight, right?"

Molly nodded. "Yeah."

"Why don't you ride with us?"

"Sure, I'll have Renata take my car home."

They reached the end of the wall. Carlos used his teeth to remove the appliance. "Thank you, Molly." He walked slowly down the tunnel. Molly noticed the bandages around his leg.

"Ian, what happened to Carlos?"

"Nasty McDuffy's cleats tore a hole in the back of his leg."

"Ouch."

"Now you two have something in common." Ian lifted Molly's stitched hand and kissed it.

Before meeting Carlos and Ian, Molly had to check out from work. She changed the dressing on her hand. Renata helped her friend. "Are you going to the team party?"

"Yeah, Ian asked me to come. Could you take my car home?"

"Sure, beats taking that slow ass bus. I'll call you tomorrow. Besides, I want to hear all the juicy details. I can hold your car for ransom."

"You wouldn't," Molly said in mock horror.

"I would." Renata winked as she took the keys.

Freshly bandaged, Molly walked through the now quiet stadium. The only ones left in the seating area were the cleaning crew sweeping up all manner smashed cups, nacho cheese boats, and peanut hulls. She felt as if she had run 90 minutes, just like her man. Except her running happened to be up and down stairs. Her knee cramped a bit; a bit of arnica gel and a few drinks should take care of the pain.

She entered the north end inner lot and easily spotted Ian's car. The top was still down. She hopped into the Jaguar and sank back in the soft leather seat. She closed her eyes and relaxed, as she waited for Ian and Carlos.

Her cell phone rang. She fumbled through her purse and answered it just before it would have gone into voice mail. "Molly, where are you?"

"Ian, I'm in your car."

"Okay, we'll be out in a minute."

Seconds after she hung up, it rang again. She looked at the caller ID. It was not a number she recognized. She answered it anyway, thinking it might be from a pay phone or something. She knew a few people without phones at all. It was Jack. "I want to pick up my stuff. You changed the locks on me, you bitch."

"Yes, I did, asshole."

"Where the fuck are you?"

"I had to work tonight and now I'm going out."

"I need to get my stuff tonight. You come straight here, right now, or I'll just have to break down your door."

"If you do that, I know where to send the cops to arrest your sorry ass."

"Woman, I want you to come home right now."

"No fucking way. You'll pick up your things when it's convenient for me not you. You'll just have to do without your leather girdle tonight."

"Fuck you, bitch." Jack shouted and hung up with a loud bang.

By this time, Ian had approached. He witnessed the tail end of the conversation. "Who was that?"

"That was just my ex. There's still some of his crap at my apartment. He wants to pick it up tonight, but I told him no. That I was busy." She tucked her phone back in her handbag.

Ian got into the car. He put his arm around Molly and gave her a little squeeze. "That's right, you are busy." He gave her a quick kiss.

Carlos had already eased his way into the back seat. He stretched out across the supple *piel*. His knee and calf throbbed, but he ignored the pain. Tonight, he intended to have fun. "Where are we going?" Carlos tried out his English.

"The team likes to go to Axis—it's a nightclub—after matches sometimes. I think Mirek has arranged for us to have a private room, but no one is obligated to stay in that room, of course. *Hay gringas bonitas allí*." Ian smiled as he looked over his shoulder at Carlos.

"Gina say, no dancing." Carlos looked at his knee.

"You'll have fun anyway," put in Molly.

Ian started the engine and pulled out of the stadium.

CHAPTER VII

Later at The Filling Station, Jackie circulated among her soccer buddies. Matt was ignoring her. He was probably irritated about her hanging out with Sean in Section 12.

Madeline cornered her. "Hey, girl, what's up with you and Sean?"

Jackie shrugged.

"You two looked like you were getting pretty cozy at the match."

"Oh, that, that's just match-time adrenaline, or something like that. We probably just got caught up in the moment."

"I think Sean might want something more." Maddie winked.

"He's a sex-crazed teenager. I know that. Trust me, I know how to handle the lads. Besides, a boy toy might be fun for a while."

"He's only seventeen, you know."

"Oh yeah, that's right. I'll definitely steer clear then."

"Atta girl. Besides, Matt's sweet on you."

Jackie looked over at the pool table where Matt was bending over to take a shot. He looked so goddamn sexy in his kilt. A rush of energy jolted her loins. "I don't know. I think he might just be playing me."

"Well, he is a hard cat to figure out. I've known him since high school and he's always been hard to read when it came to emotions. He's pretty jaded about relationships after getting jilted at the altar a couple of years ago."

"Whoa, yeah, that would be enough to screw anyone up." Jackie began to look at Matt in a whole new light. A lot of his strange behavior around her started to make sense now.

Both women were silent for a while as they sipped their respective brews and watched Matt. The jukebox started playing "The Stroke" by Billy Squier. Both of them cringed simultaneously wondering who would have selected that tune.

Another lady supporter came over. "Hey, Razor. Hey Maddie."

"Hey, Paulie," Jackie greeted with faked enthusiasm.

Pauline set her empty pint glass on the bar. The bartender asked if she wanted another, but Pauline waved him away. She flipped her recently dyed strawberry blonde soft blonde curls. "I heard all the players are over at Axis celebrating Carlos joining the team."

Madeline's eyes bugged out. "Really? I'd sure like to get my hands on that Iceman."

"Really. I'm headed over there if anyone wants to go with me." Pauline was a full-figured woman with ample breasts and a heart of gold, on the surface. She tended to be pushy when it came to trying to meet the players, so most of the supporters did not want to align themselves with her too often, for fear of being accused of the same. She developed the reputation when she was a high school student in the 1980's around the Chicago Sting of the long defunct NASL. "But the Iceman is mine."

"Count me in," said Madeline. "I'll go grab Lawrence. I know he would want to go."

"As long as he stays away from my Iceman."

"Oh, chill out, Paulie. There's no way in hell that Brendan is gay," Madeline replied before bounding off to tell Lawrence.

"What about you, Jackie?"

"Oh sure, why not. I need a bit of distance between myself and Matt right now and Sean, too."

Pauline looked around the room. "Sean isn't even here right now. Someone checked his ID while he had a beer in his hands and he was kicked out."

"Oh, that sucks. Someone has got to get that boy a good fake ID." Jackie shook her head. "Oh well. Let's go."

Word circulated quickly. Over the next fifteen minutes, waves of supporters left The Filling Station and headed to Axis.

The team had gathered in their private room at the club. Carlos settled himself on a couch with his feet up. He wore his hand prosthetic on his right arm. He was drinking Tecate complete with salt and lime, the Mexican way. He was only 19, but no one had bothered to check his ID. He smiled at his victory in this. It was good to be the superstar.

Tomás, with vodka neat in his aging Polish paw, pulled up a chair next to the kid. The two men clinked glasses. "*Salut!*" Tomás looked at Carlos' bandages as a concerned father would. "How is your leg feeling?"

"Bien."

"Don't lie to me. I know better." Tomás smiled. "Do you want me to find some women for you?"

"*Sí, mi amigo.* I would like that very much."

Tomás rose. "Anything for my new teammate." He slapped the kid on the back in a friendly guy-like sporting way.

Carl grabbed Ian to help him translate while he chatted to Carlos. Carl's command of Spanish consisted of being able to pick up women and order *cerveza* in a bar. When he heard them, He also knew some soccer-related terms. But was unable to carry on any meaningful conversation in the language.

Tomás departed. Carl continued to talk to Carlos through Ian. Tequila flowed like water in honor of the new teammate, but no one on the team could match Carlos' affection for tequila like Carl could.

Jackie, Madeline, Pauline and Lawrence all arrived at Axis together. They begrudgingly paid the cover charge, but were given a dollar off for still wearing their fan gear. It was a deal that Carl had made with the management for every home match. He had tried to get his faithful flock a half price deal, but the club manager was stubborn and would only offer a dollar discount.

Lawrence headed for the bar and bought his girl friends a round of drinks. The ladies scanned the room looking for players and other Stampede personnel. It was Saturday night, but the club was not too crowded yet. After all, it was only 10:30 pm. The night was still very young.

"So, Paulie," began Jackie, "how do you propose we find the boys?"

"Yeah, this place is huge. I've never been in here before," added Madeline.

"Oh girls," replied Paulie. "It's easy. Just follow me. I come here all the time."

The bass thumped loud in their guts as the DJ spun dance tunes at a volume that might break one's eardrums. The little group had to shout to make themselves heard. Meanwhile, Lawrence had put in earplugs.

Pauline led the pack as she headed for a set of stairs. She paused when she spotted one of the waitresses that she knew. Pauline asked where the Stampede players were. She was told that it was one of the private rooms on the uppermost floor. Pauline passed on the information, and then suggested a conference in the ladies' room. It was quieter, somewhat.

Without skipping a beat, Lawrence followed them in. A lady touching up her makeup gave him a funny look until she noticed the rainbow trim on his cape. Then, she asked Lawrence, "How do I look?"

"You look fabulous, darling," he obliged her. She grabbed her clutch and left.

"Okay, girls, here's the deal," Pauline started, clasping her hands together. "Our boys are in a suite upstairs, one of the private boxes overlooking the main dance floor. The probably won't stay in there. They'll be going in and out. So all we have to do is just circulate around that general area. I don't think we should cluster. We'd look like a pack of wolves or stalkers or something. It would be too obvious. The security here has instructions to bounce anybody who looks like they are stalking anyone in the suites."

The other three nodded. Jackie spoke up, "I don't know about you guys, but I can handle myself around celebrities. It's just their job, you know, playing soccer—just the same as mine is accounting."

Lawrence and Madeline looked at each other, then at Jackie. "Whatever, Jackie," breathed Madeline.

"I'll show you guys, then everyone's on their own." Pauline turned to head out.

When the foursome arrived at the location leading up to the suite, Tomás was coming out. The Polish player leered at Madeline. He took her hand and kissed it as he bowed to her beauty. Madeline blushed. He did not immediately release her hand. He tugged on her ever so gently. Madeline grinned broadly as she followed Tomás to the dance floor.

"Wow, that was quick!" said Jackie.

Lawrence nodded as he scanned the area for eye candy and possibilities, red clad or not. The bartender caught his eye. "I think I'm going to go freshen my drink." He headed for the bar and settled himself on a rare vacant stool.

"Well, Jackie, I think I'm going to circulate a bit to see who else is working that I might know."

"Sure, Paulie, see ya later." *Finally, by myself again*, she thought to herself. *I mean, I like all these folks and all, but sometimes, they just get on my nerves. I wonder if Matt will be here*, she sighed. She leaned back against the wall and tried to blend with it as she nursed her lager.

Tomás and Madeline cut a mean rug. The more he watched her dance all over him as if he were a stripper's pole, the more he wanted to take this little firecracker home for a ride.

Jackie watched Madeline. *God, that girl is shameless. Tomás is one of the ugliest guys on the team.*

Brendan appeared next on the main dance floor. Before Jackie could congratulate him on the match, he crossed to the bar and sidled up next to Lawrence. *Oh, it's a good thing Pauline's not here to see this*, thought Jackie as she watched Brendan's approach.

Brendan extended his right fingers and ran them up Lawrence's spine. He leaned in, whispering lustily in Lawrence's ear, "Hi, darling."

Lawrence's heart skipped a beat upon turning to see who spoke. He gazed into Brendan's ice blue eyes. "Hi." In that instant, he knew that Brendan swung his way, and even more importantly was interested in him.

"Darling, don't talk. Just follow me."

The bleached blonde stud turned to head back upstairs. He said something to the gatekeeper just inside the door. Lawrence was able to pass by easily. Like a puppy, he followed the Iceman. There was a catwalk around the perimeter of the dance floor, with doors that led into luxurious suites of various sizes. Huge windows overlooked the floor. The team was in one of the largest suites opposite the stairs to the main floor.

Brendan pulled a key out of his pocket and unlocked one of the doors in a dim corner. Lawrence followed him in. Brendan locked the door and made sure the hotel style curtain was drawn. The room was quite cozy and lit only with candles. Brendan unfastened Lawrence's cape and laid it carefully over a chair. He crinkled his nose at Ian's jersey. "I'll have to give you one of my jerseys, lover."

Lawrence unbuttoned Brendan's black silk shirt to reveal his solid build. Lawrence ran his fingers through the futbolista's light chestnut fur. As Lawrence bent to kiss his nipples, Brendan removed Lawrence's jersey. There was a bit of a fumble because of the tight fit. It was laid on top of the cape. Lawrence continued his trek down the Iceman's washboard abs. One-handed, Lawrence unbuckled the belt . . . top button on the black slacks . . . zipper . . . red silk boxers, bulging, rock hard desire spilling out through the vent. The slacks fell to the floor.

Kneeling, Lawrence knew what to do. He cupped hot cock in his hands and smelled its essence. His tongue flicked, licked, wrapped around the tip. Brendan sighed. "Yes, I want to feel your lips around me."

Slowly, the fan pleased him. Lawrence always prided himself in his ability to deep throat. He was fast becoming legendary in Boys Town. And pleasing the Iceman tonight was no exception. Hands free and locked on either butt cheek, Lawrence took in all eight thick throbbing inches and pumped and sucked him like Brendan had never felt before. Brendan struggled to hold back, to lengthen his pleasure, but the fan was too good, damn good. Brendan erupted with an explosion that rivaled Krakatau. Lawrence swallowed every delicious drop.

The two men pulled apart. Lawrence's own dick throbbed in anticipation of a favor returned. Brendan pulled up his pants and tucked his half flaccid flesh inside before zipping up. Lawrence watched and started to speak. Brendan laid a left-hand finger on Lawrence's lips. "Don't speak."

Lawrence noticed a gold band on Brendan's left ring finger. Without saying anything, he touched the ring and looked up questioningly.

"Yes, I am married. I am still in the closet. Don't even start. This is the perfect arrangement for me, especially in this sport. I trust you can keep a secret."

Lawrence nodded.

"Good. I rent this suite from the manager. No one else uses it. It is where I come to get some relief, because my wife can't suck dick for shit. She doesn't even like the taste of cum."

"I'm sorry," Lawrence said as he rose.

Brendan scolded, "I told you not to speak. I don't even want to know your name. I just want you to promise me two things. One, this is our little secret; and two, you will come by after every home game."

Lawrence nodded.

"I wish I could take you into the private party, but it would be too suspicious, since you're a rainbow warrior. Sorry." Brendan reached for his wallet and pulled out a hundred-dollar bill. "Take this. Enjoy yourself tonight." He pressed it into Lawrence's hand.

Lawrence shook his head. "I can't. I'm not that kind of—"

"Shh!" scolded Brendan again. "Okay, now I'm going to step out. You wait five minutes then go back downstairs. There is a small washroom here with some mouthwash, so you can freshen up. And make sure the candles are out before you leave." He held Lawrence's face in both hands. He kissed him on the lips, first slowly, then more passionately. Before leaving, Brendan said one more time, "Our little secret."

Lawrence's loins ached as he watched the blonde beauty leave. He could barely believe what had just happened. He wished that Brendan had returned the favor, but maybe next time, definitely next time. He pocketed his ill-gotten gain. He then took full advantage of the tiny bathroom, relieving the great pressure below.

Lawrence managed to do as Brendan instructed him, and slinked quietly, undetected by anyone who knew him, out of the club.

Carlos had the coaching staff move the couch to a location where he could see out the window. If he could not go dance, he might as well be able to watch the chicks gyrate. That's when he spotted Tomás on the dance floor. *"Pinche pendejo, pinche Tomás."*

Ian and Carl were standing nearby engaged in a tête-à-tête. *"¿Qué?"* said Ian.

In rapid Spanish, Carlos started going on about how Tomás was going to bring up some girls for him, but then there he was dancing down there with one, and not sharing.

"Carlos, *tranquilo, wey.* Tomás never goes back on his word. He's probably just testing them out for you," Ian tried to assure the lad. He looked out the window and saw what Carlos was looking at. Oh hell, Tomás is having too good of a time. He knew his friend pretty well, but the way Tomás was dancing with Madeline looked a bit too close to sex with clothes on.

Carl peered out. "Wow, Tomás can sure move on the floor. Almost as down and dirty as he moves on the pitch." His eyes scanned the room. "Hello, who do we have here?" He spotted a woman, with a figure like Venus, leaning against the wall near the stairwell. Her shape looked familiar to him at a distance. Her red replica jersey cried out to him. "Excuse me a minute."

"Señor Costello, bring me some *chicas, por favor,*" pleaded Carlos.

Carl nodded as he rushed out of the room.

"Ian, I'm never going to get a *chica* tonight." Carlos sighed.

Carl's long legs glided quickly around the catwalk to the stairs. He could not take his eyes off Jackie. He remembered being near her in Section 12. She oozed fire and spice, the dark-haired beauty. He bounded down the stairs, taking two at a time. Maybe it was the tequila shooters starting to take hold, but he felt that he must talk to this woman.

An Eastern European matron with a basket of roses was coming up at the same time. Carl intercepted her. He purchased six of the fullest blooming roses from her basket. He pressed a generous tip in her hand. *"Dziękuję bardzo,"* she said.

"Proszę bardzo." Carl replied. Tomás had been teaching him Polish.

He went down. Jackie was still in the same spot. Carl slyly reached around the corner and presented the roses to his target. Smooth like satin, the rest of his body followed the hand clutching the blossoms.

Jackie's eyes followed the arm until it connected to the body. She looked up at Carl. "Thank you." A remix of Madonna's "Skin" started to play.

"Would you like to come upstairs?"

She, who bragged about being able to handle being around celebrities, found herself flustered. "Uh, wow . . . uh, yeah, sure." Unconsciously, she ran her fingers through her hair. She did not feel that way when she was near him in Section 12, why now?

"We have a private room upstairs. The whole team is up there. Well, except for Tomás." Carl gestured toward the star defender. "I just don't see how he can dance like that after playing a full ninety."

Jackie smiled, shook her head and shrugged.

"By the way, darling, what's your name?"

"Jacqueline."

"That's a beautiful name. I saw you in Section 12. I hope you're not dating the high school lad."

"Oh, heavens no." Not when I have a wealth of other possibilities, like you. She drank in the scent of the roses.

"*. . . put your hand on my skin . . . kiss me I'm dying . . .*"

Carl smiled, keenly aware of the song lyrics. He bent closer to her. She almost swooned from the scent of Polo and salty sweat from drumming.

"Before we go up, I need to find some cute girls for Carlos."

"*. . . do I know you from somewhere / why do you leave me wanting more . . .*"

"Okay." She wanted to lick him.

"I thought you could help me."

"*. . . kiss me . . . kiss . . .*"

Jackie wanted to grab him and kiss him, test his rhythm. She breathed deeply, trying to gather her senses. Jesus Christ, girl, get a hold of yourself. "Okay."

Carl kissed her cheek gently. He noted the nearly empty glass she clutched. "First, let's freshen your drink."

They crossed to the spot where Brendan had picked up Lawrence. Jackie wondered for a moment what happened. She did not see Lawrence come back down, but she did notice Brendan walk by himself into the party room.

Carl ordered two Petrón frozen margaritas. "I hope you like margaritas, Jacqueline."

She normally did not like the sound of her full first name; it was too girly. Yet, somehow, it sounded right when Carl used it. "Yes, thank you."

"Any ideas for finding some *chicas* for Carlos?"

"We could try the front entrance, see who's coming in. Maybe there's a fresh pack. All these gals in here are pretty well settled in, if you know what I mean. There is one who'd like to come up there, but, trust me, you don't want to even set foot near her."

"Is she some kind of stalker?"

"You could say that."

"Is she at least attractive?"

"Nah, she's a fat cunt. Her face isn't even that pretty. Problem is, she thinks it is. I've seen drag queens better looking than her."

Carl was taken aback by her choice of words. "Well, then, we'll just stay away from her."

Carlos watched Carl and Jackie leave his field of vision for the front room. "Damn, even *el señor Costello,* is betraying me."

Molly brought over a tequila shooter for him. "Here, this will ease your pain."

"*Gracias, mi bonita.*" He smiled flirtatiously.

Ian shot Carlos a territorial look, subtle enough for Molly not to notice, but just enough for Carlos to pick up on.

Fifteen minutes later, Carl and Jackie entered the party suite with five of the hottest, cutest chicks in tow. All were exchange students from Europe. Each wore a soccer jersey from one club side or another, with tight mini skirts and stilettos. "*Ay, muchos gracias por las bonitas,*" Carlos said trying to contain his enthusiasm.

Introductions were made, and Carlos began conversing with the raven-haired lady from Barcelona. The brunette from southern France started massaging Carlos, who let out a moan of pleasure. The other three began to circulate, talking in native tongues to those appropriate and in decent British to those Americans. Baumgartner and his fiancée, who was also from Germany, conversed with the fraulien.

Carl and Jackie retired to the back of the room and found a loveseat to relax on. She still clutched the flowers. Carl ran his fingers through her hair. "All this is crazy, isn't it?" He smiled warmly as he looked into her eyes.

She sipped her margarita. "Yes, it is." She thought it was crazy that Carl had picked her out of the crowd in the first place. "Do you plan on coming down to Section 12 for most home games?"

"Yes, I do. It's so boring up in the owner's box."

"But you get all the booze and food you'd ever want, right?" Jackie struggled to make conversation. Normally, this was not a problem for her, but somehow, looking into Carl's piercing eyes left her almost speechless.

"Yes, but it's more fun where the real fans are. That's what I am first, a fan. And that's what makes it so damn hard to make important business decisions regarding the club." He paused, touching her cheek gently. "I don't want to talk about that right now. I want to explore you."

She crinkled her nose. Her defenses struggled to stay up. She heard standard lines and hoped that they were sincere. Still, she asked, "Aren't you married?"

"Never did."

"Girlfriend?"

"No, and if I did I wouldn't be here with you like this right now." He pulled her into a kiss. She yielded to his desire. She hoped he was not just feeding her lines to get her into bed. She wanted this to be more than just a one-night stand.

He pulled back. "Are you sure you want this?" He cocked his head to study her face.

She swallowed and nodded. Jackie found herself at a loss for words.

"I want you to be comfortable around me. I want to be able to talk to you."

"Yes, Carl." She exhaled slowly. "I'm sorry. I'm usually not this—uh—flustered." She nervously ran her hand through her hair.

Carl wanted to tell her to relax. But he was nervous, too. He slipped his arm around her and pulled her closer. "If it helps, I don't want you just for tonight. I see a person I'd like to get to know, not just your body."

"Same here." Her voice cracked. She finished her drink just in time for a waitress to bring the pair a fresh round. Carl tipped the waitress. Jackie looked at him quizzically, as he didn't seem to pay for the drink.

"The bill for the drinks and the room are sent to the Stampede office. There is mandatory gratuity added to the drink bill, but I like to give the girls cash on the spot. They deserve to have their own money."

Jackie smiled. "Good idea." She took a drink. She should not worry about Carl. So far, he had proven to be nothing but a gentleman. She snuggled closer to him. He felt good, lean, strong. She ran her hand down his thigh and allowed herself to relax.

He pulled her into a deep kiss. She responded fully to him.

Across the room, Mrs. Novotny and Leah, a stunning African-American woman who was Capt. Dan's girlfriend, decided to put together an all women's outdoor team to play in a co-ed league. They circuited the room recruiting.

Molly befriended the pair. After chatting briefly, the ladies told her about their idea.

"I've never played, but I'd like to try," replied Molly.

"No worries, sweetie," assured Leah. "I'll teach you."

"Hey, who's that girl in the Stampede jersey talking to Carl?" said Mrs. Novotny in a gossipy tone.

Leah shrugged. "I don't know, but she looks like she might know how to play. We do need one more."

"I don't know if we should interrupt them or not. They're starting to look like they need a room," Molly added.

All three giggled. Mrs. Novotny pushed her glasses up and said, "I'm going to ask. Carl needs to be interrupted before he goes off and does something he regrets." She crossed the room.

Leah said to Molly, "She's always been a mother hen type."

"Excuse me, Carl, can I talk to your lady friend for a minute?"

"Agnes, dear, why of course." Carl pulled back from his embrace of Jackie. "Jacqueline, this is Mrs. Agnes Novotny. Agnes, this is Jacqueline."

Jackie extended her hand. "Nice to meet you. Please, call me Jackie."

The two women shook cordially. "We're putting together an all-women's team for the summer session to play in a co-ed league. You look like you might have played before."

"Yes, but it's been since junior high."

"That's okay. It's something to do more for fun anyway. A lot of us are sick of just watching our guys play. We want to get in on the action." Agnes licked her lips. "Molly over there, you know Ian's new honey, has never played before, but she's going to give it a go."

Carl looked at Jackie. "What do you think?"

Agnes added, "Carl has agreed to buy all our equipment and uniforms with names and numbers. The last games the league sells tickets to for charity."

Jackie thought for a brief moment, and then said. "Yes, I'll do it."

"Oh good, now we have a full 22. Give me your number and I'll call you later this week with all the details."

Jackie searched her pockets for a scrap of paper. Agnes had already whipped out a small pen and notepad. "Just write it down here, honey. That way I won't lose it."

Chapter VIII

Sunday, APRIL 12, 1998: Tomás never made it back upstairs. He snuck out with Madeline. No one seemed to notice, until the end of the night. And if they did, they just assumed something illicit was going on, because they had witnessed simulated sex on the dance floor.

Carlos ended up taking Miss Barcelona and Miss France home. The other three went back to the hostel where they were staying.

Paulie went home alone and pissed about being 'abandoned' by the other three.

After the party, Ian circled in loops and figure eights around Molly's apartment building for 45 minutes looking for free parking. They finally saw one about a block away. He insisted on walking her up to her place.

She was glad, because the whole evening, she could not get Jack's phone call out of her mind. As she climbed the stairs, an overwhelming sense of doom descended over her. Ian followed closely behind. She arrived at her door only to find it open. She froze. Ian nearly bumped into her. She held up her hand. "Don't go any further. Just call the cops."

Dutifully, Ian whipped out his cell phone and dialed 911. "We'd like to report a break in."

Molly sat down on the top stair. "Hand me the phone," she said wearily.

Ian complied.

"Hi, yes, it's my apartment. I'm pretty sure I know who did it. Just send some officers out to take a report and dust for prints, etc. We're not going inside until they get here." She gave them her address and hung up.

Ian sat down beside her. "I'm sorry, honey. I'm here for you." He pulled her close and held her tight. He did not have to ask. He knew who had busted into her place. Molly started to punch the wall with her healing hand. He caught her arm, just before potentially painful contact was made. He held her even tighter, rocking her comfortingly.

"Molly, it's too early to say that I love you, but I want you to know that I care very deeply for you. And whatever problems you have with this ex of yours, I'll be behind you." He cupped her face in his hands and kissed her soft lips. She embraced him as she responded.

The police arrived and did their thing. Molly gave them a quick list of likely places to find Jack so he could be arrested. It was nearly 6:00AM when the officers left and Molly secured the place. Ian then took her to his place.

Ian's condo was a warm place in a vintage building in the Gold Coast. The doorman buzzed them in; a valet parked the Jaguar.

Inside, Ian turned on the lights and said, "Welcome to my humble abode."

"It's beautiful," she gushed. Humble was certainly an understatement. The vintage details were well preserved. Mahogany woodwork was the dominant feature. It was decorated in warm earthy tones, antiques and velvets. Molly felt like she had stepped inside a dream.

"Thank you." He closed and locked the door behind him. "I'll give you the grand tour tomorrow. We're both too exhausted, you from work and me from play." He took her hand. "Let me show you the bedroom."

He led her down the hall. She said nothing, but he could sense her awe at the grandness of his mahogany four-poster bed. He started to remove her blouse. She unbuckled his belt and undid his trousers. They fell to the floor, spilling change, clattering loudly on the hardwood floor. He cupped her ample breasts in his hands and kissed each one as he unhooked her bra. Her hands lifted his golf shirt over his head. She ran her fingers over his solid muscles, licking his already erect nipples. Her hands slid down his ripped physique to his groin. The bulge through his drab plaid cotton boxers was more than apparent. They both wanted the same thing, each other.

Ian breathed in her ear. "Are you sure?"

"Yes," she breathed back, "I am."

He lifted her onto the bed. He removed her shoes. Slowly, he eased her tight black jeans off. She felt a bit embarrassed about her holey white cotton bikini panties, but Ian made no comment as he took them off. His hands felt good on her skin. She thought to herself, I sure am glad that I shaved my legs before going to work.

She eased herself further back on the king-size bed. Ian lay down beside her. He asked as he looked at her face, "Are you sure you're not too tired?"

She lied, "No. I want to make love to you."

She rubbed his engorged flesh. It was not too big, nor too small, it was just right. She pulled him closer to her.

"What about a condom?"

"I'm on the pill."

"That's not what I'm worried about."

"I'm sorry. You're right. You have one?"

"Yeah, just a minute." One-handed, he opened the top drawer to the nightstand and pulled out a Trojan. With his teeth, he ripped the package open. She helped him roll it on. Face to face, on their sides, he entered her. He slipped in easily. She sighed in satisfaction. Motionless, they laid.

He wanted to, she wanted to, but both were so tired they couldn't move.

His level of hardness started to fade. He wanted her, but just could not summon enough energy to do it right. He kissed her, slow and gentle. "I'm sorry, honey. I'm too tired," he said softly.

"That's okay. I think all we have the energy to do is lie here in each others arms." She smiled.

They eased apart and he removed the latex. He dropped it on the floor and turned back to his new lover. He snuggled in her soft locks. "Sweet dreams, my dear."

She kissed him. "Good night." She rolled over to sleep on her side; he draped his weary arm and leg over her and before long both were sound asleep.

Jackie awoke to Carl stroking her hair. He was spooning her. She could feel his engorged loins pressed against her buttocks. She smiled. His touch was gentle. It had been over a year since she had been touched like that.

Slowly, she rolled over to face him.

"Good morning, Jacqueline." His husky voice felt good to her ears, especially the way he said her name.

"Good morning." She peered into his eyes and felt the sensation that she was falling.

He leaned in to kiss her. She was now fully aware of the tenderness of his lips caressing hers.

A throbbing pain in her head interrupted the moment. She eased herself upright. "Do you have some Excedrin?" she asked.

Carl smiled. "In the medicine cabinet. Help yourself." He pointed in the direction of the bathroom.

She swung her feet to the floor. She was still dressed except for her socks and shoes. Her head swooned. A brief spat of nausea hit her. "God, what did I drink last night?"

"I don't know what you had before we met, but you knocked back quite a few margaritas, then passed out about three-quarters of the way through the bottle of Vueve Cliquot."

She glanced over at him. "We drank champagne?"

"Yep."

"Oh god, no wonder my head is spinning." She padded into the bathroom and shut the door. Her head was not just spinning from the aftereffects of drinking; she was still stunned that she, Jackie Harris, was actually in Carl Costello's condominium. This had to be a dream.

She opened the medicine cabinet. It was filled with a variety of prescription muscle relaxers in addition to Excedrin and Advil: Xanax, Valium, Demerol, all nestled neatly next to a bottle of the truck stop classic, white crosses. She took two Excedrin tablets and finger-combed her hair.

There was a clock in the room. It read 12:36 PM. "Shit!" she exclaimed. "I've got work to do." She racked her brain for a tactful exit strategy.

Carl expressed his disappointment. "I was hoping to cook for you."

"I'm sorry. I've got a lot of work to get done today."
"On a Sunday?"
"I'm a CPA."
"Oh, say no more. I understand."

Jackie took a cab to her car. She was surprised that there was not a parking ticket on her car when she picked it up from the metered space near the club; she remembered that Chicago police did not issue parking tickets on Sundays.

At the loft, Jackie's message indicator was blinking. She hit play. "Jackie, it's Matt. I'm just wondering if you made it home okay. It's 4 am. I'm sorry, I'm drunk, and I can't get you off my mind. I wish you had said something before you left the bar. Call me."

<beep>

"Jackie, it's Lawrence. I need to talk to someone and you're the only one I can trust with this. Call me. You've got my number."

<beep>

"Miss Harris, this is Cassie Matthews. I want to know if you'll be done with my taxes tonight. I want to set up an appointment with you before they are filed. Call me."

<beep>

"Hey, Jackie, I found those receipts you needed. I'll bring them by and leave them with your doorman if you're out."

<beep>

"Jacqueline, it's Carl. I know you're going to be very busy this week. So I want to ask you this now. Would you like to fly to Miami with the team and myself for the match? Call me either way. My number is 312-555-3473."

<beep>

She had to replay the last message to get the number. True, she was not looking forward to meeting with all these clients this week to wrap up, but capping the week off in Miami sounded deliciously tempting.

She would call him later this evening, once her headache was gone. She disconnected her phone so it would not ring. Her body pleaded for a nap, so she collapsed on her own bed and closed her eyes. Everything else could wait a few more hours.

When Jackie woke up, she procrastinated by checking the discussion board for the Chicago Stampede. It was more social and childish most of the time instead of the serious match analysis that she craved. But that did not stop her from checking it at least once a day.

Post number 699:

Pauline: Where did everyone go last night? I looked around at Axis, but I lost all three of you. Did you meet anyone? I missed everyone.

Post number 700:

Maddiemay: Tomás and I had a ball on the dance floor. I'm surprised you didn't notice us.

Post number 702:

Pauline: I'm really ticked that I missed meeting Brendan, or anyone else for that matter. Maddie, how could you have ended up with someone who looks like Tomás? I know he's a player, but he's old and ugly and married.

Post number 703:

Maddiemay: Shut up, fat broad. You're just jealous because you didn't get ANYONE to dance with you that night. Back to the list topic, where is everyone meeting this weekend for the Miami match? Is Sueños del Fútbol still our official bar?

Post number 708:

Seaner: Whoa! What a show by Sin Brazos last night. I could barely believe my eyes. What a treat to have witnessed a perfect bike live. If that's not going to win goal of the year, I don't know what will. Matt, dude, I know you would have won our little bet if he hadn't have been subbed out. Does anyone know his status?

Post number 710:

Gdoc: Hi, Doc Gina, here. Wanted to give you an update on Carlos' condition. His calf was stitched up as he watched the second half. On Monday, we will examine his knee to make sure there are no tears or any other pressing problems. He should be fine for the Miami game on Saturday, provided he doesn't bust the stitches during practice this week. I think Nasty McDuffy, the bastard, may be facing a fine from the FLA and a longer suspension than just the one game for the red card, but that's just rumor. I think he might have had illegal cleats.

Post number 711:

KiltedOne: It's good to hear that Nasty will have to pay for what he's done. That looked so awful. I'll bet you were picking grass out of that gash for a while, Gina. On a related note, I've heard a rumor that the FLA might outlaw metal cleats due to this incident. There is no clear ruling on that yet. Jackie, dear, where did you end up last night? You're usually the first one with a drunken post match post.

Post number 715:

Pauline: Jackie, Madeline, Lawrence and myself went to Axis where the team was. But I lost track of them. They either cut out or ended up partying with the team. Knowing Jackie, she probably ended up with the team upstairs in one of the private party rooms.

Jackie quickly typed a response to the post, which appeared as

Post number 745:

Razorgirl: I thought my ears were burning while I took a long nap today. I didn't get home until close to noon, FYI. Where I was and whom I was with is nobody's business but my own, so piss off.

The next three appeared in rapid succession.

Post number 746:

Ccostello: She was with me.

Post number 747:

Pauline: That backstabbing bitch!

Post number 748:
Seaner: Take it off the list, you fat cow.
As soon as Jackie read post #746, she dialed Carl. "What in the hell do you think you're doing?" she roared.
"Whoa! Jacqueline, what are you talking about?"
"Your post to the list. What are you doing to me?"
"Calm down, Jacqueline. I only said you were with me. I didn't say anything else."
"Oh, that's enough. Last night may just be a drunken one night thing."
"We didn't do anything you'd regret and you know it, darling. I don't know if you got my message, but I think it should be fairly obvious that I want to see you more. I'm inviting you to come to Miami this Saturday. I don't know why you are ashamed of me, but it sure as hell seemed like it on the list."
Jackie took a deep breath before responding. She mulled over his words for a moment, and then replied, "I'm not ashamed. I don't like to kiss and tell. Plus, I didn't want to piss off Paulie. Surely you noticed how agitated she was about not meeting any players."
"Is she the one you warned me about?"
"Yeah."
"Then why do you even care?"
"Because we have to see each other all season. We both stand in Section 12, watch parties—"
"Don't go to the watch party on Saturday. Come see the match in Miami. The game is on the 18th, after tax day. You deserve to be swept off your feet and taken on vacation, if only for a few days. I want you to come with me, with the team."
"Carl, I don't know," she mused.
"Think about it. I promise you that nothing will happen, unless you want it to. I'll be a perfect gentleman." He did not want to make such a promise, but felt it was necessary.
"Carl," she said softly.
"Yes, Jacqueline," he replied tenderly.
"I had a great time last night."
"I did, too, Jacqueline. I did, too."
"Call me Wednesday night. I'm just not sure yet. I may have extensions on a couple of my clients if they don't give me all the info." It would be easy to dump everything and run off, but she wanted to try to take this one slow. Carl was a catch, and she knew it.
"I understand. I'll call you on Wednesday."

Matt read Carl's post and reality hit him like a brick upside the head. He was going to lose his chance at Jackie. He clicked on Jackie's e-mail address to send her something directly. Fingers poised over the keyboard, he found himself at a loss for words. He clicked 'cancel' and picked up the phone instead.

"Hello, Colin, I need some advice about Jackie."

"Talk to me little brother. I just read the posts myself."

"I think I'm starting to fall for her. But I'm afraid I've blown it. I failed to ask her out."

"You both have been busy. Especially her being an accountant and all."

"I know. But now I'm losing her. If it were Sean, I wouldn't mind, because I know that wouldn't last long. He's too young for her for anything long-term. But with Carl Costello, I have no way of competing. He's got money and power. How can I compete against that?"

Colin scratched his head. "I know you don't want to hear this, but just be there for her as a friend."

"It's going to be hard."

"I know. But you could try asking her out on a date," Colin suggested. "Call her and see what she has to say. Maybe nothing happened while she was with him last night. And what if it did? You know how she is; she flirts with everybody. Carl could have just been using her. He's got a reputation as a player, you know."

Matt sighed. "Yeah, that's why I don't want to move too fast with her. I don't want to come across that way. I know she wants to fuck me. But I want to get to know her first. I don't want to become another notch on her bedpost."

"Then tell her that. She'll probably respect you more."

"I'll call her."

"Remember, you are a MacNaughten. We are proud warriors. You will get what you want. But you have to fight for it. Okay, my brother?"

"Okay."

"Now, go get her."

Matt called Jackie, but her phone was busy. Disappointed, he replaced the receiver.

Jackie rang Lawrence. She barely got out a hello when he started in on his dilemma. "Did you see who came up to me last night?"

"Yes, what happened between you and the Iceman?"

"I'm trusting you to keep a secret."

"You have my trust. You know you do."

Lawrence took a deep breath. "Brendan is gay."

"Well, duh, that was obvious from the way he was picking you up. So, I know you're dying to tell me. What happened?"

He took me up to a private room, and, well, I, we, uh . . ." Words failed him.

"So, did you fuck him or what?" Jackie bit off the tip of a carrot stick.

"Jackie, such words," Lawrence sounded shocked.

"Hey, I never claimed to be a lady. So, spit it out, did you guys get it on or what?"

"I only sucked him off. He didn't reciprocate."

"That's all? Ugh, you got the short end of the stick."

"Please, Jackie, keep this between us. I'm not even supposed to be talking to you about it, but I trust you."

"Hon, don't worry. Your secret is safe with me."

"So, whom did you end up with, girlfriend?" He had already read the posts. He knew, but he wanted to hear it from her.

"Carl Costello."

"So, what happened?"

"We hung out in the party suite for a while. I met some of the players. I didn't talk to Carlos much, but he's pretty cool. He's not good with English and my Spanish is minimal. Carl and I brought up five Euro chicks in kits. So, he was occupied the rest of the night. I met Mrs. Novotny and I think I got signed up to play in a summer league. Then, Carl took me to his place in his limo."

"You rode in a limo?"

"Yeah, it felt strange, but it was fun. I'm not used to being treated like that."

"So, then what?"

"I passed out. Way too much tequila and champagne later."

"I hope you didn't do anything stupid."

"I don't think so. He wants to take me to Miami this weekend."

"Miami, how nice. Are you going?"

"I don't know."

"Why wouldn't you?"

"I don't know. I told him I might still be working on a few accounts, as a cover. It's just that I just have an odd feeling about all of it. I mean, why me? What do I have to offer Carl? He could have any woman he wants. He could have a penthouse full of supermodels with his money. I'm certainly not supermodel material."

Lawrence cut in. "Girl, shut up. Don't worry about the whys. Just live in the moment. Enjoy yourself and for god's sake take advantage of Carl's offer and go to Miami."

"Okay," she mumbled.

"If the man wants to spend money on you, for crying out loud, let him. I met Carl at a fundraiser before the season. He's a nice guy. If I knew he swung my way, I'd fight you for him. If I thought he was a jerk, I would tell you not to go. Just go and have fun. You deserve it."

She perked up a bit. "You're right. I do deserve it. I am worthy of Carl."

"That's the spirit, Jackie."

"You know, I even feel comfortable with him calling me Jacqueline."

"Wow! You won't even let me do that."

"Yeah, but when Carl says my name, it feels right."

"Take that as a positive sign. Hey, if you don't see me at the bar after the next home game, don't be surprised."

"Yeah, I'll just tell folks you have to work early the next day or something."

"A little white lie," Lawrence said.

"To cover up the big one," she finished.

Chapter IX

WEDNESDAY, APRIL 15, 1998: NEW YORK CITY: Fútbol League America has issued an additional suspension to San Francisco Fog Dog midfielder Jack "Nasty" McDuffy. In addition to the normal one match suspension, McDuffy has been suspended for three additional matches and fined $5000.00.

Lance Merton, FLA president, stated, "McDuffy was found to be wearing illegal metal cleats during the match against Chicago. The league owners have now passed a rule effective immediately that outlaws metal cleats of any kind."

McDuffy refused to comment when contacted by this reporter.

San Francisco head coach Dalton James said, "Losing McDuffy for four matches will hurt, but the team does not approve of his behavior on the pitch. We agree with the punishment. I encouraged the FLA to pass a clearer rule than what FIFA states on metal cleats."

Carlos Cortez is recovering from the injury sustained by the tackle from behind. Team officials for Chicago have placed Cortez on the questionable list for Saturday's match in Miami.

Chapter X

FRIDAY, APRIL 17, 1998: The team jet landed in Miami early in the evening. Jackie was onboard, sitting next to Carl. He held her hand most of the flight. As they deplaned, Carl even carried her overnight bag.

A hotel bus awaited the team and staff. They were headed to Hilton. Mirek, Carl & Jackie stepped into a white limousine.

When they were settled in, Carl asked, "So, Mirek, what's your strategy against El Sol?"

Mirek poured himself two fingers of cold Bak Zubrowka vodka. He slung it back. "Well, we were doing well before Carlos came on. I'll use the same 3-5-2 line-up we used before Carlos."

Carl opened two bottles of Newcastle and handed one to Jackie. "Are you sure that will be enough to stop their strong attack? I've been watching the Miami game tapes from the past few weeks. Cairn & Miklos are unstoppable."

"Sure they are. They haven't played against our defense yet." Grinning, Mirek poured himself another two fingers.

"Didn't Tomás play for Poland when Miklos played for Greece in some Euro Cup match?" Jackie put in, not wanting to be left out.

Mirek swirled his vodka in the glass. "No, that game, Miklos was out with a pulled hamstring. But you're right, Jackie. Tomás knows Miklos' style of play better than anyone else on the team, including myself." He sipped the clear liquid. "I do think that Tomás might have played against Miklos during a club side Champions League qualifying match. If he had, he didn't say anything to me. But, Carl, don't worry. We are prepared to defeat El Sol."

Carl lifted his bottle in toast. "That's what I like to hear."

The three drank, "To victory!"

Chapter XI

SATURDAY, APRIL 18, 1998: An hour before kickoff, 12-Steppers, as the supporters group jokingly referred to themselves, began spilling into Sueños del Fútbol. Soon, the place was awash in red.

Matt had been at the bar since noon, even though kickoff was not until 6:00 PM. Jack Daniel's whiskey saturated every cell. He never tried calling Jackie again. He was afraid to. Whatever Carl Costello went after, Carl got. Sean, of all people, had pointed that out to him on the list. Despite his warrior heritage, Matt could not compete against a man like Carl.

Lawrence sat next to Matt, who brooded over his whiskey at the far end of the bar. Without so much as a hello, Matt turned to his friend and said, "So, exactly what the fuck happened at Axis last weekend?"

Lawrence, who was not much of a drinker, sensed Matt's obvious level of inebriation. "You're upset about Jackie and Carl, aren't you?"

Matt glared at Lawrence; he slammed the rest of the Jack.

Lawrence continued, "I really don't know. I was on the dance floor when Carl supposedly picked up Jackie. I left after a while, but I didn't see Jackie with Carl. I never even made it upstairs to the team's suite. I did see Tomás' mack daddy moves on Maddie, though."

"I don't care if Maddie fucked Tomás. I just want to know about Jackie and Carl," growled Matt.

Joe set a glass of water in front of Matt as he removed the empty rocks glass.

"Damn, guess I've been cut off." Matt dutifully drank the water.

"From the looks of you, I'd have to agree with him." Lawrence smiled. "Whiskey will not make the problem go away."

"No, but it sure as hell dulls the pain for a while." For the first time all week, Matt smiled.

Lawrence put his arms around the lad and pulled him into a strong hug.

"Thanks, man, I needed that," Matt said.

Lawrence glanced up at the television. "Look, the game's about to begin."

Jackie wore a red jersey with #7 on it for the injured lad, still recovering from his entanglement with Nasty McDuffy. She walked proudly beside Carl as they made their way around the pitch sidelines. The teams entered the field to the traditional FIFA anthem. Jackie and Carl clapped as they stood near the visitor's bench.

A reporter with a cameraman in tow vied for Carl's attention. He asked Carl for a brief pregame interview. Carl nodded. The reporter straightened his tie. Carl rolled his eyes. Jackie tried not to laugh.

Camera on, the reporter began, "I'm standing here with Carl Costello, owner and general manager of the Chicago Stampede. Carl, El Sol de Miami is undefeated so far with very lopsided scores. How do you see the Stampede faring against their attack?"

"Quite well, actually. Defender Tomás Lozowski and keeper Captain Dan have had shut outs so far. And, by the way, our offense scored seven goals last week." Carl beamed with pride. He reached for Jackie's hand and squeezed it. She squeezed back.

"But two of those goals were from Sin Brazos. What is his status?"

"Well, Mike, Carlos didn't make the trip. The stitches will be coming out tomorrow. He practiced very lightly this week. Thankfully, his knee will be fine."

"That's certainly good news for Chicago. Will Sin Brazos be available for next week's match against defending champions DC Eagles?"

"It looks like it, yes."

The reporter stole a quick glance at the cleaved hands of Jackie and Carl. "Who's the pretty lass?"

Without hesitation, Jackie answered, "I'm Jacqueline Harris, no relation to Ian."

"Carl, we've never seen you with a lady at your side. What's going on?"

"That's for us to know and you to find out," Carl replied with a grin.

Matt launched the water glass at the closest TV. "Fuck you, Carl!"

Joe came out from behind the bar and hauled Matt out by his shirt collar.

Chapter XII

MIAMI, FL: The Chicago Stampede visited Lockhart Stadium in Miami Saturday night and left with a 6-1 victory.

It was clear that Chicago did not need the scoring abilities of Carlos Cortez who did not make the trip due to the injury suffered in the last match.

Juan Cristobal began the goal fest in the 10th minute with a blistering bender of a free kick. Michael Cairn answered for Miami six minutes later.

But it was all Chicago from there. Brendan Glazier logged two more in the 20th and 55th minutes. Juan Cristobal got his second of the match in the 49th. Even the rookie Tom Simpson who came on in the 53rd minute for Ian Harris scored on a penalty kick. Tomás Lozowski scored the sixth off a second penalty kick in the 83rd minute.

Yellow cards were issued to Miami's Alexander Boozman and Carlton Mills. Boozman's was booked for dissent. Mills received his booking for an illegal tackle on Ian Harris. Lozowski and Miami's Alex Saxon tangled late in the match resulting in Saxon receiving a straight red card ejection. Saxon will automatically sit out the next match.

Chapter XIII

April 19-24, 1998: 'The morning after the match, Carl woke and decided that he wanted to spend some time with Jacqueline without the team or any of her friends or work interfering. She had already risen and started to run the shower. He walked into the bathroom. Leaning against the doorframe, he asked, "Want to go to Key West for a few days?"

Not thinking clearly, she quipped, "I only packed for a couple of nights." She ran a brush through her hair.

He expected that light argument from her. He had only packed for a couple of nights as well. "We'll go shopping."

She stepped into the shower and let the warm liquid saturate her hair. "Sounds good."

He dropped his red silk boxers and pulled back the curtain. Water glistened off Jackie's skin. He fought back a boner. Despite all the time they had been spending together, Carl did not want to push sex on her. She made no advances in that direction either. He cleared his throat discretely. "Mind if I join you?"

"Sure, but you'll have to scrub my back."

"With pleasure, Jacqueline." He stepped into the shower. He grabbed the bar of soap and a rag and began rubbing her back. The items fell and he found his fingers flowing effortlessly over her slickened skin. He could fight back his urges no longer.

Jackie turned slowly, laying her hands on his chest. She made a move to the soap and washcloth. He quivered as she touched his engorged member. She let her mouth slide over him.

"Oh, Jacqueline," he moaned.

As she sucked him, licking him as if he were a lollipop, she groped for the soap. She slicked her hands with it before fondling his balls.

Carl decided it was worth waiting for her to make the first move toward lovemaking, well worth the wait.

They finished the shower foreplay and moved into the bedroom, where it was less awkward. Both felt they wanted their first time together to be slow and gentle and normal.

As he laid her on the bed, he found her absolutely beautiful without makeup. She spread her legs apart to welcome his engorged member. Unhurried, he made love to her until they were both a quivering pile of flesh. He climaxed himself inside of her not once but twice.

They lie naked, still half wet from the shower. He gazed at her. He wanted to spend the rest of his life with her.

Carl rented a Jaguar to drive down to the Keys. Jackie marveled at the length of the bridges connecting each island. The conversation was kept light. While Jackie was curious about where Carl's money came from, she did not pry for fear of appearing like a gold digger.

By the end of the week, she had shopped in the most expensive boutiques, where the price was never displayed on the item, because it simply did not matter. She had dined in the finest restaurants. She had learned about the history of the Keys and partied in the bars that Hemingway was said to frequent.

She felt like a princess. She chose not to be too forthcoming about her past. She did not really have much to discuss anyway and her mother and grandmother had taught her to be a lady in discussing former lovers. She did not ask Carl about his past loves either.

Each day, Carl checked his voice mail and email. He did not respond to any, though, choosing to focus wholly on Jacqueline. He told his secretary, Carrie, to cancel all his appointments or reschedule them for next week. He enjoyed having that luxury.

Being the boss was fun, but it left him lonely. Sure he could call up an escort service or pick up a bar bimbo. He was not immune from succumbing to such devices when he just wanted to get off. He had grown tired of doing things that way. He was only 25, but he felt much older. He wanted some stability in his life. He wanted someone to share his success with on a daily basis. Jacqueline was the first woman he had met who might be able to fill that role.

Chapter XIV

Wednesday, April 22, 1998: The phone woke Molly at nine in the morning. "Collect call from—Jack—Will you accept the charges? Press one for yes, two for no." She dutifully depressed 2 as loud and as hard as she could. She slammed the receiver down.

"Who was that?" Ian mumbled.

"Fucking Jack."

"Leave the receiver off the hook."

"Good idea." She flicked the phone off its hook. They listened through the obligatory burps, beeps, and complaints before it fell silent to the busy signal.

Molly curled up next to Ian. He held her tight. He breathed in her ear. "I love you."

She twisted around and kissed him deeply in reply; still she could not take her mind off the phone call. "Even in jail, the bastard refuses leave me alone."

"Didn't you put in for a restraining order?"

"Yeah, but county jail doesn't have much control over who he dials."

"Report the attempted call and maybe they'll take his phone privileges away."

She sighed. "Yeah, maybe I'll try that." She rolled him onto his stomach and ran her hands over his naked supple body. As her right hand touched the back of his right thigh, she asked, "How is your hamstring feeling?"

"Fine, but Doc Gina's afraid I'll aggravate it if I start on Saturday."

"Are you going?"

"No, I don't think so. It wouldn't be worth it to sit on the bench. Carlos should be back on Saturday."

She gently massaged his legs. "So, I'll have you to myself this weekend?"

He emitted a sharp sound of pain, followed immediately by one of relief. "Oh my god, yes!" he exclaimed. "Yes, yes, my lover, you will."

They were quiet, except for his utterances of pleasure as she massaged him from foot to head.

Slowly, Ian rolled over to face her. "Do you want to go to Sueños del Fútbol to watch the match?"

"Where?" She blinked.

"That's where the 12-Steppers go to watch the away matches. I haven't been there, but I guess it's cool, according to the supporters' discussion list."

"Oh my god, you trawl that thing, too?"

"Yeah, but I never post."

"Neither do I. I do just the get info on what the hooligans might be planning to celebrate the next goal or victory or whatever."

"I do to get a good gauge of what the fans think about the team. Carl does, too, but he actually posts occasionally."

Molly nodded. "Yeah, did you see the one where he came out and pretty much claimed that Jackie chick?"

"Yeah, but she's cool. She went down to Miami with us. I've known Carl for a while, and I've never seen him this smitten with a woman. He usually just gets bubbleheads for a night or two of fun, then sends them on their merry way."

"Yeah, probably after paying them." Molly knew the types. She used to be one, a long time ago, sort of.

Chapter XV

SATURDAY, APRIL 25, 1998: Matt called Colin. "I tried calling her, but I think she's still with Carl."

"My brother, just bide your time. Leave very strong, but unquestionable hints to her and, maybe, she'll hear them."

"She hasn't posted to the list this week."

"She's probably still with Carl. She'll likely be at the DC match with him."

"Don't say that. Even though I know it's probably true, don't say it."

"I guess you aren't going to Sueños del Fútbol later?"

"Yeah, I got red-carded last weekend."

"Come over and watch the match here with me and Charlotte."

"I'm not going to watch it."

"It's supposed to be a great match. Both teams are undefeated. And DC is the defending champion. You know we are poised to upset them."

"I know," Matt sighed. "I'll listen to it on Polish radio."

"But you don't know Polish." Colin scratched his head in wonder.

"I know enough to understand what's going on and I know that Carl doesn't speak Polish, so there's no chance of hearing him."

Carl and Jackie were guests of the owners of the DC Eagles, Jon and Betty Eagle. They chitchatted about league politics before the match. Carl even made a friendly wager with Jon. Closer to kickoff, however, Carl and Jackie headed for the Stampede bench.

Jackie, in her full fan garb, cheered on the kickoff. Carl, smiling at her, just clapped. He had finally found a woman with the same passion that he had for the beautiful game.

A slightly limping Ian and Molly walked into Sueños del Fútbol. They found two open seats at a table shared by two 12-Steppers. "I'm Sean and this is Lenny."

"Ian Harris and this is Molly."

Lenny offered, "Can I buy you two a drink?"

"Sure," replied Ian. "I'll have a Goose."

"Make it two," said Molly.

"I'll just get a pitcher for the table," said Lenny getting up.

"Tough break last week, Ian," said Sean.

"Yeah, if I had stayed in the game we might have scored at least one more goal," he joked in reply.

Molly rolled her eyes. "He's usually not this full of himself."

Lenny returned with the pitcher and four glasses. "Molly, haven't I seen you working at Soldier Field?"

"Yes, I work in the yellow seats. I'm an usher supervisor."

Sean started to pour. Lenny said, "Is that how you met Ian?"

"Yeah, he introduced himself to me after the first match. I was afraid I would get fired for talking to him. I watched his back while he was signing autographs." She smiled broadly.

Ian kissed her lightly on the cheek. "She did such a good job I just had to give her my number so she could watch my back more often."

"You are so full of it today, Ian," Molly said.

"Hey," said Sean, "game on."

On the pitch in RFK Stadium, the Stampede received the ball first. They launched a full-on attack. Novotny passed it back to Starkov, who sliced up field. Brendan was open, as planned, so Starkov passed the ball to the Iceman. It was a high pass. Brendan headed it to Carlos who took a few control steps with it before knocking a hard left-footer toward the net from the top of the box.

The Eagle keeper lunged. He was not expecting this fast or clean of an attack. It was like there was no defensive response from his teammates. Cursing loudly, his fingertips grazed the leather, but it was not enough to stop the ball from finding the back of the net.

In celebration, Carlos did a front flip. Brendan, followed by several teammates, rushed to congratulate him.

On the sideline, Jackie squealed with delight and jumped into Carl's arms. He lifted her up and kissed her.

Back in Chicago, Sueños del Fútbol erupted. Ian kissed Molly. "We're going all the way!" he shouted.

"Yeah, baby!" Lenny agreed. "Look out LA. Here we come."

In the 23rd minute, DC's Darin Milano answered.

The score remained tied at 1-1 at halftime.

Jackie accompanied Carl on his ritual trek to the locker room. Mirek let Carl speak to his sweaty warriors first. "You guys are not going to lose this match. We've won our first three games because no one expected us to. I'm not saying that you guys suck, but, I will say this much. Tomás' yellow card foul on Tellum was a cheap shot that cost us the lead. Mirek, I want him subbed out in the second half."

Mirek nodded. He was not going to question the man who signed his paycheck. But Jackie was. "Carl, darling, let Tomás stay in the match. You can't afford to sub him out now. If we were up by three, then, yeah. If he's dumb enough to allow himself to get red-carded, we can afford to be without him against the Bulldogs next week. If you are going to sub anyone out right now, sub out O'Connor for Byron Jameson. Not right away. But go ahead and shift Starkov up to midfield, move Cristobal up to left striker, Carlos in the middle and Iceman on the right, you start out with a 3-4-3. Tomás would anchor the back as sweeper."

Carl and Mirek looked at each other and digested her suggestions. Carl stroked his chin.

She added during the awkward silence, "A 3-4-3 is the best balanced approach against the Eagles. They are not going to stop. They will score from the field. If it wasn't for our four-man back and Captain Dan, they might be up two or three on us now. But in order to penetrate their tightened defense, we need three up front."

Mirek nodded. He could come up with nothing to counter her suggestion. "Carl, your lady is a genius. She's right. The way the Eagles have been playing us, her idea of 3-4-3 is probably the only one that will work."

Carl was speechless.

"Team, did you catch what Jacqueline said? Starkov up the midfield. Cristobal, left striker. So, guys, how many are we going to score?"

"Many!" the team shouted in unison.

"And how many are you going to let DC score?"

"None!" they yelled again.

Carl grabbed Jackie by the forearm and hauled her out of the locker room. He pinned her against a wall. "What the hell did you think you were doing in there?"

"Helping the team defeat the Eagles." She blinked at him. "I'm sorry, but I just wanted to help."

"My god, don't be sorry. Jacqueline, how in the hell did you know that?" He softened his grip on her shoulders.

"I've been watching the game ever since I learned how to play. I'm not a great player, but I have a good—uh—feel for strategy."

"You just caught all of us off guard. Frankly, I'm surprised Mirek even entertained your idea. He's from the old country, you know." Jackie nodded. He smiled. "Are you bucking for his job?"

She laughed. "No, he's a great coach. Don't replace him with silly ol' me. I just have these occasional flashes of brilliance. But, Mirek, well, he's great all the time."

Carl whispered in her ear. "You're great all the time." He pulled her into a long kiss.

Some of the team was starting to come out. "Looks like she's being punished for speaking out of turn," quipped Cristobal.

All those around him laughed.

"Would you look at that?" said Lawrence. "Our boys are switching to a 3-4-3 in the second half."

Lenny picked up his refilled pitcher off the bar. Staring at the television, he said, "My god, you're right. I wonder where Mirek got that idea. I don't think he's ever used the 3-4-3 when he was in Europe. Hey, Ian, what's up with the line-up?"

Ian shrugged. "I don't know. We've never practiced it. Unless they started this past week."

Sean added, "I don't think Mirek would have thought of it either. It's such a weird line-up for him or anyone on our team for that matter. But, you know, after watching the first half closely, I think it might work."

Work it did!

Brendan scored off of Starkov in the 53rd minute.

Tomás headed off a DC attack in the 57th minute.

Jameson came in for O'Connor in the 62nd minute and made an immediate impact. The young rookie headed the ball into the back of the net off a corner kick from Cristobal in the 64th minute.

Larsen even shined by making some great tackles late in the 2nd half.

But in the 83rd minute, old predictable Tomás did just as predicted and drew a red card with a blatant tackle from behind on Tellum at the top of the box, but thankfully, it was spotted outside the box. On the ensuing free kick, Captain Dan knocked the ball high out of bounds, for a corner kick.

The final score would stand at 1-3. The Stampede had just upset the defending champions on their home turf. The rest of the season would not be the same.

Chapter XVI

Sunday, April 26, 1998:
Post #1193:
Seaner: Where do you think 3-4-3 came from in the 2nd half yesterday? Even Ian Harris couldn't come up with any ideas.

Post #1194:
KiltedOne: I should have actually watched the game. But man, were the Polish radio announcers excited! Does anyone have a tape I could borrow to dub? (Only as long as Jackie's not on screen.)

Post #1195:
HappyLarry: Matt, I taped it, and no, Jackie was never on screen. I didn't even see Carl get any face time like he usually does.

Post #1198:
CMacNaughten: What little chance I've had to talk with our razorgirl at matches, she might have had something to do with the 3-4-3 2nd half. If so, the fucked up thing is that #1) Mirek listened to a woman (you know how eastern European men are when it comes to women) and #2) That it worked!

Post #2000:
Seaner: You're damn right it worked. But I still want to know how Mirek came up with it.

Post #2002:
Len1976: Are you kidding, Sean? Mirek will never admit it if he didn't come up with it himself.

Two days later—
Post #2045:
PolakCoach: I know this thread is a few days old, but only here do I want to say where I came up with the 3-4-3, a line-up I never would have considered if it was not for Carl's girlfriend, Miss Jacqueline Harris. I hope that she's not after my job. But I must give credit where credit is due—to Miss Jacqueline and to our boys for making it work so well.

Chapter XVII

Dreams of footy colored red
Shadows dancing in my head
Contrast green pitch, bright blue sky
My heart bleeds, as you draw nigh.
Sun blisters my Scottish skin,
Yet I feel a cold, cold yen
Watching you across the pitch
Be with him, you fucking bitch.

SATURDAY, MAY 2, 1998:

Matt laid down the pen with a heavy sigh. Every time he tried to write a beautiful lyric to try to woo Jackie, he ended up with a cursed ending. All the previous attempts littered his feet as wadded crumpled bits. He started to do the same to this one, but could not.

He stood and flexed his slender, naked frame. Donning his kilt, he looked at himself in the full-length mirror on the bathroom door of his tiny studio apartment. He frowned. What did he have to offer Jackie that Carl could not? Carl was the rich owner of not one but two soccer teams. He was just a regular bloke who worked nine to five and had to worry about bills. He stared at himself. His boyish chest glared blindingly back at him. Chances were Carl had a manlier chest, too. Carl had more of everything. Carl had Jackie. Dammit! Matt turned away from the mirror.

"What could I offer Jackie?" he mused, pacing about. "I can't even come up with a good poem." He picked up his last attempt. "Maybe I should give this to her."

He shouted it out the open window, prompting more than one strange look from the passers-by below.

One man stopped to listen to the whole tirade. "Has she heard it?" he called up.

"No, I just wrote it."

"Tell her. She needs to know how you feel."

"Just give it to her?"

"No, you need to read it to her, just like you just read it. You have a passion for this woman that needs to be shouted from the rooftops."

"You think so?"

"Yeah, man, go for it! If you don't, you'll regret it for the rest of your life."
"Thanks, man."

The tailgating began in the late afternoon. The early May sun shone brightly. Maddie arrived early, as it was her turn to help the tailgate group. She iced down the bottles and set out the chips and condiments on the table.

Lawrence was one of the first to arrive. "Maddie, it's good to see you. We didn't get a chance to talk the last couple of weekends."

"I know. We haven't really seen each other since after the last home game at Axis." They hugged.

"So, are you going to tell me what happened between you and Tomás?"

"Like a hetero story would do a thing for you," she retorted.

"I'll take that as a no."

Maddie just smiled and went back to work.

Carl's stretch white limo descended the west ramp of the north end of Soldier Field. Jackie sported a rather risqué red leather cat suit with a plunging neckline. Her flesh was tan from lying on the beach. Her footwear elevated her by six inches—black stiletto heels. Her nails sported the numbers of the day's starting ten field players. Her dark locks flowed naturally, delicately framing her face.

She stepped out first. Carl followed. He was proud of how she looked in that outfit. He was falling in love with her body, mind and soul. He felt that she was falling in love with him.

Jackie strode tall and proud, like a supermodel, toward the tunnel area to the Stampede locker room. Carl walked behind her. His eyes never left her flawless figure. He questioned her about wearing it, but once she put it on, he could not protest anymore. The weather was still cool enough for her to be comfortable in it. It was one of the outfits he had purchased for her in Miami. It had been too warm for her to wear it down there.

Mirek spotted her. "Holy, mother of god! Is this the same woman who told me how to do my job last week?" He tried to look at Carl, but could not.

Carl grinned broadly. "Mirek, quit staring at my woman!" he scolded jokingly.

"Carl, my god, you can't help yourself whenever the—uh—goddess—is wearing—uh—oh, never mind." The coach forced himself to look Carl in the eyes. "So, has your goddess suggested anything for today's match?"

Jackie spoke, "No, I haven't, actually." She kissed Mirek in a traditional European greeting. "Good to see you, darling."

Mirek responded in kind. "Good to see you, Jacqueline, my assistant coach."

"Oh, please, I'm not even on the payroll." She laughed. "Ian's back in good form, right?"

"Oh, yes, healthy as a horse on race day—or so they say in America."

"Good, then you won't be needing any of my input." She smiled.

"No input on defense? Tomás is serving out a red card penalty."

"Hey, like I said last week, against the Bulldogs, missing Tomás shouldn't be a problem. Good lord, they are one and three; we're undefeated."

Carl tugged lightly on her elbow. "You wanted to go to the 12-Steppers tailgate?"

"Yeah, sweetie." She kissed Carl on the lips briefly. "Mirek, honey, you know what to do. That's why Carl put his trust in you." She kissed Mirek on the cheek, a bit fuller than a European good-bye.

"Jackie, you scare me," Mirek said.

She placed her hands on her hips. "Why's that?"

"For one, you see things I don't. Which, by the way, is fine. I'm open to suggestions, as should be clear from last week. And two, I feel compelled—Carl is, too—to listen to you."

"And that scares you?" Puzzled, she looked at him.

"Carl's in a position to void my contract and replace me with whomever he wants. Even if that might be you, my dear. I don't know, but I have this vision that you could be a great coach. And I really mean that."

Carl added, "He's right. But enough of this. I'm craving a bratwurst."

Colin and Matt arrived together fully kilted. Colin worried about his brother. Matt had been silent the entire ride.

Matt palmed the poem he shared with the stranger. Jackie was sure to appear at the tailgate with Carl. Matt was counting on it. He was going to read his poem to her as loud as he possibly could. He no longer cared what anybody thought of him. Today would be the day he would be outed as a poet. Not even his brother Colin knew about his secret creative outlet.

Two hours before kickoff, Jackie with Carl in tow arrived at the 12-Steppers tailgate. Matt laid eyes on her and could not avert them. She was whorishly stunning. Colin watched his brother closely.

Carl secured two brats fresh off the grill and handed one to Jackie. The two ate and drank. Matt watched the new couple interact. It was like they had known each other all their lives. Matt's jealousy level began to boil. The near empty can of beer crinkled as his grip tightened on it.

Sean spotted Carl. "Hey, good to see you, Carl. Everyone's healthy for today's match, right?"

Carl nodded and finished chewing the last of the brat before answering. "Yeah, Ian will be back today. We decided to rest his hamstring last weekend, but he's up to full speed now. Gina gave him the go ahead on Wednesday."

"Ian came out to watch the match at Sueños del Fútbol with the group last weekend."

"That's good to hear. We, meaning all of us, need to work together to really build soccer in the States. That's why I tell the players to interact with the fans beyond the scheduled appearances." Carl smiled.

Sean said, "I know you aren't from around here. Why did you move to Chicago for your home base?"

"I fell in love with the city during World Cup '94. I saw how the locals were in their fervent support of the beautiful game. I wish I were offered the opportunity in 1996 to give Chicago a team. I supported the Bulldogs while in Boston, but wrote daily to Lance Merton about the faux pas of not putting a team here in the beginning. Early last year, Lance finally responded and said they were going to expand the league by two teams and would I be interested in owning one. Hell yeah! But one had to be in Chicago; otherwise I would not do it. I love this city, so I moved here and helped the FLA establish the Stampede."

Jackie listened intently. She had not had any conversations about money with Carl. Granted, she was curious, but she purposefully avoided it. She preferred to get her information from casual conversation. She also liked the fact that he never felt the need to brag to her about his holdings and wealth. Then again, maybe she should do some investigating on her own into his true worth. She had the know-how. Nah, that would show lack of trust if he were to catch her at it.

Sean said, "Don't you also own the Philadelphia Minute Men?"

"That's right. It was between Philly and Denver, but the fans in Philly wanted it more. They worked hard to land a team there ever since the inception of the league in 1995."

"And Denver didn't?"

"The city and surrounding area, it was my impression, that they couldn't care less. They are so wrapped up in their Broncos right now. And that's fine. I do know they are still on the table if and when the FLA expands again."

"How long do you think that will be?"

Carl shrugged. "The next steps will be getting soccer-specific stadiums built and boosting and keeping attendance. Columbus' and Kansas City's owner Clark Logan began construction late last year in Columbus. Next season, the team should be moving in. He's having a harder time in KC though. The Columbus stadium should be nice, but it's too open. I much prefer the roofed ones in Europe."

"Wow," Sean exclaimed. "I will be majoring in architecture at IIT. Could I design something? I've been dreaming about the perfect stadium all my life."

"Sure, on one condition, that the stadium be residential like Arsenal's or here in the city like Wrigley Field. I want a culture to be built up around it, a whole neighborhood of atmosphere. I don't want it surrounded by parking lots like Comisky or here, for that matter."

"Yes, sir, I'll give you a whole plan, complete with locations scouted."

"Are you sure you'll have time for all this with your studies?"

"Oh, absolutely. I won't have classes this summer. Plus, I can talk with my advisor about getting some advanced credit for it."

"If I like it, I'll pay you. When it's built, I'll give you a bonus, more if it's in a location you've chosen."

The two gentlemen shook. "You've got a deal, Carl."

Carl gave the lad a business card. "Feel free to call or email me if you have any questions about the design or logistics."

"Thank you." Sean went to chat with some of his buddies who just arrived.

Carl turned to Jackie. "Do you think he'll really do it?"

"Oh, he'll do it. I think he almost has one finished. Before I met you, we chatted on-line one night about it. Why do you ask?"

"I already have plans drawn up, but I didn't want to discourage the lad."

Matt paced. He tried to distract himself, but failed. He kept looking at the happy couple. He saw Carl squeeze Jackie's hand. He looked at his watch. It was getting close to kickoff. Carl and Jackie would be heading in. Matt reached inside his sporran and retrieved the poem. He jumped on the hood of his brother's car.

Colin and Lawrence rushed over to try and pull Matt down before he did or said anything stupid. But it was too late. Matt began reading. His voice boomed over all other conversations, forcing all attention toward him.

"Dreams of footy colored red
Shadows dancing in my head
Contrast green pitch, bright blue sky
My heart bleeds, as you draw nigh.
Sun blisters my Scottish skin,
Yet I feel a cold, cold yen
Watching you across the pitch
Be with him, you fucking bitch."

As he recited, he stared at Jackie. When he finished, he jumped down and headed toward the stadium entry. Colin and Lawrence chased after him.

Jackie's mouth fell agape. She nearly dropped her beer.

Carl looked at her. "What just happened, Jacqueline? Were you seeing him?"

Jackie took a long last swig of brew then flung it into a nearby garbage can. "I don't know. We flirted, but I didn't think he ever wanted to go out with me. Oh my god, Matt has a huge crush on me."

Carl pulled her into a long hug. "And to think I was worried about Sean. Jacqueline, we've spent a lot of time together over the last few weeks. And I've grown to like you, a lot."

"Same here," she said softly. "Don't worry about Matt. He's just got a lot of issues right now. Colin and Lawrence will handle him. Let's go inside."

"I think we need to avoid section 12 for the first half," he suggested as they started walking.

"Agreed."

After the match, Lawrence entered Axis and situated himself as close as he could to the same spot that Brendan had picked him up from. He ordered a single malt scotch, straight up. He downed it and waited patiently.

Saturday night swirled around him—bumping, grinding, gyrating. He witnessed Brendan's true hat trick less than an hour ago. His victorious lover would be here soon.

Brendan entered the club. The rest of the team had all gone their separate ways. A few might stop by, but he doubted it. Carl did not reserve a room this time. That was good, because the more teammates might be around, the more likely it would be that his secret would be discovered.

He spotted Lawrence and gave a toss of his head. Lawrence met him; together they went upstairs. The love nest awaited.

In the room, Brendan remained the dominant one, but this time he wanted to romance his lover. "Get comfortable, darling."

Lawrence sat down on the couch. Brendan opened two long neck bottles and handed one to his lover. He sat next to him. Lawrence reached out and squeezed Brendan's thigh. The player smiled in encouragement and took a swig.

"Have you told anyone?"

Lawrence lied, "No."

"I know you know my name, but I want to know yours."

"Lawrence."

"A strong name. I like it." Brendan touched Lawrence's cheek. "I'm sorry about leaving you so abruptly last week."

"I felt like a whore."

"Aren't you?" Brendan smiled. "I'm joking. No, seriously, every first encounter, I always pay off. But your commitment tells me that you came back for me and not the money, am I right?"

Lawrence nodded.

"I'm glad." Brendan pulled him into a long, probing passionate kiss. Both men grew. Lawrence set his beer on the table behind him, and then did the same with Brendan's bottle. Brendan worked his lips around to the ear. "I want to make love to you. I want you to be satisfied this time. We have plenty of time. There is no rush tonight."

Lawrence breathed in reply, "Yes, Bren, anything for you."

Brendan lifted Lawrence's shirt off. He was still offended at him wearing Ian's number. "I have something for you later."

Lawrence just nodded. Too many words would have ruined the moment.

Brendan's hand rubbed Lawrence's soft flesh. He worked his way down. He unfastened Lawrence's khaki trousers. Lawrence's hard cock sprang forth in full glory. "It's beautiful," Brendan exclaimed. He immediately set to sucking. He took it all in.

Lawrence sighed. "Oh my god." Brendan slid his lips up and down the shaft. He stopped, kissed Lawrence's balls, and then stood. He disrobed teasingly, but not too slowly. Lawrence finished taking off his own clothes as he watched his firm lover. He thought to himself briefly that he really needed to get to the gym. Lawrence stood. Both men were fully naked and erect. They rubbed each other up and down, drinking in each other's scent.

Brendan pulled him close. "Fuck me." Lawrence turned his lover around to reveal the firm backside. He cupped and separated the cheeks as Brendan bent over and braced himself on the couch. Uncovered, Lawrence sunk himself deep in the athlete's tight ass. Brendan grunted loudly with each stroke. The fan's left hand gripped Brendan's hard ass cheek, while the right hand curled around the slender perfect waist and pressed his dick against his abs. Lawrence's fingers rubbed as the rest of the body thrust. He did not want to come so soon, but it felt so good. He could not hold back. With a loud finale, Lawrence filled Brendan. He pulled out.

Brendan stood up and positioned his new lover face up on the couch. Lawrence smiled. He was glad that Brendan wanted to do missionary. He spit on his own cock before easing it inside his lover. Lawrence grunted. Brendan liked to pump it hard and fast, just like he ran up the pitch. Both men grunted and panted. Brendan began to drip sweat onto his lover. Usually that bothered Lawrence, but not tonight. It was honeyed nectar dripping on his flesh.

The Iceman unleashed his mighty load inside the snug hole. His mouth fell on Lawrence's. "God, that felt great," sighed Brendan. The pair cuddled for a bit.

Slowly they at least put on their underwear as they chatted and sipped drinks. Brendan was truly interested in getting to know his lover on a personal level. Lawrence felt himself falling. Here was a man he could love, but was in the closet and heterosexually married. It was not going to be easy keeping up appearances, but he knew he could manage. He had to.

Before they parted, Brendan handed Lawrence a plastic bag. Lawrence peered inside and pulled out a dirty jersey, still damp with sweat. "It's the one I wore tonight. I want you to have it," said Brendan.

Chapter XVIII

Wednesday, May 6, 1998: "Molly, I don't want you working the games anymore."

"But I like to, Ian. The company counts on me to pull together all the loose ends. Besides, I'm the only one the 12-Steppers trust."

"But I want you to enjoy the matches." He held her hands. They were at her place. A replay of a Premiership match danced on the television screen.

"Then, take me with you to Dallas."

"I'll have to clear it with Mirek and Carl, but I think you'd be able to."

"I'd love to."

Chapter XIX

FRIDAY, MAY 8, 1998: Molly and Renata had a girls' night out. They went to Smiler Coogan's to see a decent local band play and pound bottles of cheap domestic beer. Molly caught Renata up fully on her blooming relationship with Ian.

They cheered on the band, devil-horned hands held high. Two o'clock came and went. The two sat at the bar. One of Jack's friends came in. "Molly, so it's your fault Jack's fucking locked up."

Molly stood to face him. "The mother fucker trashed my apartment. Damn right he deserves to be locked up." Renata placed her hand on Molly's shoulder. Molly brushed it off. "It's okay. I can handle this pussy."

The man pushed Molly in the chest. "You cunt, you told the cops it was him."

Molly caught the man's wrists and twisted his arm behind his back. "Not only did he call and threaten me that he was going to do it, his fingerprints were all over the place. That motherfucker's going down. And I know that he's had enough previous arrests for this to count as a felony. So, it's not my fault, you bastard. Jack brought it all on himself. Now get the fuck out of here." Molly shoved him the few feet toward the door and threw him out. The man tumbled down the steps and rolled onto the sidewalk.

Two broad-chested bouncers and Renata stood behind her. All three were ready to interfere. But there was no need. Molly had everything under control. One bouncer placed a firm hand on her shoulder. "Is everything okay?"

Molly nodded. "Absolutely." She cracked her knuckles. "Just make sure he doesn't come back in."

The second bouncer said, "Renny gets thrown out of here all the time. I'm just glad a chick did it this time." He chuckled. "Where in the world did you learn that move?"

"I'm a licensed security guard," was all Molly said.

Chapter XX

SATURDAY, MAY 9, 1998: Ian, Tomás, Carlos and Brendan decided to go out without the rest of the team or any women in tow. They went to Calo's, an Italian restaurant in the Andersonville neighborhood, for dinner. They lingered over big bowls of pasta, but resisted the urge to drink. Mirek frowned on his players drinking the night before matches.

"So, Bren," said Tomás between huge mouthfuls. "I've been meaning to ask. Early this week you looked like you got laid. And I know you haven't been getting it at home."

Brendan looked down at his fettuccine and twirled it. He was not sure how to answer.

"Looks like we'll have to drag it out of him." Ian winked.

Brendan swallowed hard.

Carlos asked, "How come I never see you talking to ladies when we go out after games?" His English was greatly improved, thanks to Ian's lessons.

Brendan did not answer. He shoved a forkful of noodles in his mouth.

His three mates stared at him, like a pack of cats wanting fed.

Brendan took a long swig of water, and then faced his attackers. "What? My private life is my own personal business." It was the best answer he could come up with.

"That still doesn't answer my question," said Carlos, pointed his fork at him.

Brendan pointed his fork right back at the lad. "Your English is getting too good." Carlos grinned from ear to ear. "Ian, stop teaching him."

"No way," said Ian. "Especially if it helps to give you hell."

Tomás laughed as he nodded in agreement.

Ian continued, "We all know that you are hiding something from all of us. And we are going to hound you about it if it takes all season."

Oh shit, Brendan thought to himself.

Carlos lowered his voice. "Brendan, I've seen how you look at me in the showers."

"You are not my type," he replied.

Tomás and Ian looked at each other. There was an awkward silence. Carlos finally found the right words. He looked lustily at his fellow striker. Blinking flirtatiously, he said, "Why not?"

Brendan breathed deeply. He was attracted to Carlos. Oh sure, he could not give hand jobs, but his sweet little brown mouth. Oh stop! He thought to himself, don't think like that.

Ian sensed the Iceman's discomfort. "Back off, Carlos. No teasing the animal." Carlos sat back and started eating again. "Bren, I think the cat's out of the bag. I'm amazed you've been able to keep the secret for this long. But it's been obvious lately that your dam is about to burst. We catch you looking at us in the changing room. That's why the three of us asked you out."

"Does your wife know?" asked Carlos.

Brendan shook his head. "No."

"Do you love her?" Carlos cocked his head. The whole gay thing made him uncomfortable, but once he had talked with Ian about it during one of his English lessons, he began to tolerate it. He was still not sure what possessed him to flirt with Brendan, but it was effective at flushing him out.

"I love her as a friend and I know she loves me, but I can't bring myself to make love to her like we used to. She's beautiful, but . . ."

"How do we know? We've never seen her," said Tomás.

"Yeah, Bren, how come you never bring her to the games?"

"Sheila hates soccer."

All three mouths fell agape. "What? You married a woman who hates fútbol?" Carlos said. "Do you remember the ladies that Carl brought up for me a few weeks ago? Now, those ladies love fútbol." He grinned.

"Are they still around? I thought they were just here on vacation." Tomás said salivating.

"You never saw them. Yes, they were on holiday. They were at the game, too. That's what Gemma said, the Barca chica. Gemma said she will come back to see me. We e-mail each other."

Ian redirected the conversation. "Bren, look, we know you're gay, and, frankly, we don't care. But to help keep up appearances you have to be seen with your wife. Put her in the skybox with the players' wives. I keep trying to get Molly up there, but she won't stop working. Then, go to some functions with us with her."

"I know, I know." Brendan lowered his head and rubbed his temples. "She used to. But when we moved here, she stopped. Sheila ran into an old friend from high school and they started hanging out. I think we've drifted apart. But I don't want me being gay to be the final blow."

"How long have you known?" Carlos asked.

"Since high school. But I've always kept it quiet. I don't want it to ruin my career in soccer."

"But, this is America," said Ian.

"Yes, but I play soccer. I want to get signed to a Champions League quality club. A scandal like this would ruin my chances. Remember Fash the Bash?"

Tomás laid his napkin on the table. The waitress spotted the move and cleared the empty plate away. "He wasn't nearly as good as you are, Brendan. You will go far. But you are right. The world of soccer is very homophobic. I was until I started playing here. I found a condo I liked in Lakeview and most of my neighbors swing your way.

But, sorry, they are all committed couples, as far as I can tell anyway." He put his arm around Brendan. "We want to make a pact with you."

Ian said, "This whole conversation will not leave this table. You will come out on your own time to the rest of the world. We are not here to ruin your life."

Carlos added, "We are your teammates and your amigos."

"Thank you. I'm glad you guys understand. And, I'm sorry, Carlos, if I've made you uncomfortable. I will invite all of you over for a dinner party sometime."

Chapter XXI

Sunday, May 10, 1998: Molly heard the presale ticket count before placing her ushers. She was unsure if the increase was related to the "Soccer Mom" promo for Mother's Day, or if it had to do with the Stampede doing so well.

The giveaway for the day was logo seat cushions, which the 12-Steppers scoffed at. They never sat down. They were always chanting and singing, waving scarves, the way soccer fans should.

Molly also heard that the Ultras were going to be joining the 12-Steppers. The Ultras were a group of Polish fans who started coming out to mainly support Tomás and coach Koneki. It was clear that they fell in love with the team. But as fans go, the security considered them hooligans. Molly attended a meeting earlier in the week and volunteered to help monitor them. The Ultras leader, Jacek, thought that Molly was the only one working who really understood what the atmosphere was supposed to be like in a soccer stadium. Jackie, as a rep from the 12-Steppers, and Sean were also at the meeting. They said they would welcome the Ultras with open arms as long as no one got hurt with a flare. The head of security agreed to a hands-off approach, unless Molly thought they needed extra policing. All parties agreed.

So section 12 was more boisterous than ever.

Agnes Novotny organized a pregame luncheon with the ladies who had signed up for the league team. Jackie was there. The others were Baumgartner's fiancée Margaret Jaeger, Leah, Sheila Glazier, Michelle O'Connor, Cristobal's twin sister Juanita and wife Maria, Julie Mathison, Arí Amat, Mirek's daughters Księżnicka, Róża, and Magia, Natasha Starkov, Doc Gina, Jameson's girlfriend Jennifer Melkirk and, from the Stampede front office, Stacy Dennis, Paula Strum, Winnie Harrison, and Carrie Andrews. Agnes excused Molly, who was busy coordinating the official blending of the Ultras in with the 12-Steppers. She would fill her in later. The idea was to discover everyone's strengths and weaknesses, and get to know each other without their men distracting them.

Most had never met Sheila. She said, "I'm Sheila Glazier, Brendan's wife. I regret that I haven't been out much since we moved to Chicago, but dear Agnes finally flushed me out. I've never played soccer and don't even go out to watch my husband play. I don't understand the game, but I guess I'm starting to cave. So what better way to learn the sport than by playing. Then, maybe, I'll understand why they jump all over each other when they score."

The table clapped.

Later, it came down to positioning. Magia said, "Agnes, you're a great manager, for pulling all this together, but we are really going to need someone to coach us. I suggest Jackie. My dad told me about her in Miami. She was the one who came up with playing the 3-4-3 in the second half. If it wasn't for that, our boys might have lost."

"Magia," cut in Jackie, "no one was supposed to know about that."

"But we all know," said Carrie. "Mirek announced it on the list. Plus, it's no secret among us at the office. We all think it's great. That a woman could upstage a man in a man's world."

"You have to. Play, too, of course," said Julie. "Coach us, Jackie. You're the only one among us with the vision to win this league."

"Wait, I thought this was a rec league," interjected Sheila, who was beginning to get a bit nervous.

"Ha! Fooled you. But at least now we believe that Brendan has a wife," Księżnicka said.

Róža punched her in the arm. "Be nice, sister."

Agnes barked in a firm motherly tone, "Behave, girls."

By kickoff, most everything had been sorted out. The first match was slated for next Saturday.

During the match, Molly had her hands full with section 12. It was louder and more boisterous than ever. Streamers and confetti were not the only things tossed from there after goals anymore. Added to that mix were register tape and smoke bombs.

At halftime, Matt cornered Molly. "Hey, I'm worried about Lawrence. The Ultras are giving him a lot of shit."

"What's going on? Is he wearing the wrong jersey today? If so, I can relocate him."

"No, no, Lawrence is one of the 12-Steppers, but he's gay."

Suddenly Molly understood. "I'll go talk with Jacek."

"I'm not quite sure which one that is."

"He's one of the two chant leaders."

"Oh, then I think they are down by the Beers of the World stand."

Molly thanked Matt then hurried inside the smoke-filled concourse. She surveyed the beer line from the upper level. Spotting him, she approached.

"Jacek, can I talk to you a minute?"

His friends glared at her. In Polish, he told his friend to buy him a beer and shoved a twenty-dollar bill in one's hand. They stepped to the side. "Molly, everything is okay, right?"

"Actually, no. Someone has told me that your buddies are harassing the gay supporter." She used her most motherly sounding voice.

"Oh, did the faggot complain?"

Molly narrowed her eyes. "No, but that's not the point. Just stop it, okay? Or you're going to have to deal with me." Jacek looked like a scolded child. "And I guarantee you that I'm a damn sight tougher than you guys think you are."

"Okay, okay, I get the point. I will talk to everyone."

"You'd better. Remember, everyone cheers for the same team."

"*Tak, tak*, Molly. Everything will be okay." He reached for Molly's hand. They shook. He patted her on the back before heading back to his friends.

"What was that all about, Jacek?" asked the tallest, sturdiest one in Polish.

"We have to leave the faggot alone."

"That's no fun."

"Look, just leave him alone, okay? I don't like it either, but we have to do what Molly says. She could have fun things like smoke bombs taken away from us."

"She can do that?"

"Yes, she can."

"*Kudowa!*"

Molly headed for the track, so she could see Ian for a brief moment before the second half. Her timing was perfect. He was emerging just as she arrived at the corner field gate. "You looked stressed, my dear," he said.

"Just the Ultras harassing one of the 12-Steppers."

"Why?"

"Because he's gay."

"Hang tough, sweetheart. But you know you don't have to do this anymore."

"I know, but I can't break my promise. I'm the only one the Ultras trust."

"We'll talk about it later. Maybe we could go dancing or something at Axis."

"How about dinner?"

"They have a grill in the basement kind of like a sports bar."

"Okay."

He kissed her. "I love you, Molly."

"I love you, too. Now go score some damn goals." She smacked him on the ass.

The Stampede started the second half tied at 1-1. There were no line up changes, but Molly noticed Ian started to limp a bit after a hard tackle. She could not worry too much about her man. She had to stay focused on Section 12.

The referee decided not to card the KC player, or even call a foul, for the offense against Ian. The fans protested vehemently. Calling the referee every horrible name in English, Spanish and Polish that one could think of. Molly hovered nearby the track. She wanted to watch the match but could not.

The stadium announcer's voice boomed. "Substitution for the Stampede. Number 21, Maxwell Harp for number 14, Ian Harris."

Molly swallowed hard. *That can't be good. I hope it's not too serious.* She glanced at the time clock, 59th minute. She tried not to worry and turned her eyes back toward the boisterous fans.

Molly watched Jacek balance seemingly precariously with one foot on the wall and one foot on a chair in the front row. His ass shook as the drums beat. She could not help but watch it wiggle and bounce rhythmically. Everything seemed to be going rather smoothly. Slowly she turned her eyes her toward the pitch.

There was a murmur of puzzlement among the 12-Steppers. "Ian for who?" "Ian was limping." "But Harp? Come on. What was Koneki thinking?"

From the ladies-only skybox, Jackie studied the situation on the pitch. She wanted to use this time to begin to sharpen her match analysis skills. She made notes in a steno book. She knew that Harp at this point was the right choice in this situation, even though he had never played in an FLA match. The 20-year-old had something to prove. Jackie had seen him at practice at Halas Hall earlier in the week. Carlos and Harp were running drills together up front. Mirek had made the right decision. Ian would be needed for the Lone Stars match on Thursday.

Cristobal won a header at midfield off a KC goal kick in the 67th minute. The ball went toward Harp. He brought it down and ran a few paces up field before crossing it to Carlos. Carlos saw the huge hole in the defense and took the opportunity. The hard shot bounced off the goalkeeper's wide chest. Novotny was on top of it. But shot it off the far post. Harp had pushed forward to the perfect position to knock the ball past the 'keeper into the back of the net. Stampede 2—KC United 1.

Molly turned her attention back to Section 12. The Ultras lit a smoke bomb and passed it haphazardly around the section. The security guards tensed, but looked to Molly for the cue, as per prematch instructions. The sun still shone brightly, but the effect was perfect. She watched the smoke rise and curl around Jacek's head. He was unaffected and led the crowd into a bouncing "Lo, lo, lo . . ."

Molly caught his eyes as they fell on her. She thought, *why is he looking at me that way? It doesn't make a lick of sense.* She found herself smiling at him. He grinned back. Had to be the moment.

Ian came up behind her. She jumped. "What's the matter?" he asked.

"Hi, sorry, you startled me, that's all. I'm just watching the 12-Steppers, making sure the Ultras don't do anything too crazy." She turned to face him, but kept one eye on the stands.

"These guys are cool. You know that. Just relax and let them be."

She nodded. "I know, but it's the guards I'm worried about. They don't understand soccer at all. Actually, while these guys are more rambunctious, they are actually better than the Bears fans." She shrugged.

"I keep telling you to quit. I'll take care of everything you need, dear." Ian gave her a squeeze.

"Why were you limping on the pitch, dear?"

"Just pulled something." He gestured at the ice pack taped around his left calf. "I should be fine after some rest. At least that's what Gina told me a few minutes ago. I probably could have played out the match, but Mirek made the right decision."

"I saw." She smiled. "That kid Harp is good."

"I agree." Ian looked up at section 12. He spotted Carl banging on the drums. "I'm going to go up and hang with Carl."

"Shouldn't you be sitting down?"

"I'll be fine, honey. You'll just have to give me a good rub down later." He winked. The injured warrior made his way up the stairs to Carl. He joined in the chanting. Molly smiled as she watched him. The crowd respected him, not bugging him for his autograph or photo ops. There was a match going on. No time for that silliness.

Not missing a beat, Carl acknowledged Ian. The one, who was usually serenaded on the pitch, joined in the song. "*Go Chi-ca-go. Hey, Stampede go, a—lo lo lo lo lo lo lo lo lo lo . . .*" Molly watched her man clapping, being a fan.

The score remained 2-1 for the rest of the match. Carl and Ian chatted as they descended the stairs to the track. Molly had already moved down to her usual autographing area position.

"Hey, Carl, do you mind if I take Molly with us when we fly down the Dallas for Wednesday's match?"

"Sure, I don't mind. But I think the ladies might be preparing for their inaugural match all this week. They had that luncheon today. I don't know what was decided on. I wasn't invited."

They started walking toward the tunnel. Ian paused a few times to sign autographs. "I'll check with her."

"Do you think Mirek will let you make the trip? You looked like you were limping pretty badly on the pitch."

Ian sighed heavily. "I'll have to see what Doc Gina thinks, unfortunately. She's the one who says if we're one hundred percent match fit or not. Personally, I don't know. I may have to sit this one out and watch the ladies practice, if they are that day."

Agnes spotted Molly on the track. "We missed you at the luncheon today."

"I had to set things up for work. Had my hands full coordinating Section 12. How did things go?"

"Well, I think Jackie is going to be our coach. I don't quite have that ability. She'll play, too, but she's better able to help the team organize on the field. I'm just more of an administrator." Molly nodded. Agnes continued, "What are your strengths?"

Molly shrugged as she handed a Sharpie marker to Carlos who had returned with his appliance. She held objects steady for the lad to sign. "I've never played. I watch the guys on the pitch and I understand the game, but I've never kicked around in the park with Ian or anyone."

"That's okay. You're not the only one. We'll practice all this week and figure stuff out. We'll have access at Halas Hall starting Monday after the guys are finished."

"They're not going to stay and watch us, are they? I hope not."

"I'll talk to Mirek about it. I certainly think that we need the place to ourselves the first week or so." Agnes started helping Molly hand things back and forth between Carlos and the autograph seekers. "How are you and Ian doing, by the way?"

"Fine. My ex keeps trying to bug me."

"You should move and change your phone number."

"Ian keeps pushing for me to move in with him, but I'm not ready for that step yet. It's too soon."

"You'll know when the time comes. That's how it was with Paul and me. We got married just before he came over here to play for the Stampede. We had only been going out for about six months, but I knew. Just a intuition thing, I guess."

Carlos looked at his two helpers. "Gracias. I'm done now." Molly took the marker. The lad jogged down the tunnel for a well-deserved shower.

"Agnes, just let me know what time for tomorrow. I see Ian down the track with Carl with no security."

"Okay, dear. I'll be in touch."

Molly trotted off to the pair.

Księżnicka, Róża, and Magia all came down from the skybox. They strolled through the concourse. Sean left section 12 and headed for Gate 0. He stopped in his tracks when he saw the three coach's daughters. Księżnicka's blonde hair fell in waves down her back. Her slim athletic build curved in all the right places. She stood about three inches taller than her two older sisters.

Magia, at 19, the oldest of the three, was the shortest. Her hair was dark like her mothers. The waves framed her face and tumbled down to lightly brush her ample bosom. Sean liked her slender waist and full hips.

Róża was also a blonde, but her hair was only shoulder length. She was built more like her younger sister. Actually, at first glance, one might mistake Róża and Księżnicka for twins.

Sean liked the looks of all three. They were wearing team scarves, tight red summer weight sweaters, and hip hugger jeans. He thought he had just seen three angels.

Księżnicka said to Róża in Polish, "He's kind of cute."

"*Tak*, he is a handsome lad. Looks about our age, too. Let's go talk to him," Róża replied.

Róża boldly walked up to him. "Hi."

Sean stammered a bit before spitting out a "Hello."

"I'm Róża, and these are my sisters Księżnicka and Magia."

"I'm Sean. Great game today."

Księżnicka shrugged. "It looked a bit rough. When Ian went out, the whole momentum changed."

"I agree." Sean met her deep blue eyes. She was beautiful, a soccer fan, and, he hoped, single.

"Where were you sitting?" Róża asked.

"With the 12-Steppers. You?"

"We were in a skybox," she replied.

Księżnicka added, "The view of the pitch from there is good for an overview of the match. You get a feel for the flow of the game, but for atmosphere, it's not so great."

Sean nodded. "Yeah, I'll bet. Who were you with?"

"We were at a luncheon for our league team. Our summer season starts on Saturday," Księżnicka said. She was not about to tell him yet that they were Mirek's daughters. She sensed Magia breathe a sigh of relief.

"What are you doing now?" Róża asked.

"I'm headed over to the bar to see if I can get in again. I think different staff works there on Sundays," Sean replied. "It's all ages because they serve food. Do you want to come along?"

"Sure, but let me call our dad and let him know," Księżnicka said. "Magia, you have your phone?"

"Yeah, I'll make the call." She reached in her purse and stepped aside. She really wanted no part of this red-haired hooligan. She was engaged to Jerzy Josefczyk, one of the top young players in Poland. She would let her sisters fight over him. She called their father and spoke briefly.

The four exited the stadium.

Sean waltzed into The Filling Station with Mirek's three daughters in tow. Lenny turned to Matt and commented, "That boy has two too many."

Matt nodded.

Paulie, flirting shamelessly with Matt, sat at the same table. "I think those three are Mirek's daughters," she said.

"You're kidding, right?" Lenny said.

"No, I'm not."

"How in the fuck did that little bastard manage to meet them?" Matt swore. Messing around with any one of those three would be enough to forget all about Jackie.

Sean headed for the back room. Księżnicka and Róża flanked him. Magia tagged along, but a few paces behind.

Matt rose and followed them back. He caught up with Magia. Gently, he tapped her on the shoulder. "Magia?"

She spun around. "*Tak?*"

"I just wanted to say that your dad coached a good game today." Matt failed to think of any other legitimate opening line.

"Thank you." She looked him up and down. He was not bad looking, just a bit boyish. She could tell from the legs emerging from beneath the kilt.

"I'm Matt." He extended his hand.

She shook. "Magia."

"Can I buy you a drink?"

She shrugged. "Sure, I'll just have a glass of red wine."

Matt went to the bar and ordered a glass of merlot. He watched her. She pulled a compact from her purse and checked her hair and lipstick. Adjusting little, she put the mirror away. Matt liked a low maintenance woman. He thought that was what Jackie was until he saw how she behaved around her new boyfriend Carl.

Matt presented the glass of wine to her. "*Dziękuję,*" she said.

Matt blinked at her.

She smiled. "Thank you. *Dziękuję* means thank you in Polish."

Matt nodded with a smile. "You're welcome." She was beautiful. "Let's go sit somewhere and talk. We stand the whole game in section 12. I really need to sit for a while."

"I know. I saw you guys from the skybox."

He took her by the arm gently and guided her to an empty table. He pulled a chair out for her. Matt put on his best gentleman airs for this woman. It was something he should have done for Jackie but completely missed his opportunity.

During their long conversation, he noticed her delicate gold and diamond ring on her left ring finger. He did not bring it up, hoping she would, but she never did.

Around midnight, the two sisters came out of the back room. Sean was not with them.

"What happened to Sean, Księżnicka?" asked Magia. "Did you kill him?"

Matt raised his eyebrows.

"We got his number. We said we'd call him, but we don't know if we will yet or not."

"He's a nice enough boy, and it's kind of fun that he hasn't figured out who we really are yet."

Matt snickered.

Róża pointed at Matt. "Does he know?"

Magia nodded. "He knew before he even talked to me. But so far, it seems like it doesn't matter." She winked at Matt.

"But you're engaged to Jerzy," said Księżnicka.

"I know. But Matt could be a good friend."

"If you screw up your engagement to Josefczyk, Dad's going to kill you," Róża added.

Matt blurted out, "You're engaged to Jerzy Josefczyk?" Oh my god, I'm messing around with . . . oh never mind, just go for it. If she wants to, then I will, he thought to himself.

Magia met his shocked expression with a soft gaze. How could he know who Jerzy was? Matt was obviously not of Polish extraction. "Yes, I am. I came over here to help my dad and sisters get settled in. I'm sorry I didn't tell you." She reached for his hand.

"You are a really nice guy, and I enjoy talking with you. I'd let you date one of my sisters in a heartbeat, but me, my heart is with Jerzy."

"That's okay," he said. But it was not okay. Inside he was dying again. He bit his lower lip, and said. "Any chance your dad might be trying to get Jerzy to play in Chicago?"

Róża spoke, "I think I overheard Dad talking one day about that. Magia's already applied for her green card."

"One has nothing to do with the other. Dad insisted on me applying so I could work if I needed to without having to give up on Jerzy and marry an American. No offense, Matt. But I want to marry for love and not for some silly government paperwork. Jerzy wants to play in Europe. Right now, he's with a lower division team in Rzeszów. The FLA does not have enough clout," said Magia.

"Give us a few more years, and he'll change his tune," said Matt.

Chapter XXII

Tuesday afternoon, May 12, 1998: Mirek called Quigley. "I've got a proposition for you."

"What is it, coach?"

"Since you were so successful in getting Sin Brazos up here for me, you were the first person I thought of."

"Thank you, I think." Quigley scratched his head. What could Mirek be up to now, he thought. The team is doing well.

"My oldest daughter Magia is engaged to Jerzy Josefczyk. He's playing for a team in Rzeszów, Poland. But I really want him to come over here for a while. We can make a roster cut if need be to bring him in. I'd like my daughter to stay in America, but I don't want her to mess things up with Jerzy. The kid is golden. He's a great midfielder and I want him in Chicago."

"Have you mentioned this to him?" asked Quigley, trying to feel out the situation.

"Indirectly, yes."

"You know I don't know a lick of Polish."

"I know. I will arrange for an interpreter, but I'd like you to fly out to Rzeszów just to check him out. Get back to me and we'll see if it's possible."

"Are you buying my ticket there and back?"

"Save all your receipts. I'll make sure that he talks to you. Jerzy does speak fluent English, but I'll make sure an interpreter meets you at the airport."

"You're crazy, Mirek. You know that."

"Just wait until you see him play. Getting him over here to the FLA whether he's in Chicago or not, would be a major coup for the league."

"I'll do my best."

Chapter XXIII

THURSDAY, MAY 14, 1998: DALLAS, TX: The Chicago Stampede suffered their first loss of the season to the Lone Stars. Argentine star Sebastian Tuffatore scored the game winner in the 89th minute to win 1-0.

Lone Star coach, Dave Dunkirk, said of the win, "This is huge for us. We upset the team that most were saying couldn't be beaten."

The red card ejection of Carlos Cortez in the 64th minute made a huge impact on the Stampede offensive attack. Yellow card cautions were also issued to teammates Lozowski in the 66th minute and O'Connor in the 70th. No cautions were issued to the Lone Stars.

Stampede coach Mirek Koneki said of the match, "We were missing key playmaker Ian Harris. And the red card foul on Carlos was absurd. I can believe the first yellow handball call, but the red card foul was a blatant dive by [Frank] Magione. Check the tape, I'm sure most would agree with me."

"We play a very defensive game. It's been said before and I'll say it again, offense scores goals, but defense wins games," said Dunkirk.

Cortez will sit out the next match against the San Francisco Fog Dogs on May 23rd. Ian Harris is expected to be back from injury for that match.

Chapter XXIV

SATURDAY, MAY 16, 1998: Jackie was the first to arrive at the field in the park for the inaugural match of the Stampedistas. She drove herself for the first time in weeks. It felt good to be behind the wheel again. Carl insisted on his limo driver taking her everywhere. This time she refused, if only for the sake of her feminine independence.

The Stampedistas had practiced all week with anticipation of this first match. Jackie took on the role of coach as if she had been one for many years. She had her starting eleven planned out, but did not say anything until an hour before the match. She decided to utilize a 3-4-3, with the Koneki sisters up front, Agnes, Michelle O'Connor, and the two Cristobal ladies at mid, Winnie Harrison and Carrie Andrews in the back with Natasha as sweeper and Margaret Jaeger as goalkeeper. Jackie felt this less popular formation would provide a nice balance on the pitch.

In ones and twos, the ladies arrived. When all were present, Jackie announced the line-up. She liked coaching so much that she did not even want to be a field player herself.

The ladies looked sharp in their kits, supplied by Carl. Each sported a name and number on the back. Their opponents wore plain yellow T-shirts with crude numbers done in electrical tape on the back.

Promptly at 2pm, the match began.

Banana Monkeys versus Stampedistas.

The ladies received the ball first. The Monkeys tiptoed around the ladies until Michelle made a strong run up left field. At the only legitimate challenge, she knocked a crisp back heel pass off to Magia who went for the shot. The Monkey keeper was barely able to handle the hard rocket from tiny Magia.

After that attack, the Banana Monkeys took the Stampedistas seriously. At halftime, the score stood at 0-0, thanks mainly to spectacular saves on both ends of the pitch.

During the 10-minute break, Jackie talked to her charges. Agnes, wheezing, said nothing. She knew that she had made the right decision. The league was governed by FIFA rules, so Jackie could only have three subs and a keeper, if necessary, the whole match. She asked if anyone wanted to come out. Agnes immediately volunteered. Jackie instructed Doc Gina to go in for her at the start of the second. She would make more subs later, primarily to get some of the new girls on the pitch.

The Banana Monkeys received the ball to begin the second half. Evidently, someone had mentioned that they might lose to a bunch of girls. The guys with their token lady on the pitch as a right-winger, sliced through the Stampedistas. Natasha attempted a sliding tackle on the left-winger who was racing for the box. She mistimed the tackle and clipped the guy's right ankle. The referee whipped out a yellow card. The Monkeys went up 1-0 on the ensuing successful direct free kick.

The ladies launched a strong counter attack, but each attempt was thwarted by good clean tackles up field or by the goalkeeper. Jackie decided to sub in Molly for Natasha and Leah for Maria. The fresh legs made an immediate impact. Molly threw the ball in on the restart. It was well placed toward tall Leah who out leaped the man marking her. Braids flying in a beautiful whirl, Leah headed the ball toward the far post. The Monkey keeper lunged but failed to get even a fingertip on the ball. The Stampedistas had equalized.

Even the soccer-hating Sheila squealed with delight as she recorded the stat on the sheet for Jackie. As Mrs. Glazier began to understand the game, she was beginning to love it.

The final score would go down as a tie. The Stampedistas showed that they were a brutal force to be reckoned with.

Carl came down from the bleachers. He picked Jackie up and spun her in the air. "You were great, babe!"

Mirek was there to watch his daughters. He shook Jackie's hand. "Your choices were great. I applaud you, rookie. Are you sure you're not after my job?" He winked, grinning broadly.

All Jackie could do was laugh.

Ian came over to hug a sweaty Molly. "That was a great throw in, honey."

"Thanks. I used to play basketball in high school. That's where I guess I picked up that skill." She kissed her man.

"Captain Dan and I have a celebration picnic set up under that tree over there," said Ian.

"Good, I think we all worked up an appetite," she replied.

Dan put in, "We have enough for both teams."

Jackie said, "Great, I'll go over with you to invite them."

They walked over to where the Banana Monkeys were cooling off. "Good game, guys," Dan began.

"Thanks," replied one.

"We've got plenty at our picnic table over there," Jackie said. "You're welcome to join us."

Dan added, "We just tapped the keg."

Half the team jumped up. "We're there," said a couple in unison.

Jackie found herself chatting with Agnes at the picnic.

"How do you like it?" Agnes asked.

"I feel at home on the sidelines. I never thought about coaching before, but it feels natural to me."

"I knew you had it in you. Paul even thinks so. He told me that Mirek values your opinion and that is hard for Eastern European men to do, you know, value a woman's opinion. Most of them can't handle strong women." She took a sip of her Pilsner Urquell.

Jackie nodded. "Carl scolded me with a smile." She lifted her keg brew to her lips. Budweiser disgusted her, but she wanted to be a team player. "I always felt like I knew more instinctively than I should, but I just don't have the athleticism to be a player."

"What about coaching at the college level or youth girls?" Molly suggested as she had been listening to the conversation.

"I don't want to coach women, no offense to you gals of course. I prefer to play with the boys."

"What's wrong with us?" Molly countered. "Aren't we good enough?"

"Oh, that's not what I meant. All you girls are great, but I'm just saying that my game knowledge skills don't translate well in general to women's soccer when it's all women in the league. You girls are different because the league is coed. I can get away with being more male-oriented."

Agnes polished off her bottle. Paul tossed her another one. She sighed. "I've got a good man."

"Yes, you do, Agnes," Molly agreed.

"So," Agnes began, "what do you do now?"

"I'm a CPA," Jackie replied.

"Ick," said Molly.

"I hate it. I haven't taken on any new clients since tax day. Thankfully, none of them were late filers."

"Why accounting?"

"My father pushed me into it." She finished the last drop of her Bud. "I didn't know what I wanted to do when I went to college. Unfortunately, I always have had a gift with numbers and statistical analysis. So here I am."

Agnes commented, "If things work out with Carl, you may never have to crunch numbers again. I think you two make a good match. You are bringing him out of a dark place."

"What do you mean?" asked Jackie.

Agnes placed a motherly hand on Jackie's shoulder. "Come over here and we can talk, just the two of us." She looked at Molly. "I'm sorry, dear, but this is not for public consumption."

"Oh, hey, no problem. I'll go see what Ian is up to." Molly gracefully excused herself.

Agnes pulled Jackie well away from the rest of the group. Jackie grew nervous. Then, she remembered what she had seen in his medicine cabinet the morning after they met. She had an idea of what Agnes might tell her.

"Jackie, dear, Carl's taken on a lot of stress by owning two teams, new teams."

"I'm aware of that."

"He would work late, then go home and take painkillers to help him sleep. Or so I've been told. And to wake up, ephedrine with espresso. I don't know what was really going on but I think there's more to it than just the stress."

"He hasn't talked to me much about his personal life. He did tell me once that he was an orphan. It wasn't for lack of trying to get him to open up about his past, mind you. But every time I try, he changes the subject."

"I know, dear. I've even offered my ear for free, but he refuses to take me up on it."

"Something painful must have happened. I can just sense it." Jackie paused. "What do you mean by 'for free'?"

"I'm a psychologist. But I haven't been working here. No work permit for me, just a visa to be with my dear Paul." Agnes smiled. "I've applied for a teaching position at one of the community colleges. If hired, they would help me sort out the paperwork. But I digress. Jackie, I just want you to be aware. Many of us fear that if you leave him or hurt him in any way that Carl may reenter that dark place and drive himself over the edge with the abuse of prescription painkillers."

Jackie nodded. "Thank you. I'll keep that in mind."

"And if you ever need to talk, I'm here."

"Thank you." The women hugged before rejoining the party.

Chapter XXV

MAY 19-21, 1998: A bit nervous to be in such a strange land, Quigley stepped off the plane in Rzeszów. He thought it was nice that he could stick with the same airline all the way. He feared that he would have to changed planes more than twice, but when Mirek handed him the tickets he saw differently.

A translator, a beautiful young college girl, held up a sign with Quigley's name on it. Quigley stumbled over the pronunciation of "*Dzień dobry*." The blonde giggled then introduced herself in perfectly fluent English. Anna Wzorek was slender with long hair cascading to her waist. Her piercing blue eyes struck Quigley's heart in a way he had not expected. He was becoming less anxious about this trip already.

"I have your schedule," said Anna. "It will be nice to meet Jerzy Josefczyk in person. You are trying to get him to come play in the States, *nie?*"

"*Tak*," said Quigley, trying to show off another word he recalled from the tourist tapes. The two walked toward baggage claim. "Anna, I have my doubts about how successful this trip will be. Mirek Koneki is the one who was insistent on the matter, since Jerzy is engaged to one of his daughters."

"He is a great player, too. I think you will have a fight on your hands. He has been on record as being pretty insistent about staying in Europe."

Quigley was impressed at her knowledge. A beautiful young lady who also knew the sport, too bad she lived in Poland. "He hasn't heard my offer yet."

She smiled, and then changed the subject. "The first thing on our agenda is getting checked into the hotel. Then we are meeting Jerzy for dinner at 8pm. The Resovia match is tomorrow. He's a beauty to watch on the pitch. So tell me about this new league in the States."

Quigley filled her in on the three-year history of the league and how it was mainly set up to help increase the competitive level and quality of the United States national team. He told her about the Chicago Stampede and how well they were doing. He told her about the league being a single entity despite having individual owners of teams and how there was no relegation and the awful shoot out clock to resolve regular season ties, which was gotten rid of for the 1998 season.

She listened intently, nodding upon occasion. He quizzed her about how the Liga was set up in Poland and about the money situation for players' salaries, and her opinion as to why Jerzy was playing for a third division and not a first division team if he were so good.

"Koneki and the national team coach seem to have been the only ones to have noticed his skills so far. He's young. He needs time to develop. While he plays well, he's still rough around the edges on finishing. That, in my opinion, is why a first division team in Poland or any other European country has not signed him. Given that, you may have a chance."

Quigley nodded as he loaded his bags into the trunk of a taxi. Anna told the driver the location and name of the hotel and negotiated with him on the price. Once the amount of zlotys was agreed upon, the driver took off. Anna settled back in the seat. "The hotel is near the stadium."

He looked at her. "How do you know English so well?"

"I've always wanted to be a translator. Besides English, I'm fluent in German, Russian and Czech. I just graduated last year."

"I'm bilingual in Spanish," he put in.

"I haven't tackled any of the romance languages yet. I do hear, though, that once you learn one, it's easy to pick up on the rest."

"True, I do find myself being able to pick up the gist of written Italian and French now because of it."

"How did you become an agent?"

"During law school, I specialized in contract negotiations, since I didn't want to be a trial lawyer. It was a natural step actually from there, especially given my love for sports and music. I do represent a couple of musicians when they need to renegotiate contracts with record companies and booking agents. I got into representing soccer players in 1996 when I helped broker the Nasty McDuffy deal, a five-year contract with a no trade clause. It was a sweet deal for the Irish lad and myself. My last big deal was getting Carlos 'Sin Brazos' Cortez signed to the FLA and the Chicago Stampede. That's how I came to know Mirek pretty well. We worked together to get the *niño* up to Chicago. Now it seems he wants me to pull off a miracle. His reasoning is more of a personal nature with Magia being engaged to Jerzy."

"So if you can get him over to the States, he doesn't necessarily have to play for Chicago?"

"No." Quigley thought for a moment about the other eleven teams' rosters. "While signing another Polish player to Chicago would help, Chicago doesn't really need anyone like Jerzy right now. I may be able to broker him to San Francisco or to the New York Mad Cabbies. Both teams are beginning to show signs of struggling, even though it's early in the season." He shrugged. "We'll see how things go at dinner tonight."

They made small talk during the rest of the ride. At the hotel, Anna paid the driver the agreed upon amount. The driver began to protest pointing at the larger amount on the meter. She all but gently reminded him of the agreement, indicating that there was another witness. Somehow Quigley managed to throw in a "*tak*" at the right moment and the driver shut up.

They checked into the hotel. One room with two beds awaited them. Quigley was a bit surprised that she was staying with him in the same room. "I snore," was all he could manage to say about the matter.

"Don't worry. I do, too." She grinned, and batted her eyes flirtatiously.

Later that evening, Jerzy Josefczyk met the pair for dinner at a nice restaurant. He was 19, the same age as Magia. He stood 1.8 meters tall. His ice blue eyes could grab any woman's attention in a heartbeat, so it was no wonder that Magia fell for this young lad, thought Quigley. Jerzy's dirty blonde hair was short but gelled into a modern Western style. It was hard to gauge his muscular firmness beneath the khaki pants, but his golf shirt clung to his upper body. Anna nearly swooned when he entered the room, but she managed to maintain her composure and professionalism as she approached. Quigley watched her. He thought to himself, a dumpy troll like me probably has no shot at dating Anna.

Anna facilitated the introductions as they sat down to dinner. "I know why you are here," said Jerzy in Polish. Anna translated.

Quigley responded, "And that would be . . ."

"Magia's father sent you. He wants her to stay in the United States and me to be with her there. I don't know what American fútbol has to offer me," shot back Jerzy.

Quigley took the verbal volley and ran with it. "I know you want to stay in Europe, but look at you. You are only playing for a third division team. You are a star here, yet languishing in the third division. No one is looking at third division Polish teams for players. In the United States, you could flourish. European first division coaches do look at the FLA for players to steal away for lots of money." He paused for Anna to catch up on the translation.

Before Quigley could say more, Jerzy said, "I do miss Magia." His eyes were downcast. He swirled the water in the stemware. Anna looked at Quigley and winked. "I have not seen Magia for nine months. I wanted her to stay but she insisted on helping her father and sisters get settled in Chicago, since her mother died in that awful car accident."

Quigley raised an eyebrow. He always wondered why Mirek's wife was not by his side, now he knew. It had never come up in prior conversations.

Jerzy continued, "The season ends this weekend. My contract is up. I'm planning on visiting Magia over the summer." He looked up. "I want you to represent me."

Oh my god, thought Quigley, this is going easier than I thought. Mirek had to have known.

Over the rest of dinner, Quigley and Jerzy ironed out the terms of a representational agreement.

The following day, Quigley and Anna attended the match. Jerzy provided them with tickets better than what Mirek had arranged. They sat at midfield a few rows up from the home bench. Anna, already a fan of the team, wore the team colors. She lent Quigley her scarf.

The match ended in a 2-2 draw. Jerzy scored one goal. It was clear that he was one of the fan favorites. Little did the crowd know that this was to be one of the last games with the team.

After the match, Jerzy met Anna and Quigley and led them to the small gathering of reporters. There, along with the coach, Jerzy made an official announcement that he was not interested in renewing his contract with the club. Anna whispered the translation into Quigley's ear.

Reporters bombarded Jerzy with questions.

Jerzy simply replied, "I want to be with Magia, my fiancée, who is with her father in Chicago."

"Will you play for the Chicago team?" one asked.

"That has yet to be worked out. It may be with Chicago, or it may be with another team." Jerzy glanced over at Quigley. Anna finished translating. Quigley nodded.

Quigley stepped up. "We have yet to enter into full negotiations with the FLA. A contract must first be agreed upon with the league, since they are a single entity, unlike the way things are in European fútbol." Anna translated.

"Why go when there is nothing definite?"

"I'll field this one, Jerzy," Quigley said. Jerzy nodded. "There is a contract spot waiting in the FLA for Jerzy. It is just a matter of working out the salary end and which team has the salary cap room."

One reporter grumbled to another that Resovia should have signed Jerzy to another deal then sold the contract to the FLA. Jerzy overheard, as did Anna. Both rolled their eyes. They knew how the club was financially, but even such a feat could not have helped. The problem would have been if the deal to the FLA had fallen through, then Resovia would be stuck with a high-salaried contract they could ill afford.

Jerzy decided it was time to end the press conference. He said, "Thank you for your years of support. I will send word back to the local papers of my career as it continues in the United States of America." With that, he began to walk away. Quigley and Anna followed.

Chapter XXVI

THURSDAY, MAY 21, 1998: Brendan began to grow restless. It would be harder for him to get his jollies with Lawrence with Sheila growing more involved with the other wives, girlfriends and ladies in the Stampede front office. He received a notice in his private post office box regarding the renewal of his private room contract.

A few players on the team knew, but they made a pact to keep quiet about his sexual preferences.

He stuffed the renewal notice in his back jeans pocket and walked outside. He wished the times were different, like in tennis, where he could come out and not sacrifice his career. If it were not for his desire to play in a European premiership, he would do it. He would shout it from the press box for all to hear, regardless of Sheila's feelings.

Sheila. She was another reason. Maybe he should start dropping hints. He needed to cut her loose, before the big outing. He was afraid the outing would come before, that she would find out, and she would be the one to blow his cover. It was not Carlos, Ian and Tomás he feared so much as he feared his own wife.

He walked instinctively to the Boys Town neighborhood. On the way, he pulled out his cell phone and dialed Lawrence.

"I really need to talk to someone," began Brendan.

"I'm here for you, Bren. Just name the time and place if you want to meet in person."

"How soon can you make it up to Sidetrack?"

"I'll be there within the hour. I live in the south suburbs." Lawrence sensed uneasiness in Brendan's voice. "Just don't do anything rash. I'll be there as soon as I can."

Brendan walked into Sidetrack on Halsted and chose a seat close to the entrance. He ordered a single malt scotch from a gorgeous young waiter. Brendan only drank scotch when he was close to making a major life decision.

In the past, all those decisions were good. Like the one to pursue professional soccer. And the decision to help cover up his preferences by marrying his best friend Sheila.

Sheila. The last thing he wanted to do was break her heart. But it was the best thing he could do for himself psychologically. Maybe she wouldn't care. After all, she was his best friend. Maybe she already knew. Hopefully, that was the case.

About a half hour later, Lawrence arrived. The two lovers embraced and kissed cordially. Lawrence was cautious to follow Brendan's lead. In this neighborhood, they were among their own kind and could express themselves freely without fear of being outed if they were not already.

"Bren, you sounded so shook up about something on the phone. Talk to me, darling." Lawrence signaled the waiter as he seated himself across from Brendan.

"I'm so confused, Lawrence. I don't want to hurt Sheila, and I don't want to ruin my career chances, but . . ." He trailed off.

Lawrence encouraged him. "But what?"

"I feel trapped. I'm sick of acting straight. I can't act anymore. I just can't do it." He stared at his rocks glass, which was nearing the bottom of the second scotch.

Lawrence extended his hand and gripped Brendan's arm in a supporting manner. "You have to come clean with yourself first." He gently tilted his lover's face so he could look into his eyes. "Keeping your true self secret is not doing you any good. I can see in your eyes and your heart that this agony of living in the closet is going to begin to affect your game. Then what are you going to do? You'd be stuck here regardless because you would be seen as a fucked up mediocre player. You are so beyond mediocre. If the managers in Europe can't see that in and of itself, regardless of your personal preferences, then fuck 'em."

Brendan thoughtfully swirled the ice in his glass. In his heart, he knew Lawrence was right. The waiter brought another scotch on the rocks to the table. With a heavy sigh, Brendan lifted the new glass, but set it down without taking a sip. He reached for his cell phone and dialed Sheila.

"We need to talk. I'm at Sidetrack in Boys Town with a friend. I need to talk to you now."

"I was just headed out to do the shopping, but I'll stop by there first. I know something's been gnawing at you. I'll be there as soon as I can, honey."

Brendan folded his phone closed. "I think she knows."

Lawrence nodded.

The two changed the subject and conversed about the upcoming World Cup until the wife arrived.

Sheila came in and took one look at her husband and Lawrence together and just started laughing. "So you're finally decided to come out, Bren." She gave Lawrence a strong look up and down. "Surely you could've picked a better physiqued boyfriend. Like that waiter over there."

Lawrence bit his tongue. He knew he needed to hit the gym more often, but the venom in the woman's mouth. He sighed. She was probably being defensive to hide the pain.

Brendan said, "So you've figured it out?"

"Bren, I've known for a long time." She placed her hands on his. "I had a feeling when we got married. Your mannerisms, the way you look at men when you should be looking at women that way."

He sheepishly looked at her eyes. "Thank you."

She continued, "I know how much your career means to you. And I know enough about the world of soccer to know that a huge public emergence will possibly destroy your chances of playing in Europe. Honey, I want to travel to Europe with you. I want to live the high life as a rich soccer wife. So I'll be damned if I'm going to ruin your chances of that."

She signaled the waiter, who oddly recognized her and the fact that she drank Absolut fuzzy navels without her saying a word. Lawrence looked at her in disbelief. The waiter set her drink in front of her and commented, "She's one of the original fag hags."

"Thanks, Bailey," she said as she stuffed a generous tip down his shirt.

"If only I could get your soccer superstar husband to touch me that way," he commented as he walked away.

Brendan narrowed his eyes at both of them.

Sheila took a long drink. "Don't worry, Bailey's cool." She leaned back for a moment, then back in shaking her head. "You honestly thought I was a stupid straight bitch?" She laughed. "My god, we've known each other for what seems like forever! I knew exactly what I was getting into when I married you, buddy. I knew without you even saying a word. All the awful sex we had. Completely obligatory. And while we're laying everything on the table, darling, I might as well tell you that I'm really a lesbian."

Now Lawrence's jaw dropped. Fag hag was believable, but this? Whoa!

Brendan said nothing. He knew that she was not finished with her tirade.

"I know you've been cheating on me, but I don't care. So have I. We don't do the hetero thing anymore because neither of us can stand it any longer."

"So, Sheila, what do you want to do?"

"We have the perfect cover for you right now. Divorce is not an option. Until you decide to retire from soccer or decide to come out to the world of sports, it's best to maintain the status quo. I'll continue to keep my sexual orientation quiet for you. I do love you, you know. And the last thing I want to do is ruin your career." She hugged him as a sister would a brother.

Brendan responded. "I love you, too."

And they both knew exactly what it meant.

Chapter XXVII

Friday, May 22, 1998: Sheila rang Lawrence early Friday morning. "Saturday's match is in San Francisco. What would you say to going out there?"

"I don't know if I could afford it, especially at the last minute."

"Don't worry. That's what Brendan's credit card is for."

"Does he know?"

"No, I thought we'd surprise him. I've got the team schedule down to the precise minute. I know he'll hit some of the clubs tonight, and that's the part that scares me. I want to make sure he doesn't blow it."

"I think he'll be okay. But, you're right. He is in a restless state right now. San Francisco's team isn't drawing well. I don't think he'll be spotted."

"But what if one of those with a kit fetish recognizes him?" speculated Sheila. She knew the scene as well as anyone. She had seen the email lists with the photo exchanges. She had subscribed to one to keep an eye out for anything related to her husband.

"You're right." He looked at the calendar in his planner. "I can clear my schedule. Not letting Bren ruin his career is top priority."

"Thank you. I'll call you with the flight and time."

She called Agnes next to say she was not going to make the league match. Then, she began to pack an overnight bag.

Molly and Jackie opted to stay in Chicago for their team. They would all head over to Sueños del Fútbol after their match to watch their boys play.

Jackie decided to take on no more new clients. Carl offered to support her. She was hesitant at first, but she felt so comfortable with him. Everything seemed perfect. Being a kept woman could not be that bad.

She checked her email. Lawrence wrote a long missive about Brendan coming out to Sheila. She deleted it, as a precaution. She, too, knew how dangerous such information could be to Brendan's career. She logged off.

She dialed her friend. "Lawrence, I got your email. How are you doing?"

"I'm okay. Sheila and I are flying to San Fran to surprise him," Lawrence replied.

"And keep an eye on him, too?"

"Yeah, I just wish we were going in tonight, but Sheila couldn't get a flight booked until early Saturday morning. Are you going with Carl?"

"No, Molly and I are staying to play in our league match. I was going to invite you, but it sounds like you have other plans."
"That's okay. Thanks for the thought."
"Have fun in San Fran."
"You know I will, girlfriend." He chuckled.

In Poland, Jerzy began to arrange his life for a quick move overseas. Saturday would be his last match in Poland for a long while. He tried to call Magia earlier in the week, but Mirek answered the phone instead. The future father-in-law advised that it would be a good surprise for Magia.

Quigley, Lance Merton, Carl and Mirek met at 11:00 AM to discuss Jerzy's impending arrival.

"Mirek," said Carl, "I'd love to arrange to have Jerzy play for you, us. But I don't think we have much wriggle room. At this time, given the salary cap and the limit on international players, I don't rightly see whom we can trade. Everyone loves Carlos; Baumgartner is a solid anchor in the mid. Our defense would be wanting without Tomás. We are going to have to bring in other owners."

"I was afraid of that. My heart went before my brain on this one. Sorry, Carl," said Mirek.

Quigley asked, "What about Philly? Is there any room on the roster there, Carl?"

Carl shook his head. "I wish we could keep him in the CSG, but, again, given the restrictions of the FLA we can't." Carl cast a sidelong glance at Lance.

Lance shot back, "You know damn good and well the reason for salary caps and limits on international players."

Carl tossed his hands in the air. "Whatever, Lance."

Mirek said, "I can vouch for Jerzy's quality as a midfielder. He would be a welcome addition to any team."

Quigley mused, "Isn't there a large Polish population in New York as well?"

Lance nodded. He had his ear glued to his cell phone. "I'm already on it. Olufemi was in a horrible car accident last night. He's out for the rest of the season, at least. That opens up an international slot for New York. I'm trying to get through to Alexi Taman."

Carl stood. "I'm headed back to the office. Stop in before you leave, Mirek."

Mirek nodded. He knew he could leave, too, since Jerzy had little chance of ending up in Chicago this summer. He checked his watch. He could wait another fifteen minutes. After all, he still had a personal interest in the matter.

Lance was connected. "Alexi, it's Lance. How's Olufemi? . . . That serious? Damn, that's a shame. I hope for soccer's sake that the doctors are wrong and he'll be back next year . . . Uh huh . . . Uh huh . . . Well, the reason I'm calling is that I have a midfielder for you. Jerzy Josefczyk . . . Yeah, Polish, third division . . . Mirek here in Chicago wanted him, but we couldn't make it work . . . Yeah, yeah, I know, league parity . . . Sure, ticket sales may increase. That's another reason I thought of you, Alexi . . . The agent's name is Michael Quigley. I'll have him set up a meeting with you early next week. Whatever you two agree on will be fine with me . . . Keep me informed on Olufemi's progress, okay? I wouldn't wish that kind of tragedy on any player . . . Great . . . I'll be out next month. I'll see you then. Ciao."

Lance turned to Mirek. "See what you can do about finding any game tapes for Alexi to give to coach Hartford."

"I can't promise anything. It may be easier to fly Jerzy in for a try-out. I'll see what I can do, though." Mirek leaned back in the chair. He was glad there would be a place for Jerzy in the States. Magia will be so surprised.

"I'd like to see the tapes, too," added Lance.

Mirek stopped by Carl's office.

"I wish you would have told me," scolded Carl.

"Sorry. My heart went before my head in this case. But he is an excellent player, regardless of whether or not Magia's engaged to him." Mirek sat.

"What if Olufemi had not had been in an accident? All the FLA teams are full-up on internationals."

"He had all summer to sign with a European squad. But it would not do any good for Magia."

"She's old enough. You should let her go be with Jerzy."

"I insisted that she come with me to help watch over her two younger, wilder sisters."

Carl nodded. "I understand." He stood. "Get out of here." He pointed to the door. "And win me another soccer match."

Chapter XXVIII

Saturday, May 23, 1998: Ian awoke in the San Francisco hotel. He was the first up. Tomás still slept soundly, but Brendan was not in the room. He recalled Brendan not being there when they all went to bed. He assumed that Brendan had hooked up with some local friends. Maybe, hopefully, he crashed at their house. Mirek would be furious if Brendan failed to catch the bus to the stadium.

Ian pulled on his warm-ups and grabbed his cell phone and hotel key card. He took the stairs down to the lobby. He liked to take the stairs in hotels as an extra workout or a warm-up, even when he was on a high floor.

He dialed Brendan's cell phone. It went straight into voice mail. Ian left a brief message. He tried not to think the worst, but his mind could not help but go there.

He ordered a steaming cappuccino from the lobby barista. With his back turned to the counter, he scanned the scene. It was quiet. A few people in sweats returned from jogging. A few checked out.

The barista tapped him on the shoulder. "Here's your cappuccino, sir. You're charging it to the room?"

Ian turned. "Yeah, room 1224." He signed the authorization and took the steaming cup. He found a cozy spot in a chair and relaxed, as much as possible.

About halfway through the cup, an odd couple walking in caught his eye. Both looked familiar at a distance, but they seemed like they did not belong together. As they got closer, Ian realized the woman was Sheila Glazier. He had seen the man before at the matches in Section 12.

Ian stood. "Sheila?" he called out.

She turned on her heel.

"What are you doing here?" Ian caught himself. "Oh, yeah, right."

Sheila bristled. "What do you mean by that?"

"You're just out to surprise your husband. That's all." Ian made a motion with his hands for her to settle down. "Who's your friend?"

"This is Lawrence." Pleasantries were exchanged between the two men. Lawrence was wearing Brendan's game jersey. Ian raised an eyebrow, and then glanced at Sheila briefly.

The desk clerk called Sheila over to finish the check-in process. She excused herself, leaving the two men by themselves.

Ian said in a hushed voice, "She knows?"

Lawrence nodded. "So I guess you know, too."

"Yeah. He was supposed to room with Tomás and me, but he didn't make it in last night."

"Oh shit, that's not good. Sheila and I were afraid of this happening. That's why we came out here."

"I'm glad you did," said Ian. "I wouldn't know where to begin looking." He ran his hand nervously through his hair. "Am I to presume you are his lover?"

Lawrence nodded. "That's why Sheila brought me along. She may be a lesbian, and a fag hag, but I probably know of more places to look for Bren."

Sheila had walked up. "What do you mean, look for Bren?"

"Sheila, Brendan didn't come back to the hotel last night," Ian said. "He went out by himself, against team policy. One of us should have insisted on going with him. I didn't know he was this close to breaking."

Sheila placed her hand on Ian's shoulder. With a heavy sigh, she said, "That's why we're here. Let's go put our bags in the room. Walk with us, Ian."

They headed toward the elevator. When the doors closed, Sheila rammed her fist into the wall. "That son of a bitch! He's going to ruin his career."

"He's thinking with his dick," said Lawrence. He grabbed Sheila's arms and tried to calm her down. "It happens to all men no matter what their orientation. We just have to try to think like he does. Ian, do you recall him saying anything before he took off last night?"

Ian crinkled his forehead. "I think he many have mentioned Haight and Ashbury, but I don't recall any more than that."

"Okay, Sheila and I will start there. I'll give you my cell phone number so you can call me if he checks in, and we all hope he does."

Ian nodded. "Sounds good."

They all walked down the hall to the room. Once inside, Sheila asked, "Did you try to call him?"

"It went straight into voice mail," Ian said. Lawrence and he exchanged cellular numbers. "I'm in room 1224, if you want to leave word at the desk."

"Well, Sheila, we need to get moving if we want to find him and make sure he gets to the match."

Ian headed back to his room. He hoped to find Brendan there, but he thought it unlikely. He paused in front of the door. Why shouldn't Brendan be allowed to come out? he thought. After all, there was a rainbow brigade of loosely networked FLA fans in nearly every city. He's an excellent player and it should not matter. If it doesn't matter to an old school Eastern European like Tomás, why should it matter to anyone?

Brendan slowly shook the sleep from his head, if you could call it sleep. He was naked except for soccer socks. His whole body ached. He found enough strength to lift his head and look around. He had no idea where he was or how he got there.

The room was littered with clippings ripped from soccer magazines and empty bottles of wine, beer and booze. There was no furniture. Rings were placed at various points on the walls and floor. Long athletic socks were strung through those rings.

He tried to move his arms, which were positioned slightly above his head. He found that they were still tied to the wall. His head began to spin. He closed his eyes in hopes of awakening from this nightmare scene.

Late Saturday morning, Molly happily snatched the keys to the Jaguar from the counter. It was a beautiful day for having the top down. She slung her soccer gear bag into the tiny trunk and hopped in.

The engine roared to life. Her hands caressed the steering wheel. She had never driven a Jaguar. Plus, she was surprised that she did not have to beg Ian to leave the keys.

She wanted to take it for a spin on Lake Shore Drive before her match. As she pulled out of the parking space, she laughed wickedly, thinking how jealous Jack would be.

Her cell phone rang as she approached the first stop sign. It was Renata. "Hey, what are you up to today?"

"I've got Ian's Jag. Are you working anywhere today?"

"No, why? You want to hang out?"

"Yeah, I'll come pick you up. You can watch me play soccer then we're all heading over to Sueños to watch the Stampede."

"There a good show later out at Riley's, if you're up for it."

"Who's playing?"

"Dismembered Hedz, Jack's old drummer's new project. There are some other bands on the bill, but I don't remember whom. We can always check the *Illinois Entertainer* later."

"Well, it should make for an interesting evening, to say the least."

At ten minutes before noon, Mirek began knocking on his players' hotel room doors. It was time for roll call and group lunch.

Ian told his roommates that Brendan never made it back. Tomás knew nothing more than Ian did about Brendan's plans.

Tomás put in, "Mirek's going to be pissed. Team policy is that you don't go out alone, always at least in pairs."

Ian nodded. He tried Brendan's cell phone again. Voice mail. "Now, I'm really worried. I hope Sheila and Lawrence have some luck."

Mirek knocked on the door. "Open up. I hope everyone's up and ready to go."

Tomás opened the door. "*Dzien dobry*, Mirek."

"*Dzien dobry*," replied Mirek. "I only see three here. Where's Brendan?"

Tomás looked at Ian, who still clutched his cell phone. "I'm trying to reach him, coach."

"Keep trying. And tell him that if he misses lunch, he's off tonight's starting lineup."

"Sure thing, coach."
Mirek left the room.

At lunch, Mirek saw that Brendan was missing. He would have to talk to Ian and Tomás. He looked at his planned lineup and dutifully scratched Brendan's name off. He scanned the table. He decided he would not announce the replacement until they got to the locker room.

After they ate, Mirek pulled Brendan's two roommates aside. "Okay, boys, I want to know where he is," he demanded.

"I wish I knew," said Ian.

"What do you know?" the coach pressed.

Ian put his arm around coach's shoulders. "Let's step outside, out of earshot of the rest of the team." They exited the restaurant into the bright sunshine. Ian looked Mirek in the eyes. "Carlos and Tomás already know everything I'm going to tell you, but the rest of the team does not. Brendan would prefer them not to right now."

"I'm listening." Mirek nodded.

"Brendan is gay."

"Isn't he married?"

"Yes, he just came out to Sheila. She wasn't surprised. Then she added that she was a lesbian. But that's not really the point. He also has a lover who is one of the 12-Steppers. Anyway, Brendan has been struggling to keep his orientation secret because of the prejudices in sport. I think when he came out here last night, he arranged to hook up with some friends. Sheila and Lawrence had a feeling that he might snap this weekend. They came out here this morning and started looking for him immediately."

Mirek hung his head.

"Coach, at this point, even if Brendan shows up at the stadium, he probably won't be up to playing at all."

"Don't worry. Even if he were up to playing, I wouldn't use him as a sub. Punishment, you know."

"I have a feeling that he may not be responsible for his own disappearance. It's so unlike him. Coach, I'll keep you posted. I hope Sheila and Lawrence find him soon."

"I'll keep this quiet for now. Say he got hooked up with a girl or something in case the press asks."

"Good, anything to keep the gay part under wraps for now."

Sheila and Lawrence arrived at Haight and Ashbury. She closed her eyes slowly and tried to imagine the vibe after dark. She had known Brendan a long time. She knew that he had a dark side, a gothic side. The two had grown up together. That was why it felt so comfortable for the two of them to be married. Both their families were happy with the union.

After about a minute, Sheila spoke. "There's an underground Goth club nearby. I just don't know exactly where."

Lawrence said, "I'll ask somebody."

"It's fucking noon. Don't you know anything about the Goth scene? No one who is up in the daytime is going to know where the hell an underground Goth club is."

"What about a record store?" Lawrence suggested. "Someone working there might know."

Sheila shrugged. "It's worth a try. We really can't afford to wait until nightfall."

Molly and Renata pulled into the park's lot. Jackie parked next to them. "Wow, Molly, I'm surprised Ian let you drive his car."

"He trusts me." Molly grinned. She introduced Renata to Jackie.

The three hiked over to the field. Renata threw a blanket down to sit on. Molly and Jackie shared corners of it as they put on their cleats and shin guards.

"So, Jackie," began Renata, "how did you meet Carl Costello?"

She shrugged. "I guess I was in the right place at the right time. I think he saw me in Section 12 first before we hooked up later at Axis."

"I remember you coming up with Carl," put in Molly. "You two looked so natural together."

"Thanks. I felt a chemistry between us from the start." Jackie began stretching. "Molly, I want to run you through a few drills before the rest of the girls get here."

"Sounds good," replied Molly as she bent over for a full-side stretch.

The captor entered the fetish room. He wore a Stampede scarf and nothing else. He had strong well-developed legs and a firm solid ass. His thick dick was semi-erect and surrounded by soft curly fluff. His torso was that of a Grecian statue. His knees bore scars of deep invasive surgery. A tattoo of a soccer ball with devil's horns and flames graced his upper left arm. His skin was olive. Dark curls tumbled to just past his shoulders. His nose was crooked, like it had been broken at one point in his life. His mahogany eyes beamed at his captive Brendan.

He reached down and ran his hands through Brendan's platinum short locks. Brendan stirred, opening one eye slowly then two. His eyes focused. His captor smiled wide enough to fully expose his highly pointed teeth. "Fuck," Brendan breathed.

"Good morning, slave."

Carl arrived at the park field just as the Stampedistas match was getting underway. He initially told Jackie he was not going to go, but changed his mind. He could not stand being away from her for very long. He had never felt that way about a woman before.

Jackie gathered her tribe just before kickoff. She named her starters, some of which were starting for the first time. She wanted to spread experience throughout the squad. After all, it was supposed to be a recreational league.

She felt natural as a coach and wanted to get more training to be more qualified. But she did not want to coach just women's. She wanted to coach an FLA team. She desired to be the first woman to coach a men's premier division team in the world. It was a man's world, but she always thought of herself as one of the boys.

Jackie had been devouring books on technique and strategy ever since she learned to play and fell in love with the sport. After all, she reasoned, the best players did not necessarily make the best coaches later in life.

The starting eleven of both teams took the field. Carl found a spot on the stands. Jackie still had not noticed him. He liked that. It meant that she was focused on the match, like any good coach should be.

Kickoff.

Jackie watched her players intensely. She read the other team and helped her players by yelling instructions. Carl sensed she was keenly aware of each player's abilities. He would keep a close eye on her performance with this rag tag team of women. His business sense had overridden love as he watched her. She was going to be big and he was going to help her.

The defense let one slide in the back of the net. Margaret Jaeger dove heroically, but could not even get a glove tip on the cannonball shot. Regardless, Carl smiled when he heard Jackie's reaction, "That's alright, ladies. Counter attack. That's our key and our strength. We won't let them shut us down."

The opposing coach laughed hysterically.

The Stampedistas won their match 2-1. The women lay sprawled on the surrounding park turf. Carl descended from the bleachers. Jackie sat among her team and doled out post match comments. Carl paused and listened. She really sounded like a coach. And all the ladies listened to her. She was a natural.

Carl came up behind Jackie and placed his hands on her shoulders. "Good job, Jacqueline," he breathed in her ear.

She reached up and patted his hand. "Tell your girls that." She smiled.

Carl addressed the team, "Well done, ladies." He clapped.

Jackie stood. "Everyone is welcome to come to Sueños to watch the Stampede match and rehydrate." She turned and kissed Carl. He dipped her.

Magia sighed heavily and whispered to her sisters, "I miss Jerzy."

The team arrived at the stadium sans Brendan. Ian, Tomás and Mirek grew increasingly worried. Ian kept looking at the other three and signaling that he did not know anything. He kept his cell phone as close to him as possible.

Mirek decided not to tell Carl just yet. He decided to wait until closer to match time.

CHAPTER XXIX

Sheila and Lawrence entered a record store. Lawrence began browsing casually. Sheila studied the flyers tossed in haphazard piles near the door and on the counter. She picked up one that advertised a fetish weekend at a place called the Blood Bank. No address was listed, but a phone number was given.

She stepped outside and called.

"Who dares disturb my sleep?" hissed the voice on the other end.

"I saw your flyer and had some questions."

"The Blood Bank is located at the end of an alley near H&A. Look for a red light bulb. We don't open until after sundown." The voice hung up.

"Shit!" spat Sheila. "We can't wait that long." She punched redial.

"Who dares—"

"Oh, stop the bullshit and listen to me. My husband is missing. I think he may have gone to your club last night. I want someone to meet me at the club who worked last night."

"Okay, okay, I guess you won't leave me alone until I meet you."

"Damn right."

"Okay, find the alley and call me back. Let it ring once. Watch for the red light to blink three times. At that point, the door will be open where you can come straight in." The voice hung up.

Sheila poked her head back inside. "Lawrence, let's go."

The pair hustled back to Haight and Ashbury where they started peering hard down alleys, looking for the door with the red light above it. "I think I see it," announced Sheila. She went through the prescribed procedure. The light blinked three times. The pair scurried to the large metal door.

Once inside, a tall skinny pale man bolted the door behind them.

The sounds of Mozart softly filled the air. Sheila detected an odor beneath cedar and clove cigarettes that reminded her of a butcher shop. Lawrence ran his fingers along the red crushed velvet curtains that lined the entry foyer.

The slender man led them inside the club. He offered two barstools at the first bar. It was dark inside. Sheila and Lawrence's eyes were still adjusting from being outside. The man had no trouble navigating in the blackness.

He sat two long black taper candles on the bar and lit them in a manner that seemed like magic, like he just had to touch the wick with his fingertip.

The firelight reflected off the red jersey Lawrence still wore. The man spoke, "You are seeking the Iceman, yes?"

Sheila spoke, "Yes, was Brendan here last night?" She studied the wan features of the man.

"He was here." He reached a long finger and touched Lawrence's jersey. "I will never forget meeting the Iceman."

His tone made Sheila's spine crawl. The man reached for a pack of clove cigarettes. He flipped the top and tapped one out. He used the candle to light it. As he exhaled, the smoke swirled around his head.

"What went on here last night?" Sheila probed.

"We had a lot of soccer fetishists here last night. I think they were hoping the Iceman would show up." He dragged hard on the incensual cigarette. His other hand stroked the jersey. Lawrence grew nervous. The man continued, "The last time I saw him, he was talking with Alex."

Sheila reached out and removed the man's hands from Lawrence's arm. "We have to find him. Where would Alex take my husband?"

"And my lover?" Lawrence added.

"Alex has a dungeon, but I don't know where it is. I have only heard stories. Soft bondage, with scarves and socks." The man tapped the long ash into a tray.

Sheila grew impatient. "Look, the Iceman is supposed to play today. He has not reported back to the hotel, or with his coach. We fear the worst. The last thing Brendan would do no matter how fucking horny he got would be to ruin his career. He's chosen a homophobic career because he's damn good at it. This Alex person has to be holding our Iceman against his will."

The man sat silent for a minute, finishing his cigarette. He crushed it out. "Fuck," he finally breathed. "Damn him, I didn't think he'd be capable of something like that." He slammed his palm onto the bar. "Fuck!" He paced back and forth behind the bar. "Fuck! Fuck! Fuck!"

"Where is Alex's dungeon? You do know, don't you?" Sheila pressed.

The man grew increasingly agitated. "Excuse me." He disappeared into the shadows.

Sheila and Lawrence looked at each other. He said, "I think he knows."

"Stay here. I'm going to try to follow him." Sheila took off in the general direction that the man went. There was a dark spiral staircase. Candles flickered in a few places as it wound down. Sheila heard footsteps as she descended. She followed the sound. At the bottom was a conference room. There was nowhere else to go. She entered the room. Scalps were mounted on the walls. What kind of place is this, she thought. There was a door, partially hidden, at the end of the room. She pushed it open. A long hallway, with black walls. In the distance, she saw the man turn a corner. She ran toward him. She turned the corner. He waited for her. He grabbed her upper arms and dug in his bony fingertips.

"Don't follow me," he hissed. His breath smelled of death. He towered over Sheila.

She froze, momentarily. Instinct took over. She kneed him in the balls. He released his grip. He took a step back and bared his teeth. Then he slapped her, his nails raking across her cheek. Blood trickled down. The man licked her cheek.

She pushed him back. "Take me to Alex and Brendan."

Another figure appeared at the end of the hall. "Kierakos!" the figure said in a deep baritone. "What is going on?"

"Find Alex and the Iceman," Kierakos called back. "Bring them to the conference room."

Kierakos spun Sheila around and marched her to the conference room.

Alex untied Brendan and led him to a bathroom.

Brendan pissed long. His whole body ached. He could not remember what happened last night. He did not even know what time it was. He guessed it was morning, but he could not be sure since there were no windows.

He splashed water on his face and looked in the mirror. His eyes were bloodshot. Dark circles ringed his eyes. His neck and chest bore scratches, some had bled and crusted over.

Alex pounded on the door. "Hurry up."

Brendan stuck his lips under the faucet and rinsed his mouth out. He swallowed thirstily. He felt so dehydrated.

Alex thrust his way in. He grabbed his captive and spun him around. The two men faced each other. Alex was slightly taller, but physically they were evenly matched. Alex pinned Brendan's shoulders against the cold tile of the wall. He smashed his mouth on the Iceman's. With impassioned intertwining of tongues and the dominating aura of Alex, suddenly Brendan was drunk again.

Hours seemed to pass as Lawrence watched the wax drip down the tapers. He looked at his timepiece. The team would be headed to the stadium. He tried to call Ian, but could not get a signal in this dungeon-like club. He dared not move either, in case Sheila should reappear from the darkness.

He felt the air conditioner flip on. The chilly rush of air felt more like the breath of death.

Sheila was forced to sit in a chair. She agreed to cooperate just so Kierakos would not tie her up. That did not stop her from bombarding him with questions.

"What goes on here?"

"Bondage and fetish shows."

"What's up with the scalps?" She gestured at the walls. "What else goes on here?"

"It's art." Kierakos shrugged.

Sheila narrowed her eyes at him. She knew he was hiding something.

The ladies streamed into Sueños. Carl held Jackie's hand as he often did.

From a barstool at the far end, Matt watched them. He closed his eyes slowly, hoping that when he opened them Jackie and Carl would not be there. No such luck. But he did spot the three Koneki sisters.

Róża and Księżnicka approached him. They flanked him, each draping one arm around him. "*Dzien dobry*," they greeted. Maybe this afternoon would not be that bad after all, thought Matt.

Magia sat at a table with Carl and Jackie. "Carl, what is my dad up to?"

Carl gave her a funny look. "What do you mean?"

"Is he trying to get my fiancé over here?"

Carl shrugged. Mirek had sworn him to secrecy. "I don't know. He wouldn't be able to play for the Stampede. We don't have the salary cap room, and we are at our limit on foreign players." At least that much was true.

"I think he and Jerzy are up to something." She ran her hands through her hair. "I hope they are. I really miss Jerzy."

Jackie extended a sympathetic hand. "It must be rough."

"If it weren't for my two sisters." Magia gestured at the younger Konekis who had draped themselves all over Matt. "I'd be with him right now."

Carl's cell phone rang. "Excuse me." He looked at the caller ID before answering. Standing, he said to the caller, "Hello."

"Carl, are you by yourself?" said Mirek.

"No, I'm with Jackie and the Stampedistas at Sueños."

"Step outside for a minute. I fear your verbal reaction, when I tell you what I have to."

Jackie gave Carl a quizzical look. He mouthed, "It's Mirek." Carl walked toward the back door. Jackie's and Magia's eyes followed him. They looked at each other with a 'this can't be good' look.

"I'm outside, Mirek. What's so terrible?"

Mirek sighed heavily. "Brendan is missing."

"Why the hell didn't you call me the minute he missed the first roll call?" Carl nearly shouted.

"I kept hoping he would show up. Sheila and Lawrence are actively looking for him as we speak."

"Son of a fucking bitch!" Carl slammed his palm against the building. "How? How in the fuck could he pull a stunt like this?"

"I don't know. Brendan went out alone last night. Yes, I know he broke team road policy, so don't even start. But, I don't think he disappeared on his own free will." Mirek glanced over at Ian, who shook his head. "Sheila suspected something might happen. That's why she came out here, with Lawrence. But they couldn't get here in time."

Carl tried to calm down. "What did Sheila suspect? And wait a minute, you mean with rainbow warrior Lawrence from Section 12?"

Mirek replied, "Yes."

"Why Lawrence?"

"Lawrence is Brendan's lover."

Carl's mouth fell agape.

"Don't breathe a word to anyone, not even Jackie."

"Shit, San Francisco. That son of a bitch! Are you sure it's not his own free will?"

"Come on, Carl. Yeah, he probably has friends out here, but I know Glazier would not risk his career like this. We all know he wants to play in Europe and being outed would be the stupidest thing he could allow to happen right now."

"Damn it all to hell, Mirek!"

"Look, I've been thinking about this a while, about how to handle the press."

"What did you come up with?"

"Food poisoning, which would also explain why he didn't make it to the stadium."

"Okay, fine. Do what you have to. And call me the minute he shows up." Carl snapped his phone shut. He looked up at the sky, clear blue with a few fluffy clouds. Despite all its beauty, he cursed God.

Jackie peeked her head through the door. "Honey, is everything okay?"

Carl shook his head. "Magia with you?"

"No, she went to try and pry her sisters off Matt."

"Come on out."

She stepped fully through the door and shut it most of the way.

"How close are you to Lawrence?"

Raising her eyebrows, she replied, "What does that have to do with—oh, OH! What's wrong with Brendan?"

"You've known all along, huh?"

"Yeah, so what's wrong?"

"The Iceman is missing."

"How? Ian and Tomás were supposed to keep an eye on him."

"Jesus H. Christ, woman, how do you know all this?"

"Molly and I talked today before the match," she said.

"Molly knows that Brendan is—"

"Yep." She studied Carl's wrinkled brow. "Look, Sheila and Lawrence will find him. How is Mirek going to handle the press later?"

"Food poisoning."

"Good call." Jackie nodded. She touched both sides of Carl's face. "Everything will be okay. Don't worry. Just come back inside and act like it's just food poisoning, okay?"

Carl nodded, partially forced by Jackie's loving hands. As Carl kissed her, for a moment all the worry melted from his mind. "I love you, Jacqueline."

Jackie and Carl went back to the table. He nervously clutched his phone. He switched from his usual lager to Bushmill's black Irish whisky neat. No matter how Jackie tried, he just could not calm down inside.

Mirek turned his starting eleven in to the press box. He still listed Brendan as a substitute, in case he decided to grace the stadium with his presence.

The strains of the FIFA anthem filled the stadium as the teams and referees entered the pitch. A high school choir sang the national anthem. As beautiful as they sounded, the Stampede could not bring themselves to enjoy it.

Matt read the graphic that gave the starting line up. He turned and hollered at Carl. "Hey, where's Brendan? Why isn't he starting?"

"Food poisoning," he answered. Jackie squeezed his hand for support.

The one who was ordered to find Alex and the Iceman poked his head in the conference room.

"Kierakos, Alex took the Iceman to his private dungeon. He's not anywhere to be found."

Sheila fingers flexed out of impatient anger. It was close to kickoff and still no Brendan.

Kierakos spoke slowly. "The lady needs to find the Iceman. His career is at stake. Maybe even his life, if Alex is playing this serious of a game with him. Do you know where Alex's dungeon is?"

"I've only been there once. Alex blindfolds you coming and going."

Sheila slammed her hand into the table. She got up. She grabbed a pen and a scrap of paper from her pocket and scrawled her cellular number on it. She shoved it across the table. "Call me if the Iceman and this Alex creature show up back here."

Kierakos nodded as he picked up the paper.

She dashed up the long winding staircase, grabbed Lawrence and entered the daylight.

Brendan melted into Alex. He had never felt this strong of a pull before to a man.

Alex gripped Brendan's cock. It was firm, the pulls almost painful. Alex worked his mouth downward. Brendan sighed. He did not even know his captor's name, but he did not care. Intense paradise, strong vibrations electric prickled every cell of his being. It was a feeling transcending all space and time.

Brendan rode on the brink. Alex knew how to keep him there. Alex controlled everything. Alex's tongue flicked the Iceman's head. Then he took it all in. Brendan grabbed handfuls of silken dark hair. Alex clamped down with his teeth. Brendan released.

Alex stepped back. Red oozed from the bite marks. Alex lapped hungrily the sweet red nectar.

When the bleeding subsided, Alex left the room. "Clean up, Iceman. I'll bring you some clothes."

Brendan nodded. He was shaking. He turned on the shower and stepped under the water. Slowly he came back to life, to reality. If only he knew what time it was. He at least needed to check in with Mirek.

Alex had brought Brendan a large fluffy red towel. Underneath a Fog Dog kit was placed.

Brendan emerged and found the towel. He dried off and reached for the clothes. He froze when he saw what team's kit it was. "I'm not wearing this," he hollered. "Where are my clothes from last night?"

Alex laughed. "Today, you will wear a Fog Dog kit."

"No way." Naked, Brendan picked up the clothes and stormed out of the bathroom. Enough was enough. No more games. He had to figure out what time it was, find a phone and get to the stadium.

He found Alex dressed in full fan gear, lounging on a sofa. Strong sunlight streamed through small slits in hotel-style blackout drapes. Brendan sensed that it might be afternoon.

Brendan tossed the enemy kit in Alex's face. "I'm not wearing this piece of crap team's kit."

Alex tossed it back. "Yes, you are. The Fog Dogs need you." He smiled.

"Who the fuck are you?" The clothes lie at Brendan's feet.

"You're best lover and you're worst nightmare." Alex smirked. "Now put on the kit. It's almost time."

Reluctantly, Brendan pulled on the doggie shorts. "Time for what?"

"Match day."

"Are you trying to keep me from playing today? Is that all this is, some sick twisted game to you?"

"Life is a sick and twisted game. We are all players." Alex sat up. "The shorts look good. Now, put on the rest."

Brendan reached for the top. Shuddering, he pulled it over his head.

"Oh, you look so good as a Fog Dog," Alex sighed. "You're going to play for my team someday. You just don't know it yet."

"What time is it?"

"Almost match day."

"May I at least have my cell phone, please?"

"You want to call your coach. You want to tell him what exactly?"

"I . . . I don't know." Brendan had failed to formulate a good excuse. He sat next to Alex. "I'll call Ian."

"Tigger knows you, well, eh?"

Brendan nodded. "He knows." He looked hard into Alex's eyes. His tone turned serious. "I don't know who you are or what your intentions are, but I have a job playing soccer, and I will not let you or anyone else ruin my career."

"I am Alex Rodriguez. And I will ruin your career." He whipped a blindfold out from between the cushions. Quickly, he masked the Iceman. Then with a soft, deft hand, he bound Brendan's hands behind his back. Alex forced socks and shoes onto Brendan's feet. He stood his captive up. "It's match day."

Chapter XXX

Sheila briefed Lawrence on what went on. The trail had dead-ended. She had a sinking feeling that Brendan was not going to reappear until after the match.

"Well, should we just go to the game?" asked Lawrence.

"Might as well." She shrugged.

The eleven Stampede starters huddled. Ian began. "We have to do this for the Iceman. We all know he's missing. For all we know, a crazed fan could have kidnapped him. We are going to destroy the enemy for him."

The team joined hands in the middle. In unison, they shouted, "One! Two! Three! Four! Stampede! Stampede! Here we go!"

Mirek held Ian's phone. He hoped it would ring. As the ball was put into play, he gave the object a wishful squeeze.

Alex pulled into the parking lot. Brendan heard the crowd noise rising from the stadium. He knew where he was. Alex pulled off the blindfold and released his hands.

Brendan blinked, adjusting to the light. Alex handed him his cell phone. "Now, you can call."

Brendan drew in a deep breath and exhaled slowly. He one touch dialed Ian's number.

Mirek felt the vibration against his thigh. He whipped the cellular out and on. "Hello."

"I'm okay," said Brendan.

Alex yanked the phone away and hung up.

Ian was playing the ball down the right side. Out of the corner of his eye, he saw Mirek on the phone. Ian deliberately knocked the ball off the Dog defender. Ian made the move to get the ball. A quick communication with Mirek confirmed that Brendan was okay.

Mirek dialed Sheila.

A minor wave of relief washed over the pair.

Alex instructed Brendan to get out of the car. They were in the media and stadium personnel parking area. Brendan wondered exactly who Alex was. He thought about running. Alex sensed that and slipped a choke chain collar and leash around Brendan's neck.

Alex led his captive into the stadium. They walked through the underbelly. The Stampede scored their first goal of the match. Brendan smiled. Alex jerked the leash. Brendan's hand flew up to protect his throat. They turned and went through a gate that led toward the Mongrels supporters' section, known as the Dog Pound.

Brendan stopped. He could not be outed like this. Alex snapped the chain hard. "Continue," barked Alex.

Brendan gagged, but managed to eek out a "No!" He grabbed the chain with both hands. A tug of war struggle ensued. Brendan fought to free the leash from Alex's iron left grip. Alex pushed Brendan's front side up against the concrete and steel. Brendan's lip oozed blood from the forceful impact.

A security guard rounded the corner from the tunnel. "Alex, who's your slave this week?"

Alex's head snapped around. He spun Brendan so he could see the guard. The guard gasped. He reached for his radio.

Alex twisted Brendan's arm behind his back. He marched the Iceman into the daylight, into the public eye of the Dog Pound.

Brendan felt like he was in a slow motion movie. His body went limp. Images blurred with the sound of barking hecklers. Flash bulbs popped, immortalizing him in the Fog Dog kit, leashed to Alex. His head spun. He felt sick. His whole world was crashing down around him.

Alex pulled Brendan into an embrace. His lips crashed forcefully on his. Brendan was weak. He wanted to fight, but Alex infused him like a drug. Everything went black.

Doc Gina noticed the commotion, recognized Brendan and raced over to the scene. Security guards surrounded Alex and wrested him away from Brendan's body. He was handcuffed and led away.

Gina touched Brendan's pulse points and checked for breath sounds. Stadium EMT's rushed to her assistance. Brendan was lifted onto a litter and whisked back to the locker room area.

Sheila and Lawrence arrived at the stadium just in time to see the commotion and her husband being taken away. She cornered a security guard to get an escort to the lockers. The guard did not believe her until she showed him her Illinois driver's license. Reluctantly, he acquiesced.

Gina tried to wake Brendan. The pair of EMT's called for an ambulance. Gina called Mirek and briefed him, who told her to stay at the stadium. She instructed the EMT's to make sure a psychological consult was ready for him when he woke up.

The escorted Sheila and Lawrence arrived. Sheila rushed to Brendan's side. She touched his face gently and spoke softly in his ear. "Brendan, my dear, wake up. You're safe now." She ran her fingers through his short platinum locks. Bren, honey, come back. You're with people who love you now."

The ambulance arrived. Sheila was allowed to ride with him. Gina briefed the ambulance crew, adding at the end, with Sheila's nodding approval, "Treat him as if he were a rape victim."

The game itself was going well. Brendan was not missed. On the pitch, Baumgartner scored the first goal. Juan and Ian connected for three more making the halftime score 0-4.

Even so, Carl's heart skipped a beat when his cell phone rang at halftime.

"Carl, it's over and it's not over," began Mirek.

Carl walked to the back. Jackie trotted after him. "What do you mean?"

"Brendan has been taken to the hospital. His captor was arrested. But it was all in front of the Dog Pound."

Carl stepped out. "Damn it! So that's what the commotion was all about down there. One of the damn TV cameras caught part of it. The commentators thought it was just a scuffle between fans, thankfully."

"The still photographers were closer. The fall out is not going to be pretty."

"*Kudowa!*" spat Carl. Jackie raised her eyebrows.

"Gina arranged for a psych consult at the hospital."

"Good."

"Sheila went with him in the ambulance."

"Good."

"So what about the press?"

"Well, it is a police matter, so just say that we can't comment due to the pending police investigation."

"That's exactly what I was thinking."

"Good. That's why I hired you, Mirek. Now as for the rest of the game, continue to punish those damn dogs."

"I really don't think that will be a problem." Mirek smiled for the first time all day. Both men hung up.

Jackie looked her boyfriend in the eyes. "Well?"

"Brendan has been found. Unfortunately, the media are going to have a field day with this one."

"Damn, I had a sinking feeling about the incident near the Pound."

"So did I." He squeezed her hands. "Let's go back inside."

Matt watched Jackie come back to the front with Carl. The younger Koneki sisters were still at his sides. Magia failed in her attempt to get them away.

Księżnicka said, "You really like Jackie, don't you?"

Matt nodded.

"You're better off with one or both of us," said Róża. She stroked his spine.

"Yeah, we share very well," Księżnicka put in.

Matt's spine tingled. Maybe the girls were right. But he hesitated. They were only sixteen and seventeen.

Sean walked by and shot a jealous look his way. Matt laughed, for the first time in a long time.

"Róża," he began, "when is your birthday?"

Her eyes sparkled. "June 21st."

"Ah, 'twas a beautiful midsummer night when you were born." Matt cupped her chin gently in his hand. Their eyes met. He wanted to kiss her. She was beautiful. All the Koneki girls were. His hand dropped slowly. He sighed.

She swooned.

"I will call you, Róża."

Księżnicka shot her sister a jealous look. Róża failed to notice. Księżnicka stepped away. She tugged her sister's jersey. "Ladies room," she said curtly.

Róża sneered. So much for sharing. Księżnicka stomped off. Where was Sean? She thought as she scanned the room.

Sean seated himself across from Carl. He knew something weird was going on with the team; he was determined to break the story on the discussion board. But no matter how Sean tried to squeeze the truth out, Carl kept saying that Brendan had a case of food poisoning, and that the incident involved some actors. The two were completely unrelated.

Sean tried to pump Jackie for information, then Molly. Jackie told him the same thing Carl did. Molly pled ignorance.

Księżnicka approached him and draped her arms around the young redhead. Sean reached up as naturally as if she had been his girlfriend. Molly and Jackie smiled at the exchange. "I didn't know you two were dating," said Jackie.

Startled, Sean turned and looked at Księżnicka. "Hi," he said. Gently, he kissed her hand. Księżnicka flushed at the feel of his lips. Sean stood. "Excuse me."

He took Księżnicka by the hand and led her to the back room. He pressed her back against a wall. "Księżnicka, what kind of game are you girls playing?"

She cocked her head.

"Do you really want me? Seriously?"

She cast her eyes downward. He forced her to look at him.

"Answer me."

"Sean," she began slowly. She could not find the words. She gripped his head on either side and pulled him into a long kiss.

Amazingly, Sean forgot that there was soccer or the Stampede on the television.

Sheila nervously flipped through the pages of a six-month old issue of *People*. The ER doc came out. "Mrs. Glazier?"

She looked up.

"Physically, he's dehydrated. We are treating him for that. He has suffered some minor contusions and cuts and scratches to various parts of his body. We've taken samples with a rape kit, per your instructions. We don't see any physical reason, so far, for his state of conscious, however."

Sheila nodded. "That doesn't surprise me."

"Shall I have the psychiatrist talk to you about what happened?"

"Please, doctor."

"I'll leave word. In the meantime, it may be best if you stayed by his side. We'll be transporting him to a private room shortly."

Sheila followed the doctor through the swinging doors. Brendan lie peacefully on a bed in an exam room. She touched her husband's hand tenderly. Despite it all, she loved him.

"Bren, my husband, my best friend, please wake up," she whispered in his ear.

His hand flexed.

Sheila smiled.

About a half-hour passed and an orderly arrived to transfer him to a room upstairs. Sheila followed, holding Brendan's hand the entire way.

Within an hour of settling into the room, Doc Gina arrived. "Hi, Sheila," she greeted quietly.

"Hi, Gina," Sheila replied. "You can talk normally. He's not sleeping. He's still unconscious."

As the two women chatted about what happened and speculated why he was in the state, Brendan's fingers twitched. Gina noticed the movement. "I think he's hearing us."

Sheila nodded. She stroked the top of his head and touched his cheek gently. "Brendan, you stupid son of a bitch, wake up this instant."

Gina raised her eyebrows, but Sheila's behavior did not surprise her. True, theirs was an odd relationship, but it worked well. And that is what counted the most.

Brendan's eyelids fluttered. Sheila continued her verbal reprimands. She was careful, however, not to bring up the possible ruining of his soccer career.

Gina added at an opportune moment, "The team needed you today."

Brendan's eyes flew open and he said, "No, they didn't."

Sheila said, "Welcome back, Bren." She kissed him on the cheek.

Gina started checking his vitals. Everything was normal. She slipped out to report his status to the nurse on duty and call Mirek and Carl.

Shortly after the match was over, Carl and Jackie headed back to the condo. He hunched over the computer surfing for press releases on the match and any rumors no matter how true they might be regarding the incident and Brendan.

Jackie set a steaming mug of Irish coffee in front of him. She knew he would be up all night. She kissed him on the cheek. He did not even take his eyes off the screen. That did not bother her. She understood.

She headed back to the kitchen and grabbed the phone. She dialed Colin MacNaughten's cell number. "Colin, it's Jackie. I need to run something by you, but it needs to be under attorney-client privilege."

"Hold on. Let me get somewhere quieter." Colin excused himself from his friends. He stepped on to a nearby balcony and closed the French doors. "Jackie, the clock starts now." He jotted down the time in a small notebook.

Jackie told him everything she knew about the incident in San Francisco. Then added, "Do you think there may be grounds for a defamation of character suit?"

Colin paused and chose his words carefully before answering. "Maybe. Was Brendan actually being courted by any top flight European teams?"

"Nothing serious, but after his performance so far this year, there is a strong possibility."

"What a bit, Jackie, and see what actually hits the press. Then we'll figure something out."

"Okay, I'll keep you posted. When Brendan and Sheila get back, I'm going to set up an appointment in your office."

"Sounds good," said Colin. "By the way, where should I send the bill?"

"To my business address will be fine. I don't want Carl to know that I'm doing this for them right now."

Chapter XXXI

Molly and Renata did not discuss soccer for the rest of the day. Top down, Molly drove out to Aurora. They pulled around back and parked. It was still early. They spotted a band loading in. Molly hopped out and approached. Renata watched her friend. Molly tossed her hair a little as she chatted. Molly's moves were subtle, but in just a few minutes, she was waving Renata over. They headed in the back door. Each carried a small item. No cover charge was to be paid by either lady that night.

Renata had always admired her friend for her ease around celebrities. That is why, Renata reasoned, that her friend was in a relationship with a soccer star. She wished she could be as comfortable as Molly.

The two settled in at the bar. Nearly every barstool had a good view of the stage. Molly ordered a pitcher of the darkest tap beer and shared glasses of it with the band that let them in. The two conversed casually.

The first band began to play. Renata and Molly chided them. In between bands, Renny, Jack's friend, approached. Renata seated herself. She rolled her eyes. She knew who would win this encounter.

"Well, well, well, Molly, long time no see," he began sidling up to her. He ran his fingers obnoxiously along her shoulders.

Molly stood. She challenged him as if she were a man. "You and I, outside, right now."

Renny's jaw dropped, as did Renata's.

"What's the matter, asshole? Are you chicken?" She poked him in the chest.

"Afraid of you? Ha!" said Renny.

"Okay, then, let's go." She grabbed his arm firmly. "You can bring whoever you want to."

He swallowed hard. Molly sensed his fear. She started walking toward the front door. Renny froze. Molly paused by the entrance. "Well, are you coming or not?"

He shook his head.

"Then spread the word that I'm not to be fucked with." She strode back to her beer. She poked Renny in the chest for emphasis. "Understood?"

He nodded with a slight whimper. Molly reseated herself and took a long drink.

Renny walked to the opposite end of the bar. He glowered at her the rest of the night.

Renata scolded her friend. "Are you fucking crazy?"

"All of Jack's friends are all talk and no action. They wouldn't dare hit me. It's just not in their pussy cat nature." Molly paused. She wondered if she should tell Renata what Jack was really like with her. It was worth telling the secret she had kept. She continued, "But Jack, on the other hand, that bastard likes to hit women."

Renata just stared at her in disbelief. "I can't believe you never said anything."

"I know. I should have."

"So a lot of those bruises weren't from mosh pits or work scuffles?"

Molly shook her head. "Nope, they weren't."

"Why didn't you have him arrested?"

She shrugged. "I don't know. I guess I was under his spell. But I used to do just as much damage to him from time to time. Threatening to cut his dick off stopped most of it."

Renata forced a laugh. "You should have. You might have saved a lot of women a lot of headaches in the future."

Molly nodded. "You're right. Might have helped me with my traumas, too." She looked at her scarred hand. "I should have never gotten involved with him. It's been affecting my relationship with Ian. He's understanding, but we can't seem to get Jack to stop calling."

"Sounds like it's time to file a restraining order."

"I have. You would think that would stop it. I've tried pleading with the wardens at the city lock-up, but they keep saying they don't have the power to control who Jack he dials."

Renata nodded. "They would if you have a restraining order, or so you would think. If he tries to contact you again, he could be in a world of hurt with the law. You need to file a formal complaint."

"I'll call a lawyer on Tuesday."

"Smart move."

Chapter XXXII

Monday, May 25, 1998: Sean invited Księżnicka to a private picnic. Her sisters were not with her, which was a relief for both of them.

Sean drove to a random quiet spot in the countryside. Of course, getting out of the Chicagoland sprawl took almost two hours. He did not want any distractions from anyone he might know or from other picnickers on Memorial Day. That was why he did not go to the Forest Preserve or the lakefront.

Księżnicka asked what the holiday was all about. Sean explained the meaning and history of it, and then added that most folks, sadly, just thought of it as the beginning of summer and a day off from work. They had conversed the entire drive down. He felt comfortable with her. He hoped that something more serious might develop between them.

Sean laid out the blanket. He set out the picnic items. He even brought a bottle of pinot grigio he stole from his parents' wine cellar. He watched her get comfortable. She was wearing a long skirt and a white lacey blouse. Her blonde locks framed her face. She was beautiful; she was interested in him.

"Good choice." Księżnicka smiled.

"Thank you," he replied. "Only the best for my lady." He knew it sounded silly and scripted but too late.

She blushed. "Did your father teach you about wine?"

He pulled the cork effortlessly. "No, my dad is a recovering alcoholic. He sobered up a few years after my little brother was born. My mom still keeps some wine around for special occasions."

"How much younger is your little brother?"

"He's four years younger." Sean poured her glass first.

Taking the goblet from him, she asked, "So you probably don't remember much about him being drunk."

Sean shook his head. "No, I don't. What about your father?"

"Well, being Polish Catholics, we are predisposed to enjoying a drink from time to time." She smiled and raised her glass. They toasted. "Seriously, my father likes the vodka. He's—um, how do you call it?—Ah, I remember, a snob."

Sean laughed. He could not fathom being a snob about vodka, but he supposed it was possible.

She took a sip and continued, "He began drinking more after mother died. Then, we came over here. He found a substitute for mother, I think, with the Stampede. He never before approached a team like he was married to it. I've even heard old Tomás say that his coaching style has changed from what it was in Poland."

Sean pulled out the food, mostly finger food, from the picnic basket. "Did you want to come to the United States?"

"Oh yes, Róża and I both wanted to come. Magia wanted to stay with Jerzy, but Father insisted that she had to come to the United States with us, to help keep Róża and me in line. I think Father had plans all along to get Jerzy over here to play in the FLA."

Sean raised his eyebrows. "Really? But there is no way he could play for the Stampede."

Księżnicka shook her head. "Yes, I know all about the politics and crazy rules in the FLA. I think he might end up in New York."

Sean stroked his chin. "Yeah, you're right. Olufemi's tragic accident opened up a spot for this season." He reached for a soft breadstick. "Enough about soccer." Wow, he never thought he would ever utter such a phrase.

"I agree, enough about *piłka nożna*." She playfully reached for the breadstick he was holding, but instead leaned in for the kiss. His mouth responded to hers. Her inner strength and outer beauty turned him on. His whole body tingled.

She pushed him back. He lay half on, half off the blanket. He felt himself getting hard as she crawled atop him. He did not know how far she was willing to take things, but he was certainly going to enjoy the ride.

Chapter XXXIII

TUESDAY, MAY 26, 1998: Quigley flew into JFK airport early. He had a meeting with Alexi. He had only spoken to Alexi's secretary and really had no idea what Alexi looked or sounded like. Alexi did not make many public appearances that he could recall or remember.

Quigley first met Jerzy near the ground transportation. Jerzy had already found the old bilingual limousine driver. Jerzy and the driver were discussing the World Cup. At least that is what Quigley thought due to the country names dropped. The driver greeted Quigley warmly.

"Jerzy's bags are already in the trunk, Mr. Quigley." The spry Polish-American picked up Quigley's overnight bag and placed it neatly in the trunk. He opened the door for his charges. The two men crawled in.

Jerzy reached for the vodka decanter and poured himself two fingers. He gestured to his agent. Quigley shook his head. "It's too early," he said, gesturing at his wristwatch.

Jerzy nodded. He found a container of orange juice. "Juice?" he pronounced slowly.

Quigley smiled. "Yes, please. You've been working on your English."

"Yes, I studied a lot." Jerzy poured some juice into a glass and handed it to him. "I need to learn more. Magia will teach me." He formed the words slowly. His pronunciation was thick but understandable.

The driver left the partition lowered in case translation services were needed. "You are madam's only appointment today," the old man remarked.

Quigley gave the driver a quizzical look. "Madam? I thought we were meeting directly with Alexi."

"Yes, Alexi, *she* said she was looking forward to meeting the agent who brought Sin Brazos to Chicago."

Jerzy smiled and tried not to laugh as he sipped his vodka. Even he was smart enough to do his proper homework on the team that he might soon be playing for.

Alexi Taman sat behind a large slate and stainless steel desk. The surroundings were simple. A small cell phone rested near her hand. A slender laptop was open. She had the bio page of Jerzy pulled up.

Her secretary announced the morning's appointment. Alexi motioned for her to usher them in. As the three men entered, Alexi rose.

She shook Quigley's hand. He had to look up. Alexi stood six-feet tall in her stocking feet, but she was not afraid to tower over men. She added three more inches in heels. Her build was slender, as a runway model. Her long dark mahogany locks hung loosely but neatly around her face. Her visage was angular with sharply defined cheekbones and a Grecian nose. Her manner of dress oozed money and power.

She shook Jerzy's hand firmly. "I've seen some of your game tapes, pan Josefczyk. I like what I see."

"Dziękuję," replied Jerzy.

"Please, have a seat." She gestured to the leather chairs with stainless steel frames.

Quigley cleared his throat. "We all know about the salary cap situation. I'm glad that Lance is going to allow the Cabbies this opportunity."

"We won't be able to do much this season, but can reevaluate things over winter," stated Alexi.

Quigley looked over at Jerzy to see if he understood. Jerzy said, "I understand."

Alexi continued, "We have arranged for an apartment and a vehicle."

"Good," said Jerzy.

"Hmm, I'm impressed. Jerzy, your English is good," commented she.

"Thank you," he replied.

Meanwhile, Michael had reached for some paperwork in his briefcase. "The agreements that I have drawn up are fairly standard, but I'll understand if you wish to have your lawyers or the league's attorneys look it over." He handed the papers to her. It was a struggle for him to maintain an aura of professionalism in the presence of such a beautiful woman. That was why he never tried to represent supermodels.

As she took the papers, she said, "Thank you." She turned her attention to Jerzy. She motioned for him to stand up. He complied. She circled the desk and approached Jerzy. She ran her right hand over his muscles, squeezing occasionally.

Jerzy grinned from ear to ear. Quigley grew concerned. What was she doing? She was looking him over as if she were buying a horse. He had never seen any owner or manager treat a potential player in this manner.

Alexi's fingers paid careful attention to Jerzy's knees. He was instructed to raise his pant legs one at a time. She quizzed him on his injury history. The old chauffer stepped forward to translate. Jerzy removed his shoes. Alexi examined his ankles, feet and toes. Quigley wanted to stop her, but the look of enjoyment on Jerzy's face kept him from doing so.

She rose. "You may sit down now." She gestured. Turning to Quigley, she said, "Before we sign anything, I will want our team doctor to run a fitness test and an MRI on his legs from hips down. It's my standard procedure." She retook her seat. "My initial exam detected nothing out of the ordinary. Seeing recent game tapes from Poland is a testament to his fitness. But please, understand that we want to be sure that he will be able to start immediately."

Both men nodded.

She scribbled down an initial offer and slid it across the desk. "This offer is, of course, contingent of him being fully fit."

Quigley reached for the paper. He read the numbers. He showed Jerzy the figure.

Jerzy crinkled his brow as he tried to convert the figure into zlotys. "Is this good?" He looked at his agent, as a young boy would a father.

"You can live on that here, but we would have to get you set up in a car and an apartment." Knowing that Alexi had heard that, Quigley turned back to her.

"We can discuss transportation and housing allowances once the fitness test is deemed satisfactory," she said curtly. "Usually, we like to assign roommates."

"What if my Magia wants to move in with me?" Jerzy asked.

"Do you really think that Mirek will let Magia move in without getting married first?" Quigley asked.

The old man started to translate, but Jerzy held up his hand. He understood. "I will talk with Mirek."

"In the meantime, Jerzy can stay with Jon Harper. We just traded his roommate to San Francisco for a draft pick." Alexi made a note to call Jon about the arrangement. "Do you have a hotel room for tonight? If not, we'll take you over to Jon's place."

"I think Magia is coming in later this afternoon," said Jerzy. "So we have hotel."

Quigley nodded in agreement. Mirek had purchased tickets for his eldest to fly into New York to see Jerzy.

"Okay, let my secretary know where you are staying. We'll be in touch regarding the physical." Alexi stood.

The men followed suit. Handshakes all around. The deal was nearly complete.

For all Magia knew, she was just being allowed a vacation away from her sisters. Her father and the Stampede would be in town later that weekend. She deplaned, retrieved her luggage, and then went in search of the right hotel shuttle.

She gazed in awe at the hustle and bustle of Times Square. She could not wait to see it after dark. She had always wondered if it would be like what she had seen on television and in the movies.

She entered the lobby of the five-star hotel. Her mouth fell agape. Quigley was in the lobby. "What are you doing here?" she exclaimed.

Quigley looked up from his laptop. "Hi, Magia, good to see you. I had some client meetings. You?"

"Dad decided to give me a break from my sisters. I'll go back with the team on Sunday."

"Oh, that's right. The Cabbies play the Stampede on Saturday." He was doing well playing dumb, so far.

"Who's the client?" Magia felt that something was fishy about the two of them running into each other in the same hotel lobby. Way too convenient. Had to be more than coincidence.

"Do you want to meet him?"

Magia raised her eyebrows. "Depends."

"He said to bring him a pretty woman for dinner companionship tonight. You certainly fit that description."

"Oh, I don't think that would be wise. I'm engaged you know." She could not quite figure out what Quigley was up to.

"Come on. Help me out here, Magia. You know you can trust me." Quigley added after she still looked apprehensive, "Tell you what. I'll go to the same restaurant and be there, just in case something funny starts to happen."

She shrugged. Might as well have some fun. "Okay."

"Have the bellhop follow with your bags," said the agent.

Magia narrowed her eyes at him. "Can I at least check into my room first?"

"Okay. I suppose that would be a good idea." Quigley did well to keep a poker face throughout. She was right to be cautious. Now, he only hoped that the desk clerk would not blow the surprise. Michael watched her carefully. She got her key card without any whoops of joy.

"Okay, I'm ready. Room 3029." They headed for the bank of elevators.

"Wonderful," he said. "My client and I are on the same floor."

She swiped the card in the lock of room 3029. Quigley watched to the side, waiting for her reaction. He was supposed to alert Mirek after he got Jerzy and Magia together.

She pushed the door open. Familiar cologne wafted up her nostrils. "Jerzy?"

He beckoned to her in their native tongue. She ran into the room. Quigley smiled. His job was done. He headed to his room; he had a call to make.

Magia fell into Jerzy's arms. He held her tight. Their lips collided. The kiss bore deep longing. Each savored every moment of it. "Don't ever leave me again," he murmured.

"I won't, Jerzy. I won't."

Chapter XXXIV

Brendan was released on Monday morning but was instructed to stay in town. The district attorney wanted to speak with him Tuesday morning. Sheila brought her husband back to the hotel. Lawrence, obligated to work Tuesday night, had flown back early Monday.

Brendan was glad that Lawrence had left. His lover's presence compromised everything. Instead, he spent some quality time with his wife. The pair was best friends and that is what made everything easier and harder at the same time.

He had lamented to her, "I wish I could love you as a hetero man loves women. I'm sorry."

She reached out and lightly, tenderly caressed his cheek in response. "Don't be. I wish I were attracted to you in that way myself. But we are closer than most husbands and wives will ever be."

The two arrived at the courthouse at 7:00 AM. Alex was to be arraigned today. Brendan balked as he put his hand on the door handle to the building. Sheila placed her hand on his shoulder and squeezed. He sighed heavily and entered.

The district attorney was a hard-boiled brunette with short, no-fuss hair. Sheila took an instant liking to her. The woman approached them in the lobby. "Brendan Glazier?"

He nodded his head.

"I'm Lisa Santorini." She thrust her hand at him. Brendan shook it. "Follow me. I want to go over a few things before the arraignment."

Brendan started shaking as they entered the courtroom. Sheila squeezed his hand.

Alex was already seated next to his attorney at the defendant's table. Alex's hair was slicked back smooth. The controlling oil glistened under the fluorescent lights. His suit was black on black, befitting his gothic ways. He smiled crookedly at Brendan, as if to say, "Why?" He winked at the Iceman, and then blew him a kiss.

Brendan swooned. Sheila guided him to a seat at the prosecution's table. She whispered in her husband's ear, "You are really drawn to him, aren't you?"

Brendan nodded. Alex was the best fuck he had ever had. He felt like a smitten schoolgirl when he was in the same room with Alex. That was how he felt when the dominant first approached him at the Blood Bank. He sighed.

Sheila hissed under her breath, "You fucking sadist."

The judge entered the courtroom. Alex stood accused of rape and kidnapping. He pled not guilty to both charges, as anticipated. Lisa argued for no bail. The judge set bail at $100,000. Sheila signaled Lisa to ask for a restraining order. Brendan shook his head.

"It's best," said Sheila, placing a hand on his shoulder.

Lisa agreed. She raised the issue. "Your Honor, we request that an emergency restraining order be instated, since the defendant is expected to make bail."

"So ordered."

"Thank you, your Honor."

The judge banged the gavel. "Call the next case."

Sheila and Brendan left the courtroom. Alex's eyes followed the Iceman. Brendan felt his gaze. As soon as they were in the hall, he tore into her. "Why did you have to insist on a restraining order? I want to see Alex again."

"No," she insisted, "it's for your own good." She tugged on his arm. "It's time to go home."

He stood firm. Glowering, he said, "No, I want to say good-bye to Alex."

Sheila slapped him with a hard open palm. Her fingers stung. "Snap out of it, Bren."

He stared at her in disbelief. She had never slapped him before. Not even when they were kids. He was not quite sure what drove her to it now. "Fuck you, Sheila!" he spat and headed for the exit.

Sheila chased after him. "Damn it to hell, Bren."

Brendan raised his arm to hail a cab. Sheila caught him and whirled him around to face her. A taxi pulled up. "You and I are getting in this cab together and going to the hotel for our bags then straight to the airport." She shook Brendan. "Do you understand me? There will be no seeing Alex tonight or any other time, until we are due back in court. Are we clear on that?"

Brendan cast his eyes downward. "Yes, okay, fine, we'll do it your way."

Chapter XXXV

Wednesday, May 27, 1998: Mirek, Carl, Jackie, Colin MacNaughten, Sheila and Brendan met in the conference room of the Stampede office. Carl closed and locked the door. He still could not figure out why Jackie insisted on being involved in this, but she was the one who initiated the meeting with Colin. Carl instructed her to just take notes and keep her trap shut. He did not like being harsh with her, but it was needed. She was becoming too pushy, too involved.

The six were seated. Carl assumed the chairman's seat.

"The first thing," Carl began, "we need to address is Brendan's blatant breaking of team road rules."

Brendan hung his head. He knew this was coming.

"Do we have a set policy, Carl?" asked Mirek.

"Yes, we do. It is in writing and every new team member must read and agree to it before playing for our organization." Carl directed his answer more toward Colin than Mirek. "The first violation is being benched for one match. In this case, I suggest that Brendan not even be allowed to make the trip on Saturday."

"Okay," said Brendan meekly.

Carl folded his hands on the table. "Good. That was the easy part. Now for the media fallout."

Colin cleared his throat and pushed his glasses up. "Jackie has provided me with printouts and clippings from major media and underground outlets. She has suggested that I look into a libel or slander suit. The problem here is that the implications that Brendan is gay turn out to be true. If it's true, then we can't sue."

Brendan laid his head on the table and folded his hands over it. Sheila laid a reassuring hand on his back and rubbed.

Banging his fist on the table, Carl barked, "Sit up, Brendan Glazier."

The player bolted upright.

Carl continued, "You were not aware of this, but Lance and I recently had a conference call with the owner and manager of Derby County about a transfer. Even though you are not considered national team material, they still are talking about a nice chunk of change for you. This was before last week's match. Yesterday, I received a call again from them. They are no longer interested."

Brendan spoke, "It's because I'm gay, isn't it?"

"They said discipline problems, Brendan." Carl leaned into his face. "And they are right. Mirek has been telling me you've been late for practice a lot lately, even coming in hungover."

Sheila interjected, "How long has this been going on?"

Mirek said, "For about a month."

Carl leaned back. "So what are we going to do about it?" He placed his hands behind his head.

Silence befell the participants. Carl waited patiently. Colin finally spoke, "I think it's time to make an official announcement."

Carl leaned forward. "Go on."

"First we need to get Brendan some counseling."

Brendan nodded with a heavy sigh. Sheila squeezed his shoulder.

Colin continued, "I'm no psychologist, but it's clear to me that it's time for Brendan to come out loud and proud. Questions, of course, will be coming more at Sheila, as his wife. Are you ready for this?"

"I'll come out publicly at the same time," she stated firmly.

Colin cocked his head and raised his eyebrows. "Hmm, Jackie didn't tell me about this little tidbit."

Jackie shrugged, but she remained silent per Carl's instructions.

"So," Colin stroked his chin, "how long have you known each other was—you know—swung the other way?"

Sheila answered, "Bren and I have been friends since we were kids. He never told me that he was gay and he thought that marrying me would help to hide it. But I've known for a long time that he was gay. He just never seemed to pick up on my being a lesbian."

"Was the marriage consummated?"

"Ugh! Worst sex partner I've ever had," Sheila spat with a grin.

"Speak for yourself. You think I liked the weekly at first?"

They both laughed.

"Okay, then, sorry I asked." Colin smiled. He turned back to Carl. "I'm no marketing wizard here either and maybe Jackie has some ideas you can discuss later, but you are going to open up a huge market and perhaps pave a path for future closeted sportsmen to come out."

Carl nodded thoughtfully. "Yes, Colin, you're right. And in a sense we would be beating them at their own game."

Colin folded his hands on the table. "Exactly."

Alex logged onto the Internet and checked the price of a one-way ticket to Chicago. A nude picture of the Iceman was taped to his monitor. He had snapped it himself. Brendan was posing like a model.

"I will have you," he said to the image. He clicked on the cheapest flight. "I will see you soon, my lover." He kissed his fingers and touched the image.

Chapter XXXVI

THURSDAY, MAY 28, 1998: Jerzy passed the team physical with flying colors. With permission of Michael Quigley, he signed on the dotted line. The next day, he was at Cabbie team practice.

Magia joined him. They arrived early. She put on her shin guards and cleats. The two liked to go one on one. She helped him stretch out, and he returned the favor.

Cabbie coaching staff and trainers were arriving. The head coach watched his new player and girlfriend. Jerzy and Magia toyed with each other, a light work out. He appeared to defend as well as attack. She went at him harder than he did at here. Her skills were fairly impressive, considering she was a woman, thought the coach.

When the rest of the Cabbies arrived, coach blew the whistle. Magia kicked the ball toward the coach. The pair jogged over. Introductions were made.

The coach smiled warmly at Magia. "I should have known you were a Koneki. You have your father's moves."

"Thank you."

Jerzy handed his bride-to-be a bottle of Gatorade. She took a slow sip at first, wary of what quick rehydration could do. Jerzy gave her a peck on the cheek. He liked the taste of her salty sweat.

Jerzy was introduced to the team. No one on the staff or on the team was fully fluent in Polish. Magia was allowed to stay closer than most guests were allowed at Cabbie team practice.

While drills were underway, Magia stood next to the coach. He commented, "I should call Alexi and have her hire you as a translator."

She smiled. "I also speak Russian and German. German, not so well, though," she added for conversation's sake.

"Well, I'm thinking the only one in the whole organization who speaks fluent Polish is Alexi's personal driver. I'm looking at you and I see you translating out here until Jerzy can handle things on his own, then maybe in the front office working in marketing." The whole time, his eyes never left the pitch. During the one touch drills, Jerzy's passing was crisp and precise no matter what the speed of the receiver. It was uncanny how he seemed to know the relative speed of each new teammate. Coach stroked his jaw.

Magia blinked at him. "You're kidding, no?"

"No, I'm not." He reached for his cell phone. "Alexi, darling, you should come out today."

"How does Jerzy look?" Alexi asked.

"Good. Don't wait until Saturday. Besides, I have an idea."

"I'm afraid to ask. Most of your early morning ideas are nut ball."

"Hire Magia Koneki."

"Why would I do that?"

"We need a pitch side translator until Jerzy is fluent. Then, I figure she could help with marketing to the Polish-American neighborhoods to put more butts in the seats."

"Fucking brilliant. I'll be by as soon as I can get out there."

Alexi arrived as coach was dividing the team up for a full field scrimmage. Jerzy lined up as a midfielder. "Five minutes, then we mix it up," he hollered, and then blew the whistle.

Coach introduced Magia to Alexi. The two women went off to chat. "Magia Koneki, so you must be Mirek's eldest daughter."

Magia nodded. "Yes."

"And Jerzy's bride?"

"Yeah," she replied more dreamily.

"You've picked a looker." Alexi sighed as she recalled how Jerzy's body felt underneath her manicured fingers.

Magia sensed the older woman's desire, but held back any jealous-sounding comments.

"Well, Coach Hartford thinks you might be a good addition to our organization as well. What do you think?"

She shrugged. "My only job in Chicago is keeping an eye on my sisters."

"Did you work in Poland?"

"No, just school. I'm only 19."

"You love soccer."

"*Piłka nożna, tak.*"

"Here in the United States, we have problems getting people into the stadiums to see the games. Our attendance is averaging less than your Chicago Stampede. We have a huge Polish market here, but little means to tap it. Hartford and I both think you might be an asset to us as much as Jerzy will be."

Magia nodded. "It's sad, but true. In Chicago, it's a bit of a novelty, but we've done well. It would be nice, though to see a full stadium." She smiled and pushed a strand of loose hair behind her ear.

"I don't think we'll ever fill Giants Stadium the way it was in 1994 for the World Cup matches, but I'd like to see some better numbers."

"It will not be easy," mused Magia. "Jerzy is a good start, but he is not a well-known player in Poland yet. I think he should be, but I am biased." She turned her eyes back toward the action on the pitch.

Alexi noticed Magia's boots and shin guards, which had not been removed yet. "You play?"

"Jerzy and I were going one-on-one earlier. I help him warm up a lot. Women don't really play sports and aren't traditionally supposed to even like sports in Poland. My sisters and I all play. We just started playing on an all women's team in a coed rec league. We are the Stampedistas. All of us are committed to either a player, the front office, or in Jackie's case, the owner."

Alexi smiled. She was listening. She liked Magia's pluck.

Hartford's whistle blew five minutes. All the players jogged over. He rearranged the line-ups. Jerzy was shifted to left forward.

Magia crinkled her nose. He's a better right to middle player. She wanted to point that out to the coach, but held her tongue. It was wrong for a woman to speak her mind out of turn. Instead, she mentioned her thoughts aloud to Alexi.

"Hmm," said the owner. "Well, Hartford likes to experiment. We think it gives our players better experience come match time. Next five minute scrimmage, he'll be placed on the other side."

Magia nodded. "Yeah, Dad does that, too, sometimes."

"I like you," said Alexi. "But before I say yes to a front office gig for you, I want to hear some ideas." She looked the young lady in the eyes.

Magia knew so little about marketing and how Polish immigrants here were. Sure, she knew some of the Ultras in Chicago, but her father tried to keep the three of them sheltered from the main Polish immigrant neighborhoods in Chicago.

She ran her hand through her hair, still damp with sweat. She exhaled. "I don't know. *Piłka nożna* is as natural as breathing in Poland." She tapped her lips in thought. "I think going after the—hmm, what's the right word—ethnic—yeah, that's it—market just because you have a certain player from that country could be bad in the long run. You may gain in the short term but not in the long run, and maybe not overall if the player retires or is traded."

Alexi nodded slowly. "You're right. I've never liked that strategy. May be good for baiting and a short term increase in turnstile numbers, but long term—that's what I want and what the FLA needs."

"I agree," said Magia. "We have to get them hooked on a new team, their new home team, because this area is their home now."

"I like you," repeated Alexi. "Screw the marketing department. I want you to work directly with me."

Magia swallowed back a squeal of disbelief. "Thank you," she said as calmly as possible. Money did not matter. That would be worked out later. The two women shook on the initial offer.

"I need to head to the office. Come by later this afternoon when you get a chance and we can talk about compensation," said Alexi as she rose to her full statuesque height.

Magia stood out of respect. "I'll be by later."

Alexi crossed to Hartford. They exchanged pleasantries. Hartford blew the whistle and had Jerzy shift to right forward.

Jerzy breathed a sigh of relief. He felt unnatural on the opposite side. He could play it well enough; it was just a comfort factor.

They restarted on a free kick. From that side and a couple of touches, Jerzy knocked the ball past the keeper.

Alexi said to Hartford, "Start Jerzy on Saturday."

Coach nodded.

"Then work him to where he's just as fluid on the left side."

"Yes, ma'am. Can't say I don't agree with you."

With that Alexi walked in long graceful strides back to her limousine.

Chapter XXXVII

F RIDAY, MAY 29, 1998: Lawrence grew worried. He could sense that something bad was going to happen. He spent Friday afternoon listening to Hildegard von Bingen and cleaning his parents' house. Washing dishes by hand, staring out the window at the backyard, his mind wandered.

He never intended to, but he did, fall in love with Brendan. At least, that's what it felt like. It bothered him that neither Brendan nor Sheila had called him. He had no idea how the arraignment had gone.

He dried his hands and walked to his room. The sounds of Hildegard wafted through the house. He lit a pair of candles and some incense. He reached for his well-worn tarot deck. He mouthed the name of his lover, projecting energy into the cards.

One by one, the cards were laid. He only had time for a quick reading, a three-card spread. The symbolic reality of the third card hit Lawrence in the chest like a shotgun blast—Ace of Swords.

"Alex," seethed Lawrence.

Magia quickly found her niche in the Cabbies' front office. Alexi had bestowed the fancy title of assistant to the general manager on her along with a tidy paycheck.

She had not told her dad yet. She decided to wait until the three of them sat down to dinner. Mirek was coming in later that afternoon.

The team jet landed at the Newark airport. The Stampede were transported to the Sheraton at the Meadowlands. Mirek arranged for a cab ride to a prearranged restaurant where he would be meeting Magia and Jerzy. Carl crawled into a limousine supplied by Alexi.

Alexi awaited her target like a spider in the middle of her web. She had been following Carl's life for a while.

Carl was born out of wedlock. His mother was a prostitute and did not know who the father of her child was. Ms. Costello also liked to play the lottery. One day, his mother hit a large jackpot, $163 million. Carl was 17 at the time. He thanked his mother daily for taking the annuity.

His mother had the foresight to write a will even before the winnings and take out life insurance on herself in the amount of two million dollars. But even after the winning, his mother could not break away from being a prostitute. An angry housewife ended Carl's mother's life when he was 18.

Carl suddenly found himself a very rich man, even though he had no idea his mother had been that wealthy due to a winning lottery ticket. Somehow, his mother had kept him from finding out.

He invested carefully in the early 1990's and cashed out of the market at the right time. Alexi admired him for that. Obviously, Carl's most risky investment was the FLA. Alexi herself did not even know if the league would ever turn a profit, but she was for damned sure going to have fun trying. She hoped that she could form an alliance in more ways than just the FLA with Carl.

Alexi's driver opened the door. Carl climbed in. Alexi fought back a sigh. Her long lean superman was joining her.

The decisions Carl had made with the inherited jackpot were outstanding. He had increased his worth tenfold. This was a fact that his little girlfriend Jackie was probably not aware of, she mused. Ha, Alexi scoffed to herself, Jackie's no match for me. I will have whom I want when I want and tonight I want Carl Costello.

Alexi greeted him cordially and offered a glass of merlot. Carl accepted the glass and the two toasted to a good match.

Alexi sipped her wine and flirted shamelessly. She was getting turned on just from the sight of him. Even though some of her players had better physiques, Carl's skinny ass was still the one that made her wet at mere sight. Maybe it was a power thing. Maybe it was . . . oh, hell, even she did not even know.

The driver headed for the prearranged location. Alexi fought her attraction and engaged Carl in conversation. She did not want to be obvious, at least not yet. "I want to thank you for Jerzy and Magia."

Carl looked puzzled. "I didn't have much to do with Jerzy's deal. That was all Mirek's underhanded dealings to get his eldest's beloved over here."

"Then thank you for not being able to add Jerzy to your roster. I was at practice yesterday and the boy looks great." She raised her glass. "As for Magia, what a little unknown package she is going to be. The Cabbies are going to gain a lot in the marketing department from her."

Now Carl was really clueless. He shook his head and shrugged.

"Oh, wow, Mirek must have really left you out of the loop. Although I don't think he planned on *pani* Magia to be a part of the deal." Alexi smiled. She was amused by Carl's lack of knowledge. She clarified, "I hired Magia as my personal assistant."

Carl raised his eyebrows. "She's so young and has no college experience."

"Oh, Miss Koneki wasn't looking for a job, but when I met her at practice, the way she understood things, the game, American marketing, the challenges, oh it was so cute, actually, she said, 'In Poland, piłka nożna is as natural as breathing.'"

"She's right, you know." Carl sipped his wine.

Alexi nodded. She leaned closer. "I know. It was her observations and knowledge of the game why I hired her." Alexi's heart rate increased and a rush of electric warmth hit her loins.

Carl simply said, "I don't know why we never knew that about her. Mirek must have been keeping secrets from me."

"I think," said Alexi, "knowing Eastern Europe, that her knowledge of the game and business was probably well-concealed from her own father."

Alexi patted the seat next to her. It was subtle. She wanted Carl, by her side. Between the two of them, she knew they could be the most formidable force in the world of US Soccer. She held on to the hope that Jackie was one of his long string of bimbos.

Carl did not budge. He preferred to look her in the eye. "You're probably right, Alexi. But Mirek isn't completely adverse to suggestions from a woman. He took Jacqueline's suggestion during halftime at a match."

Alexi leaned back. "Oh really." Sounds like Jackie's not a bimbo after all, she thought to herself.

"Her suggestion based on her reading of the first half was tactically brilliant." He finished the wine. As she refilled his glass, he asked, "So where are we headed for dinner?"

"I made reservations at Chez Paysan. I hope you like French."

Mirek met Magia and Jerzy for dinner in a quiet Mediterranean café.

During dinner, Mirek and Jerzy chatted about adjustments to living in the United States, his impressions of the Cabbies, and what his living arrangements would be.

Magia listened politely and finally interjected, "I got a job."

Jerzy smiled. He knew, but her father reacted with, "You what?"

"Papa, Alexi Taman hired me to help translate at practice and as her assistant."

"What?"

Jerzy interjected as he squeezed his beloved's hand under the table, "Magia met Alexi. Pani Taman liked Magia so much that she hired her. I will need help at practice until my English gets better. At first, it was only going to be that. Then, I guess Magia impressed Alexi so much that it turned into something more permanent."

"Papa, I am not flying back with you on Sunday," she stated flatly. "I am staying here with Jerzy."

"You are not married yet. I forbid you to live with Jerzy until you are married." Mirek scowled.

"I am 19 and am free to do as I please. It was bad enough that you forced me to come here instead of staying with Jerzy in Poland."

"What about your sisters?" protested Mirek. "I can't take care of them myself."

"Papa, they are nearly old enough to leave, too. They are not babies. If anything, it's been the three of us taking care of you."

Her words cut straight to his heart. He laid his napkin on the table in a dramatic fashion. He shoved his chair away from the table. Rising, he said, "Excuse me." Mirek headed in the direction of the bathroom.

Magia pushed her half-eaten entrée back. "I'm no longer hungry."

Jerzy kissed her on the cheek. "It will be okay, my love. He is like my father was when my older sister Agnieska decided to go to college rather than get married out of high school." He gently turned her face to his. "You were at our family dinner that Christmas. Everything is fine between Agnieska and Pappa. Our fathers' values are backward to us, but they say all of those things out of love."

She nodded. A frown slowly turned into a smile. "Thank you."

"If you think it will help, we can move up the wedding."

"No, that's not necessary right now."

"Shall I go into the restroom to talk to your dad?"

Magia shook her head. "He'll be fine. He just doesn't want to curse in front of me. I don't know why. I hear him on the bench and at practice."

Jerzy laughed. "I love you, Magia."

She kissed her fiancé. "I love you."

They chatted about other things for another five minutes. Mirek emerged from the restroom. He appeared calmer. He seated himself.

"I'm sorry, Magia. I overreacted." He rubbed the spot in between his eyes. "Jerzy, I love you like a son. I had you come over to the States for Magia. I trust you will take good care of her."

"I will, Mirek," Jerzy replied. "I will." He squeezed his bride's hand under the table.

Chapter XXXVIII

MATCH DAY, SATURDAY, MAY 30, 1998: Giants Stadium's lower bowl filled slowly. The section next to the main supporters began to fill with a large number of Polish men mostly in their early twenties. Word had spread quickly of not only Jerzy's signing but rumored starting position. Many were garbed in Polish national team jerseys. Scarves were draped around necks or tied around their waists. As each descended the stairs, they fisted 16 ounce cups of brew in each hand. The national anthem just finished. The starting lineups were announced. The Cabbie supporters booed each Chicago player. Their behavior riled the Polish group, especially when they booed Lozowski. They responded by pounding on a big bass drum and chanting in Polish. "Lozowski!" Even though Tomás was on the opposing side, to insult Lozowski was to insult Polska. Lozowski heard the tribute and raised his hands to applaud his countrymen.

When Jerzy was introduced, the shouts and chanting grew louder. After all, he was playing for the home side.

Magia was invited to sit with Alexi and Carl in the owner's box, but she politely declined. She wanted to meet the New York Ultras. She knew some of them through a soccer bulletin board web site, but even then only by their nicknames. She had selected the moniker JERSEYGRRL and gave no indication that she was affiliated with the Mad Cabbies, Jerzy or Mirek. She felt that by building street credibility, she could make initial inroads into the close-knit community of hardcore supporters.

Kickoff.

Magia descended the steps between the Garage and the NY Ultras. She spotted about ten Stampede supporters, all but two Polish, who had made the trip from Chicago. She crossed a row of empty seats and headed toward Jacek, a familiar face.

He turned to say something about a play when he spotted Jerzy's bride. "Magia? What are you doing here?"

"You know I'm Jerzy's fiancée." She smiled.

Jacek looked at her team supplied polo and the fancy all-access laminate around her neck. He just shook his head.

"Alexi Taman hired me. One reason is to help Jerzy adjust, which I would have done for free, but she also wants me to help reach out to the Polish community here."

Crowd noise intensity swelled. Jerzy was driving up the right side. He crossed the ball to an open teammate. Tomás was dropping back as fast as he could. Capt. Dan poised himself for a save. The Cabbie floated the ball to the top of the box where Jerzy was charging. Jerzy and Tomás leaped for the ball at the same time, but Jerzy got the flick on to the top left corner of the goalmouth. Dan could not react fast enough. The Cabbies were up by one in the 5th minute.

"*Kudowa!*" spat Jacek.

Magia found herself being sucked into the revelry, receiving *piwo*-soaked kisses from fellow countrymen.

In the owner's box, Alexi leaned over and kissed Carl firmly on the lips. "Thank you."

Carl pulled back. "For what? I'm blaming Mirek for this." He tried to appear offended but failed. Alexi's mimosa-flavored lips were actually quite tasty. He forced himself to turn his attention back to the pitch, rather than look at her.

The Stampede regrouped and pressed. Jerzy played back in the midfield. Tomás stuck close by. The old man was damned if he was going to let himself get schooled again. Carlos and Ian were working together up front for the Stampede.

The New York defense was effective at intercepting and getting it back to the midfield, but before Jerzy could get his foot on it, Baumgartner or Novotny won possession and passed it forward.

Carlos was able to get a shot off but the opposing keeper, Brady, got a glove on it. Corner kick for the Stampede. As one of the shorter teammates, Carlos took the kick. The ball floated into the middle. A mass of male flesh leaped for it. Stampede midfielder Byron Jameson got his forehead on it and directed it to the far post. Brady had committed himself to the near post. He tried to change directions, but it was too little too late. The ball flew into the inner side netting. 1-1, in the 23rd minute.

Carl turned to Alexi and stuck his tongue out playfully. She had inched her way closer to him. She wanted to have his tongue probe her, not tease her.

Magia found herself filled with mixed feelings. Jacek pulled her aside. Gripping her upper arms, he pressed her into a kiss. She tried to stiffen her reaction. The kiss was clearly not intended to be a quick peck, but a long one. She should not feel, but she did. Whoa! Jacek was a good kisser.

He looked her in the eyes. "Please come back to Chicago," he said.

Magia felt herself caught in a weak moment. She had tasted the forbidden fruit, the bad boy. And it felt good. She forced herself to speak with her head. "I can't. My future is with Jerzy."

The New York Ultras were undeterred by the loss of the lead. They resumed their chanting. The Garage followed their lead this time.

The restart had the Cabbies trying to keep the ball in their possession. But things almost appeared like a combination of aerial and ground level volleyball over the halfway line. This continued with a few good attempts on either end until the halftime whistle.

By this point, Alexi had slid as close as possible to Carl. Their thighs were touching. Carl found himself being seduced by her scent, her eyes, her lips. He placed his hand on her leg. Her painted talons raked through his thick hair and down the back of his neck, sending shivers down his spine. He had been successful so far in resisting her wiles, but a man could only take so much. He pulled her closer. Carl wanted her. Their lips met in a sea of frenzied passion. His fingers found their way through her hair. He was glad her locks were not too hair sprayed. They slowly eased away from the window to a navy leather couch.

She laid back and gently tugged on him. He followed willingly. Her fingers nimbly unbuttoned his red shirt. She raked the carpet on his chest. He grunted his pleasure. "I want you, Alexi," he purred.

His hands slid up her tight jade suede skirt. She was wearing thigh-high stockings with a garter belt. He eased her silver-sequined g-string to the side. She moaned her encouragement. She lifted her pelvis to him. His fingers stroked her. She was already dripping wet.

Her hands scrambled to unfasten his belt and pants and release his throbbing desire. One-handed, he helped her. Time was short. He knew he would not be able to last long once inside of her. His cell phone rang. He grabbed it from his front pants pocket and tossed it aside. Whoever it was could wait. Alexi was all that mattered. He thrust himself inside of her. She squealed. Pumping hard and fast, his mouth covered hers. She was pulsating, her muscles squeezing his dick, encouraging him. Just as he was about to pull out and come inside her mouth, the door to the box swung open. The startle made him release his juice deep inside her.

Magia announced her presence with, "Oh my god!" Mouth agape, she quickly shut the door.

Carl and Alexi scrambled to regain composure. She adjusted her clothing and reached for her makeup bag to touch up and check her hair. Carl poked it all back in. He hated to do so without wiping off, and hoped it would not leave a damp spot through his pants. He poured himself a shot of vodka and knocked it back before going to the door.

Magia was still frozen. Carl yanked her inside. Magia was too close to Jackie, even though she would not be returning to Chicago for a while—there was always email. Alexi and Carl looked at each other knowingly. The Polish girl's silence had to be bought.

Carl spun Magia into a chair.

Alexi spoke first. "How much did you see?"

Magia found English words hard to come by. She blurted out, "*Ty brudna kurwa!*"

Carl slapped her. He knew what it meant. "Speak English."

Magia rubbed the left side of her face. She looked down and tried to regain her composure.

"You saw nothing. That's what you saw, nothing," said Alexi.

Magia looked up at her boss. "Or what?"

"Feisty one, eh?" said Carl. "Just like your dad."

Alexi had to think fast. She knew that her underling had gone down to the New York Ultras section. She gestured to the binoculars near the window. "Or else I tell Jerzy and dear old dad what you've been up to with the Ultras."

Magia swallowed hard. "You could see me down there?"

Carl backed Alexi, knowing this was the perfect card to play even though he was not even sure if Alexi had seen anything that might get Magia in trouble with either man. "You were getting quite cozy down there, weren't you?"

Magia's face turned red. "Okay, okay. I won't say anything." She hopped up and went straight for the vodka bottle. She poured herself three fingers and knocked back the entire amount in one drink. Slamming the glass down, she reached into the fridge and grabbed two beers. Methodically, she popped their tops and poured them into the required plastic cups. Without another word, she left the skybox, slamming the door behind her.

Alexi and Carl just looked at each other for a second. Carl stated, "I've seen men do that, but never a woman."

"The girl has spunk. Gotta like that." Alexi gestured for Carl to bring her another drink. She went over to the window to see if the second half had started yet. "And that is what scares me. Actually, it should scare you."

"Did you see anything down there with the binocs?"

"No, but she is guilty of something. If she wasn't, she would have played out something else, like blackmail for money."

Carl handed Alexi her cocktail. He kissed her. "Why are you so afraid for me?"

"Your Jackie is not going to go away quietly. She will fight for her man. And she has every right to, because you are quite a catch." She winked. She took a sip. Thoughtfully, she added, "You know, it's funny how you and I were on the same page, thinking the same thing without any collaboration."

Carl nodded and smiled. He looked out the window just as the start of second half whistle was blown. He gestured. "We have a game to watch. Care to make a friendly wager?"

Alexi offered, "If my boys win, Chicago's first round draft pick. If your boys win, you can pick any of our bench players in the off season."

Carl smiled. "You're on." He extended his hand to shake. She grabbed and pumped it firmly. "But let's get this in writing, especially since we've been drinking."

"A deal's a deal. I never go back on my word, drunk or sober and I've never been drunk enough to forget any business deal or bet that I've made." She flipped her free hand. "But have it your way and I'll sign it if my handshake is not good enough for you."

Carl sensed that she was quite offended. But he was not going to take any chances. He jotted down the bet, dated, signed and slid it over to her. She scrawled her signature with flourish. Both turned their attention to the action on the pitch.

Jacek chatted casually with his Big Apple-based Polish friends. They were to the side of the beers of the world stand. The New Yorker was asking Jacek about Magia. "You know, I didn't really have a shot at even kissing her until today. She's Mirek Koneki's oldest girl. And word has it she's going to marry Jerzy Josefczyk," Jacek stated simply.

"If she's a Koneki, how come you haven't had a chance to hit on her?" asked the friend.

"Mirek keeps his girls sheltered from us. He thinks we're hooligans or something." Jacek laughed with a shrug. All of them drank.

"I hope our JERSYGRRL comes back for the second half," sighed another New Yorker.

"I think it's going to come out whether she's a Stampeder to the core or if she's already turned traitor on us because of Jerzy. Who will she support? Daddy or her man?" chimed in a very scarred Chicago female supporter with a shaved head.

"You got the flares in okay, Chrissy?" asked Jacek.

The woman patted her chest. "Right here, daddy-o. Buy me a beer for carrying this shit for you, Jake." She scowled at him.

He obediently hopped in line.

Magia made her way back to the Ultras section. She paused at the top of the steps. She had promised the group that she would be back. On her walk back, she had consumed half of one of the beers she carried. She wanted to get drunk. She could not wait until the vodka kicked in. She wanted to erase the vision of Alexi and Carl and the ensuing conversation from her mind.

As she walked down on the Garage side, she watched Jerzy on the attack up the left flank. He nutmugged Tomás and streaked straight for the goalmouth. Captain Dan was all that stood in the way.

Magia squealed with delight. She stopped as she watched the play develop.

Jerzy reached the top of the box. Capt. Dan stayed close to his line. After witnessing Tomás being fooled like that, Dan was not going to take any chances. Tomás was coming up fast. He was pissed. Just before Jerzy was going to get a shot off, Tomás slid in from behind. Cleats up, Tomás swept Jerzy off his feet. Jerzy pitched back then forward.

The linesman signaled for a foul. The referee fumbled for his card set as he jogged to the spot.

Jerzy bounced up. He tore into Tomás something vile.

The ball trickled toward Dan who gently placed it on the penalty spot. He knew what the call would be.

Tomás stood and shoved Jerzy. The younger Pole did not retaliate. The referee jumped in between them. The linesman dashed over to help maintain order. Dan caught Tomás from behind and under the arms. He pulled his teammate back. The two Poles continued exchanging words in their native tongue.

The referee said, "I don't know what the hell you two are saying, but I want both of you to shut up and play." He showed the yellow card to Tomás.

The Garage erupted. They were glad that at least there was a yellow card, but many were muttering that it should have been straight red. Magia had to agree. She had made here way down to the front.

Alexi and Carl said nothing to each other in the box.

Dan released Tomás once he was sure that he was not going to deck the lad. "You're damn lucky that wasn't a red, Tommy."

The old man merely grunted. He lined up for a possible rebound on the penalty. Dan jogged over to the goal line. He had to focus on the shooter.

Akeem Williams, the other New York forward on the pitch, lined up to take the kick. When the referee was assured that everything was in place, he blew the whistle. Akeem ran for the ball hard and buried a left-footed shot in the right corner of the net. Dan jumped to left, expecting a right-footed shot.

2-1 Mad Cabbies, 51st minute.

Alexi jumped up and did a little happy dance. Carl shook his head.

Magia joined the celebration in the Garage. Akeem ran toward the supporters after scoring. Jerzy followed him. He spotted his fiancée and blew her a kiss. She responded with a similar gesture. She could have run down to the track, but decided not to. She would have to play nursemaid to his bruises soon enough.

The remainder of the match was uneventful. Counter attacking soccer was seen from both sides. Koneki arranged to have Tomás subbed out in the 62nd minute. Manny Larsen took his place. Coach Hartford decided to keep all his players in the full 90. The final score was the same as what it was after the successful penalty kick.

Magia headed to the locker room. She was not going to go near the owner's box again. Besides, she wanted to hug and kiss her man. The alcohol had hit her hard in the 75th minute. She had swooned a bit. The fans around her made sure she sat down and managed to get her some water. The Ultras were good folks. She never understood why her father was so against her associating with them.

Alex stepped out of the taxi across the street from Sueños. He looked at his watch. The match would be over soon. He crossed to the bar and looked in the window.

All eyes were affixed to the televisions. Brendan and Sheila were seated at the bar. A large man in a red cape was on Brendan's other flank. The man had gotten as close as possible without touching the player.

"Don't worry, Iceman," Alex muttered. "I'll get you away from him and your dyke wife."

Alex watched Sean pat Brendan on the back and say something. Brendan shook the kid's hand and smiled. Alex pulled a folded ball cap out of his back pocket. He purchased a Cubs hat at the airport. He tucked his hair underneath and pulled it tight.

Inside the bar, he blended in at the end and ordered a drink. He eyed Brendan. Lawrence had stepped off to talk to some other friends. Brendan appeared relieved. Sheila had gone to the ladies room. Alex got his drink, paid, and then made his way toward the object of his desire.

Brendan signaled the bartender for another lager. Sheila had told him no more, but he wanted another one. The bartender set him up and marked appropriately on his tab.

Alex slapped Brendan on the shoulder. "Aren't you supposed to be in New Jersey?" he said.

Brendan froze when the sound of Alex's voice fell upon his ears. He turned slowly. "Koneki wanted me to recover another week." It was the same stock answer he had been using all night.

Alex's hand lingered on his shoulder. Brendan did not mind. Alex's touch excited him. Alex reached in his pocket and pulled out a small folded piece of paper. He pressed it in Brendan's hand. "That's too bad. Perhaps Chicago would not have lost tonight if you were there." Alex, beer in hand, headed back to the end of the bar and tried to immerse himself in a baseball game, which the nearby television had been switched to.

Brendan glanced at the writing on the paper: Alex's cell phone number, no name, just the number. Brendan slipped it in his back pocket and turned to finish his ale before his wife got back.

Alex polished off his drink quickly and left. He hailed a cab and disappeared into the night. All he had to do now was wait for Brendan to get a moment alone.

Carl and Alexi went to her limousine. Carl wanted to go to the locker room like he usually did post match, but Alexi talked him out of it. She never did, and did not wish to change her *modus operandi* even for one night.

Magia passed a showered and dressed Tomás. She sneered at him. "You should be sitting out the next match," she spat.

He shrugged. "Maybe. But the ref just gave me a yellow."

"I think you should apologize to Jerzy."

He cupped her chin in his hand. "My dear sweet girl, I never apologize for what occurs on the pitch in the heat of battle." He turned from her and headed into the locker room for the customary debriefing.

Alexi and Carl arrived at her downtown Manhattan condo overlooking Central Park. She opened the double doors wide and made a sweeping invitation to her guest. Alexi called out to her housekeeper. "Cara, honey, bring out a bottle of the Tunuta Caprazo Brunello di Montalcino, the 1993 Riserva."

"Yes, madam. Would you like the good crystal goblets?" responded Cara. She was dressed in a traditional maid's uniform.

Alexi waved her hand. "Yes, that will be fine. Carl is special company after all." She kissed him. "We'll be on the balcony."

"Yes, madam."

As Cara disappeared around the corner, Alexi grabbed Carl's hand and led him to the balcony. She liked to show off the view. She flung the French doors open. "Come on out here, Carl," she cooed.

He stepped out. The view was impressive. He gathered her in his arms. The game seemed so long ago. He engaged her in a long kiss. He did not intend on going to his hotel until the next morning to gather his bags. She was too good to abandon tonight. Strong women attracted Carl like picnics drew ants. And there was no woman stronger and more desirable than Alexi in Carl's eyes. He forgot that Jackie even existed.

Carl said, "I don't know why we haven't gotten together sooner."

"Opportunity," she replied. "We haven't really had the opportunity until now. I wish I would have been able to go to Chicago for the last match, but I had business negotiations to attend to."

Carl leaned in closer. "Let's not talk about that now."

His lips caressed her soft cheek. He tasted her foundation as it rubbed off. He eased down her neck. She moaned quietly in pleasure.

Cara tapped on the door glass. "Madam," she began. The maid was carrying a silver tray with the requested bottle of elixir and two Mikasa crystal goblets. She set everything on the table and poured the first serving. Quietly, she excused herself.

Carl did not want to stop. He remembered all the fantasies he had as a young teenager about Alexi Taman, supermodel. Never in a million years did he ever think he would be her peer, much less that she would physically be putty in his hands. She was older, but she was still flawless.

Alexi gently pushed back and sat at the table. Carl chose to pull his chair around to where he could see both her and the view. She lifted the goblet and sipped slowly. "Carl, it should be obvious by now that I want you. But I want to be clear that my desire is for more than just what happened at the stadium, for beyond what will happen later."

Carl reached out and touched her face lightly. She laid her hand on his. He spoke softly, "I know."

"Together," she said slowly, "I want to be with you." She looked into his eyes. Carl sensed her loneliness. He knew what she was feeling. He often felt the same way.

"Alexi, I will be with you." He pulled her into a tight embrace. He kissed her tenderly, lovingly, as a lover would.

Chapter XXXIX

SUNDAY, MAY 31, 1998: Sheila, Brendan and Lawrence stayed at Sueños until after midnight. Sheila found herself flirting with a barmaid who might be at least bisexual. The front tables and chairs were cleared away from the front window so a Celtic band could set up for a performance. The three danced and drank, trying to forget that the Stampede had dropped a game.

After the band's second set, Sheila tabbed out and tipped generously. The trio walked the eight blocks to the Glaziers' condo in Lakeview. With his right hand, Brendan held Lawrence's hand. With his left, he fingered Alex's phone number in his pocket.

Sheila ducked out shortly after the guys were settled in. She said she was heading to Andersonville and not to expect her back until after sunrise. "If all goes well." She winked.

Brendan poured his lover a scotch on the rocks. "It does feel good to be partially out."

"I'm glad," replied Lawrence. "I didn't mind sneaking around to see you, but this is better." He lifted his glass in salute. "So what really happened in San Francisco?"

Brendan sank into the white, puffy, leather couch next to Lawrence. He let out a long slow breath. "I don't know. I barely remember going into the Blood Bank."

"So, where do we stand?"

Brendan did not answer immediately. He leaned forward and set his drink on a coaster on the coffee table. He sat upright, torso turned to face Lawrence. He gathered the man's hands into his own. "We haven't had much opportunity to get to know each other. I do care about you, Lawrence."

"I care about you, too, Bren."

"It's just that after last weekend, I'm not sure about what's going on." He paused. He gave Lawrence a loving look. "I think we need to take things slow."

Lawrence freed his hand and touched Brendan's cheek. "I understand." He leaned up and kissed the striker's lips softly.

"The team suspended me for the match earlier. They put me down as injured on the roster. Don't tell anyone else."

"You can trust me."

"They also instructed me to get some counseling. Sheila is on their side."

Lawrence rubbed his chin. He felt a bit rough. "It might be a good idea. That bar, the Blood Bank, Sheila and I were there in the daylight and it was creepy enough then. So were you really kidnapped or not?"

Brendan stood up. "I'm not comfortable talking about this right now."

Lawrence saw Brendan's hands begin to shake. He rose and pulled Brendan to his chest. "You don't have to."

Alex sat on a park bench near Glaziers' condo building. He saw Sheila leave and waited for Lawrence to do the same. He gave up waiting at 3:00 AM and returned to his hotel room.

Sheila came back at nine in the morning. She found Lawrence and Brendan cuddled up in the master bedroom. She picked up her husband's khakis and smoothed out the wrinkles. As she laid them over the chair in the corner, the piece of paper with Alex's phone number fell out. She retrieved it, looked it over and set it on the chair.

The phone rang. Sheila quickly scurried to the kitchen to retrieve the portable. "Hello."

There was no voice on the other end.

"Hello," she repeated. "Is there anybody there?"

She heard a click, then dial tone.

That's weird, she thought as she hung up.

Chapter XL

Monday, June 1, 1998: Carl called Agnes late in the morning. "How are you with counseling homosexuals?"

"What? Who is this?"

"I'm sorry; it's Carl. I thought you would know my voice by now."

"Oh, yes, that whole fiasco in San Francisco. You need me to counsel Brendan off the books?"

"Yes, I'll pay you."

"Now, you know I can't legally take money for counseling yet, Carl."

"Off the books, under the table."

"That's fine, but give the money to Paul." Agnes reached for her daily planner. "Do you want me to call him or will he call me?"

"I think you need to call him. I don't think he'll follow through even with Sheila nagging him."

"With everything going on, I'll probably need to counsel her, too."

"Just let me know and I'll take care of it. I know Paul's salary living here in Chicago makes things a bit tight. I wish I could have paid him more. He's certainly worth it, but it's that damn salary cap that the FLA imposes."

"I appreciate that, Carl. I really do."

Agnes hung up and flipped her planner open to G. She dialed Brendan.

Sheila answered, "Oh, hey Agnes, what's going on?"

"Carl has hired me so to speak to counsel Brendan as per some kind of team punishment."

"Oh, that. I didn't know you did that sort of thing."

"Yes, it's my life's work. I'm waiting on paperwork to clear here in the States before I can do it legally. But for the team, I'm always available."

"Great, I may need someone to talk to as well."

"I figured as much. I'll take care of you too."

"Good, I'll put Brendan on." Sheila covered the mouthpiece. She hollered, "Honey, it's for you."

Brendan picked up, "Got it. Hello?"

Sheila hung up.

Agnes spoke, "Brendan, it's Agnes Novotny. Carl wants me to counsel you."

"Oh, yeah, that." He let out a sigh. "I don't know. I didn't know you were a shrink."

"Yes, Dr. Novotny to you. I have plenty of time this week."
"I'll call you back. I have to check the practice schedule."
"Don't wait too long," Agnes cautioned.
"I won't."

Brendan clicked the off button on the portable. He picked up the scrap of paper with Alex's number. He dialed it.

"Alex."
"It's Brendan. I don't have much time. I want to see you tonight."
"Good."
"Meet me at Axis at 8pm in the grill section."

As Brendan hung up, Sheila entered the room. "Who are you meeting for dinner?"
"Lawrence," he lied.
"Tell him I said 'hi'."
"I will."

Brendan arrived a few minutes before eight. He stood outside the building for a moment. A bad case of nerves hit him. His hands shook. He dug deep and gathered the courage to open the door.

Alex awaited his prey in the furthest corner booth from the entrance. Brendan sensed his lover and headed directly for Alex's table.

"Hello, Iceman," hissed Alex. He appeared to be wearing sanguine lipstick, but Brendan could not be sure.

"Hello." Brendan slid into the booth.

Alex invited him closer so he could kiss him. It was a quick peck on the lips, but the player felt himself melting on the inside. "I hope you don't mind, but I went ahead and ordered for the both of us."

"That's fine." Brendan slid over a bit so that he could face the dark one. "What are you doing here? Why did you pick me out? This whole thing is ruining my career."

"Are they really that homophobic in Europe? It seems to me that they would be a bit less Puritanical about it all, especially in the Eredivisie." Alex blinked. "Are you really that good? You didn't have a great year the A-League last year."

"Coach told me that he had someone call from England who was interested in me. But called back after the stunt you pulled and said that they were no longer interested."

"You're kidding, right?"

"It's not bullshit. The world of sports—well most male team sports are still very homophobic. You know that. That's why I married Sheila. I wasn't planning to come out of the closet until I retire from soccer."

Alex reached out to stroke Brendan's cheek. "I'm not sorry."

"What do you want with me?"

"A transfer to San Francisco for starters."

Brendan shook his head. "That will never happen."

"Don't be too sure. The wheels are in motion for a trade for a draft pick." Alex smiled.

"Oh bullshit," spat Brendan.

"Such a filthy mouth." Alex grabbed Brendan by the shoulders and pulled him in for a deep probing kiss.

Brendan tried to remain stiff, but could not resist this man. He surrendered.

An hour later, Brendan took Alex up to the private room. Their lovemaking was a much gentler affair than when they first met. Brendan remained the submissive.

Alex slipped out after Brendan fell asleep. It was nearly 3:00 AM.

Brendan awoke to the sound of sharp knocking shortly before 4:00 AM. The club was closing. He yelled back that he would be out in fifteen minutes.

He rolled over and placed his hand on something sticky. He flicked on the lamp. A small pool of blood was congealing on the sheet.

Brendan leapt up. He turned on all the lights and stared at the stain. His heart fluttered. What the hell happened? He did not remember injuring himself or hurting Alex.

He went into the bathroom. Splashing water on his face, he noticed two small cuts on his neck. "You've got to be kidding," he said aloud. "Alex must think he's a vampire."

Brendan hopped in the shower and rinsed off. He dressed and, taking the stained sheets with him, left the club.

Chapter XLI

TUESDAY, JUNE 2, 1998: At Stampede practice, Ian and Carlos noticed Brendan's neck. Brendan did not have bandages. The cuts did not seem deep and they were scabbed over fairly well.

Carlos spoke, "What happened?"

"Huh?" Brendan gave him a puzzled look. Carlos touched Brendan's neck. "Oh, those. Shaving?"

Ian shook his head. "I don't think so. Those look pretty deep. You should have Gina look at them."

"Maybe." Brendan bent over to tie his boots. Then he helped Carlos tie his shoes. Carlos continued to probe, "You look tired. Did you go out last night?"

Brendan nodded. "I stayed out too late."

"We'll have to have a talk with Lawrence about that," Carlos joked sounding rather fatherly.

Brendan swallowed hard. "Yes."

"Brendan Ramone Glazier! What's the matter with you?" barked Mirek. Coach noticed that he was not running full speed during drills. "I will not let you lose your hunger for this game."

The rebuked forward jogged slowly over to face his grizzled master. The scabs on Brendan's neck had broken open and were oozing blood.

Mirek pulled on a latex glove over his right hand and examined the wound. "Go see Gina. We'll talk later."

Brendan removed his practice jersey and perched on the cold metal table in the locker room where Gina set up shop every practice day.

Gina entered and gloved up. "What's going on with you? Mirek tells me that you have a couple of cuts that need proper dressing. And you have been dogging it today."

Brendan simply nodded.

Gina took his vitals. "Well, that's all normal," she pronounced. "Now as for these cuts." She probed and irrigated the wounds. "How long did these bleed? They are deep enough to require stitches."

Brendan shrugged. "I don't know."

"How did you get them?"

Again, a shrug. "I don't know."

Gina gripped his chin and made him look directly into her eyes. "I don't know what's going on. But you've been acting so strange lately. Does this have anything to do with what happened in San Francisco?"

He blinked at her.

She stomped her foot. "Answer me."

"Yes," he replied sheepishly.

"That's better." She loosened her grip and went back to clearing out the beginnings of infection. She wrapped his neck in clean gauze and removed her gloves. "I'm going to call Agnes. You are going to have a session with her before you leave today. Doctor's orders. I'll whip a few stitches in each of those cuts while we wait for her."

"Okay."

Agnes flashed her team credentials to the gatekeepers. She asked which room Gina was in. She hurried down the hall. "Hey, Gina, I got here as fast as I could."

Shirtless, Brendan sat on the examining table. "Hi, Agnes."

"Hey, Agnes, thanks for coming so quick." Gina shook her hand. "Brendan is not very forthcoming about everything. Today he turns up in practice, not working out at full speed according to Mirek, plus he has these oozing fresh wound on his neck."

Agnes put on her glasses to examine the wounds. She used two fingers to gauge the spread, and then compared it with the spacing of her own canine teeth in her mouth. The closeness in measurement was eerie.

"Let me talk to him; I'll get to the bottom of this."

Gina covered the two cuts with a bandage. "Call me when you're done." She left the room.

Agnes locked the door.

"So what happened in San Francisco? Tell me as much as you can remember."

Brendan began to spill his guts. It felt good to let it all out. Agnes listened. She barely had to ask any leading questions. He hungered for therapy.

"It's weird, but every time I'm with Alex, I black out a lot of the events," he concluded.

Agnes stroked her chin. "Hmm, do you think he might be slipping you something in your drink or food?"

"Last night, I'm pretty sure he didn't, because I know all the bartenders and waitresses at Axis. That's my territory, not his."

"Okay, so you woke up and found blood on the sheets and these cuts on your neck. Alex hangs out in a bar called the Blood Bank in San Francisco, which is known for industrial music and goths. Do you remember if Alex was wearing fangs? Or if he had his canines sharpened?"

Brendan shook his head. "I suppose it's possible. But why can't I remember. I only remember having three beers last night. That's not nearly enough to get me even feeling a little buzzed."

"But my question is, why, if he is drugging you, does Alex feel the need to drug you? Would you like him and date him if he didn't drug you?"

"Probably." Brendan took a sip from a water bottle. "I feel drawn to him, but everything about it is wrong."

"How do you feel when you are with Lawrence?"

"Different. He's a very different lover than Alex. Lawrence makes me feel like a man and he is the wife to my husband. Alex—well—I'm the submissive with him."

Agnes thought for a moment. "How do you feel when you are playing soccer? In control?"

Brendan mused. "Sometimes. But it's a team game, so we all have to be ready to control the pace of the match. If one of us is off, it throws the entire game off—oh, Mirek must think that's me now. I need to start staying in on school nights."

"That would be a good start." Agnes smiled.

"You've really helped today, Agnes. Thank you."

"Good. Now I want you to go home and get some sleep. Also, I want you to cancel this lease you have on that room at Axis. It's too much temptation. You are out of the closet enough now that you should not have to be that secretive about your comings and goings." She pressed a business card in his hand. "Program my cell phone into yours. I want you to call me before you see any more of this Alex. He is not good for your health and well being, never mind your career."

Brendan nodded. "I will."

Chapter XLII

THURSDAY, JUNE 4, 1998: Carl avoided Jackie for the next week. She would send email love notes, but he would send curt replies: "I'm sorry. I'm tied up with work this evening."

Jackie tried to brush it off and occupy herself with a new client, a small business who wanted her to handle the books and payroll. She swore she was not going to take on more clients, but the owner was an old friend from high school. She grew worried, though. She began to wonder if he was pulling away for a reason. She started to think that he might be scared of commitment.

Thursday, she broke down and called Agnes. The ladies arranged to meet for coffee at the Chicago Cultural Center.

The cappuccino stand was at one end of the museum. Agnes was already there and had staked out a table. Jackie ordered a tall mocha and joined her.

"It's full today," Agnes commented as she looked around.

Jackie nodded. "If you don't mind, I think I'd feel more comfortable chatting in Grant Park. Less ears."

"I agree," said Agnes. "A lot of them look like *babská hubas*."

Jackie laughed. She was not sure what the word meant, but she knew it had to be a good, if not insulting, descriptor.

The ladies left and crossed Michigan Avenue. Grant Park was in full bloom. Jackie needed the walk. Moving around sometimes helped her think.

"Agnes, please assure me that everything I tell you will be held in the strictest of confidence."

"Jackie, I may be a gossip myself, but I was sworn to a strict code of ethics when I became a psychologist. I know we're not just having girl talk."

"Thank you." Jackie took a few more steps in silence. She sat down on an unoccupied bench. Agnes joined her. Jackie exhaled long before saying, "I think I'm losing him."

"Oh, Jackie, no. What's going on?" Agnes emoted shock.

"Last Wednesday, he went up to Philadelphia to check on things there. He came back on Friday only to fly out to Jersey. He barely said hi or bye to me on that day. I didn't hear from him all weekend. He usually calls me when I can't go to the away matches. And you know I haven't been able to because of our team."

Agnes nodded. "What do you think made him 'pull away'?"

Jackie shrugged. "Maybe I was getting too pushy. I mean we've only been together for a month and a half. I have been at his condo a lot. I was beginning to hope that he would ask me to move in and I would have to find a good excuse not to. Especially since I own my loft. I'm hoping it's one of his hang-ups and not mine." She paused and stared at a couple of tourists with a video camera. "Maybe I should just play hard to get and stop emailing and calling."

"That may work. I do suspect that Carl might be the type that likes to hunt and chase a bit. Try it," Agnes concurred.

"But what if he really doesn't want to be with me?"

"I don't think that's true. I've seen the way he looks at you." Agnes smiled warmly.

"I just hope he didn't meet somebody else." Jackie's words came out slow and soft. She shocked herself by even thinking it. "Agnes, what am I going to do? I don't want to lose him."

"What do you like about Carl?"

"He's handsome. He treats me like a lady."

"In what ways?"

"He presented me with a rose when we first met. When I passed out, he took care of me and didn't try anything. He calls me Jacqueline, which I usually hate, but it feels right when he says it."

"Why does having your full name spoken bother you otherwise?"

"Because I think it sounds too feminine. I've always been a tomboy."

Agnes nodded. "Tell me about your last serious relationship."

"It was with a guy named Jim. He works in my father's accounting firm. In fact, I really think my dad hired him so he could set us up. Jim comes from a good family. But I know more about the way Jim really was."

"And how was that?"

"He treated me like dirt."

"In what way?"

Jackie hated to talk about it, but maybe she needed to. "It was never physical, always mental." Jackie drew a deep breath and blew out long. She shuddered as she heard Jim's voice in her head. "He would call me a whore. I would dress in the latest fashions for him to go out to dinner and he always found something wrong. I dressed like his mother once and that was a disaster. He accused me of trying to be with him for his money. I said I never wanted to be with him in the first place. After the mother costume fight, I gathered my stuff and bought the loft."

"Go on," Agnes encouraged.

"Well, little Jimmy went crying to my dad. My dad put a lot of pressure on me to get back with Jim. For the good for the family and the firm, he kept saying. Jim turned into a stalker almost. He left things on and in my desk. He would sit for hours outside my loft building. Once I called the cops to at least give him a scare, but the cops never came, especially not when I told them Jim's last name. Turns out, the family were huge

FOP contributors. A couple of months of this went by and I told my dad that I quit. Just went in on a Friday and said I would not be back on Monday or ever."

"Have you talked to your father much since then?"

"No, the last time I saw him was the obligatory Christmas dinner. Neither of us brought it up, for the comfort and well-being of the rest of the family."

"How do you think you've changed since?"

"I've become more assertive. I've created my own circle of friends instead of just my dad's friends' kids or work-related contacts." Jackie stopped short. Agnes said nothing while she allowed her to find the right words. "I'm a happier person now. I want to pursue my newfound interest in coaching soccer."

"Do you think Carl will hold you back from exploring that option?"

Jackie shook her head.

"Do you think you might be too demanding on his time? I know you have been with him a lot lately. Every couple needs time apart in order to grow. Even Paul and I enjoy the mild separation that soccer season gives us."

Jackie nodded. "You're right. I probably shouldn't worry about it. I don't think he's going to Tallahassee this weekend, so maybe I'll have my chance. In the meantime, I'm just going to wait for him to call me."

"Good." Agnes reached out to her friend and squeezed her hand. "It will work out. Everything will be okay."

Chapter XLIII

Friday, June 5, 1998: Carl woke up in a pool of sweat. He was shaking. He had the nightmare again. He had not had the flashback dream since he started seeing Jackie. It usually made an appearance every other night.

He reached for the phone and dialed Jackie's number from memory.

The ringing phone pierced the still night air in her loft. Jackie rolled over and glanced at the clock, 2:51 AM. She hoped it was a wrong number and considered just letting the answering machine get it. She picked up the receiver and mumbled, "Hello."

"Jacqueline, please come over." He did not allow her to respond before he hung up. He hoped she would just come over. She had to. He needed her.

Jackie listened to the dial tone as she processed the voice and request. Something did not sound right in Carl's voice. It was not a drunk voice; he sounded like a frightened boy. She set the handset back on its cradle. She had to go. She loved him too much.

Jackie drove over as fast as she could. She used Carl's guest parking spot and her passkey to gain entry. The doorman was napping in his chair. The elevator seemed excruciatingly slow. Jackie grew worried. She hoped that Carl did not take anything stored in his medicine cabinet.

She found Carl still in bed. The lamp was on. He was propped up. His skin was a ghastly pallor. He smiled weakly at her.

"I'm here, honey." She approached him. She kicked off her sandals and crawled onto the bed. She embraced him tightly. She felt his shaking. His trembling gave way to sobbing. She continued to hold him, caressing his back. She could tell that he had to let it out; whatever it was, it had to come out.

A half hour passed. Her should was soaked in Carl's salty tears. He pulled back. "I'm sorry," he mumbled.

"It's okay, Carl." She brushed his cheek. "I love you."

"I want to tell you something." He gathered her hands in his.

She looked at him. His red puffy eyes, his tear-stained face. She found herself more attracted to him than ever.

"I found my mother shot dead when I was 18." His face scrunched up in pain. "I never cried about it until tonight. Thank you."

Oh my god, she thought, that explains so much. "I'll always be here for you, my love." She held him tight. She was not going to pump him for details. It was a big step alone for him to admit what happened. She wanted to call Agnes for advice. She hesitated. All Carl needed right now was to be held and loved.

Carl fell asleep as Jackie held him. Her touch and love was the best drug to make the feelings and memories that had haunted him for nearly the past decade go away. The nightmare did not return.

The smell of fresh brewed coffee wafted up his nostrils. Carl stirred. Jackie was standing in the doorway holding a tray. The image reminded him of his mother and how she would take care of him when he was sick.

"Good morning, sleepyhead," she cooed.

Carl's mother would say those same words to him. Good memories were what he needed. He smiled warmly. "Good morning, Jacqueline."

She set the tray in front of him. "I hope you like scrambled eggs. I'm not too good at anything else."

"That's fine. Anything you make will be fine." Alexi's maid popped into his mind. Alexi probably could not even boil water. A wave of guilt hit him. He had to make sure that Jackie never found out about last weekend.

"What's wrong, honey?"

Jackie's voice startled him. "What?"

"You look pensive."

"I'm sorry." He stabbed at his food. "I've had a lot on my mind lately." He stuck a forkful of fluffy egg into his mouth.

Jackie waited patiently for him to continue. She sipped her coffee and gazed at him tenderly.

"Thank you for coming over."

"I'll always be here for you." Even if you're not there for me, she thought coldly as she recalled the past week.

"I hope so, Jacqueline. You are my everything. I've really fallen in love with you, but I didn't truly realize it until last night."

"I love you, too, Carl."

Chapter XLIV

Saturday, June 6, 1998: Alone in his office, Carl typed out an email:

"Dear Alexi, I've been doing a lot of thinking lately. As much as we would be a force to be reckoned with in a marriage partnership, I cannot entertain that idea at this time. While it is true that we have grown closer and have shared a lot in the past week, I must profess my love for Jacqueline Harris. I intend to make her my bride. I will not allow you to interfere with this in any way. I do not consider myself to be a vengeful man, but if you do anything to harm Jacqueline or damage my relationship with her in anyway, I will not hesitate to exact revenge.—Sincerely, Carl Costello."

He hesitated before hitting the send icon. The last sentence he deleted before sending it through cyberspace.

Jackie watched the match prior to the Stampedistas match on the city park pitch. One of the teams, the ladies were scheduled to play next Saturday. The league was supposed to be recreational, but many of the teams took it very seriously, including the Stampedistas. She enjoyed competition. It brought out her best.

Matt came up behind her and placed his long slender fingers on her shoulders. She jumped and whipped around. "Hi," he said.

"Hey, Matt. You startled me."

"I just saw my chance and took it." He grinned from ear to ear. "You were concentrating pretty hard."

"Scouting next week's opponent," she replied. She lifted her notebook.

"Wow," he breathed. "You've really taken a liking to this coaching gig." He sat on her right side.

"I really like it. I'd like to pursue it further, but I'm not sure how to proceed."

"You could contact US Soccer."

"They're busy with the World Cup right now," she stated. Her eyes followed the action on the pitch. A flashy forward was making a run up the left side. He crossed back to his partner, but the sweeper intercepted and pushed it forward. The back line of the Barclay's Pub team seemed impenetrable. She had some stats and they had only allowed two goals so far this season. She had to find a hole.

Matt watched with her. "Which team?"

"I'm taking notes on both, but the Barclay's Pub team in the green jerseys are the ones we are playing next Saturday." She jotted a couple of notes about the sweeper.

Matt let his left leg touch her right thigh. She did not shift. She pressed back lightly, subconsciously. Matt smiled. He still wanted her. He gazed at her profile. A gentle breeze blew her hair. He emitted a soft sigh.

"I love this game," she said. "I would love to coach on a professional level."

"You could ask Mirek or Carl what is required."

"Mirek might be intimidated by me. He keeps saying that I'm after his job. He makes it sound like a joke, but I can tell he's a bit spooked by some of my comments."

"Like the 3-4-3 suggestion?"

Jackie nodded. "Exactly. And Carl, well, I just don't know. We're at an awkward stage in our relationship right now."

Matt's ears pricked up. He had to be careful. He had to be the supportive friend. He had to be the one she would run to when things began to fall apart. He would catch her. "I'm here if you ever need to talk."

"Thanks, Matt. I appreciate that." She glanced at him. He wore a concerned look, but it was more than that. "It will be okay. We had a breakthrough the other night. I think we'll be stronger once we are past this issue."

Matt raised his right brow. The word 'issue' hung in the air like an albatross. He fought the urge to query further. He hated the fact that he found himself soliciting and holding gossipy information a lot. It was an outgrowth of his natural curiosity. Instead of saying anything, he extended his left arm around her and pulled her into a gentle hug.

She patted his hand. "Thanks."

His hand slipped away slowly. The final whistle blew. He let out a near silent sigh. Matt felt like it was a *Pretty Hate Machine* kind of day.

Jackie tucked her notes in a messenger bag and pulled out her game plan. She gathered her team and announced the starting lineup. It still seemed weird to be missing a Koneki sister. Last week, Jennifer Melkirk filled Magia's position, but Jennifer twisted her ankle in practice. Natasha Starkov would get the nod today. Ankle propped up on a red cooler, Jennifer supported her teammates.

The opponents, who dubbed themselves Springfield's Finest, had not won a game yet. They sported jerseys the color of Marge Simpson's hair and each team member was nicknamed after a character on *The Simpsons*.

"Okay, ladies, the cartoon hoolies obviously don't take themselves too seriously," she began her pep talk. "We've had a good few weeks and I think we are really starting to gel. What I want is for you to name the score on them. I mean, come on, their goalkeeper's nickname is Chief Wiggum. And if you are as familiar with the show as I am, you know he can't catch anything."

Laughter erupted.

"Hush up. We don't want them to think we're not taking them seriously. Because that's when they'll sneak up and put a few in the net. ¿*Comprende?*"

The red clad warriors nodded.

"Good. Now get out there and show them that women really rule the planet."

They broke huddle with a loud, "Hear us roar!"

Jackie took her customary place by the bench in the coach's box. The match kicked off with the Stampedistas taking the ball first. The women immediately pressed toward the box. Ari Amat came flying up the middle and received a well-timed pass at the top of the box. She bounced the ball up in the air then took a flying swing at it with her left leg. Neither sweeper nor keeper had time to react except to watch the ball fly into the net.

Jackie's jaw dropped. Ari must have been practicing on her own with Virgil, her husband and backup keeper for the Stampede. They certainly had not tried anything like that in practice.

Sheila recorded the goal as happening at the 32-second mark, but the official stat sheet would read merely the first minute.

By the 24th minute, Ari had recorded a true hat trick. Jackie decided to think about pulling her in order to get another Stampedista some experience. She looked over at Sheila, who shook her head.

"Maybe later, I've been so tired lately keeping Brendan out of trouble."

"Okay, just be ready by halftime," Jackie stated. She pointed at Winnie Harrison. "Get ready."

Winnie gathered her long red locks into a scrunchie. She began stretching.

Jackie turned her eyes back to the pitch in time to see Róża win an aerial battle. She directed the ball to her sister. Księżnicka dribbled past three of Springfield's Finest and had a one-on-one shot at Chief Wiggum. Fake left, fake right, right down the center, goal! Wiggum did not know which way to go.

Jackie heard a familiar voice rise up from the stands. She turned to see Sean on his feet.

"Księżnicka! Woohoo!" Sean shouted at the top of his lungs.

Księżnicka looked over at him and grinned, fist raised in the air.

Winnie jogged lightly back and forth behind the Stampedistas bench. Jackie signaled for a substitution. The referee allowed it before the next kickoff. Winnie entered the match for Ari. Ari was still giddy from her hat trick. "Great job," Jackie praised. She patted Ari's sweaty back.

"Thanks, coach. I just hope to be able to repeat next week." Ari took slow sips of Gatorade.

"You'll get your chance."

Carl arrived at the park at halftime. The score was 5 to 0. He beamed. Maybe he should get these ladies formalized into a W-League team. At the very least, he needed to get Jackie her coach's certification with US Soccer. He vowed to bring it up later.

Matt spotted Carl and approached. He kept it casual, just two guys making small talk about soccer. "Hey, Carl, checking up on your mini investment?"

"Hey, Matt, good to see you." The men shook hands. "All of them are doing a great job." Carl gestured toward the pitch.

Matt nodded. "You should've been here earlier. Ari's first goal was a true *golazo*."

"First goal?"

"Yeah, she recorded a true hat trick. Księżnicka had the fourth goal and the fifth was knocked in by Natasha."

"Really?"

"I'm not kidding. A true hat trick. Winnie is in for Ari now."

Carl looked at Jackie. "Wow." She really does have a knack for coaching. "So what brings you out?"

"I wanted to see some good soccer," Matt lied partially.

Carl saw right through it. "I see." He stroked his chin. "Which of my Stampedistas are you here to see?"

Matt did not hesitate. He had anticipated this line of questioning. "Róża," he responded confidently.

The Scotsman's reply threw Carl off. He raised his eyebrow. "You're dating Róża? Róża Koneki?"

Matt grinned. "I'm waiting until her birthday to begin officially. Róża didn't want to but I insisted."

"Does Mirek know about this?"

"Probably not." Matt shrugged.

"I'm not sure he'd approve of her dating you. Age difference and all," Carl pointed out.

"I'm sure the whole older man thing is part of the appeal. I was wearing my kilt when we first met."

"Ah. Well, I wish you luck, my friend," said Carl. He patted Matt on the back of the shoulders. And stay away from my Jacqueline, he wanted to add, but kept that sentiment to himself.

The whistle blew signaling the start of the second half. Jackie had made one more substitution, Maria Cristobal for Natasha Starkov. Sheila had successfully convinced Jackie to wait until past the 60th minute to put her in.

For the most part, Springfield's Finest employed a bunker with mild counter attacks. Their forward attempts were often thwarted by the Stampedista midfield.

Matt and Carl expressed mutual admiration for Jackie's abilities. Sean even came over and joined the two rival suitors. They were all on even ground for the moment, as they watched the second half.

Maria and Juanita Cristobal created havoc in the midfield. If it were not for the bunker defense, the Stampedistas might have been up by ten.

In the 62nd minute, Jackie subbed in Sheila for Księżnicka. Sheila ran hard and received a nice pass from Maria. She just launched a shot at the goal. It was not anything spectacular, but it still went in. She celebrated her first goal as if it were the come from behind game winner. The entire team joined her.

The referee did not allow the celebration to last long. He and the Springfield's Finest expected to catch the Stampedistas off guard on the ensuing kickoff. To no avail. Maria performed a perfectly legal slide tackle and the ball was back in the control of the ladies.

Jackie viewed the bunker defense as a good trial for next week's match. She hoped the girls did, too. They still were pressing which was a positive thing, much to the opposing team's chagrin.

The final whistle blew. A score of 12-0 was recorded. Jackie beamed with pride. She gathered the team after all post match customary handshakes. "Ladies, great match. I didn't want you to stop pushing and you didn't. Next week will be harder. So we're going to work on some drills for penetrating tight defense this coming week. From what I saw today, no confidence was lost against the bunker. That's good. If you're not going to Sueños later, I'll see you on Tuesday for practice."

Carl approached as the huddle broke. "Great match, love."

She smiled. "Thank you." She welcomed Carl's embrace and celebratory kiss. Carl enjoyed her being close. He drank in her scent, her pheromones mixed with the outdoors. "I love you," he whispered in her ear.

"I love you, too," she replied.

Matt and Sean singled out their respective Koneki girls. Matt still wished he were with Jackie and not Róża. He looked over at Jackie and Carl, trying to find a flaw in their relationship, but found nothing. Everything looked perfect.

Chapter XLV

After the Tallahassee versus Stampede match, Carl whisked Jackie home. He wanted to get her alone to ask what he had wanted to all evening.

They were at her place. Carl desired for her to feel comfortable. He marveled at her place. It would be a shame to ask her to leave it, sell it.

Both of them had a mild buzz from drinking tequila at Sueños del Fútbol. He took her hand and led her onto the balcony.

"Why haven't I been here before?" he asked.

"You've never asked about my place," she countered.

"I'm sorry." He did know without asking that she did indeed own the loft condominium; it was not a rental. Maybe she would be able to rent it for investment's sake, he speculated. He made a mental note to read her association's covenants.

He gathered her hands in his. "Jacqueline," he began. His eyes were full of hope, love and desire.

"Yes?" She blinked.

He slipped one hand in his pocket and pulled out a small box. Deftly, he popped it open. He had been practicing the maneuver all day. "Will you marry me?"

Jackie's jaw dropped. The ring was gorgeous, but the question hanging in the air meant so much more. This ultimate declaration was not what she had been expecting. Still, she did not hesitate in her giddy response, "Yes! Yes, I will marry you, Carl Costello."

Carl slipped the two-carat diamond and platinum band on her left ring finger. It fit perfectly. Jackie threw herself around him. He held her in a tight, passionate embrace. "I love you, Jacqueline Harris," he murmured, face buried in her soft curls.

That night, they made love on the balcony before curling up in her bed.

Chapter XLVI

Sunday June 7, 1998: TALLAHASSEE, FL: The Tallahassee Tempests and the Chicago Stampede battled to a 2-2 draw last night.

The first half was uneventful until the 42nd minute when Tempest midfielder Indie Marisco was yellow carded for a tackle from behind on Stampede defender Tomás Lozowski. Lozowski was assisted off the field for an injury to his left knee. The Polish international did not return to the match and was replaced by Manny Larsen at the half. MRI results are expected on Monday.

Tempest Socrates Kosmos scored the first goal of the match in the 63rd minute. It was the Grecian international's first FLA goal. The Stampede were able to salvage a tie in stoppage time when Ian Harris headed one in off a corner kick.

Tempest coach Matt Eider was pleased with his team's performance. "This is an important win for us. My boys played fairly clean throughout and the match was fairly called. Granted the last minute goal for the tie was a bit disheartening, but we played hard. I am very proud of everyone."

On the possibility of missing Lozowski for at least the next match, Chicago coach Mirek Koneki was upbeat. "Manny Larsen has been a great defender off the bench. I do not think our back line has been compromised at all."

In other FLA news, San Francisco has recorded their first W of the season by upsetting Boston 3 to 0. This is also their first win under new head coach, Steve Mercado. The Fog Dogs fired Coach Dalton James last Monday.

Chapter XLVII

TUESDAY, JUNE 9, 1998: At the next Stampedistas session, all the ladies gushed over Jackie's news. It was hard to get everyone focused on drills. Finally, Jackie with Agnes' assistance got them going.

Carl sat in his office staring at the phone. A sense of impending doom had settled over him.

Maura, who was filling in for Carrie, paged him. "Keith Watson is on line one. He said it's urgent."

Keith Watson was the general manager of the Philadelphia Minute Men. Carl punched the call through. "What's the word, Keith?"

"I'm afraid I don't have good news, Carl."

"You never do when you say it's urgent." Carl let out a heavy sigh. He hoped it was something minor. Keith had a knack for blowing things out of proportion. "Coach Bierkov had a stroke this morning. He's in ICU now at Jefferson University hospital. It doesn't look good."

Carl pounded his fist on the desk. "Fuck."

"I've appointed Tom Nederson to fill in until we know more."

"Do you think he's up to the pressure?"

"There's only one way to find out," said Keith nonchalantly. "This weekend it's the CSG cage match."

Carl looked at the schedule magnet on his desk. "Yes, it is. Are you going to make the trip?"

"I'll be there. Tom's going to need some moral support."

"I'll see you Friday night, then."

Keith added, "I'm sending you an email with Bierkov's hospital room info."

"Thanks." Carl clicked off. He jiggled the mouse to bring his computer screen to life. The email from Keith was waiting. He dialed the hospital and requested the attending ICU physician. Carl was informed that Coach Bierkov was in a coma. If he woke up, he may be paralyzed and would require extensive physical and mental therapy. He was also told that Mrs. Bierkov had signed a Do Not Resuscitate order.

Carl gently hung up the phone. He blew out slowly. It would be wrong to let Coach Bierkov go, but it was clear that the search for a new coach had to begin. He decided to wait until he had a chance to discuss the matter with Keith in person on Friday.

He called the hospital again, this time to query after Mrs. Bierkov. He was patched through to the room.

"It's so good of you to call, Carl." Her voice sounded choked with tears.

"How are you doing?"

"As well as can be expected." She sniffled. "It's all so sudden. I almost feel like he's already dead. The doctor said there is little chance of a full recovery. Mikel made it clear to me that he did not want to live as a vegetable, so I signed a DNR. My hand shook so hard, but I know in my heart it's the right thing."

"I support you. As long as he's alive, he'll get a full paycheck."

"Thank you, Carl. You know that's not necessary. He'll never coach again. We both know that."

"It's okay." Carl had a feeling Mikel Bierkov would not last through the week. "Mrs. Bierkov, I want you to call me if you need anything."

"Yes, Carl." She paused. "Carl, dear, do you have any good news? I could use a bit of cheer."

Carl had intended to keep the engagement quiet from his end. "I'm getting married."

"Oh my, congratulations. Who's the bride? That wonderful brunette you've been seen with?" The happiness in her voice was clearly forced.

"Yes, her name is Jacqueline Harris."

"Good. Let me know when the date is set."

"I will," he promised.

"I need to go. The doctor is coming in."

"Keep me informed." He ended the call.

Carl stared out the window. His office sported a lovely southeast view of Lake Michigan.

Carl kissed his date goodbye. She lived across the street. He held on to the hope that Maria would become his girlfriend, but he feared that her father would forbid it because of Carl's mother's profession.

As he stuck his key in the front door, a middle-aged woman shoved him as she burst through the entryway. He nearly fell backwards down the steps. The strange woman had a crazed appearance despite her accoutrements. Carl shouted, "Hey, watch where you're going!" but she provided no indications that she heard him.

He watched her round the corner and disappear from view. Carl shrugged, chalking it up to the neighborhood and city life. As he rode the elevator to his apartment, his mind drifted to the recent memory of Maria's lips on his.

He made his way down the hall. Subconsciously, he checked for the sign that his mother was entertaining. She would leave a rubber band around the doorknob. There was one, but the door was slightly ajar. That was not right.

With a single finger, he slowly pushed the door fully open. "Mom?" *he called out.*

She did not answer.

He called louder, "Mom, are you here? Are you okay?"
Still nothing.
He cautiously peered into her bedroom. She was home.
Staring up at the ceiling, her lifeless body lie naked on the bed. A neat bullet hole in her left temple. Blood soaked the pillow and dripped onto the floor. Lying nearly on top of her was her date, his fat, pale carcass almost shimmering in the low light of the candles. He was shot in the right temple and in the back of the head. Congealing scarlet ribbons contrasted harshly against his skin.
Carl neither cried nor screamed. Instead, his autopilot kicked on. He dialed the police, then sat outside on the stoop until the authorities arrived.

Carl had locked his emotions in a steel box that night. Only now, years later, did the pain begin to ooze out. He felt for Mrs. Bierkov. It reminded him of the night he found his mother murdered.

Maura's urgent buzzing startled Carl back to reality. "Carl, there is a sheriff's deputy here with some papers for you."

"What?"

"A deputy sheriff is here to see you," she repeated slower. "Shall I send him in?"

Carl could not think of what might be going on. Could be something related to the kidnapping case in San Francisco. "Yes, send the officer in."

"Are you Mr. Carl Costello?" the deputy began.

"Yes."

"I have a summons to serve you."

Carl took the documents from the officer's outstretched hand. He glanced over them. He was being asked to appear at a parole hearing for Kassie Milpenny, his mother's murderess.

Numb, he signed for them. The officer thanked him and exited.

Chapter XLVIII

Jackie spent every spare minute devouring books and training videos on soccer. She intended to get certified as a coach by US Soccer and FIFA. She knew she probably ought to take formal sports education classes at a college, but decided to see how far she could get without having to do so. After all, she would likely have trainers and assistants on staff later.

Surprisingly, she found Carl supportive. He would watch the videos with her and request in depth match analysis after watching World Cup matches together.

At times, she let her mind wander as she stared at the crystallized carbon on her finger. It was at these times when she was most in tune with Carl. As the week progressed, however, her worry that he was hiding a dark secret from her increased.

FRIDAY, JUNE 12, 1998: Jackie accompanied Carl to meet Keith and the Minute Men at Midway airport. Keith and Tom crawled into the limousine.

The silence in the car was eerie. Jackie delicately poured Bruichladdich 26-year-old single malt scotch whisky. She hated scotch, but poured herself a finger anyway. She knew what had been going on. The weekend was not going to be a pleasant one.

Keith spoke first to break the quiet. "As soon as we landed, Mrs. Bierkov called. Mikel passed away an hour ago."

Carl replied, "It's for the best." He raised his glass. No one had drunk yet. "Here's to you, Mikel Bierkov."

"May I hope to be as great a coach as you," Tom added.

The foursome drank. Jackie found herself impressed with the smoothness of the whisky. She could learn to enjoy scotch the way her fiancé did.

Dinner was a somber affair. Carl's left hand rested on her right thigh most of the evening. After Tom and Keith were dropped at the hotel, Carl snuggled with Jackie in the limousine. He instructed his driver to just drive.

Carl gazed into her eyes. "Jacqueline, I love you and I trust you. You've been very patient with me. I have not been fair to you lately." He paused.

She waited with bated breath.

He gathered her hands in his. "I need to tell you about the nightmare that wakes me when I'm not with you." His words came slowly. "I told you that I was an orphan. That is only a small part of the truth. I never knew my father. My mother raised me

184

alone, until I found her bloody body in the bedroom. She had been shot in the head." He stopped. A tear welled up in his eye.

Without saying a word, she reached for a tissue and dabbed it away.

"Thank you." He smiled weakly. He drew a deep breath and continued. "The woman who was convicted is up for parole. I have to go to the hearing."

"What happened? I mean, why would this woman shoot your mother in her own bed?" Jackie realized the absurdity of the question as soon as it left her lips. She had an inkling of what might have happened.

"It was a crime of passion, per se. My mom was a prostitute. The woman, Kassie Milpenny, was the wife of a longtime regular client. He was shot too." He shuddered as the scene flashed through his mind. Jackie ran a loving, reassuring hand down his arm. "Mrs. Milpenny confessed to everything. That's why she's up for parole so soon. It's hard to believe it's time already."

"Are you going to fight to keep her in prison?" Jackie cocked her head.

He shrugged. "That's just it. I don't know. On the one hand, I thank her for freeing my mother from the lifestyle trap she had fallen into, plus that's how I got my inheritance from some secretly stashed lottery jackpot. I don't blame Kassie for reacting that way. On the other hand, she killed my mother."

"It's a decision you'll have to make for yourself." Jackie felt powerless.

Carl said, "Call Agnes. I need to talk to her tonight." His voice sounded like he was admitting defeat.

Jackie pulled out her cellular phone. Luckily, Agnes was on speed dial. "Agnes, it's Jackie. Carl needs you. We're coming by." She hung up before Agnes had a chance to protest. She then used an intercom to relay the address to the driver.

"Pour me some more of that Bruichladdich." Carl shook the ice cube in the glass.

"I don't think you should, but we haven't really drank much tonight," she protested lightly. She decanted the potent potable into his glass.

He swallowed half. "Jacqueline, you will be with me no matter what decision I make, right?"

"Yes, honey, I will." She touched his cheek lovingly. "From what little you've told me, it sounds like she has served her time."

"I love you, Jacqueline." He pulled her into a tight embrace. Their lips locked. He did not want to let go.

Chapter XLIX

SATURDAY, JUNE 13, 1998: Carl awoke refreshed. Telling Jackie about his mother lifted a big weight off his shoulders. Opening up to Agnes and getting some guidance about the Milpenny parole hearing helped as well.

He looked over at Jackie sleeping peacefully. He kissed her gently on the cheek and slid out of bed. Breakfast needed to be cooked.

Jackie awoke to the sounds and smells of bacon frying and coffee brewing. She smiled. "I have a wonderful man," she thought.

She stepped down and padded into the bathroom to freshen up. There, she spotted a pile of personal letters in a shoebox-sized plastic bin. Her nosiness got the better of her. She scooped up a few.

Kassie Milpenny.

She sat on the toilet and pulled out a few to read.

9/12/1995

Dear Carl,

Thank you for your last letter. I've been well. Reading Aristotle's Nicomachean Ethics has shed some new light for me on how the world is. I find his ancient words soothing. I would like to learn to read the original Greek. I have nothing but time in here. Perhaps you could help me.

Yes, every day, I think about how I robbed you of your mother. But you and I both know that we are all better off. I got rid of my scoundrel husband who never respected me and you were spared further embarrassment by her chosen profession . . . .

Jackie skipped to the next one in her hand.

12/7/1997

My dearest Carl,

I, too, feel like we have started to develop a mother son relationship. I do not wish to take Miss Costello's special place in your heart, but you have certainly filled an empty hold in mine.

The prison years for me have been lonely, but productive. I've learned Greek and Spanish, the former thanks to your generosity, the latter from my cellmate Gloria. If I had to do it all over again, I would make the same choice. I really hated that I had to say that, but I do feel that way.

According to my count, I'm up for parole next summer. I hope the above paragraph does not come back to haunt me. The State will probably call you to keep me in, but I hope you think about my side of things. Write me back and let me know what you are thinking. If there is a delay, I'll understand. I know you've been busy with your new endeavor, your soccer teams. It all sounds like too much work for me. I admire you. Miss Costello raised a fine son. She would be proud of you.

Love, Kassie.

Jackie carefully put the letters back. No wonder he was conflicted. She began to feel creeped out by the whole situation. If she were to marry Carl, it seemed highly likely that Kassie Milpenny would become part of her life, as a mother-in-law figure. She wondered what he had written in letters to her. She decided to try to read the rest as soon as she could.

She flushed, washed her face and brushed her teeth. As she opened the door, Carl was preparing to knock. They kissed. "Breakfast is ready," he said.

She ate, but the letters haunted her. Part of her said, leave it alone, but a larger part said to bring it up. Still another part wanted to read them all and copy them for Agnes.

Best not to dwell on them, she decided to herself. She looked at the time. She needed to get moving so she could grab her match notes.

The two discussed the day's plans. Carl tossed her the keys to his Mercedes-Benz SLK 230. He said that he would need the limousine for Keith and himself. She kissed him goodbye and dashed out the door. She needed to breathe.

Chapter L

STAMPEDISTAS versus BARCLAY'S PUB: Jackie lined up her best eleven in a 4-3-1-2 formation. Arí and Księżnicka were up front with Róża in that midfielder/forward position. The plan was to attack hard and fast and utilize any and all openings the ladies could find.

There were holes in the tight defense. Jackie had confidence in Ari and Księżnicka to work together to find them. Both vowed to make Swiss cheese out of their keeper.

Barclay's Pub received the ball first. They played a 4-4-2. Their lady forward ran strong up the middle to the top of the box, whereupon she passed to her partner. Margaret Jaeger stuck to him tight. She was able to win the ball and push it forward.

Księżnicka dribbled up the sidelines. Passing back and forth to Ari and Róża as needed. They worked the ball, seemingly slowly through the Barclay Pub defensive back and eventually slotting a shot on goal. The ball found it's way past the keeper. GOAL!

The Stampedistas were up in the 3rd minute. Jackie held back her excitement. She knew their lead would not last long. "Way to go, ladies!" she yelled as her team jogged nearby. "Don't back down. Keep pushing hard."

Possession ping-ponged. Most changes were in the midfield. Tackles were clean, until late in the half.

Margaret slid into the Barclay lady striker. The ball was missed. The angle of approach was intentionally clean, but the contact between Margaret's exposed cleats swept the striker off her feet. The referee whipped out the yellow card. Margaret cursed in German, and then walked to the goal line to calm down.

The striker lay crumpled in the box. She was holding her left knee. Two of her teammates assisted her to the sideline.

Jackie shook her head. Chances are the score would be tied going into the break. The only possible consolation would be that Barclay's Pub might have to sub in their weakest player, the only other lady on the roster.

The penalty kick was converted.

In the stands, Carl had arrived with Keith. Keith had insisted on coming. Carl was going got be content with missing the pivotal match for the Stampedistas. He was glad that Keith wanted to go.

"I'm impressed. I'm actually seeing some good soccer," Keith commented. He cringed upon seeing the yellow-cardable tackle.

Carl nodded. "I'm glad Jackie got involved. She thinks she's found her calling."

Keith looked toward the Stampedista bench. Jackie kept a cool head. She did not scream in protest or fling her clipboard. "I'm simply impressed with how calm she looks, especially with how intense the game is. Do you think she'll sub out the gal who go the card?"

Carl shook his head. "No, Margaret's the anchor in the back. I'm positive that Jackie will take the risk. Besides, Margaret did not intentionally mistackle. She's a clean player."

"You're right." Keith watched the penalty shot go in. "Do you think Jackie might entertain an internship on the Philly coaching staff?"

Carl was startled by the question. A pain struck him in his heart. He knew that she would jump at the opportunity. But he did not want to be away from her for long periods. "You'd have to ask her."

"Fly her out to Philly when you get a chance."

Jackie checked on the status of the opposing player at halftime. The striker was still insisting on going back in. The blonde had a lot of spunk. "No," their coach kept telling her, "you'll blow your knee out again."

"It's just a bruise," she insisted. "And you need me out there. Katie can't play for shit," the blonde spat.

"Lisa, I'm putting Katie in. You are staying here under ice."

Jackie went unnoticed. She fought back a wide grin. She spoke to her team.

Keith had moved in closer to the Stampedistas' bench so he could listen.

"Okay, ladies, you've played well so far. Lisa, their striker, will not be coming back in. Katie is not as good, but that doesn't mean that you can leave her uncovered. The worst players have been known to score." She glanced over at Sheila, who grinned at the reference. "I want every one on the bench to warm up some. I don't know if I'll make any subs today, but I want everyone to be ready." She broke the huddle and pulled aside Margaret. "Thank you for staying calm."

"I deserved the card. It must have looked bad."

"It looked intentional," Jackie said frankly, "but it was mistimed. We all know that. I'm keeping you in, so just be careful. We can't afford to lose you in the back line."

Margaret nodded. "Is she okay?" She gestured toward Lisa.

"Just a knee contusion, I think. But their coach is keeping her out."

"After the match, I'll invite her to the tailgate at the stadium."

"Good plan, and stop feeling guilty." Jackie patted the fraulien on the back. "Just go play some soccer."

Keith rejoined Carl. "I want her on my coaching staff."

Ari scored in the 84th minute. 2-1 would be the final at the whistle. Margaret finished the match without another card.

Before kickoff of the Stampede match, the stadium had a moment of silence for the Minute Men's fallen leader, Coach Bierkov. Molly continued to work the stands. She had Renata as a backup supervisor working in the Section 12 area.

Renata approached a six-pack of *piwo*-infused Ultras who insisted on heckling the dead during the quietness. Molly watched her friend from two sections away on the track. She hoped to spot Jacek, but he was not at his usual leadership post. Carl was not in the section yet either.

Renata confronted the six men, three of whom towered over her small but stout frame. Molly lifted her radio to a ready position. She could sense that something bad was about to happen. The lime green security force did not know, was not paying attention. Insults in Polish were being heard across the stadium as the moment of silence was ending.

Ian turned toward the source of the commotion. He saw his girlfriend raise her radio to her mouth to get assistance. He saw Renata get punched.

Molly ran. "Need backup. Row 10, Section 12. Fight. Need backup immediately." She bounded the stairs two and three at a time. Protocol was that she could not hit a customer unless they hit her first.

Renata, though outnumbered, did not panic. She caught the next swinging fist in her hand and twisted the man's arm over. His body followed his arm bones. His comrade grabbed her arms from behind. She made her body go limp to escape his grip.

By this time, Molly joined the fray. She first grabbed the one who had tried to hold Renata. Molly knew exactly how to apply the correct amount of pressure on a spot on the trapezoids close to his neck. Howling in pain, the attacker dropped to his knees. This allowed enough time for the security guards to handcuff him.

The rest of Section 12 backed away. They wanted no part of this chaos.

Molly and Renata continued trying to subdue the remaining five. Molly pushed one back. He had jumped onto the front row chair seat in an attempt to leap atop her. He lost his balance and fell head first over the concrete wall.

Television cameras caught the horror of the fan breaking his neck.

Molly froze.

Renata rushed down to track level. Medics scrambled to the scene.

"Oh my god, what have I done," Molly said quietly. She barely felt the knife plunge into her back.

"This is for Jack," came the voice in her ear, as the blade was pulled free.

Molly spun around to see who her attacker was. She swooned.

Jacek had pushed his way to the front of the section. He caught Molly just before she would have hit her jaw on a chair back.

"*Kudowa!*" He lifted her in his strong arms and carried her down the field access stairs. He laid her on a gurney.

Molly was about ready to pass out. She looked up at Jacek.

He bent over and whispered in her ear. "I saw who it was. I'll take care of him." Before she could thank him or protest, she blacked out.

The distracted Stampede fell to the inspired Minute Men 0-1. Carl decided that Tom would make a fine head coach. He instructed Keith to put together an offer. The sooner the interim tag could be lifted, the quicker Philadelphia could heal from the sudden loss of Coach Bierkov. He was not yet aware of the details of the Section 12 chaos before the match. He did not bother to even inquire. He would learn about it all soon enough.

Jackie met Carl near the locker room. Carl sent the limousine on with Keith. The couple embraced. "Are you ready to go home?" he suggested.

"Yes, I'm not up for any post game stuff. It's been a long day." She handed him the car keys.

Chapter LI

Sunday, June 14, 1998: CHICAGO: Piotr Kodwyck died at Soldier Field Saturday evening before the kickoff of the Chicago Stampede match.

A scuffle between security and fans erupted during a moment of silence honoring Mikel Bierkov. Bierkov, coach of the Philadelphia Minute Men, passed away Friday from complications after a massive stroke.

Team officials, Soldier Field personnel, and security and ushering service contractors all refused to comment pending an investigation of the events.

Kodwyck was a 23-year-old Polish national visiting his family for the summer. His friends and family cited his love for soccer and that he was an avid fan of the Chicago Stampede.

Funeral arrangements were pending as of press time.

Ian laid the Sunday paper aside. He could not finish the article. He sat by Molly's side, holding her limp hand.

The doctor said that she had lost a lot of blood. The knife barely nicked her right lung; thankfully, there had been no major damage. During surgery overnight, the tear was repaired, and the bleeding stopped. She had needed three pints of blood. The sedation should be wearing off in the next few hours.

Ian remained in his Stampede uniform. He had only removed his boots, socks and shin guards in his haste to get to the hospital. He had been unable to focus on the game. Mirek subbed him out in the 66th minute. Ian was relieved.

He looked at the clock. It was five-thirty AM. He had not slept. The nurses tried in vain to get him to take a shower. One had even gone to the trouble of finding him some scrubs to change into. They lay undisturbed on the windowsill of the private room overlooking Lake Michigan. Ian did not want Molly to wake up alone.

Renata came by at eight. She, too, had been up all night. She was still in her work clothes. Molly remained asleep.

Ian stood. The two hugged. "What happened, Ren?"

She shook her head. "I'm not sure. I've been with the cops all night trying to get it all figured out. But I have a feeling that Molly's stabbing is not related to the fight." She gave her friend's hand a light squeeze.

"What makes you say that?"

"Neither the guards nor the cops found any knives on the five hecklers."

"Her ex is still in jail, right?" Ian asked.

"As far as I know." Renata shrugged. "We'll just have to wait until Molly wakes up."

Molly came to around noon. She blinked at the sunlight streaming through the window. Ian came into focus. She smiled weakly.

Ian pushed the call button for the nurse. He stood up and kissed Molly lightly on the lips. "You gave everyone quite a scare, sweetie," he said.

"What happened?"

"Someone stabbed you in the back. You're in Northwestern Hospital."

"Was it during the fight?"

"It was someone else. Renata will be back soon. She knows more, I think."

A couple of nurses entered and began taking her vitals. The doctor came in a few minutes later. He explained what occurred during surgery. He informed her that she might be released on Monday if all went well.

The doctor left, but the nurse remained to clean her wound and change the dressings.

Renata arrived just as the nurse was finishing. She had gone to the cafeteria to get something for Ian and her to eat. "Oh, hey, you're awake," she said.

"Hi," replied Molly.

"Ian, go take a shower." Renata crinkled her nose.

He kissed Molly's forehead. "I'll go clean up now. I just wanted to be here when you woke up."

Molly smiled. "Thank you." Once Ian was in the bathroom, she turned back to her friend. "What happened?"

"Somebody stabbed you."

"Well, that much I have figured out. But why? I don't remember."

"What was the last thing you recall?"

Molly closed her eyes. "I helped you out during the fight with the Ultras. One tried to jump on me. I pushed him back, and he went over the edge."

Renata nodded.

"But I don't remember much after that." She let out a sigh. "Did you see who it was?"

Her friend shook her head. "No, but it's possible that one of the TV cameras caught his face."

"I hope so."

Chapter LII

T UESDAY, JUNE 16, 1998: Alexi's feet dangled over the edge of the doctor's exam table. She casually flipped through a three-month old copy of *Woman's Day*.

The doctor tapped lightly on the door before entering. "Miss Taman, I have the results of your pregnancy test."

Alexi let out a deep breath. She set the magazine aside. "Go on."

"You're pregnant. Just a few weeks along, so there is plenty of time to discuss options." The gynecologist took a measured pause. "But you may not have another chance at your age."

Alexi touched her abdomen. "I'm going to be a mommy," she cooed, smiling.

"Then congratulations." The doctor wrote a prescription for prenatal vitamins and gave cursory instructions against alcohol consumption.

All Alexi could say was, "I'm going to be a mommy."

Chapter LIII

WEDNESDAY, JUNE 17, 1998: Ian doted on Molly during her recovery at home. The blood loss had left her weak. Ian poked her full of spinach salads and red meat.

She lie on the couch. As she half-watched the World Cup matches, Ian did crunches and stretches until he was summoned to practice. "I love you, Molly."

Jacek knocked the hair off his razor before taking off the final swath. It had been a while since he took his head down to skin. Where he was going, however, blending in would be easier as a skin.

He changed to red the laces in his combat boots. He slipped a nine-inch hunting knife into a sheath strapped around his right calf. White tube socks helped hold it in place. No one but Jacek knew the knife was there once his pant legs were down.

He pulled his semiautomatic handgun from its hiding spot in the closet. Before holstering it in the small of his back, he checked to see if it was fully loaded.

The cool night called for a jacket. He tucked an extra gun cartridge in the inner pocket.

He wanted to call Molly, but hesitated. The less anyone knew about his plans the better.

Jacek parked his Harley Sportster in front of the nondescript clubhouse. He knocked thrice. A peephole door opened. "Password?" came the gruff voice from the other side.

"Rollerchain," replied Jacek without hesitation.

A heavy deadbolt slid back with a distinctive clunk. The door opened. Jacek entered a world he thought he had left behind in Poland.

On the back wall over a drum set hung a large Nazi flag. Cigarette smoke hung like a cloud over a large octagonal poker top table. Six white men sat around it.

The one who answered the door welcomed Jacek. They shook firmly. "Welcome, recruit. It will be good to add another brother to our ranks."

Jacek nodded. "Yes, thank you for the invite, brother." He stepped further into the white power lair. All of the men had shaved heads; prison tattoos graced some of the gnarled knuckles gripping beer bottles.

One of the men at the table rose. "Welcome new brother J. I am brother M. Please make yourself at home." M gestured toward a 1950's style refrigerator. "We have cold beer."

Jacek chose a Dixie. He joined the circle and engaged in the white power topic of the evening.

Club members came and went as the evening wore on. Jacek stayed vigilant looking for the one who had stabbed Molly.

Heavy metal played in the background. Some men jammed. Jacek was recruited to take Jack's place in the band. He shook his head. "I can't do that. I'm not very good."

At midnight, the one Jacek hunted appeared. He was shorter than the Pole by three inches. His bony hand extended to Jacek. "I am brother B. Welcome, new brother J." The two men eyed each other.

Jacek knew the man as Bobby on the outside of the clubhouse. Bobby was a member of a band that usually opened up for Jack's band. But he was more of a groupie of Jack's than anything else. He joined the clubhouse so he could shadow his idol. Rumor had it he was a woman-beater as well. Jacek was sure that it was Bobby who had stabbed Molly.

Hours passed. The beer supply dwindled to zero. Plans were made to support a fringe political candidate for state office. Bobby suggested ways that they might spring Jack from jail—both legal and illegal. Brother M, who seemed to be the alpha male, joked that B might be gay since he was always talking about Jack. That put a quick end to that conversation.

At three-thirty AM, Bobby left. Jacek excused himself and departed.

Bobby got into his 1968 Camaro. As he pulled out of the gravel lot, Jacek kickstarted his Hog. He put on a pair of black leather gloves before leaving.

Bobby did not live far. Jacek stopped about half a block back and shut off the V-twin engine. He walked confidently to Bobby's door and waited in the darkness.

Drunk, Bobby was slow to get out of his car. At the door, he fumbled with the lock. Jacek pressed the gun barrel into his back. Bobby froze. The Pole removed Bobby's gun from its holster on his back. "Turn around, coward," Jacek said calmly.

Bobby spun around. Jacek cocked Bobby's gun. He pressed the barrel between Bobby's eyes. "Why did you stab Molly?"

"That bitch put Jack in jail. She deserved it."

"Did Jack tell you to do it?"

Bobby swallowed hard and nodded. "Yes."

Jacek leaned over and whispered in Bobby's ear. "This is for Molly." He pulled the trigger of Bobby's gun. Bobby collapsed upside down over the steps. Jacek holstered his own firearm. Bobby's pistol was placed in the coward's right hand.

Staying in the shadows, Jacek watched for porch lights and lamps inside windows as he made it back to his bike. He waited five minutes. Seeing no curious neighbors and hearing no sirens, Jacek started the engine and rode away.

Chapter LIV

THURSDAY, JUNE 18, 1998: Carl arrived at the parole board hearing for Kassie Milpenny. He had not seen her in person since the trial. They had only exchanged letters.

He sat and pulled copies of her letters out of his attaché. He glanced through them, looking for clues on what direction to take. Even after long sessions with Agnes, he still felt indecisive.

Agnes had read all of Kassie's letters. Agnes advised Carl to say things to keep Kassie in jail. Then, to discontinue replying to the letters. Agnes highlighted passages that might indicate that Kassie thought that Carl was somehow connected by blood to her murdered husband. Agnes said, "Your life and Jackie's life may be in danger if she gets out of jail."

Carl stared at those portions. He just could not see that no matter how hard he tried.

He looked up at the parole board. Two women and one man sat behind a nondescript folding table. The gray-haired woman in the middle appeared the most curious. She wore gold-rimmed reading glasses. The three made comments quietly among themselves.

The older woman peered over her spectacles at Carl. "Are you here for Milpenny or to represent the victim's family?"

Carl cleared his throat. "I'm Carl Costello."

She looked at her paperwork. "Son of victim," she said as she made a note. She looked back up. "Did Milpenny comply with the requirement to apologize to you?"

"Yes."

"Do you believe the apology to be sincere?"

Carl hesitated. He could not be for certain. On the surface, it appeared sincere, but he had never heard it straight from her mouth, had never seen her expression or her eyes as the words were spoken. "I don't know." The letters crinkled in his hands as he tightened his grip.

"Why?"

Carl cleared his throat again. His mouth was dry. "I never saw her eyes. It was only on paper. You can say anything on paper."

The woman nodded. "Deputy, bring in Kassie Milpenny."

Kassie was clad in an orange jumpsuit. She was handcuffed and shackled. She shuffled her way slowly to the chair. Her remorseful look appeared well rehearsed. Her hair was long and pulled back into an unassuming ponytail. Lines on her face were prominent. She bore a scar on her left cheek.

Once seated, she looked over at Carl first. Her steely gaze sent a cold chill through him. He forced himself to meet her eyes. Her expression softened a little. He saw a woman who had been fucked over for years and was paying the price for merely striking back. In that moment, Carl decided what to say.

"Ms. Milpenny," began the parole board chairwoman, "you have served a third of your sentence. You have been asked to apologize to Carl Costello, son of Miss Costello, the female victim. He has provided us with a copy of the letter you wrote."

Kassie nodded.

"However, Mr. Costello would like to hear the words."

"Yes, ma'am." Kassie faced Carl. "I'm surprised you doubt my sincerity, Carl. I'm truly sorry for taking your mother from you." She seemed to stop short. Both Carl and the parole board waited for more. After a long pause, she continued. "If I had known Miss Costello had a child, I would not have killed her."

The chairwoman inquired, "Ms. Milpenny, please clarify your last statement."

Kassie turned back to face the board. She blinked. "I have had a lot of time to think about what I've done. You've had access to the trial transcripts. You know I was a battered woman, and the bastard cheated on me for twenty years with Miss Costello before I shot them both. I intended to only shoot my asshole husband, but it was so easy to take her out, too. What I meant was if I had known she was a mother, something I've always wanted to be, I would have probably just maimed her instead of the nice, clean kill shot I gave them both."

Carl's jaw dropped at the frank tone she employed.

The chairwoman nodded and adjusted her glasses. "I see. Thank you for being honest and forthright with us today. Mr. Costello, do you have any comments or questions?"

Carl cleared his throat. He was still reeling from Kassie's explanation. "I believe Kassie's apology to be sincere." There, he said it. It was out. No turning back now.

Kassie faced Carl and mouthed, "Thank you." She cast a smile his way.

The board conferred among themselves. The clock on the stark white wall ticked the seconds loudly. A bead of nervous sweat trickled down the side of Carl's face. He thought about Kassie's grandiose statement. He wondered what she meant by maim. A vision of his mother paralyzed flashed through his mind. He shuddered. Carl wanted to slap Kassie. He regretted the extended contact he had with her over the years through letters. His hands began to shake.

The three board members murmured. The clock grew louder. Carl did not want Kassie to be released, not now, not ever. He wanted to say so, but it was too late.

The board broke their huddle. The chairwoman spoke, "Kassie Milpenny, we will see you in three years. Guard, escort her back to her cell."

Carl breathed a sigh of relief.

Kassie reluctantly stood. As she walked by Carl, she spat on him. "You're probably his child, too," she seethed.

On just a few hours of sleep, Jacek managed to complete a full shift of tuckpointing work. At three, he wished he could go straight home, but he felt compelled to deliver the message to Molly.

Before firing up his Harley, he called her. "Is Ian with you?" he asked without even saying hello.

"No, it's film day. He won't be home until after six or seven. Why? What's up?"

"I need to see you for a minute. I can't tell you over the phone."

"Well, you know where I live."

"I'll be there in fifteen minutes."

Jacek was glad for his motorcycle in the city, especially Molly's neighborhood. A Cubs' game at Wrigley Field had made the parking extra tight that afternoon. He managed to park right in front of her building.

Molly buzzed him in. They greeted each other with quick European pecks on the cheek. He noted that she moved slowly as she played hostess, fetching him a *piwo*.

"You shaved your head," she said as she handed him the bottle of Okocim.

"Easier to get the brick dust off," he replied. It was partially true. "*Dziękuję*." He took a long drink.

She sat on the couch. "I'm sorry. I still feel weak."

"It's to be expected." He smiled at her. He turned a kitchen chair around and straddled it.

She cocked her head. "So what's so important?"

"I want you to know that I took care of the man who stabbed you."

She lowered her head. "Oh."

He continued, "This particular friend of Jack's won't be bothering you anymore."

"You didn't have to," she spoke softly.

"I know, but trust me, he deserved it." He took another drink. "You can't tell Ian that I was here."

She nodded.

He rose, finished the beer and crossed to her. "You have more friends than Jack does." He kissed her on the forehead.

She made no move as he left her apartment.

Chapter LV

Saturday, June 20, 1998: Renata appeared in Molly's position as lead in the yellow seats. Molly, who was still recovering from her injuries, was suspended without pay pending the outcome of the police investigation. The family of the victim had filed a wrongful death lawsuit against Molly, the City of Chicago Parks District, which ran Soldier Field, and the Chicago Stampede. Even if Molly was cleared of any criminal wrongdoing in Piotr's death, just like O. J. Simpson, she might be found liable for his death.

Molly still came out to support Ian. Wearing a team-issued credential, she stood on the sidelines. Her arms rested on the top of the chain link fence. She gazed at her boyfriend as he warmed up on the pitch.

Renata, when she could get a free moment, stood next to her. "Hey, Molly, I just heard that Jacek may have killed someone to avenge you."

Molly did not break her stare. "You're kidding. You've got to be kidding."

"It's just a rumor at this point. Jacek and you are on opposite sides of the law here," Renata said.

"In here, yes." Molly made a grand gesture with her hands at the still mostly empty stadium. "Outside," she trailed off.

"Metal?" Renata prompted.

Molly nodded. She said nothing. She knew in her heart what Jacek had done.

Renata excused herself. "I should probably go check on the trainees. The company always has us break them in at these games."

"I know." Molly nodded. "Go; go train them to our standards." She smiled and waved her friend on.

Tomás' groin was bothering him. The team joked in the locker room that it was Madeline's fault. Coach Koneki had Tomás dress, but did not start him. He was listed as doubtful on the injury list. It was too early in the season to risk aggravating such an injury any further. Still, it put a crimp in the defensive line. Manny Larsen was an adequate substitute, but he was not used to starting and playing a full ninety minutes yet.

"I'm ready, coach," Manny assured. *This is my chance to shine*, thought the defender.

Playing the defending champion DC Eagles was a challenge, even more so this time because they were bent on avenging their home loss earlier this season.

Molly wandered over to section 12. She helped Sean and some others hang banners. Sean eyed her skeptically when she offered to help, but in the end welcomed the extra pair of hands.

Section 12 was being punished for the minor riot last week. No flags or poles, large flags, or drums were allowed. If everything went well, next match they could have either drums or flags back but not both.

Molly found herself standing next to Lawrence. He gave her one of his trademark bear hugs when he saw her. "So good to see you, Molly." She winced in pain.

"And to you, Lawrence." She lifted a plastic cup of Budweiser she had been sipping on.

He tapped his cup to hers. "How are Ian and you getting along?"

"Good," Molly said. "I think last week was a bit of a scare for both of us, but we are getting along okay. How about Brendan and you?"

Lawrence thought for a brief moment before answering. Things were still shaky at best, especially with Alex still in the picture. "Good. We have some things to work out, but then again all couples do."

Sean interrupted, "Molly, thanks again for the help with the banners. It's good to see you with us rather than against us."

"Oh, whatever. The usher supervisor thing is just a job. You know that."

"One day, you'll be on our side permanently; you'll see."

"I already see. I see that some of your group are dicks and those make the whole lot look bad. One fuck up and the whole platoon is punished. Be good; focus on supporting the Stampede, and your flags and drums will be allowed back. Continue fucking up, and the Stampede could end up playing without section 12-style support. Nobody wants that, but the soccer moms and dads pay the team a lot of money for tickets and they don't want to see or participate in riots."

Lawrence placed his hand on her shoulder. "Take it easy, Mols."

Sean made a motion like he was going to spit at her feet, but turned his back to her for the rest of the evening.

Molly patted Lawrence's hand. "I'm okay, but if he wants to learn to be a leader, he needs to realize that life is all about give and take."

The big guy nodded. "I couldn't agree more."

The stadium announcer's voice boomed. "Please join us for a moment of silence to honor the memory of Stampede fan Piotr Kodwyck and for Philadelphia's Mikel Bierkov."

Lawrence bowed his head. Molly tried to follow suit, but her radar was up. About halfway into the moment, she relaxed and bowed her head.

Nothing happened.

On the field, Ian stole a glance at section 12. He did not like that his girlfriend was right in the middle of the scene of last week's crime. There was no arguing with her. She was a fan at heart. Besides, Lawrence and Renata would keep an eye on her. Ian resolved to focus on the match. He owed it to his team to perform well.

The first third of the match was relatively uneventful. A lot of back and forth. Captain Dan thwarted a couple of early DC chances. In the 25th minute, Ian earned a quick yellow card for a handball in the box. He found himself rattled after that incident and reacted by not playing as aggressively for the remainder of the first half.

Team captain Baumgartner pulled Ian aside after DC's Honduran signing Raul Cardenas put one in the onion bag. "Ian, pull your head out of your ass. We've got to beat these guys."

Ian nodded. He stole a glance at Molly who was chanting with section 12. He smiled. *I'm glad she's enjoying herself.* "Tigger, wake up!" he heard a teammate yell. Ian glanced around and found the ball coming through the air at him. Fabian, one of DC's defenders, came in hard as both sturdy men leaped for the ball. Fabian's elbow connected hard with Ian's cheekbone. Ian crumpled to the turf. Fabian fell on top of him. Ian heard the muffled sound of the referee's whistle.

The official showed Fabian a yellow card for an obviously reckless foul. Tellum got into the referee's face. "Oh, shut up, Juan," came the curt reply as he calmly gave the Eagle captain a booking for dissent.

Ian had to leave the pitch because he was bleeding.

Action resumed with the Stampede playing a man down temporarily. Scrappy play concentrated itself in the midfield.

Doc Gina worked feverishly to get the bleeding stopped long enough to allow Ian back on the pitch. Mirek barked at Brendan to start warming up.

On the field, Novotny finally managed to squeeze a crisp pass through a narrow lane to Sin Brazos. He knew what to do. One on one in the penalty area, Carlos nutmegged the Eagle keeper, then put the ball easily into the goal. 44th minute, 1-1.

They would go to the locker room tied at the half.

Molly crept down to the track. She walked with Jackie back to the north end. "I hope Ian's okay," Molly lamented.

Jackie shrugged. "Worst case, he's got a broken cheekbone. He's tough, so it's likely just a couple of stitches."

Mirek asked Gina, "What do you think?"

"I can't get the bleeding to stopped long enough for him to be allowed back in the game."

Ian sat on the stainless steel examining table. He lowered the ice pack. Mirek looked at the angry wound on his player's left cheek. "Sorry, Ian, it's best that I pull you out."

"Whatever," Ian acquiesced.

Gina added, "It might be cracked."

Molly opened the door to the room. "Oh, Ian." She hurried to him and kissed his boo-boo. "Is it as bad as it looks?"

"Probably not. I used to be a boxing doctor, so I've seen these types of injuries all the time." Gina gestured for Ian to keep the ice on it.

"But my eyeball feels like it's freezing solid."

"You have to keep the swelling down."

"Fine." Ian reapplied the cold pack. Molly placed her hand over his. He gave her a half smile.

Brendan took the field in Ian's place for the second half. Lawrence cheered even harder for his boyfriend.

From the opposite side of the stadium, behind the home bench, Alex began to cheer for the Stampede. The red-clad supporters around him looked at him strangely. Alex had spent the first half as a basically neutral observer.

"Good to see you rooting for the home team," commented one seat neighbor.

Alex shrugged. He did not think it so odd. "My favorite player just came on." He smiled as he watched Brendan jog by.

"Oh," came the response. The lady sipped her beer and went back to watching the match.

Alex lifted his field glasses to get a closer view. He homed in on number 9. After pacing his fluid movements, Alex moved his view to section 12. He fixed on Lawrence, his rival. *Oh, Brendan, you will be mine, all mine, soon. Lawrence is too soft for you.*

The intensity of the match did not slacken. Brendan, Harp and Carlos all took their turns at getting knocked around by the Eagle back line. Maxwell Harp managed to get the go ahead goal in the 58th minute.

The Eagles pounded at the Stampede. Hip checks, rough but legal tackles—Baumgartner pleaded for the referee to issue more yellow or even red cards, to no avail.

Eventually, the Eagles got two late goals. Peter Go scored his first goal of the year in the 85th minute to tie it up. Avila had the game winner for the Eagles in the 89th minute.

Section 12 all had to bite their tongues. They wanted to berate the officials. They wanted to pelt Avila with empty plastic beer cups. Avila taunted the fan group after his late goal.

Sean heard a distinctive eruption of Polish cursing from a couple of rows behind him. He turned to look for the source. He saw Księżnicka and Róża sandwiched between some of the Ultras.

"Matt," he hollered, "our women are here."

Matt followed Sean's gesturing hand. "Róża!" he called out. He started to move toward the sisters. Sean clamored in the same direction.

The sisters disappeared from view. Matt and Sean found nothing but a wall of sweaty Polish flesh.

"Did you see where they went?" Sean looked at Matt.

"No."

"Damn."

Księżnicka and Róża made their way to the concourse. They scurried to the tunnel under section 16. A slim man with dark hair brushed past and yanked Księżnicka's credential off her. He continued walking rapidly, vanishing from sight amidst a group of exiting fans.

"Hey!" Księżnicka yelled.

Róża placed her hand on her sister's shoulder. "Don't worry about it. I've still got mine."

"What am I going to tell papa?"

"We'll just get you another one through Jackie or one of our teammates."

Księżnicka nodded. "Okay, let's go. All the guards know us by now anyway."

Alex put the stolen all access pass on. He smiled when he saw that it did not have the bearer's name or photo on it. And it was good for the whole season. His pace slowed. He came around to the tunnel access at Gate 0. Calmly, he strolled past the security guard.

Alex went down the west tunnel to the north end. He surveyed the press conference area where the handful of reporters were gathering. He decided to join them. He stayed to the back of the group.

Mirek spoke to the media first. Alex asked one question, "Why did you put Brendan Glazier in at the half rather than in the starting line up?"

Mirek answered frankly, "Glazier must earn back his starting position."

Alex pretended to write on a note card. He saw Brendan emerge from the showers. His heart fluttered. Brendan answered a few quick questions about his return. Then he stepped down. Alex hurried to his side. "An exclusive, Mr. Glazier?" He grinned.

Brendan responded in a low voice, "What are you doing here?"

"I've come to see you."

"Well, that's obvious. All right, follow me. But keep up the reporter charade."

Brendan led Alex to his car in the north end lot. The soccer star drove away from the stadium. Up Lake Shore Drive, he pulled off at the Irving Park exit. There, he parked in the lakeside lot. They had remained silent during the ride.

Alex pulled Brendan to him. He kissed the Iceman hard on the mouth. Brendan felt himself melting.

Suddenly Brendan froze. He remembered their last night together nearly three weeks ago. His cell phone rang. Alex looked at the caller ID, Lawrence. Alex tossed it to the floor.

"But—"

Alex put a finger over Brendan's mouth. Brendan bit it—hard. Alex yelped and yanked his hand back. "What the fuck?"

"What the fuck did you do to me a few weeks ago at Axis?"

Alex licked his lips at the memory. "Oh, that? Just one of my games."

"Games? You called that a game?" Brendan started the car. "I'm taking you to the cops."

Alex pulled out a boot knife. Its steel blade caught the lamplight. Brendan drew in a deep breath. Alex plunged the blade into the player's crotch.

Brendan screamed.

Alex bolted from the car.

"You fucking bastard!" Brendan yelled. He looked down at the widening pool of red around the knife blade. As calmly as he could, he put the car into gear and drove as fast as he could to the hospital a few blocks away. He pulled into the ambulance bay and laid on the horn.

An off-duty cop approached. "Hey buddy, you've got to move your car."

Brendan rolled down the window. The officer took one look at Brendan's predicament, winced in empathy, and hollered for the medics and nurses.

Chapter LVI

Lawrence and Sheila rushed to the emergency room as soon as they heard. "What happened?" they demanded.

"Alex," was all Brendan could muster.

The attending filled in Sheila on her husband's injuries. "He was lucky that he wasn't erect when it happened. The blade grazed his inner thighs and did pierce one testicle. He should heal okay in a couple of weeks. He'll require several stitches, but will obviously have to abstain from intercourse for a while."

"Good," spat Sheila. "Serves you right for cheating on us."

"Ha, ha! Very funny," replied Brendan. "Lawrence, I'm sorry."

The big guy gently ran his hand through his boyfriend's hair. He kissed his forehead. "I'll kiss your owie later." He smiled as he pulled back.

"Better not; don't want to rip the stitches out."

"Will you come with me tomorrow to see the US match at Sueños?" he asked.

"Yes, I will."

Chapter LVII

Sunday, June 21, 1998: Jackie coaxed Carl into going to Sueños del Fútbol to watch the US National Team play Iran in the World Cup. Jackie did not like how Carl had been acting since his return from the parole board hearing. She feared he might be slipping into his shell again.

Agnes advised Jackie to inventory the pills in Carl's medicine cabinet at least daily and call in to her. Both women were worried that Carl might slip back into heavy pill and alcohol use.

Carl encouraged Jackie to hang out with her friends rather than mollycoddle him all afternoon. She tried not to but he pushed her toward them.

Matt had been watching the scene. "What's going on?" he queried.

Jackie shook her head. "I don't know. It really bothers me that whatever is eating at him is affecting his public persona. Before, he was so effective at keeping it inside." She hailed the barkeep for two pints of Newcastle.

"I've got time if you want to chat. Róża won't be here until after she is done doing the family thing."

"Oh, that's right. It's her birthday today. What do you have planned?"

"A nice dinner this evening, maybe a walk along the lakefront."

"Sounds romantic and surprisingly clean for you." Jackie winked.

"Ah, my dear Jacqueline, you know I am a poet." Matt lifted her hand and kissed the back of it.

Jackie felt a rush of warmth. Matt still had an effect on her. She recalled the short piece he read at the tailgate. As his hand lingered on her fingers, she said, "Yes, you are, Matthew MacNaughten." She felt Carl's eyes on her and pulled her hand back.

A chain of gasping surprise caused their heads to turn toward the door. Awkwardly and slightly bowlegged, Brendan Glazier walked arm in arm with Lawrence.

Carl stood and lifted his Bushmill's whisky glass high. "Welcome, Brendan and Lawrence, glad you could make it. There's room at my table."

Matt looked at Jackie who was trying not to laugh at everyone's shock. "You knew about this?" He gestured at the happy couple.

Jackie just grinned.

"I thought the Iceman was married."

"He is, but she's a lesbian."

"No way. You're joking, right?"

207

She shook her head and took a swig of ale.

"Un-fucking-believable."

Jackie's cell phone rang. She glanced at the number and excused herself to take the call. "Yes, I'm set to watch the match . . . . We're all at Sueños. I've got my notebook . . . Of course, I'm taping it at home . . . I'm still definitely interested in coming out to talk to everyone. I'm working on the arrangements. But I need to be close to Carl right now . . . . Thank you for understanding. We'll talk at halftime. Chau."

Matt's curiosity was piqued. "Who was that?"

"Keith from Philly."

Matt scratched his head. He narrowed his left eye as his right eyebrow rose. "Who?"

"You know, Keith, the general manager for the Minute Men." Her tone was nonchalant. She glanced at the clock and noted that it was close to kickoff. She opened up her notebook and poised her Mont Blanc ballpoint.

"What the hell is going on? Why would Keith be calling you?"

"Keith wants to give me a shot as an intern on the coaching staff. Tom's in support of it, as is Carl. I cannot afford to let this opportunity slip through my fingers. If I do, it will be a longer road to the top. I want to be the first woman to coach a men's professional soccer team in this country and perhaps coach a men's national team."

Her ambition did not surprise Matt. He watched her quickly scrawl the names, numbers and positions of the starting eleven on both teams. "You're crazy, you know that don't you?"

She nodded and took a swig of brew. "Yes, I am." She smirked at him.

The match kicked off. Jackie's eyes barely left the television screen. She commented once to Matt. "You know it's harder to analyze build up and true positioning from the TV broadcast. You have to be there to truly get a good feel for how the match is flowing."

"I agree with you. I'll bet Carl would have flown you over to France if you would have asked him."

She sighed. "I know."

Forty minutes passed before Hamid Estili of Iran scored the first goal of the match. A huge noise of disappointment erupted from those in the bar.

Matt looked over at what Jackie jotted down. "US not working together. Too many holes/opportunities."

At halftime, the US still had not scored. Huge murmurs of pessimism overtook those few optimists who insisted that it was only a one-goal deficit with yet another half to play. Jackie dialed Keith and the two discussed her notes.

Carl came over flanked by Lawrence and Brendan, who were holding hands. They waited patiently until Jackie was off the call. "Who was that, dear?" asked Carl.

"Just discussing the match with Keith." She smiled. "Good to see you," she said to Lawrence and Brendan.

Lawrence gave Jackie a strong hug. "We haven't talked in a long time."

"I know," she conceded. "We'll have to get together at Sidetrack some evening so we can catch up. Good to see things are going well."

Lawrence nodded. "Sounds good."

Brendan piped in, "Thank you, Jackie. I'm much happier now that things are in the open."

"We're marching in the parade next Sunday," Lawrence announced.

Jackie looked at Carl. "Do you think that's wise?"

"We all know that there is going to be some backlash," Carl replied. He reached for his next drink just as Jose set it on the bar. "But we feel that their appearance in the parade could bring butts in the gates at the next match."

She nodded. "So, Lawrence, you'll be in full Stampede regalia and Brendan will be in his kit?"

"Yes, ma'am. I can't wait. You simply must be there." Lawrence gave her a strong one-armed hug.

"If I'm in town, I will be there," she replied with a smile.

Carl pulled Jackie aside. "Please come back and sit with me."

"I've got an unobstructed view of the TV from here at the bar and am less likely to get distracted."

"We're taping it at home. You can always go back."

"Keith wants my live feelings. Pitch side, coaches don't have the advantage of instant replays. We have to rely on our observations, guts and instincts."

Carl squeezed her hand. "I admire your commitment, Jacqueline. I'll leave you be until after the match." He kissed her.

Jackie tasted the whisky on his tongue. He had been drinking a lot. She decided that she would either need to drive home or call in their driver. She reached into his pants pocket and deftly plucked the car keys from it. He whispered, "Thank you, love," in her ear as he pulled away.

Carl resumed his seat at the table. The second half kicked off. Jackie resumed her homework assignment.

The final score recorded reflected another USA loss in the World Cup. The crowd at the bar dispersed with heads shaking and hung low.

At the final whistle, Jackie began a slow walk toward the back door. Her cell phone jangled just as she laid her hand on the knob. "Keith, what in the hell was Sampson thinking? We should have dominated the second half."

"Yes, the talent is there. Give me the lowdown on what you might have done differently."

Jackie launched into a long missive on tactics and how each player on the pitch could have been placed or used differently to achieve a better end result. She ended with, "I'm still not even sure that would've worked against their keeper. He was flawless. I'm just happy we were able to sneak one past him and prevent the shut out."

"Very good. I want you to fly out here tomorrow and spend the week with us. We have an away match on Saturday against Boston. I'll make sure you are able to get back to coach your Stampedistas. You'll fly United Airlines first class. I'll email you the information."

Jackie was silent. All this was happening so fast.

"Are you still there?"

"Yes, sorry. It's all so sudden. I'll see you tomorrow." She ended the call and leaned back against the building. She cast her eyes to the sky. Her world was spinning out of control. Things were moving too fast. She fingered the diamond on her left ring finger. Engagement. Career change.

She sighed heavily as she slid her cell phone into a slim attaché. Her eyes closed.

Carl snuck up and kissed her cheek. She jumped.

"What's up, sweetheart?" he asked.

"I'm going to Philadelphia tomorrow. I'll be gone all week. Keith has already bought the plane tickets for me."

"Are you nervous?" He looked deep into her eyes. He could tell that she was.

"A little." She pushed her hair back. "Are you ready to go? I need to pack."

"What's the rush? I'd like to treat you to dinner first, since I won't be seeing you all week." Carl smiled warmly at her.

"Okay," she conceded.

Chapter LVIII

Monday, June 22, 1998: Jackie plucked her suitcase from the carousel in the Philadelphia airport. She looked among the waiting limousine drivers holding name-bearing placards for her name. Nothing. Keith said that he would arrange for transportation to the hotel. Sighing heavily, she fished her cell phone out of her attaché and punched up Keith.

"Watson."

"Hey, where's my ride?"

"Well, hello to you to, Jackie. How was the flight?"

"A little bumpy, but fine. You said were going to have a car here for me when I arrived."

"Oh dear, I think I forgot to arrange for that. I'm so sorry. See if there is a shuttle to the hotel or would you rather have a rental?"

"A rental would be nice. I've never been to Philly. It would be nice to explore on my own during downtime."

"Wait, forget the rental. I'll let you borrow Caroline's car. She hasn't been using it much lately. If you end up taking a taxi, save the receipt. I'll reimburse you."

"Okay. I'll let you know when I'm settled in at the hotel." She clicked off and dragged her baggage to the hotel shuttle waiting area. She hoped that this minor faux pas was not a sign that the entire week would be a bad experience.

She looked around at the various name-brand hotel shuttles stopping and picking up travelers, but she did not see hers, the Chestnut Hill hotel. She queried a skycap whom informed her that they did not have a hotel shuttle and would have to take a taxi. She emitted a heavy sigh. The skycap offered to assist her to the taxicab stand. Jackie smiled. "That would be wonderful, thank you."

When she arrived at the hotel, she immediately figured out why the quaint small hotel did not have their own shuttle service. The hotel consisted of only 28 rooms. She persuaded the desk clerk to allow her an early check in so she could freshen up before meeting with Keith and the rest of the coaching staff.

The bellhop led her to Room 32, a beautifully decorated room with a queen bed with an elegant headboard and comfortable furnishings. She thanked the lad and slipped him a five-dollar bill. She saw a package resting on the desk. Opening it, she found a Philadelphia Minute Men warm-up set. Her day was beginning to look up.

Jackie phoned Keith.

"We're on our way to the training grounds. We'll be by to pick you up in about twenty minutes," Keith stated.

Jackie washed her faced and reapplied a light coat of makeup with a heavy sunscreen as a base first. She slipped into the warm up suit. The fit was perfect. Keith must have talked to Carl about it.

She looked at herself in the full-length mirror. She looked odd in the red, white and blue trappings of the Minute Men. Jackie had been Stampede Red ever since the team was first announced. The dominant color of the pants was primary blue. The top was white. The jacket was primary red embroidered with the team logo and "Coach Harris" underneath the logo. A huge smile crossed her face as she fingered the lettering.

Well, she would not be betraying Carl professionally if she were to be hired by the Minute Men. After all, Carl did own both teams.

Temple Stadium served as the practice grounds. It was near the hotel. The Temple University Owls had a wonderful facility. Keith and Coach Tom Nederson led the tour of the areas the Minute Men were allowed to use. Then, Jackie met the rest of the coaching and training staff, then to the team.

Keith excused himself. He had some meetings at the downtown Liberty Place office. "Jackie, I'm leaving you in fine hands. Stick close to Tom today. He'll let you know how things are to go."

It was humid out, but that was not what was making Jackie's armpits perspire. She stood by Tom. He told her that he let the trainers run the warm-ups. He pulled out a copy of the practice drill schedule and handed her one.

She looked at it. It was very detailed.

"This is my method. Coach Bierkov always ran practice on the fly. Then again, he had been coaching for over thirty years."

Jackie studied the first page. It was a drill for indirect freekick restarts. She played through all the possible defensive moves in her head, as well as offensive responses. She had always had a knack for strategy, even was the top player in her high school chess club. "Is this a defensive or offensive drill? What is your objective?"

"Offensive," replied Tom.

"It won't work," she stated flatly.

Tom raised his eyebrows.

Jackie began to sweat less. Her tactical mind took over. "Tom, Boston will be expecting Jon Wang to move here and Luka to move there to connect with the cross. Their keeper, Wheeler, plays in the middle so he's not favoring either side and tends to be generally well-positioned, except for a shot on goal here from the top right corner of the box."

Tom nodded. "Okay, sketch out the play that you think will work."

He pulled out a blank pad of paper with soccer field markings imprinted on it.

Jackie removed a red Fisher space pen from her pocket. She inked X's and O's in the desired pattern. She drew lines to indicate directions of movements.

"The trick here is not going to be the positioning of the keeper nor the movement of the defense, but getting Wang to break his usual patterns," Jackie theorized. "Luka won't be a problem. From reviewing game tapes, he likes to switch things up—fake right, go center—that kind of thing."

Tom nodded as he looked over the plan. "You're right. Luka would have no problems with this pattern. But Wang would be better than Teren at placing the kick in the right place. Instead of Wang here, let's run it with Bobby Betis. Gathinho might be a better choice, but he's too short in most situations."

"I agree."

"Then, let's do it. Set it up." Tom turned her loose. She took over from the trainer.

"Gentlemen, we're going to run some freekick play drills. Boston has a hole in their defense against the free kick where we can bury the ball," Jackie announced. "LeCock."

"Yes, ma'am."

"You will be on the defensive team with Malek, Schultz, Sand, Randolph, Junior, Espinoza, Usman, Javier, Nate, and Vic. Come over. Tom will let you know how the Bulldogs tend to move defensively. Everyone else, step over and we'll go over the pattern."

All twenty-two jumped and divided up accordingly. Jackie's eleven gave her their undivided attention. She laid out the play. When she was confident all understood her, she broke the huddle.

Tom whistled for the play to start. It was executed flawlessly. Even Wang ran the proper direction. Tom and Jackie had them run the play a few more times to make sure everyone understood the movements. The defensive players even tried to simulate a real match time situation.

Tom clapped as he blew the whistle to stop play. "Great job everyone. Jackie will make copies for everyone's playbooks. We will use code Restart JH1. Let's switch keepers and run a full field scrimmage for the next thirty minutes."

As the players lined up, he patted Jackie on the back. "Good job, Jackie. You seem to be a natural at this. I thought Bud or Wang might give you problems because you're a woman."

She shrugged. "They may be on their best behavior today. We'll see by the end of the week."

Later before dinner, Carl rang Jackie. "Hi, Jacqueline," he cooed.

"Hey, honey."

"Are they treating you right over there?"

"Yes, darling, they are."

"Be honest with me because you know I could have them fired if they don't treat you right."

"I know."

Carl laughed. "I'm only kidding. Seriously though, all this ambition of yours is scaring me. I feel like I'm going to lose you to a non-CSG team."

"That probably won't be for a while. Relax, love, I'm still learning the nuances of how to handle the big boys," she replied.

"I know. I just worry about losing you."

Carl was letting his insecurities show, thought Jackie. "I love you, Carl. You are my number one man." She touched the diamond ring on her finger. No matter what happens, I'll always come home to you, she added to herself.

Keith picked up Jackie for dinner. She was introduced to Caroline, Keith's wife. Tom and his wife Maria were to meet them at the restaurant.

"I hope you're hungry," said Keith as he held the door open for her.

Jackie got in the back of the Mercedes sedan. "Why?"

"We have reservations at Tiramisu in the South Street neighborhood. They are really generous with their portions."

Jackie nodded as she situated herself. Keith shut the door. Caroline piped in, "Their spinach lasagna is to die for."

"Mmm, sounds good," replied Jackie.

Along the way, Keith and Caroline pointed out sights. Jackie was pleased that it was still light out, otherwise she would have missed a lot. Caroline suggested that they take a walk along the Delaware River waterfront.

Dinner conversation revolved more around general topics rather than soccer. Jackie was relieved.

Chapter LVIX

TUESDAY, JUNE 23, 1998: Mirek reviewed the medical reports with Gina.

"I recommend that Ian sit out the match this Saturday. The x-rays on his cheekbone show a hairline fracture. We've fitted him with a special mask that he can wear during light practice, but a match will be too much too soon."

Mirek harrumphed. "Well, we are deep up top. What about Brendan?"

"Frankly, he needs the rest of the season off, or at least until he can get his personal affairs in order."

"He did play well when I put him in," Mirek mused.

"I haven't seen the game tape." She paused to glance at her notes. "As for the injuries stemming from his recent attack, if he's bandaged properly and wears a cup, he'll be fine as a late sub."

Mirek nodded. "Tomás?"

"So long as he doesn't aggravate his groin strain in practice he should be okay to start."

"*Tak, dobry.*"

"Yeah, I thought our little skid might be due to our back line woes."

"Agreed."

Mirek went back to his office and studied the stats during the first twelve weeks of the season. He felt like he needed to make a trade, but whom to use as bait and whom to go after was the question.

The next opponent was Kansas City at Arrowhead Stadium. Mirek switched on the game tape. He had to find a way to win again before it was too late.

He leaned back in his chair. As he fast-forwarded the recorded Kansas City—New York match, he found himself looking more at Jerzy and for glimpses of Magia on the sidelines. If only Jerzy were a defender, he thought with a sigh.

Chapter LX

Wednesday, June 24, 1998: Tom turned Jackie loose completely. She had only an evening to plan a complete day's training regimen. She would have the other trainers to assist her, but what Keith and Tom wanted her to do was to be like the head coach for a day. She hardly slept the Tuesday night because she was so nervous.

She could not show fear. Otherwise, players like Luka Bitva or even Quentin MacElroy might show their insolence to her because she was a woman. Luka was known for his thoughts on women: they should be barefoot and pregnant and catering to his every whim. She supposed that was typical for men from Eastern Europe, but she wanted to gain his respect. Earn his, and the rest would be easy.

She parked the borrowed car in the lot at 7:30 AM. The team would begin arriving at 8:00 AM. Tom liked to practice them in the mornings during the summer. It was predicted to be a hot and humid day, so she would not mind getting in out of the sun early either. She finished the last sips of her Starbucks mocha Frappuccino before going to the Minute Men's team office.

"Good morning, sunshine!" greeted Tom.

"Good morning," she replied.

"Are you ready? I told them I was taking a day off, but I'll be up here watching you from a distance."

She breathed out fully before saying, "Yes, I am ready." Inside she was quaking like the San Andreas fault.

"Remember, Luka can smell fear a mile away. That's how he plays."

She nodded.

"He'll tear you a new one if you go in nervous. He tried some shit with me after Bierkov went into the hospital. Just bite back like a pit bull and he'll back down. I've met Luka's mother. Mrs. Bitva is one tough cookie. When Luka is around her, he cowers in her skirts. Be like her and you'll have control over him the rest of the week."

She smiled. "Thanks, Tom. That little bit of info is all I need." Her fears subsided. Feisty men usually came from very strong women, at least from her own observations. Today would be no problem, no problem at all.

After the trainers warmed up the squad, Jackie rounded up her charges. "Coach Tom is taking a day off. He left me in charge. As you all know, we've got an important match against Boston this Saturday. I want you to go in prepared. Monday, we learned restart JH1. Divide up like you were on Monday and run it through. I want to see how many of you committed it to memory."

She spoke with confidence. She felt no fear inside, so none was able to exude itself outside. "Full speed, full contact." She blew the whistle and watched.

Chapter LXI

FRIDAY, JUNE 26, 1998: When Jackie returned, she felt like a new woman. Carl picked her up that evening at O'Hare, and even he noticed a transformation. She spoke with more confidence.

"Carl, I want us to set a date."

"For the wedding?"

"Yes, for the wedding."

Carl merged into traffic on the Kennedy Expressway before replying. "What about the Cup?"

Jackie's jaw dropped. She stared at him. She was expecting an off-season suggestion. "I don't know," was all she could utter.

"I did some thinking while you were gone about all this."

"No, you didn't," she countered playfully.

Carl glanced at her briefly. His look was serious. "I did, too. I talked to Bobby Lonestar out in LA. He's the party planner in the Stars supporters group, the Starship Ultras. There is an annual event the night before the Cup called the Supporters' Ball. This year, they are looking at a beach location. I've always wanted to get married on a beach. No tuxes. Casual, surrounded by friends and well-wishers."

Jackie continued to stare in disbelief at her fiancé. She noted that he had left family out of the description. A painful reminder that Carl had none and that she was estranged from hers.

"Anyway, I suggested that the main event of the Ball be our wedding. Lonestar was enthusiastic. He's willing to be our go-to man in addition to the regular planning he does for the Ball."

"Hmm, a beach wedding," she pondered aloud. "And here I was thinking you were going to suggest that we be part of the halftime show." She smiled. "I like it."

"Really?"

"Really, I do." She leaned over and gave him a peck on the cheek. "I can just imagine the sunset as a backdrop." She gestured with a wide sweep of her right hand.

"Oh, nice. Good idea."

"Let's do it."

"Yes, let's do it. Let's get married." They squeezed each other's hands. Life was good, very good.

Chapter LXII

SATURDAY, JUNE 27, 1998: After the Stampedistas match, Jackie and Carl joined the 12-Steppers at Sueños to watch the Kansas City match. The bar was decorated in a rainbow motif in honor of Gay Pride weekend and Brendan. One of his game-worn, signed jerseys hung on the wall. The bar was located six blocks south of the beginning of the parade route, but the staging would back up at least that far.

The parade was scheduled for Sunday afternoon, barely enough time for Brendan to fly back from Kansas City.

There was a murmur that the Iceman might start, but Carl indicated otherwise. Jackie agreed. No way was Bren fully match-fit yet, close perhaps, but not quite there.

Both Jackie and Carl found it hard to be quiet about the setting of the date for the wedding. Carl wanted to be absolutely certain it could be pulled off. He had left a message with Lonestar, but did not expect to hear back until Sunday at the earliest.

Somehow, they managed, despite copious amounts of alcohol.

Chapter LXIII

Sunday, June 28, 1998 Gay Pride Parade: Sheila met her husband at Midway airport. The team had taken one of the first flights out so that Brendan could participate in the event.

Her girlfriend, Meghan, sat in the passenger seat. Meghan was a tall, stocky Chinese-American dyke. They had met at a networking event.

Brendan tossed his gear in the trunk of the Honda Civic. Meghan stepped out to let him in the back seat.

"How was the game?" she asked politely as Sheila merged into light traffic on northbound Cicero Avenue.

"We tied. I played about twenty minutes in the second half."

Sheila glanced at him through the rear view mirror. "How are your balls holding up?"

Meghan snorted as she stifled a laugh.

"I didn't bust any of my new seams. Gina made me wear a cup, which felt uncomfortable. I'll be back to my full game next week."

"As long as you stay away from Alex," Sheila put in.

"Yes, as long as I stay away from Alex."

Wearing his full game day regalia for the parade, Lawrence held a place for Brendan. He talked to the Stampede about sponsoring a float but there was not enough time to get one designed and made.

He looked at his watch. It was ten before noon. The parade was scheduled to begin at one. He called Brendan. "Where are you?"

"Stuck in traffic. But we're almost there."

Sheila spoke up, "We'll be in our home parking spot in ten minutes. Find out where he's holding a place."

Lawrence said, "I'm north of Sueños about half a block. It's the best I could do. Are any others from the team coming?"

"We talked about it, but I'm not sure." He paused as he changed subjects. "Any sign of Alex?"

"Not yet, but the precinct is on alert. He'll show up and when he does we'll get him."

"I don't know. It's a pretty bright day." Brendan bit his lip.

Sheila, Meghan and Brendan joined Lawrence about twenty minutes before the parade began. With five minutes to go, Carlos, Ian & Molly arrived. Brendan grinned from ear to ear at the open support from his teammates.

When the parade began, Brendan and Lawrence held hands. They kissed and began to march.

Alex waited in a choice spot on Halsted Street in front of the leather and sex toys store. He blended in with the other revelers. About two hours into the parade, he saw Brendan and Lawrence.

Brendan tensed when he saw Alex on the sidewalk. His stalker was dressed in a stereotypical leather outfit. He held a bullwhip. His buttocks were bared. Lawrence discreetly tapped Meghan's shoulder.

Meghan nodded and spoke into a hidden microphone on her shirtsleeve.

Suddenly, Alex found himself being tackled by two uniformed officers.

"We'll finish the parade," Lawrence said to Brendan. "Then we'll deal with Alex."

"Thank you." Brendan kissed the big lug on the mouth and gave Sheila and Meghan each a peck on the cheek.

Chapter LXIV

Monday, June 29, 1998: A motion for extradition to California was filed on Alex Rodriguez. Bail was denied on the matter of the more recent attack. Brendan was relieved. He might finally be able to piece his career and life back together.

Ian took a day off from practice to appear in court with Molly. There was a preliminary hearing in the wrongful death lawsuit. Molly's lawyer, Colin MacNaughten, argued that she had been acting in self-defense. He claimed that the security videotapes from the stadium would prove it.

The judge said that he would review the video evidence to determine whether or not to allow the case to proceed to a jury trial.

Renata gave her friend a squeeze. "Everything will be okay."

"I hope so."

"Our company hires good lawyers."

Molly nodded. "I just hope I'll be able to work again soon. I'm not sure how I'm going to pay rent on Wednesday."

"I've got you covered on that, sweetheart." Ian kissed her furrowed brow.

"Thanks, honey." She managed a weak smile.

Chapter LXV

Thursday, July 2, 1998: "Carl, I can't keep the date quiet any longer," Jackie whined over lunch. "We have to announce it."

"I know." Carl grinned mischievously. "I just wanted to wait until the fireworks and laser show after the match. I want the world to hear it through Boomin' Bob's voice." Boomin' Bob was the Stampede's stadium announcer.

ESPN broadcast the match between the Stampede and the visiting Sol de Miami. Alexi lounged on her bed. Every time Carl's name was mentioned, she rubbed her tummy.

She was just beginning to show. So far there were no complications. An early test indicated no major genetic abnormalities.

Faintly, Boomin' Bob's voice echoed through the airwaves after the final whistle.

"Ladies and gentlemen, thank you for coming. Please stick around for our fireworks and laser lights show sponsored by Blue Cross & Blue Shield of Illinois who would like to remind you to have a safe Fourth of July. Oh my, Carl Costello has just told me that a date has been set for his wedding to Jacqueline Harris. They are set to wed on October 17th at the Supporters' Beach Ball in Los Angeles."

The sports announcers then cut in. "We've just been informed that the wedding between Stampede owner Carl Costello and Jacqueline Harris will take place in LA on the eve of the FLA Cup."

"That's right, Kenny. Anyone is welcome to attend. The LA supporters group known as the Starship Ultras will host a beach party as the Supporters' Ball. The main event will be the Costello-Harris wedding."

"Are you planning on going, Tommy?"

"I hope so. All depends on where our bosses at ESPN decide to send us."

"That's certainly true." Kenny then went back to a final wrap up of Chicago's 1-2 loss to Miami.

Alexi cupped her tiny life-containing belly in both hands. "We'll be there, won't we, son," she sneered.

In Section 12, Matt's face grew pale. He steadied himself and sat down in a seat sprinkled with celebratory beer spillage. Nearly simultaneously, Róża and Colin asked if he was okay.

Matt shook his head. "I feel sick. Take me home, Róża."
"*Tak.*"
"I'll help you," offered Colin.

Tomás consoled Carlos after the match. Sin Brazos received a straight red card ejection for his collision with Miami's goalkeeper, Boozman, in the 44th minute.
"*Disculpe, disculpe,*" Carlos sobbed.
Mirek sat on Carlos' other side. "I know you are taking this hard."
"How bad is it?" Tomás asked.
"Gina was able to see the x-rays. Boozman's right wrist is busted."
That tidbit caused Carlos to wail even louder. He threw his stumps up in the air.
"*¿Porque, Dios, porque?*"
Tomás looked across at Mirek. "Where's Paul?"
"You mean, Agnes?"
"*Tak.*"
With a towel around his waist, Paul entered from the showers. He cocked his head at the sight of Carlos. "I'll call my wife."

Agnes arrived. Shooing Tomás, Mirek and Paul away, she kneeled in front of Carlos. Gently, she lifted his chin. "Carlos, I know what will help you." She spoke softly. "Come with me."
Agnes herded the Mexican into her car, parked in the north end lot. She drove to Northwestern Hospital where Boozman was being treated.
Agnes sweet-talked her way past security. With Carlos in tow, they found Boozman on a gurney in the emergency room. His wrist was on ice.
Boozman looked at Carlos. "*Jodete y aprieta el culo!*" The Cuban insult rolled off the white man's tongue just as easily as if he were a native.
Carlos just shrugged. "I deserve that."
Agnes blinked at Carlos.
"*No es importante,*" Carlos said to her. He took a couple of steps closer. "I am sorry. I know how you feel."
Boozman shook his head.
"No, I do. I used to be *un portero.*"
Boozman looked the armless Mexican up and down. "No way."
Agnes put in, "It's true."
"*Sí,* I lost my arms a few years ago in an accident. You will not lose your hand."
"But I won't be able to play keeper for a long while—maybe the rest of the season."
Carlos nodded. "I'm sorry. I never meant to hurt you."
Agnes spoke, "I know you don't believe his apology, but he's been crying about this ever since it happened."

Boozman still looked skeptical. "Really?" He lifted his right hand off the ice and elevated it above his head. "Well, right now the debate is whether or not to have it set here or just splint it and let the Miami docs handle it."

"If you have it set here, I'll stay nearby," Carlos offered.

"I'll think about it." He lowered his wrist back onto the cold pack.

A nurse stopped by to check on Boozman. "Are they bothering you?"

Boozman said, "No. They're okay." He smiled at Carlos. "So, Carlos, tell me how you became such a tough forward."

Carlos sat down and related his tale. Agnes slipped off to the psychology department. She was still looking for an employer to sponsor a work visa.

Chapter LXVI

Friday, July 3, 1998: Carl awoke and forewent his usual cup of java kickstart. Chicago losing did not bother him. It was only one match. He was on such a high that his plans to wed Jackie were going so smoothly. Telling the world that he was going to marry Jacqueline Harris, the most beautiful person in his eyes gave him a high that no drug could ever duplicate.

Then he opened an email from Alexi: "Carl, wow, you are seriously going to marry Jackie? You know I could offer you so much more."

On the surface, Carl knew exactly what she meant—money, power, greater clout. He sensed there was something else she was hinting at, but could not quite put a finger on it.

He chose not to reply and printed the message before deleting it. He filed it with the rest in a locked cabinet.

Just before lunch, a courier package arrived. It was plain except for Carl's name and address and several red-inked stamps screaming "Confidential". There was no return address, which was not unusual for a courier package.

Carl opened it, slowly removing the documents. The cover letter read:

> Mr. Costello:
>
> Many years ago, you asked me to find out about your father. I hope you haven't forgotten. I never did. I was just unable to get any solid leads until after Kassie Milpenny's parole hearing. The warden who escorted Mrs. Milpenny to and from her cell is my brother. He informed me about the incident of her spitting on you and mentioning that Arthur Milpenny might indeed be your father.
>
> That set me thinking. So I ran some tests on the sample you provided and some that I managed to obtain from police records of Mr. Milpenny.
>
> Arthur Milpenny is your father.
>
> Now, upon further investigation, I dredged up his will. He stated that if Kassie had anything to do with causing his death (he must have seen it coming), she was not entitled to any of his assets or even to read the will!
>
> Look over the copy of the will. He stated that his only son (that would be you) was to inherit everything. He has an extensive list of holdings and properties that has been held in a trust account. It is time for you to claim it.

Call me after you have a chance to look over everything.

Gary Nance
Private Detective

Carl stared at the page for a moment, rereading it even, before looking at any of the supporting documents. First was the DNA lab's report. He read it carefully. Indeed, he was 'Carl Milpenny'. He wondered if his mother knew that Milpenny was his biological father.

He rang his fiancée. "Jacqueline, I need you to find some things for me and bring them to the office immediately. First, get the box of correspondence from Kassie Milpenny. Then, go into my wall safe."

"I don't know the combination or even where it's at."

"It's time you learn, my bride," he said assuredly.

"Okay, I'm happy that you trust me that much," she replied with a smile. "I'm ready."

"Go into the room that is your office. In the closet, on the left wall toward the back, there is a panel that looks like a fuse box."

"Okay, I'm there; I see it. Got it open. Brilliant, darling, to hide it there. I don't think any thief would think of looking in a fuse box for a safe."

"Thank you, honey, that's what I was hoping when I had it installed. Here's the combination, are you ready?"

"Yes." Jackie's hand rested on the dial.

"45-28-02."

She spun right, then left, then right. Stopping on 02, she heard a click. She swung the safe door open. An internal light came on, as if the refrigerator door had been opened. "It's open. Now what do you need?"

"I need you to bring me my mother's diaries. They are bundled together with ribbon."

"I see them." She carefully removed the journals. "Is there anything you need?"

"No, just bring them. I want to look at them in light of some new information I received this morning. I'll fill you in when you get here. Make sure the safe is secure before you leave."

"Yes, I will." She closed the door and spun the lock, gave it a good tug. It was secure. Then she shut the fuse box door. Her groom was a genius. She wondered briefly what made him think of hiding a safe there instead of anywhere else in the condo. Her thoughts quickly drifted to the possible reasons that Carl needed the requested items. Something weird had to be afoot.

She tucked the items in a classic Hartmann Wings duffel and hurried down the elevator.

While he waited, Carl leafed through the holdings of his father. Detective Nance was right. Carl did inherit a lot of property. Rental buildings, mainly, were not just located in the Chicago area, but also in other cities across the United States. There was even a piece of land with a "tiki hut" on a Bahaman island and an apartment building in Paris. He wondered if he should take Jackie to the World Cup final. He could write it off as a business expense in two ways: checking up on his property and scouting talent to bring to either Philadelphia or Chicago. A mischievous grin crossed his lips.

Jackie poked her head in. "Hi, honey."

"Come on in, Jacqueline."

She crossed to him and kissed him lightly. "Here are the documents. Do you want your mom's diaries first?"

"Yes. I've never read them, actually. I was afraid. I was just wondering if she actually knew who my father was." He pulled out the books and gently undid the ribbon tied around each volume.

"Let me help you." Jackie undid one and opened it carefully.

"Thank you. I have no idea how graphic they are. The police had them for a while, but it looks like they were untouched. After the trial they were returned to me. I guess we start about one year before I was born."

Carl stared at his mother's handwriting. It was a neat, intricate script. She wrote freely with no rub outs or cross outs.

> *October 20, 1974:* Today was Carlito's second birthday. He was so cute. After he blew out his two candles, he buried his face and both hands in the cake. He was covered in frosting. I wish I had a movie camera film of it. It was a sight to behold. We both laughed. It was just the two of us. I wish it could have been shared with my mom. I've been feeling guilty the last few years, but I can never go home. She won't be alive much longer. I want her to meet Carlito, but I fear that Mom would not acknowledge my baby's existence or me. It's just you and me, Carlito, you and me against the world.

A tear trickled down Carl's cheek. Jackie found the box of tissues and dabbed it away. No words were exchanged as he closed the book and set it aside. She placed the book that she had untied in his hands. He cracked it open and leafed through the pages.

> *December 10, 1971:* Today my #1 john Arthur Milpenny bought me a condo. Well, it's his, but he's letting me stay here free. He let me pick it out. We had fun. He was my "real estate agent". I know he's married, but I do wish he could be more. So we decided to keep the relationship—strictly professional—per se.
>
> *December 24, 1971:* The mailman brought me a package today. It's Christmastime, but I am so used to getting nothing. I was so happy and surprised that I gave the mailman a huge kiss. He blushed.
>
> I raced upstairs with the package. There was no name with the return address, and even that just looked like a business. I nearly cut myself trying to get into the box. I pulled out a card first. It was from Arthur. It was standard dime store fare, but he

wrote in it, "I wanted to get something special for the special lady in my life. My life has been sunnier since we met. I wish you weren't what you are, but perhaps that will help matters in the long run. I want to be your #1 john forever. Merry Christmas." Underneath the card was a velvet box. I opened it slowly. The sparkle of the diamonds nearly blinded me. No one had ever given me anything that beautiful. I put on the necklace and did not take it off until I went to bed. I can't fall in love with this man, but he is certainly making it awfully hard to resist.

March 27, 1972: I knew I should not have allowed Arthur to ride me bareback last month. I'm fucking pregnant. Damn it all to hell.

Carl set down the book with a bang. "She knew. Goddammit, why in the hell didn't she come right out and tell me?"

"There are some things you may never know. Perhaps she wanted to preserve the integrity of the anonymity of the relationship, to protect his marriage to Kassie," Jackie offered. She came behind the desk and began to massage his shoulders.

"That's not what I want to hear, Jacqueline," he seethed. "Why didn't he divorce her and marry my mother? Why, Jacqueline? Do you have a ready answer for that one, too?"

"I don't, Carl. I'm sorry."

With a heavy sigh, he moved the diaries to the side of the desk. "This morning, I received this package from a private detective I hired years ago. I wanted to find out who my father was. Gary Nance, that's the detective, told me that the trail had run cold but he would keep the file open in case anything turned up. Well, he sent me this." He lifted the paperwork from the package. "Gary was able to use some of his connections and run a DNA test on my sample and a sample left over from the crime scene of Arthur Milpenny's DNA. It's a match. Arthur is my father. I knew he had been a long time client of my mother's, but I didn't know how far back nor how involved. I thought it strange that he was one of the few regular clients who insisted on appointments when I was home. Now it all makes sense. He wanted to see his only son grow up—if only from afar. I guess I could have saved Gary all this trouble and me some money if I would have just read Mom's diaries after she died." He rubbed the bridge of his nose.

"Perhaps, but you were not ready to. You saw a lot growing up, I'm sure. You didn't want to relive that lifestyle of hers."

"She was a good mother to me."

"I know. She raised a fine man. You are a perfect gentleman and a savvy businessman. You are loving, faithful, generous and kind." Jackie paused. She thought she had felt him tense on the word faithful. Maybe it was an early indiscretion, before they fully committed themselves to each other. "Carl, I love you and I know I would have loved your mother, too. I wish I could have met her."

Carl turned and smiled warmly. "I love you, too." He craned his neck as his lips met hers. "Well, darling, Milpenny held a lot of real estate. I must have picked up my business sense from him, well, mom, too, but still . . . anyway, do you want to go to the World Cup Final in Paris?"

Jackie spun his chair around so she could stare at him in disbelief eye to eye.

"I now own a place in Paris. Let's go check it out and catch some great soccer in the meantime."

What could she say? A trip to Paris? What woman in their right mind would say no to that? Certainly not Jacqueline Harris. "I'll go pack my bags and find my passport."

"Slow down, woman. The Final isn't until next weekend, Sunday the 12th."

"Oh, right, I should have known that." She smacked herself lightly on her forehead with open palm. She laughed.

"Let me see about securing tickets. It looks like France will be in the Final which will make it very difficult."

"Could you use your connections at US Soccer?" she suggested.

"I'm not sure how much pull they would have with FIFA and the French Fútbol powers that be, considering our dismal performance. But I'll have to start there anyway. There may be some US Federation members who aren't going now."

"Sounds good, love." She kissed him full on the mouth. "I'll leave you to the planning. In the meantime, I'll go blow the dust off my passport." She grinned.

As Jackie turned to leave, she added, "The Stampedistas won't be playing tomorrow. The league decided to take the weekend off since so many players were going out of town or had family obligations for the 4th of July. So, I'm all yours, all weekend."

"Splendid, Jacqueline. We'll find some trouble to get into." He winked at her as he lifted the phone.

She left the building feeling very happy. It was not that she was not happy before; it was more that she felt more satisfied and secure in her relationship with Carl. The wedding plans were going well. Now, a chance to see the World Cup Final. She would have to be insane to turn down a chance to see that—no matter which teams would be playing. Plus, she sensed that Carl felt a strong sense of relief about knowing who his father was. He was a little disconcerted that his mother had known all along and would not tell him. But deep down inside, he knew that she did it to protect him. At least, she hoped so.

Chapter LXVII

Saturday, July 4, 1998: Quigley invited his Chicago-based clientele to a fireworks watch party. He had a wonderful vantage point from his Lake Point Towers condominium.

The guest list included from the Stampede Carlos Cortez, Paul Novotny, Ian Harris, Brendan Glazier, Randall Silva, and Maxwell Harp. Alexander Boozman was still in town. His wrist had been set, but he was not clear to fly back to Miami yet. There were a few players from the Chicago Bears, one Cubs player who was not playing because of an injury, several musicians, a comedian, three actors, a lady golfer, a novelist and a few high-powered executives who used the agent as a headhunter. Throw in all the wives and significant others and you got an interesting mix of folks.

Wolfgang Puck catered the party, but it was still a casual affair. The televisions in the unit were tuned to FLA matches and local baseball teams. American wines and whiskeys flowed.

Carlos and Boozman arrived together. Boozman's right arm and hand were encased in plaster and rested in a red, white & blue sling. Carlos went to the party sans prosthetics. He had never grown used to wearing them. He did keep his leather gauntlet in his waistband in case he wanted to nibble on something. That way he could handle a fork.

Carlos and Boozman had become good friends in the past two days despite the ugly misfortune.

"No tequila, señor Quigley?" he asked the host.

"Not today. It's a US holiday."

"Oh, yeah, right. Jack Daniels, then."

"Coming right up." Quigley signaled for one of the catering staff to take care of the hapless pair.

Brendan, Lawrence, Sheila and Meghan all arrived as one big happy love quadrangle. "Good to see all of you," Quigley greeted. "Brendan, I've been fielding some phone calls again from second division English teams."

"You're kidding, right? I thought Mirek said that they had lost interest since the thing with Alex began."

"Well, that may have put off a couple of them, but one would like to come out and see you play in person."

"Well, hell, bring them on."

"I just have to make sure that you are going to be fit enough to start when they do."

Brendan laughed. Sheila shot him a look and mumbled under her breath, "Don't you dare screw this up."

Lawrence spoke, "We'll make sure he stays on the straight and narrow."

"Good luck," the agent joked.

Quigley enjoyed playing host and mingling with a decent portion of his clients all at once. But all the couples made him feel lonely. He wished he could have flown in Anna from Poland. He even offered to do so in one of their email exchanges. But she was busy at a convention in Warsaw. At least she was still interested in him.

After the fireworks display, the musicians got together and had an impromptu jam session. Randall Silva even joined in. Quigley was surprised at the Stampede B-teamer's ability on the guitar. He would have to make a note in the kid's file for session work in the off-season.

Agnes and the novelist found themselves off in a corner exchanging ideas. Agnes came away from the party thinking that she just might have to retain Quigley's services to help her with her work woes.

Chapter LXVIII

WEDNESDAY, JULY 8, 1998: Carl and Jacqueline settled themselves into the first class section of a Boeing 777. She had never flown first class before. She had seen the sections and always wondered truly about how they would be treated. Now she had her chance to find out.

She squeezed Carl's hand. He responded. "Are you ready to be treated like a queen?" he asked.

"Always, my love, always." For once, she felt like Jacqueline Kennedy Onassis for whom she was named. She relaxed back in the soft leather of the wide seat. Like floating on a cloud.

In the air, they were treated to a high-class meal with a French Bordeaux red wine. It was to be a non-stop flight to Paris from O'Hare. Jackie kept glancing out the window. She couldn't wait to be over the Atlantic Ocean. Then she knew she would really be on her way. She had never been to France.

Carl sensed her excitement level. She acted like a child going to Disney World for the first time. He loved the innocence she exuded. He knew that she was not truly innocent. But to be with a hungry world traveler who had not been afforded the opportunity was sheer bliss.

Midway over the Atlantic, Jackie dozed off with her head resting on Carl's shoulder. He drank in the scent of her hair and fell asleep, too.

The couple was jolted awake when the jet hit the tarmac at Charles DeGualle airport in Paris. It was early evening, local time. There was still plenty of daylight left to find the property.

Carl prearranged a driver. He thinks of everything, she thought as she climbed in the back of the hired car. Carl gave the driver the address of the Milpenny property. "First things first," he said to her.

"What if someone is staying there?" she countered.

"Then I'll deal with it as their new landlord." He smiled and kissed her.

After a thirty-minute drive, the driver pulled up to the address.

It was a nice building, but nothing really stood out about it. The tiny garden area in front was pleasantly landscaped. Rose bushes were in full bloom. The grass was neatly trimmed. A small iron gate was already open, inviting the couple in. Jackie got out first and drank in the scent of the flowers. "It's beautiful, honey."

"According to the paperwork, I now own the entire building. Good to see it's in good shape," Carl stated as he exited the car.

Together they approached. He used his key to enter. The building contained six small flats. There was a concierge who lived onsite in one of the flats. The other five were rented out as furnished units. Carl tapped the buzzer on the counter. A bell sounded inside the concierge's unit.

A plump middle-aged brunette emerged. "*Oui, monsieur.*"

Carl replied in perfect French. "*Bon jour,* I am Carl Costello and this is my fiancée Jacqueline Harris. I inherited this building from my father, Arthur Milpenny."

"Bon jour, Monsieur Costello. The gentlemen handling Mr. Milpenny's estate told me to expect you. They said you own two soccer teams in America. I had a feeling you would try to come out for World Cup so I held open a flat for you."

"*Merci a mille fois, Madam . . .*"

"*Monique, monsieur, sil vous plait.*"

"How long have you worked here?"

"Arthur bought the building so I could have a place to live and he could see me when he would travel to France on business. I was to maintain the building and keep the units full. I keep 30 percent of the rent for each unit and the rest goes into a fund for maintenance. Milpenny checked the books once a quarter and took what he felt were profits. Also, my place is included in my salary. I've been here for twenty-three years."

"It looks like you are doing a fine job, Monique. I will honor the agreement and you are free to stay on as long as you like."

"Merci, monsieur." She stepped out from around the counter. She had grabbed a set of keys from the wall behind her. "Allow me to show you your room, then I will give you a grand tour of the building."

"*Tres bien,* Monique."

The building was a compact structure. The narrow hallways were painted in a muted white that reminded Jackie of vanilla ice cream. The wall sconces were clearly as old as the building itself. Brass fixtures shone from a recent polishing.

Monique unlocked the door to a room at the end of the top floor hall. "This is the grand room. Arthur always liked it for his own visits to Paris."

"It's lovely," Jackie said. The room was elegant and richly decorated. Antiqued lace and burgundy velvets draped the four-poster canopy bed. She ran her fingers over the fabric.

"*Merci,* I decorated it myself," said Monique. "I would like to show you the rest of the building now."

"If we can pry her away from the velvets," joked Carl. He sported an ear-to-ear grin as he watched her roll on the bed.

Monique giggled. Carl crossed to her and grabbed her hand. "Come on, woman. You need to see the rest of the place."

Jackie faked a pout.

They toured the other rooms and the utility areas. The last thing Monique showed them was the small garden in the back. Jackie gushed her appreciation of its beauty more than the small fountain did its waters.

Carl had the driver bring up the bags then sent him on his way. He was on call all weekend for the couple.

Jackie found herself back on the bed. Carl saw her sprawled and suggested, "Shall we christen our new place in Paris?"

"And rub our naked bodies all over this velvet?"

"Why not?"

"Let's do it!"

As he approached his bride to be, Carl slowly took off his shirt. Her hair was splayed on the coverlet, accenting her beautiful visage. He unbuckled his belt and dropped his trousers.

Jackie smiled sexily. "*Oui, oui*, come to me," she cooed.

Carl wanted to take is slow, but ended up pouncing on her instead, as a tomcat would a heated queen. His mouth smothered hers. The kissing was frenzied and deep. As their lips were locked, Carl divested her of all clothing. Her nimble fingers removed his tightie-whities.

"Doesn't this velvet feel wonderful?" she asked when her mouth was freed.

"Not as good as you do, Jacqueline." He swished her legs apart and rammed his hardened flesh into her wet waiting pussy. Her hips lifted to receive him readily. The stroking slowed to a steady pace. She vocalized her pleasure as orgasm drew near. She did not want to cum so soon but could not help it. Carl was too wonderful of a lover.

Her quivering release massaged his dick. It felt like paradise. He fought back his own ecstatic excretions for as long as he could. When she climaxed a second time, he filled her.

The lovers lie draped over each other. "Let's stay in tonight," suggested he in a near whisper.

"Okay."

Neither had any energy left to truly enjoy any tourist activity. They sensed it in each other. Both smiled thinking the same thought, We are becoming one.

The next morning they took a leisurely stroll to a nearby bistro Monique had recommended. After a light breakfast, they had their driver take them to the Eiffel Tower. Carl wanted to enjoy it while it was not too busy.

Next they strolled the surrounding neighborhood and hit some shops. Jackie soon found herself with three new outfits complete with matching shoes. She insisted that Carl treat himself as well. He bought an Armani suit, which was altered on the spot to fit him to a T.

The driver took all their packages back to the building, whereupon Monique secured them in their room.

During lunch, Jackie said, "I saw a boutique I'd like to visit, but you can't come with me."

Carl raised an eyebrow. "Really? And where might that be?"

Jackie twisted her engagement ring as a subtle hint. "Oh, just a little dress shop."

Carl picked up on the hint. "Okay." He reached for his wallet. "Take this." He handed her one of his platinum Visa charge cards.

She kissed his fingers. "Thank you," she said taking the plastic rectangle. "You'll get to see it in October."

"The dress I hope. You will be returning the card to me after you visit the shop."

"What? You don't trust me?"

"I'm kidding, honey." He smiled.

She giggled. "I love you, Carl Costello."

"*Je t'aime,* Jacqueline Harris."

The boutique was tucked away in a small nondescript mid-block location. With a lilt in her step, Jackie entered the shop.

"*Bon jour, mademoiselle,*" immediately greeted the proprietor.

"*Bon jour, parlez vous angles?*" Jackie stumbled over the pronunciation.

"*Oui,* yes."

"Thank you, God." Jackie cast her eyes momentarily to the sky. "I'm getting married in October."

"How wonderful, an autumn wedding. The season gives you lots of fabulous colors to draw upon," the sales lady gushed. "My name is Veronique. This is my shop. Every piece I sell is as unique as each client I dress."

Jackie reached inside her handbag for a swatch cut from a torn Stampede jersey. "I have something in mind. You see, this will be a beach wedding with a soccer theme in Los Angeles. My groom owns the Chicago Stampede and the Philadelphia Minute Men. We met after a match in a club. I was wearing this color." She handed the bit of fabric to Veronique. "It's Chicago's color. I want my gown to be this color."

Veronique was unfazed. "It's a splendid color." She held it next to Jackie's face. "A good color on you, too. You know, the Chinese consider red to be an auspicious color for weddings." She reached behind the counter for a set of keys. "Let me lock the front door. I want to give you my full devotion this afternoon."

As Veronique locked the door and put up a sign in French, Jackie browsed the shop. Her fingers caressed fabrics so fine and delicate. The vision in her mind of the gown became slightly clouded.

Veronique turned back to her. "Do you see something you like?"

Jackie shrugged. "It's all beautiful."

Veronique retrieved her sketchbook. "Tell me about your perfect wedding dress." Her pencil was poised.

As Jackie described what was in her mind's eye, she aided her statements by reaching for various examples around the shop. Veronique assisted her along by asking questions about certain parts. She also suggested minor changes based on Jackie's figure. At one point, they stopped so Veronique could measure her newest client. After an hour, the dressmaker showed Jackie the sketch.

"Oh my God, that's perfect! That's exactly it," Jackie gushed.

"Step back here and let's discuss fabrics." Veronique walked as she talked. "I know you've made it clear that the primary color needs to match the swatch. I can dye to match, if necessary."

"That's good."

"I will make some suggestions on parts of the dress that need to be that particular red, but I think the lace and a few other areas could be accented with the secondary color of the team. Is there one?"

"Silver and navy," replied the bride without hesitation. "The silver is silver, but the navy I don't have a swatch of with me. Accent colors never really occurred to me."

Veronique's mind was whirling. She reached for a set of colored pencils, chose red, silver and navy, and began to color her sketch. As she worked, Jackie fondled fabrics, sometimes rubbing them against her cheek to test their softness.

"How's this?"

"Wow! Even better than all red."

They chose some cloth. Jackie promised to get a navy color sample. She thought she might have packed a Stampede jersey out of habit. If so, she could just bring it by. If not, she said she would ship it overnight to Veronique as soon as she was able to.

"How free are you to come back for a fitting?"

"My schedule is fairly open. I only have a volunteer coaching job on Saturday afternoons. I do know we are flying out for Chicago on Monday. Hopefully the girls will forgive me for abandoning them this weekend." Jackie grinned.

"I don't know how much I will have finished by Monday morning. I can call you to let you know. If there is enough to try on, especially the main body of the gown, I will want you to come down. World Cup fever has my business down right now."

"Sorry to hear that."

"It was expected. But it definitely brought me a fabulous new client." Veronique was sincere.

"I'm so glad I came in."

"Where are you staying?"

"Carl inherited a concierge apartment building. We are staying there. Let me give you the number." Jackie jotted her name and number down. "Do you require any down payment?"

"No, your trust is all I require. If you are happy upon completion, we will settle then."

"*Merci a mille fois*, Veronique."

"*Merci aussi*, Jacqueline."

They parted ways without even discussing the final cost. It did not matter. She would be getting the gown of her dreams to wed her American prince.

Chapter LXIX

SATURDAY, JULY 11, 1998: The FLA decided to suspend Carlos for two matches, so he would miss the next match. Carlos also had to pay a $500 fine for the foul on Boozman.

The punishment was the topic du jour at the tailgate. Sean and Matt butted heads over the issue. It seemed the only thing they agree on that hot late afternoon was the beauty of the Koneki sisters they were dating.

Molly and Carlos arrived together. Carlos had not yet experienced a tailgate party. Molly had suggested that he go. As they walked to the site from the north end of the stadium, Carlos had to stop several times to sign autographs and exchange ball kicks with groups of kids.

"Come on, Carlos, there won't be any cervezas left." She gently tugged on his shirtsleeve.

"I'm sorry. I have to take care of the niños," he said.

When they got there, Sean and Matt fell silent. Neither had expected the subject to show up. Matt hurried over. He handed Carlos a cold Corona. Carlos gripped it between his stumps. He put his mouth around the neck and whipped his head back to chug the cerveza. He did not come up for air until the bottle had only backwash. Molly grabbed the empty.

"Ah!" said Carlos wiping his mouth on his shirtsleeve. "*Gracias.*"

"*De nada,*" replied Matt. He gestured at Sean. "My friend over that and I were having a little discussion about your suspension. We were just wondering what your thoughts are."

Carlos had time to think carefully about how to phrase a response to such a question. His new friendship with Boozman helped. "It was unfortunate that I broke Boozman. I did deserve the red card. Lance was fair in suspending me for an extra game. I was just trying to score. I came in too hard. Boozman was just doing his job as portero. I did feel very badly for Boozman because I used to be un portero. But we are friends now."

Sean scratched his head. "Friends? How can you be friends with someone you hurt? Or how can you be the friend to someone who hurt you?" He handed Molly a beer.

"I stayed with Boozman when he got repaired," Carlos replied. He leaned over to Molly and whispered. "I want to go talk to kids again. I don't like these questions."

Molly nodded. "Okay, boys, you got your answer."

238

She flagged over some of the kids of the fan group. Carlos went to join the kids in a kick around.

Molly spotted Księżnicka and Róża and went to chat with her Stampedista teammates.

The Stampede won the match later that evening against Columbus. The score was 3 to 0. Brendan started and played the entire match. He scored two of the goals. Harp was his strike partner and scored the other one.

Chapter LXX

Sunday, July 12, 1998, WORLD CUP FINAL: Carl and Jackie decided to be paupers for a day instead of giving the hired driver more grief than he needed. Traffic would be atrocious around the stadium and with due cause, the quadrennial final pitted the home country versus Brazil. Ronaldo versus Zindine Zindane, both strikers worth of the golden boot.

Jackie would have been inclined to cheer for the underdog—well, at least in terms of home pitch advantage—but Carl had obtained the pair of tickets from the Fédération Française de Football. They were to be France's guests. So Jackie chose to wear *les bleus*. Carl wore his new suit with a smart tie the same color as the French kits. They were quite the couple and certainly stood out on the Metro. The driver did not mind the day off. He did not want to deal with the extra traffic. No one even thought twice about trying to pickpocket or purse snatch the pair. If they had been wearing Brazilian colors on the other hand, the story might have been a bit different.

At the stadium, they were recognized as VIP and quickly whisked to the appropriate skybox. Jackie wanted to enjoy the festivities outside the stadium, but Carl said that he needed to meet with the president of the FFF well before the match kicked off. He cited "good business relations" as a reason.

For the first time in Paris, Jackie was nervous. This was the first huge event that she was attending with Carl. Watching European games on television, she had observed how the faithful women sat near emotionless next to their team-owning men. That was not how Jackie ever wanted to be. She would never give up a true fan's passion for the beautiful game. She was a hooligan spirit to the core. She should be down with the rowdiest French supporters pitch-side, not inhibited by a posh skybox.

Carl sensed her growing anxiety. "It will be okay," he whispered in her ear before they entered. "I know how you feel about this hoity-toity stuff. We both know where we'd rather be." He kissed her gently on the cheek.

She began to relax. "Thank you."

With deep breaths, they entered the skybox.

The room was abuzz in champagne, wine, and all things French. A cheese table was laid out displaying the finest that the country had to offer. Various flavors of pate, freshly baked breads, a wonderfully delicious mountain of fruit. They were greeted by a garçon bearing two glasses of champagne. "*Bon jour, monsieur et mademoiselle.*" The couple accepted the offering thanking the waiter. Carl glided across the room to the window with Jackie in tow. He was looking for someone in particular. He spotted the owner of Marseille.

Courtesy introductions were made. Then Carl launched into a barrage of French about Brendan Glazier. That seemed to be one of the few words Jackie understood. Was Carl looking to sell or loan Brendan? She could not discern. But it did sound like it involved a lot of money. She politely excused herself to go nibble.

Did anyone speak English, she wondered to herself. Balancing a small plate of hors d'ouvers on top of her fluted glass, she went back to the window, but not to Carl's side. He was still deep in some type of negotiation with Monsieur Marseille. She wondered if Brendan even knew what was going on. Oh well, not really any of my business.

As Jackie nibbled on bits of fromage, she gazed at the perfect pitch. A petite blonde approached her. "It sucks being up here, doesn't it?" The voice was British.

Jackie looked down at her and blinked in slight disbelief. "Thank the Lord, you speak English. Yes, yes it does suck being up here."

"My name is Penny."

"I'm Jacqueline. I would shake your hand but well—as you can see."

"Don't worry. I'm not used to all this formality myself. You want to be down there, don't you?" Penny gestured to the French supporters section.

Jackie replied in a hushed voice, "Yeah, but I'd really rather be with the Brazilians." She pointed to a smattering of yellow-gold.

"Me, too, I hate the French."

"So how did you end up here?"

Penny replied, "I lost a bet."

Jackie cocked her head. "Huh?"

"No, seriously, I'm with the manager of Oxford United. Somehow, the bastard finagled his way up here. I think under the guise of some player trade negotiations. No one on Oxford U is good enough to play in topflight French clubs, nor does the bastard have enough clout or money to get a good player to come play for Oxford. And you, Jacqueline?" Penny signaled a waiter bearing a full tray of wine. "Hey, where can a girl get a good Newcastle around here?"

The man shrugged. He replied in English, "I will try to find some bier for you, mademoiselle."

"Merci, monsieur."

Jackie smiled. "Now we're talkin'. Anyway, Penny, please call me Jackie."

"Okay, Jackie, how did a nice American end up here? Especially when—"

"Don't even say it. I know, the US totally sucked rocks this year. Just wait till 2002 and when we get rid of that idiot Sampson."

"Right-o."

"Okay, well, I'm engaged to Carl Costello. He owns the Chicago Stampede and the Philadelphia Minute Men."

"Two teams? Wow! That's unheard of in English football."

"Well, I don't know if you know or not, but the FLA is a 'single entity'." She made a gesture for scare quotes. "It's really strange, but really it's like buying a stake into a larger business. They are all about league parity and impose salary caps. I grant that the caps are necessary right now, but I do hope that they go away as soon as the league is able to turn a profit."

"Oh, phooey, those boys just own teams to fulfill dreams that they couldn't fulfill when they were all younger. It's a power trip and a tax write off. It will all depend on how much say the players will have. Obviously, the league play experience didn't do much for your national team this year."

Jackie gave a conciliatory shrug. "That may be true, but that is more the coach's fault. If the US Federation hasn't fired Sampson's ass already, he should get the axe shortly."

"Whatever you say."

Somehow the waiter returned with two Newcastle ales in tall bottles. "Would the mademoiselles prefer glasses with their bier?"

"No, no, you've gone to too much trouble already," Penny said. She poked a few francs in his pocket. Tips were not required, but in this instance, certainly deserved. The lad had gone well out of his way.

"*Merci beaucoup*, just let me know when you need more." He bowed slightly then parted.

"Bloody hell, I was not expecting that," Penny said just before taking a long swig.

"Cheers!" Jackie replied then knocked back a large portion of the refreshing brew in the brown bottle.

Carl sidled up next to his bride.

Penny commented, "My, my, what a handsome one you are." She looked him up and down.

With a grin, Jackie said playfully, "Back off, he's mine."

"Where did you get those Newcastles?" he said.

"You just have to flirt with the right waiter," replied Penny with a wink at Jackie.

Jackie introduced Carl and Penny. They shook. Carl found it intriguing that Penny's Oxford man was here to try and strike a deal. He asked where he was. Penny pointed to a squared-jawed, balding man in spectacles with a slight beer gut. Carl then excused himself.

"Now we can get back to girl talk," Penny said with a wry smile. "I think France is one of the better looking teams, in terms of aesthetic beauty."

"Hmm, I haven't really looked at them in that manner. The Brazilians are pretty hot themselves, except for Ronaldo's teeth," Jackie replied.

Penny laughed. "So, how have you been following the matches?"

"I used them for exercises in match analysis."

"Really? You mean you haven't even bothered to swoon over Petit's flowing mane?"

"Well, I am a woman, you know. Seriously, though, I'm trying to break into coaching a professional team."

"You are out of your mind. Even if you are better than the rest of the boys who apply for the same position, you will never get them past the fact that you are a woman. It's a boy's club and they probably won't be too keen on letting you in."

Jackie grinned. "I know. That's why it's a challenge."

"You are out of your bloody mind," said Penny with a shake of her head.

Closer to kickoff, the intensity level of the throng below grew exponentially. The national anthems were sung. A rousing roar followed the French anthem from the blue-filled stadium. The two new friends hoisted fresh ales as the match kicked off. Jackie wished she had her notebook and a pen, especially since the bird's eye view provided such a great vantage point.

Carl and Penny's date rejoined their ladies. Carl planted a wine-soaked kiss on Jackie's lips. "Hi, sweetie."

"Hey, Carl." The two joined hands. "Can we go down to the supporters sections? I feel so out of place up here. So does Penny."

"I know. Maybe after a little while. I'm feeling a bit stifled up here myself." He slid behind her and draped his arms around her from behind. She stepped back a tiny bit and snuggled closer to his body.

In the second half, Carl escorted the two ladies down to the thronging sea of blue. Jackie and Penny nearly ditched Carl as they blended in with the supporters. Both picked up the French chants quickly. All three were singing and chanting at the top of their lungs.

Carl wanted to find a drum, but thought better of it. This was their time, not his. In 2002, it will be different. The USA was capable of going from worst to first in four years, especially if the right coach was selected. He shook further future thoughts from his head and submitted himself to the moment.

And just in time, too, there was a large resound of displeasure at the sending off of Desailly for his second yellow. Nonetheless, as the Brazilians took the freekick, the area resumed chanting en masse.

Carl looked down at Jackie and Penny bouncing. They were grinning. Everyone was standing. The two ladies did not have much view of the pitch, but they did not care. They carried on until Petit scored the final goal in the 90th minute and even then the air of extreme glee did not stop.

The tall, dark and handsome one tugged on his fiancée hand. "We should get back up to the skybox. It would be rude to our hosts not to be up there now."

Jackie agreed and grabbed Penny. The trio snuck out of the boisterousness and headed up to the skybox. Halfway up the elevator, the referee sounded the final whistle. The home nation had just won the 1998 FIFA World Cup.

The French federation top brass met Carl, Penny and Jackie as they disembarked the car. They held fat champagne bottles, some already opened and flowing freely into glasses and through veins.

Carl congratulated them in their native tongue. Jackie tried to mimic the message, but stumbled over the pronunciation. Penny did not care. She spoke English exclusively.

Once the French had left for pitchside and the award ceremony, the three English-speakers went inside the box. There they were handed celebratory glasses of the finest champagne. There were plenty left in the box to make it quite the soiree.

Chapter LXXI

WEDNESDAY, JULY 15, 1998: Jackie found it hard to get her Stampedistas to focus on practice. They all wanted to hear stories from France instead. Before her ladies would begin intrasquad scrimmage, she had to get tough. She promised to tell everyone later over pizza.

Carl received word that the All-Stars were selected. The starting eleven as selected by the fans included Ian Harris and Sin Brazos. Old Tomás was scheduled to be the sweeper in the back. It would be interesting to see him play with Jerzy Josefczyk of the New York Mad Cabbies.

Carl remained on a high from the trip to Paris. He drifted off in thought often. He was in love, but still held a dark secret from her. He hoped she would never find out about his infidelity with Alexi Taman. Seeing her at the All-Star match might be interesting, but he would have his fair Jacqueline at his side. Alexi would just have to deal with it. He had another ten days before that event.

Chapter LXXII

Saturday, July 18, 1998: Matt dropped by the Stampedistas match before going over to Soldier Field. He was still seeing Róża but harbored many confused feelings for Jackie. While watching Róża play, he risked hearing Jackie's voice.

The Stampedistas sat atop their league table. Barclay's Pub were only one point behind in the standings. Today's matches would decide the final standings after ten weeks. Next Saturday would pit the number one team versus the number two team. From the looks of things it would be the finest set of ladies in Chicago co-ed recreational soccer versus Barclay's Pub.

Jackie was nervous. They needed a win to assure the scudetto. Thankfully their last match was against the Banana Monkeys who were in the bottom half of the table. Statistics be damned, thought Jackie, the Banana Monkeys would be out to win as well, just because they were playing the Stampedistas. All the teams in the league played harder against Jackie's ladies. She theorized because the guys on the teams did not want to be beaten by a bunch of girls.

Matt knew all this as well. He gave Róża a kiss before she joined her teammates. He hoped to watch her score a hat trick.

The game was a midfield battle for most of the first half. Róża and Księżnicka had a few good runs on goal but were thwarted easily by the Banana defense. The ladies caught a break in the 43rd minute when Arí Amat played a deep ball forward to Michelle O'Connor. Michelle made a strong run up the left side. Róża positioned herself near the right post, struggling to stay in an onside position. Michelle saw the Koneki sisters but not before she saw a shot opportunity. She kicked the ball hard toward the net. The Monkey keeper got enough glove on it to deflect it—straight toward Róża! She quickly settled the ball with her chest and shot it hard toward the far post. The keeper had not recovered from the first missed shot. The ball found its way to the inner side netting.

Matt stood up and screamed, "Goal!" sustaining the O-sound almost as long as Andreas Cantor, the legendary Argentine Spanish-language broadcaster. Jackie spun around at hearing his voice. She waved at him, but he did not notice. He was focused on Róża as she celebrated with her teammates.

A few minutes later, the referee blew his whistle to indicate halftime.

Jackie gathered her tribe. As they rehydrated with water and sports drinks, she said, "Everyone's looking good out there. Michelle, you almost had it. Róża, great way to play cleanup. I want to see some more of the same. Is anyone ready to come out?"

Predictably, Agnes raised her hand.

"Paula, get ready. I'll have you subbed in for Agnes at half," said Jackie.

Paula nodded and went off to warm up for the remainder of the break.

"Anyone else?"

Silence and head shaking were the responses.

"Alright, let's go out and win the scudetto."

Matt stood and clapped as the teams retook the field.

The Stampedistas received the ball to kickoff the second half. Paula's fresh legs drove toward the goal. The Monkey defense backpedaled. They had made no changes and were surprised to see that Jackie had.

Księżnicka and Róża were in position to receive leading crosses in either direction. Paula settled a bit as she reached the top of the box. The Monkey keeper decided to stay close to his line. The lady Monkey made a play for the ball with a sliding tackle from behind. Paula crumpled and clutched her ankle. The referee blew the whistle and showed the tackler a red card. The lady screamed in protest at the referee. Meanwhile Paula rubbed her ankle.

"Get her off the pitch now," barked the ref at the Monkey captain.

The captain pulled his teammate aside and escorted her off the pitch. The Monkey coach yelled at his other female player to go in for one of his midfielders. Nevertheless, the Monkeys would still have to play a man down the rest of the match.

Gina attended to Paula who would be okay after a bit of the cooling power of the "magic spray".

The referee indicated that the foul occurred just inside the box. The Monkey keeper did not like that but thought it wise not to protest. After the necessary substitution was allowed, Róża lined up to take the penalty shot. She stared down the keeper and thought she saw him shudder. Matt was on his feet as she let loose. Róża put a lot of leg behind the ball. The keeper barely reacted as the bomb sailed neatly between his legs.

"Holy fuck," Jackie heard the opposing coach spit. All she could do was smile.

Matt was wishing he had a video camera. Daddy Koneki needed to see what a great player her daughter was. He did not know if Poland had a women's national team, but she was certainly worthy enough for even the United States women's coach to take a look at. She had to get into the system to be noticed. He would make sure she did. After all, the Women's World Cup was coming to the United States next year.

During the remainder of the match, both teams played hard. The Monkeys tried to score on counter attack opportunities, but they were foiled before they could even reach the penalty area. At the end of the game, Paula put one in from midfield making the final score 3 to 0.

Matt came down and gave his sweaty little girlfriend a hug and a kiss.

Jackie smiled at them. It was good to see that he was moving on from being hung up on her. She felt bad for interrupting them, but the standard post match chat was in order. After all, they were playing Barclay's Pub next weekend for the championship.

Carl donated money toward a trophy and medals. He met with Barclay's Pub who usually sponsored the trophy, so they could all agree on a design. The owner of the pub and Carl would also throw the celebratory picnic for everyone in the league.

Jackie wanted to make sure the Stampedistas won that trophy in addition to the scudetto.

Chapter LXXIII

CHICAGO—Stampede defender Vladimir Starkov will have to sit out the next match after receiving two yellow cards in last night's match against the Dallas Lonestars.

The match at Soldier Field ended in a 2-2 draw. The Stampede looked like they had it in the bag until Starkov's take down of Franco Magione in the penalty box. Ivan Smythe took the shot, which grazed Virgil Amat's fingertips.

Virgil got his first start in a Stampede uniform. Dan Danzig supported his teammate from the bench. After the match when asked if he could have stopped the penalty kick, he said, "No one could have stopped that cannon ball shot."

Both teams will get a much-needed rest next weekend, except for the designated all-star players. The FLA All-Star match is slated to take place on Saturday, July 25th in Houston, Texas.

Chapter LXXIV

Monday, July 20, 1998: "Carl, I wish I could go to the All-Star match with you, but my ladies are playing for the championship," opined Jackie over breakfast.

"But I want you by my side. The Stampedistas will be fine without you. I made sure that the girls will be well taken care of after the match."

"I know that, and I thank you for it." She let out a heavy breath of frustration. "I don't know how much you've been reading the discussion lists lately, but—"

"I haven't, especially with this inheritance stuff dropped in my lap, but do go on. I don't think I've had the pleasure of one of your rants in a while." Carl grinned over the rim of his coffee mug.

She fought the urge to melt into his gaze. "Look, I'd rather not get into that this morning." She folded the linen napkin and laid it on the table. Pushing her chair back, she stood. "I'm not going and that's final."

Carl watched her retreat to her office space. A green cast from the monitor told him that she was working on plays. She was taking the Stampedistas way too seriously. He wondered if he should just stay behind and support her.

There was little point in continuing the discussion. Jackie was a stubborn woman. As much as that frustrated Carl, it was something he loved about her.

From the office, Carl called Agnes. "Do you have time to see me today? I need some help sorting out a quandary."

"Absolutely, Carl, what time and where?"

"I'll come to you. Is one o'clock fine?"

"Yes, I'll make sure Paul is off on errands."

"Thank you."

Agnes and Paul Novotny lived in a nice bungalow near the heart of the Polish neighborhood. The lawn was neatly manicured with bright flowers growing in beds around the walk. Carl pulled into the crushed rock driveway.

Agnes stepped out and waved him inside. "Come on back to my office."

"Okay." Carl noted the Novotny's taste for old world furnishings. Embroidered hangings proclaimed things in Czech, which he did not easily recognize, except for "Už jsme doma."

Agnes pulled the pocket door shut behind him. Carl breathed in the smell of books old and new. She gestured for him to relax on an antique tufted fainting couch.

A tray containing a glass pitcher of freshly squeezed lemonade and matching tumblers was nearby.

As he made himself comfortable, she reached for a pad of paper and her favorite Waterman fountain pen. She sat across from him.

"Before we begin," Carl said, "I want to be clear that everything said in this room will remain under doctor-patient confidentiality."

"I will not go blabbing to Jackie. She is my friend, and you are my friend, but now you are also my patient. I can't charge you any fees just yet, though. I hope to have my license by mid-August. Quigley is helping me expedite that. In the meantime, I am bonded by ethical honor and the honor of friendship to you."

"Good." Carl let out a heavy sigh. He rubbed his temples as he threw his head back. He closed his eyes and began. "I wish I could be in two places at once."

"Are you talking about this weekend?"

Carl nodded slightly. "I feel like I've made a mistake by asking Jacqueline to forsake her duties as a coach and fulfill her duties has a future wife by accompanying me to the All-Star match."

"Why do you say that?" Agnes tapped the pen top on her chin. She had slipped into her serious doctor mode.

"This morning, she gave me the cold shoulder treatment after a brief discussion about it."

"I see. But I can tell there is something more. Why is it so important to have Jacqueline at your side this weekend? It can't be just for window dressing. I know she is more than that to you."

Carl hesitated before answering, "Alexi Taman."

Agnes raised her eyebrows, but said calmly, "Of course Miss Taman will be there. She owns the New York Mad Cabbies."

"No, no, you don't understand. I cheated on Jacqueline with Alexi."

Agnes nearly dropped her pen. No wonder he was so worried about keeping this conversation mum.

"I'm afraid I will succumb to her charms again. She's not right for me, but I can't resist her," Carl gushed. "It's easy when we are in separate cities. But the match in New York when I went up there, I felt like I was—oh hell, let me start this over."

"Continue when you are ready," Agnes encouraged.

As he collected his thoughts, he took a sip of lemonade. "Okay, I've had a crush on Alexi ever since I got my first hard-on."

"That's understandable. She was and still is a beautiful woman."

"In junior high, I would buy fashion magazines or use my mom's and cut out the pictures of Alexi to hang in my locker. In high school, it grew to be a wondering of why my mom didn't have those opportunities. My mom was a gorgeous woman in spite of it all. She was tall, thin, well proportioned." Carl trailed off. He bit his lip as an image of the murder scene entered his mind. He shook it off.

Agnes waited for him to continue.

"Alexi is about 15 or so years older than me. I should have been able to resist her. No, I'm painting this all wrong. It was mutual. I wanted her just as bad as she wanted me. But her wanting me was the odd part. She said that she had wanted to meet me for quite a while, like she had a crush on me."

"Crushes are poor ways to begin relationships," Agnes put in.

"I know, I know." Carl sat up and reached for the lemonade. He took a long drink. "I haven't encouraged Alexi since, but she's been sending me email. She is hinting at something but I'm not sure what. They are almost veiled threats." He paused to draw a deep breath. "I'm afraid that if I go to the All-Star match without Jacqueline by my side, Alexi will use it in some manner against me, perhaps get me into her bed again."

"Do you want to have sex with Alexi again?"

"I do and that is what bothers me."

Agnes wanted to counsel Carl to stay with Jackie, but she hesitated. "Is it that the sex is so good, or something more?"

"Alexi keeps suggesting that we have a shot at a relationship. She says that the two of us together could be the greatest soccer partnership in the United States. She falls short of just flat out asking me to marry her."

"It seems to me that you have considered it."

"I don't know." Carl leaned back on the couch. "I probably did."

"Before or after you met Jackie?"

Carl closed his eyes. "After." He leaned forward. "But I was not in my right mind. That woman can twist a boy's head."

"But you are a man, Carl Costello, a man. You are not a boy. You slipped, a moment of passion, perhaps even a bit intoxicated by alcohol, her perfume, whatever, but what was the consequence?"

"The nightmares came back."

Agnes quickly jotted down some notes. "You mean the flashbacks to finding your mother's body?"

Carl nodded. "Yes, Jacqueline was the only one who could make them go away. None of the drugs or alcohol I tried worked. Having her around helped me realize it was time to move on, that I could love somebody." He paused. "But since I cheated on her already, am I ready for marriage, Agnes?"

"I could give you some advice on that, but—"

"Please, Agnes, I need the advice."

"This is from my own personal experiences and not from any previous patients. Shortly after I met Paul, I went to college in Prague. Paul had a contract with Brno. He wanted to be transferred or traded to Sparta Prague, but the owner would not hear of it. I met a fellow student whom I developed a crush on. I made sure we were in the library at the same times, in the same areas. Eventually, he asked me out. I let things get a bit too far, knowing full well I had already promised myself to Paul. I ended up breaking Stanislav heart when I married Paul the next summer. But I made the right choice."

"Did Paul know about your indiscretion?"

"I did tell him before we got married. I needed to clear my own conscience and make things right with God. At first he was upset, but he realized that he was the winner and that I truly loved him and only him."

"Do you think I should come clean with Jacqueline about Alexi?"

"If you don't, it will haunt you."

"So what about this weekend? I am obligated to the FLA to make an appearance on behalf of both Philly and Chicago. I know that Jacqueline will be missed by the Philly contingent. Keith had wanted to talk to her a bit more about coaching opportunities. But she never allowed me a chance to talk to her about that aspect."

"I'm sure Keith will admire her commitment to the Stampedistas."

"Yes, but then there is Alexi," Carl protested.

"So what, you had your fun. Learn the power of the word 'no'. She will pressure you, especially since Jackie will not be with you. But you have to learn to resist, otherwise, you are definitely not ready for the one-on-one lifetime commitment of marriage."

Chapter LXXV

Carl walked away from Agnes' house stunned. He did not expect such a harsh reality check. However, he rationalized to himself, she was a psychologist. She was not going to give him a straight answer but let him figure it out for himself. Damn, she was good.

He was too rattled to go back to the office. There was nothing there that could not be handled by other staff members. Instead he just drove aimlessly northwest.

Within a few hours he found himself circling Lake Wisconsin. The wooded surroundings calmed his nerves. It was late afternoon. Perhaps he should just get a place to stay and relax for the evening in a nothingness kind of way.

He found a motel right on the lake that offered boat rentals. The door to the room faced the lake. The same folks also ran a nice family restaurant and a smoky workingman's bar.

Carl checked in. He found himself glad that he still kept an overnight bag for emergencies in each of his cars. He grabbed the tan Hartmann belting leather satchel and tossed it on the bed. Then he went into the bar and ordered a Jack Daniels straight with a Miller Genuine Draft chaser. This was not the place to be a beer or liquor snob.

The locals gave him a grunt of acknowledgement and turned their conversation back to how the Green Bay Packers would fare with their new draft picks in the upcoming season. Meanwhile, a Brewers baseball game aired on three televisions. The evening news was on the fourth. Up here, no one would even know what soccer was. It was exactly what Carl needed. As he ordered a second bottle of Miller, he reached in his pocket and turned off his cell phone.

Chapter LXXVI

TUESDAY, JULY 21, 1998: Jackie awoke to an empty space. Carl's side of the bed was hardly rumpled. That's odd, she thought. I could have sworn I felt him crawl in with me in the middle of the night.

She walked to the spare bedroom to see if Carl decided to sleep in there instead. It was still as perfect as the maid had left it. He was not on the sofa in the living room either. Maybe he slept at the office. She dialed his cell phone. It went straight into voice mail. "Carl, honey, I'm worried because you didn't come home last night. Please call me as soon as you get this message. I love you."

Carl did not arise until nearly eleven in the morning. Having not eaten dinner, he drank himself silly. He glanced at the credit card receipt from the bar. He knew it was not all his. He ended up paying for many rounds for the house. Thank god Monday Night Football had not started yet.

He reached for his cell phone. He turned it on and checked his messages. When he heard Jackie's from early morning, he hung up and dialed her immediately.

"I'm so sorry, Jacqueline. I should have called you," he gushed when she answered.

"Yes, you should have," she scolded. She lightened her tone a bit. "Where are you?"

"I took a drive yesterday afternoon and ended up at Lake Wisconsin. I just needed to get away from everything for a bit—no women, no soccer. No offense, darling. I just needed some time to think, clear my head."

"Will you be back today?"

"Yes, Jacqueline, I will be by your side tonight. I love you, darling, and I will never abandon you."

"I know, love, I know."

Carl checked out and drove home. He called Carrie to see if there were any pressing matters. He hoped he did not have to go by the office and could go straight to the condo. Luckily, that was the case. He was so happy that he had a good crew supporting him. It allowed him to think about what he should do on Saturday.

He must face Alexi without his fair princess by his side. It was a battle that he had to fight on his own. Despite what Agnes had advised, keeping Jacqueline in the dark about the illicit rendezvous was better than coming clean and risking losing her.

Chapter LXXVII

Saturday, July 25, 1998: A brief morning thunderstorm had dampened the pitch in the park. Jackie was not worried. Her Stampedistas had played on wet surfaces successfully in recent weeks. On muddy days, all the ladies were happy to have deep red uniforms rather than white. They felt they looked less like a laundry detergent commercial at the end of the match.

She still wished that Carl could be in the stands. But he promised to watch the video later. Matt posted on the discussion list that he would film the match. Róża wanted to send a copy of the tape to Magia, too.

All of her players arrived an hour early. Jackie insisted on it so there would be ample time to stretch out and go over final game plans. Kickoff was scheduled for one o'clock.

Mirek opted to come out and watch his younger daughters play rather than fly to the All-Star match. He did not have any participatory reason for going. The DC coach and the LA coach were the selected coaches for the teams. The FLA liked to use the coaches from the previous season's championship match as the opposing forces for the All-Star match. This was in the tradition of Major League Baseball and the National Football League's Pro Bowl. Mirek hoped to be a coach for the 1999 All-Star match. Today, he chose his daughters. Księżnicka and Róża were both elated.

Jackie did her best to calm them down. She had noted that they played better when their father was not watching. She was not sure why. Agnes suggested that it was because of Mirek being a coach. She was probably right. Agnes said she would talk to them. She did have some experience in sport psychology.

Doc Gina ran the warm-ups. She taped up those who needed it. Sheila stayed close to Jackie's side helping out with paperwork and reading off stats from notes on Barclay's Pub.

For a recreational league, winning was taken way too seriously between the two teams vying for the championship trophy.

The All-Star match was kicking off in the Astrodome. Houston was beginning to build a new stadium in hopes of bringing back an NFL team, but there was also some buzz about an FLA team being about to play there as well. Carl thought it would be a good market, but might be a difficult sell, even with the large Mexican immigrant population. There was to be a meeting about it among the owners. The FLA was using the All-Star match as a test for the market. Carl had seen the presale numbers and wondered what was going on. They were too low, even with the Dallas Lone Stars generously including the match in their season ticket package. In addition to having to deal with Alexi, Carl was not looking forward to the business luncheon. Perhaps in a professional setting, she would be on her best behavior.

Carl nervously deplaned. Alexi had emailed him her itinerary. Somehow, she managed to arrange a landing time within fifteen minutes of the CSG jet. She, too, owned her own plane, or at least leased a nice one. Carl was not for sure. He had fought the urge to knock back half a bottle of single malt scotch. He needed to stay sober to be able to resist her.

The meeting was in the Houston Grand Plaza Hotel. Alexi suggested that Carl and she share a limousine. Reluctantly, he obliged.

The limo met both jets on the tarmac. The driver loaded the overnight bags in the trunk. Carl noted that Alexi's set of luggage was from one of the designers she used to model for—Louis Vittoun—a sure sign of a high maintenance woman. In contrast, Carl just had an overnight all leather black Tumi duffle, top of the line, but certainly much more practical.

Carl allowed Miss Taman to enter the back of the stretch first. The driver closed the door behind them. He already had their destination. Both were glad, being that neither had been to Houston before.

Carl made sure he sat facing her. He noticed there was a glow about her that was not there the last time they were together. For all he knew, it might have been a new brand of makeup.

"It's good to see you again, Carl," she said.

"Same here, Alexi," he replied politely. He wanted to keep the entire weekend business-minded, so he said, "What is your take on the low numbers for presale for the All-Star match?"

"Oh, hell, darling, you want to talk shop already? We aren't even at the hotel yet."

Carl nodded. He smiled at her annoyance. "So?"

"Let's see, hmm, the past two all-star matches have been busts since they were in non-FLA markets, and were supposedly 'test matches'." She gestured with her fingers. "All-Star games are crap the way they are set up. You truly have to get a full squad out there with some history to get one, incentive for fans of that team to go, and, two, get fans of opposing teams to go. What I'm saying is, have the test matches with a foreign league team versus one of ours, not this all-star match crap."

"Damn, girl, you are bitchy in the morning." Carl laughed. He peeked inside the cooler to see if there was any bottled water. He removed two and handed one to Alexi.

"Thank you. The flight was a little bumpy over the storms in Kentucky. Sorry." Alexi hoped that Carl might take her bitchiness as PMS instead of moodiness from pregnancy. She thought that she was beginning to show. Her old clothes fit a little tighter, but it was not enough for anyone to notice. She wanted to save the drama for his wedding day in October.

"So," Carl continued, "you are saying that even if there was an all-star FLA team, they should be playing a team like the Chivas?"

"For ticket sales yes. For the good of the league, we should drop this crap."

Carl nodded. If it weren't for the league-obligated appearance, he would be rooting for the Stampedistas this afternoon. FLA President Lance Merton wanted all the owners to be present at the meeting.

"Let's talk about something else," she suggested. "How are you and Jackie getting along? I hear you are going to have a beach wedding the night before the Cup."

Whew, thought Carl, talking about Jackie is a safe subject. I hope she doesn't decide to steer it otherwise. "Yes, the plans are going smoothly. I think Jackie is having her dress made in Paris. She ducked out for several hours when we went over there for the World Cup Final."

"I wish she would have called me. I could have arranged for her to meet with Vera Wang or another designer of her choice. I still have a good relationship with all of them."

Hmm, she's up to something, thought Carl. He could sense some type of underhanded motivation between the lines. "Wow, I wish I would have thought of that." No, I don't. I don't want her anywhere near Alexi alone. "I have no idea what Jacqueline is planning on wearing, but she must have certainly liked something she saw in the boutique window. Speaking of designers, rumor has it that you have a redesign for the Cabbie kits next year."

"Yes, but I'm not going to tell you. It's good to redo patterns every couple of seasons to keep sales of merchandise fresh."

"I agree."

The pair stayed on safe subjects the entire ride to the hotel. Still sexual tension hung between them. Carl's primal body wanted to take her right there in the back of the limo. His mind repeated Jacqueline's name as a reminder of restraint. It was going to be an interesting 24 hours.

Matt thought he was over Jackie. While things had been going well with Róża, every Saturday afternoon for the past few weeks he found himself desiring Jackie. He tried watching Róża as she warmed up with long stretches, but his eyes kept drifting back to Jackie. It was not Róża who gave him the hard-on every Saturday afternoon for the past few weeks, it was the woman he could never have. Róża was sweet enough, but she was not yet fully a woman.

Jackie oozed intensity in everything she did, every move, every word. Matt loved that about her. Plus, she was absolutely beautiful. Today, her brunette locks were piled on top of her head and bound together with a soccer ball printed, red scrunchie. She wore no makeup, except for some sunscreen scented like a tropical island, which Matt smelled whenever the breeze wafted her scent his way.

Matt checked his watch. Time to set up the video camera. Kickoff was twenty minutes away.

The banquet meeting was in a small room that afforded them privacy. Carl passed a few reporters on the way in. Three of the four were from Spanish-language publications. This was to be a meeting of strictly owners and Lance Merton. Coaches and general managers were not allowed. The league had another room reserved with buffet-style fare for them. The media was given access to the coaches, but not the owners. Lance wanted to assure that business was attended to without interference.

Carl sat down near the head of the conference table. Jon and Betty Eagle sat next to him. He was glad, until Alexi sashayed in and seated herself across from him. Sugar Lipinski sat next to Alexi. Sugar made his money in acting over in Europe before crossing over to Hollywood. He owned the Los Angeles Stars. Teddy Schakelford drove down from Dallas. Evan Kingston from Miami was seated next to Betty Eagle. He also owned the Tallahassee Tempests. Paddy Kirkhoven, Sr. flew in from Boston. Clark Logan had come down from just checking up on stadium construction progress in Columbus.

San Francisco's primary investor, Frank Steele, was eager to see Carl. He wanted to begin trade negotiations for Brendan Glazier. He felt that having an out of the closet gay player on his team might boost lagging attendance, plus having a strong striker up front would help probably help win more matches. Frank was disappointed that he did not get to sit closer to Carl.

A fruit appetizer course was served. Lance called the meeting to order. "Good afternoon, ladies and gentlemen, as you know there has been some talk about expansion again. I am not sure if we want to do it this soon. We have had wonderful success in both Philadelphia and Chicago thanks to Carl Costello and the wonderful staffs in both cities."

Carl nodded. "It hasn't been easy."

"We know," Lance acknowledged. "The reason we are meeting in Houston for the All-Star match is because Diego Juan Sanchez wanted to see what the neighborhood response would be. Diego and I have been talking with Houston officials about basing a team here. We would all like to expand again, but next year we feel would be too soon." He paused.

A murmur of agreement coursed through the room.

"I have had an opportunity to speak with some of you individually. Teddy Shakelford expressed the most concern. I want him to speak out first. Teddy, you have the floor."

Teddy cleared his throat and took a sip of water. "I've had the opportunity to host DJ in Dallas. He looked around our stadium and began to bash FLA attendance numbers. That particular match was the best crowd of our entire history. Yes, we all could do better. I would love to see the pigskin-sized stadiums filled for every match and scalpers hawking tickets for hundreds of dollars."

"You're dreaming again, Teddy," cracked Frank.

"Maybe I am, but aren't you, too? Isn't this a dream shared by all of us? Is this not a dream that we could reach?"

"May I say something, Teddy?" Sugar interjected.

"Yes, sir, go ahead."

"I would permit DJ to put a team anywhere he wants in any non-FLA city so long as he builds his own stadium. We simply cannot have our teams playing in cavernous empty places. It looks bad to the rest of the world."

"You don't have to share with an NFL team," Alexi commented.

"No, but UCLA football takes precedent in Rose Bowl scheduling. Why? Because they make a lot more money off of them. We have got to get better venues. No expansion without a soccer specific stadium built first," said Sugar.

Jon Eagle said, "We need to expand two teams at a time to maintain balance."

Lance said, "Yes, that is true. Any other suggestions?"

"We have looked at Denver in the past," said Carl. "I've fielded more than a few phone calls from upset fan groups working to get an FLA team there. They are pissed that I chose Philadelphia over them."

Lance nodded. "I've gotten more, believe me." He rolled his eyes. "You don't want to take on another team, though, right?"

"No, two teams are enough for any of us," Carl said. Underneath the table, Alexi had kicked off her right pump and extended her leg to nuzzle Carl's leg. He tried not to flinch and give her a discrete look of disgust.

Alexi looked directly at Carl when she said, "We don't want any one owner having too much power in the league." Her foot was working its way up his leg.

Carl felt his cock rising. Dammit, Alexi, he thought, why can't you leave well enough alone?

"I will suggest Denver as the site of the 1999 All-Star match," Lance tossed out.

"Why not stop this test market bullcrap after this year?" Alexi spat.

"Argue your point, Alexi," Lance allowed with a heavy sigh.

Alexi went on a nearly five-minute rant. The men at the table were patient. The cater waiter set down main course dishes around them the entire time she was talking. Carl was amused, until she ended with, "And Carl will back me up on all that."

He glowered at her. "I certainly will not. Test market matches are fine, but they should not be a final gauge of interest and potential attendance and revenue streams. Season ticket deposits, now we're talking."

"What should the minimum number be?" Lance asked. The idea intrigued him.

"No one here has a team that is even close to approaching 5000 yet. I'd love to set that number for all of us, but I feel that perhaps at least 1000, even 2000 would be the ideal target." Carl had done some research on it. Rules would have to be set up to protect the money, time limits, and so on. A Denver soccer group was beginning to get together the numbers and legal resources to begin taking deposits.

Lance said, "1000 seems reasonable. Carl, I'll talk to you about the logistics later. Do we have a motion?"

Sugar Lipinski said, "I motion that in order to have a market seriously considered for FLA expansion a number of no less than 1000 season ticket deposits must be acquired and held in a trust account."

"I second that," Carl said.

"All in favor say, 'aye'," said Lance.

All but Alexi in unison voiced, "Aye."

"Opposed?"

"Nay," said Alexi.

"Motion carries. I will speak with DJ about this new requirement. Now, you all shut up so we can eat and get over to the stadium."

After the meeting, Alexi cornered Carl. "I want you and I to work on bringing Denver aboard. I know as well as you do what those fans there have been up to. DJ is serious and even with this requirement, I know the little sneak will put down 1000 of his closest friends and pay the deposit money himself just so he can get a team there."

Carl raised an eyebrow. "Really?"

Alexi nodded fully. "Yes, really. Now, you and I together have the resources and cash to take on another team. Neither of us can handle it alone."

"You're joking, right?"

"Hey, I've got a villa in Vail I haven't visited in a while."

"Holy shit, you're not."

"No, I am not." Alexi narrowed her eyes. She was insulted that Carl thought that she was joking the entire time. "I want to own another team. The league needs to expand in pairs to keep the tables even. You know this. I don't think DJ is willing to take on two new teams. I'm surprised you were, frankly. But you've done well, Carl. We both have the money and the power to pull it off."

"I'll have to think about it." Carl tried to brush it off. She was close enough for him to smell her. It was subtle, unlike her.

She extended her fingers and brushed them against his cheek. "You do that. But you'll see. You and I will be in a partnership agreement before long."

Her touch sent shudders down his spine. He watched her walk away. He sank into the wall. She wanted more than just a business partnership. That much was more than obvious. She had his number and she knew it. Yes, Alexi was a dangerous woman.

Kickoff was a little behind schedule as the head referee was late getting to the field. The Stampedistas won the toss and elected to receive the ball first. The Róża—Księżnicka tandem drove hard toward the net. Róża backheeled a backwards cross to a barely onside Księżnicka who maneuvered easily around the Barclay's Pub keeper. Their keeper had come off his line as a last line of defense. He knew he was beat. Księżnicka kicked the ball neatly into the goal. 1-0 Stampedistas in what was still the first minute!

Jackie, who should have been excited, felt a cold chill overtake her body.

As Carl shook off the sexual tension, he glanced at his watch. Jackie's game should have started by now. He wondered how they were doing.

The Stampedistas jogged back for the restart. Mirek applauded his daughters. Maybe, he thought, I should have them out at Halas Hall for practices. They'd sure give Amat a good workout.

Barclay's Pub attempted to respond with an equally fast attack. But the Stampedista back line was ready for them. A precision tackle and the girls were on the march again.

Matt regretted having to keep track of the action with the camera. He wanted to whoop and perhaps even start a Section 12 style chant. Róża's performance was actually giving him goose bumps.

Carl walked slowly back to his room. His mind was heavy. He wanted to call Jackie, but she was wrapped up in her coaching gig. He dared not interrupt her. Agnes was out, too, because she was more than likely in the starting eleven. He felt like he needed a stiff drink, but that was the worse thing he could do, especially since it would lower his resistance to Alexi's charms.

A business partnership? It had to just be a way to stay closer to him since he had no intention of marrying her. Jacqueline was to be his betrothed.

Carl opened the door to his room and unzipped his toiletry kit. He pulled out a bottle of Vicodin and a bottle of Jack Daniels. At least he would be able to numb himself enough to not feel the urge to give into the temptress. He washed back one with a long swig from the fifth.

Jackie's ladies hammered toward goal, but the game remained in the midfield. Agnes dogged her mark relentlessly in the defensive end. The Cristobals sought slots through which to get the ball to the Konekis, but the Barclay defenders swept it away. Leah found a way to drive up the left flank through a huge opening. Róża and Księżnicka struggled to stay open and in an onside position. Leah could not get a clean pass off, so she managed to nutmeg the challenging defender. Seeing a narrow strike opportunity arise from a tight angle, she struck the ball with her left foot and followed through with a hard run, in case it was deflected. The ball hovered forward inches above the turf. The Barclay keeper dove toward the far post and managed to get a glove tip on it. Księżnicka, coming up from the right wing, was in a position to tap it back the other direction. The keeper could not recover fast enough. 43rd minute, 2-0 Stampedistas.

Jackie applauded the goal. But her joy did not last long. Barclay's Pub was pumped full of vengeful adrenaline.

They took the restart and plowed toward netminder Margaret. Agnes missed her tackle and nearly twisted her ankle in the process. Carrie was the last defender before a one-on-one chance against Margaret. The top of the penalty area was crossed. Carrie was beat. With a strong arm to the shoulder, she pulled the striker to the turf. The ball trickled toward Margaret who scooped it up. The referee blew the ball dead and ran to the box.

Teammates of the fallen rushed over. The lady midfielder got in Carrie's face and screamed, "You fucking cunt!" She pushed Carrie backwards. "Don't fuck with my man." As Carrie stumbled to the ground, the woman spat in her direction.

The referee spoke in a surprisingly calm tone, "Ladies, chill out. Red card for you, Miss Andrews. And a lovely yellow for you, Miss Jones."

Margaret helped Carrie up. Shaking her head, Carrie left the pitch. No sense in protesting. She knew it was the right call.

Margaret positioned herself for the ensuing penalty kick. Miss Jones sized up the net and buried it in the left half of the net. Margaret guessed the wrong direction. 45th minute, 2-1 Stampedistas.

During halftime, Jackie could not focus. Her Stampedistas were doing well and were in position to win the trophy, even if they were going to be down a woman for the next 45 minutes. Jackie kept feeling odd chills. She knew it was not physical, at least she did not think it was. She drew a deep breath and let it out slowly. She had to focus on the match.

Agnes, as usual, was substituted out at halftime. She still had another twenty or so minutes left in her, but her ankle ached from the missed tackle. She went up to sit with her husband. Paul handed her a towel and her favorite color of cold Gatorade. "Are you alright, love?" he asked in their native Czech.

"I'm fine, but I think that something is bothering Jackie." She fumbled in her duffle for her cell phone. "I need to call Carl."

Paul gave her a funny look and a shrug. She had always been too wrapped up in her clients and friends to be concerned about her own well-being. He was certain that Carl might have been seeing Agnes for counseling. Not that it mattered to him. Even if he did know, he respected his wife profession and his boss' right to privacy.

Agnes stepped away from the bleachers and dialed Carl's cell phone. She hoped that the business meeting luncheon he was required to attend was over. The phone rang almost enough times for it to go into voice mail.

"Carl Costello," he answered in a slow voice.

"It's Agnes. How are you doing?"

The Vicodin he had swallowed was beginning to kick in. He glanced at the clock on the bedside table. "Shouldn't you still be on the pitch?"

"I always play only one half. You know that," Agnes snapped back. "Now, back to you and Jackie. You haven't done anything to forget about your fiancée, have you?"

"Not yet." A wry smile crossed his lips. He thought of how Alexi liked to get close to him. He remembered the taste of her lips. "I don't think I can resist Alexi anymore. Alexi always gets what she wants. And she wants me."

"You sound a little, um, fucked up. What have you taken or drank?"

"Mmm, Vicodin."

"How many?"

"Just one."

"What else?"

"Jack."

Agnes wished she could teleport Jackie and herself to Houston right now. She looked over at her coach. Jackie was distressed and did not know why. Carl and Jackie had a strong bond, but Agnes doubted that even it could withstand the wiles of Alexi Taman. A one-night stand with the woman, yes, but this whole thing sounded much more serious. Carl was not thinking clearly and could not whenever he was near the lithe supermodel. He had told her as much, but not directly. As a skilled professional, Agnes knew how to read in between the lines to get to the source of her clients consternation.

"How much Jack Daniels?"

Carl squinted in the direction of the bottle on the nightstand. "A lot, I think."

"Listen to me. I'm going to call your hotel and have some stiff black coffee sent up to you. You had better answer that door when it arrives and drink it. Do you understand?"

"Yes, mom."

"That's right, it's going to be coming from your mother, too. She is speaking through me. She doesn't want you to be fucked up like this. From what you've told me, she kept a clear head herself. She had to in order to survive. And so do you. Her steadiest relationship was your father, despite the circumstances. Jackie is your steadiest relationship right now. If you hurt her and fuck up that bond, I swear to God I'm going to kick your ass from here to Prague," Agnes spewed.

Carl shed a small tear. She was right. Agnes was always right.

"Do you understand what I'm saying to you?" she barked.

Carl replied in a small voice, "Yes."

"Good, now tell me the name of the hotel so I can send up the coffee."

Once Agnes had the name and number of the hotel, she called the room service and spoke with the headwaiter. Agnes gave them a generous tip with instructions that whoever delivers the coffee had to stay in the room and talk with Carl. She explained her reasons. The headwaiter said that he would be able to send up their best conversationalist.

Agnes rejoined Paul.

"What was that about?" her husband asked.

She wanted to tell him everything, but restrained herself. "Carl needed some advice." Her eyes watched Jackie.

Paul nodded. "I sometimes wish that you were not so involved in your clients' lives," he mused.

She laid a hand on his thigh. "Sometimes we all need a little extra guidance." She kissed her love's cheek.

The struggle on the grass had grown intense. If Jackie was distracted emotionally at halftime, she was certainly not now. Her lady defenders were in trouble. Margaret was being peppered with shots. Carrie's absence in the back was being felt. It was only a matter of time before a Barclay shot became a goal.

Jackie screamed at the referee for missing calls. She wanted to kill the lineswoman for missing several Barclay offside calls. She was not sure if she liked the new style of coach she had become that afternoon. Frankly, it scared her. It felt beyond just being caught up in the moment.

At one point, the referee jogged by and shook his finger at Jackie. "Watch it, Harris. This is your only warning."

Jackie simply glared in reply. She was staying in her demarcated area. She turned her attention back to her aggressive Stampedistas on the attack.

Księżnicka and Róża were pushing toward the net. Księżnicka broke away from two defenders. The Barclay keeper charged Księżnicka. Róża pushed up for any possible rebound. Just as Księżnicka let off a strong left-footed shot, the netminder lunged forward with both fists extended. He completely missed the ball and instead punched Księżnicka in the gut. Księżnicka crumpled. The referee pulled out a straight red card. He also allowed the goal, as the ball did find its way into the bag.

Róża attended to her sister. Doc Gina dashed to the scene. Jackie hollered at Leah to begin warming up. Leah would go in for Księżnicka.

No Barclay players protested the call. It was not worth it. They were already down 3 to 1 in the 68th minute. It was probably going to be 4 to 1 in just a matter of seconds.

Doc Gina helped Księżnicka to the sidelines. Jackie informed the fourth official of the change. Leah came in and lined up to take the penalty kick.

Barclay's coach had their lady on the pitch, Miss Jones, don the keeper's jersey to finish the match. Leah knocked a nice right-footed shot into the dead center. Jones lunged to the left. Róża congratulated Leah as they jogged to midfield, but her eyes kept looking toward the bench where Jackie and Sheila were attending to Księżnicka.

Sean wrung his hands. Matt reached out and patted him gingerly on the back. "Księżnicka will be just fine. She's a tough girl," reassured Matt.

Jackie had Księżnicka lie on her back. Sheila helped hold some ice on her lower ribs. "It hurts to breathe," Księżnicka moaned.

"I hope they are just bruises. Gina will have to look at you more closely after the match," Jackie said. She stroked the Polish princess' hair. "Just stay calm. Sheila and I will be here until then."

Księżnicka nodded.

The game progressed, ten on ten.

Carl failed to answer the door when the coffee arrived, so the waiter entered with his passkey. The servant set the tray down on the table and went to check on Carl.

Carl was passed out on the bed. He was still fully clothed. The empty bottle of Jack Daniels remained in his hand. A prescription bottle with the lid off was on the nightstand. The man checked for breath sounds and a pulse. Carl's pulse was weak and his breathing was shallow. Shaking his head with a sigh, the employee dialed 911 and then hotel security.

Within minutes, security arrived. The guard also checked Carl's breathing and pulse. "This guy ain't gonna live much longer unless we get him to the hospital."

"He's got friends. But I think he took more pills and drank more whiskey since I was called to have a pot of strong coffee brought up. Jamie told me what the woman who called in the order said. I just said I would do my best to sober him up."

"Tell Jamie to call back whoever called in the order so they know," said the guard. He kept an eye on Carl's chest, watching it rise and fall slowly.

"Sure thing, Marcus." The waiter dialed his supervisor and told him what was happening.

Agnes' cell phone rang. She listened; then spat, "*Kurva!*" She regained her composure. "Thank you, I'll let his fiancée know. Let me know what hospital he is taken to, please."

"I will, ma'am."

Paul turned to her. "What was that about?"

His beloved let out a heavy sigh. "You can't say anything to anybody, but Carl's overdosed on Vicodin and alcohol."

"Oh my, I didn't think he was that messed up."

"Neither did I."

"Do you want me to arrange for two tickets to Houston?"

"That would be great. I'm so glad you understand, honey." She kissed him and patted his cheek.

Agnes went back down to the Stampedistas' bench. Jackie was still tending to Księżnicka. There were ten minutes left in the match. She watched her teammates push again toward the net. Another goal at this point would be simply adding insult to injury.

Barclay's players increased their level of dirty play. The men were beyond the point of treating the ladies like ladies. They were visibly annoyed at the Stampedistas ability to play 'keep away' and still appear to be pushing for a goal. Another red card was shown to a Barclay player before the game was finished. This time for taking Róża down just outside the box. Róża bounced right back up for more. Jackie wanted to sub her out, but she refused. Leah whipped the free kick into the net.

At the ninetieth minute mark, the referee decided he had seen enough and blew the whistle the end the match. With the score line reading 5 to 1, it was clear that the Stampedistas were the league champions.

Doc Gina tended to Księżnicka and decided to take her to the emergency room for further evaluation. She feared the girl might have cracked ribs.

Agnes pulled Jackie aside. "We've got to talk."

"What's going on?" Puzzlement crossed Jackie's visage.

"Paul is booking you and me tickets to Houston. Carl is in trouble and he needs you." Agnes spoke frankly.

"I guess that explains why I've been feeling all weird today."
"It's your sixth sense and your love telling you that something is wrong."
"It's really serious, isn't it?"
"Yes, it is." Agnes' voice contained sadness.

Carl felt himself being heaved onto a stretcher. He could not move or talk. He felt life draining from his body. He just wanted to escape. He had gone too far this time. Too many pills washed down with too much whiskey.

Lights from the hallway glared through his eyelids. It was too bright. He wanted the darkness of his room. Don't take me away from my room, he said, but no words escaped his mind.

Sirens. He wanted silence. No music, no crowds, no screams of goal, no Alexi, no . . . Jackie . . . he needed Jacqueline.

"He's trying to say something," came a voice from above his body.
"Try to get him to speak. It will help."
"Come on, Mr. Costello, talk to me."

Carl's lips parted slightly, but no sounds were formed. He could not move his jaw or tongue. Jacqueline! His mind screamed, Jacqueline, I love you. I'm sorry, Jacqueline.

The motion of the ambulance ceased. So did the noise. Carl felt himself leave his body. He hovered above it.

"He's coding!" came a shout.

An EMT hopped onto the gurney and began CPR. The ambulance doors flew open. Carl sailed out. He was going to find Jacqueline.

Carl's body was wheeled into the emergency room. "What do we have?"
"Male, 25, took an unknown amount of Vicodin with a fifth of Jack Daniels."
"How long has he been down?"
"He arrested just as we got to the dock."
"We'll take it from here."

Carl floated, but did not know where to go. He was lost. He felt a tug on his arm. He looked over. It was his mother.

Momma?
Yes, Carlito, I'm here.
What's going on?
You've been a very bad boy, mio Carlito.
I know, momma, I know. Am I dead?
No, you are being given a second chance. One that I was not given. I want you to go out there and be the best husband you can be to your sweet Jacqueline.
Thank you, Momma.
I will be with you always, Carlito, watching over you. Remember that.
I will, Momma.
The two spirit bodies hugged. Mother gave her only precious son a kiss on the cheek.
It's time for you to go back, mio. I love you, Carlito.

I love you, too, Momma.

Carl felt his spirit being whisked down and back into his body of flesh. His eyes flew open.

"We got him back. Good job, team."

"Stabilize him and get him a room in ICU. He needs to be closely monitored through the night."

The earliest flights Paul could book were not until 6:35 out of O'Hare. At least that allowed a bit of time to shower and throw together a bag for a few days. Agnes accompanied Jackie to the condo. While her friend freshened up, Agnes nosed through Carl's emails.

She found nothing from Alexi that did not sound like business. Carl had deleted anything personal from her, at least on the home computer.

Jackie's mind was racing. Agnes had not told her much. She hoped it was just a car accident or something, but Agnes would not be as protective and worried about Carl's trouble being made public record if it was. She let the water run over her hair. An image of Carl dying flashed through her mind. She shuddered.

As she stepped out of the shower, she called for Agnes.

"What is it, Jackie?" Agnes replied through the door.

"How come you haven't told me what's going on?"

"I'm sorry. I should have."

"You can come in."

Agnes opened the door and leaned on the frame. "Carl finally came to me for some counseling. He said he was worried about the trip and leaving you behind. He felt guilty about not being at our championship match."

"So what's the big emergency? Was he in some kind of an accident?"

"He fell ill in the hotel room and they had to take him to the emergency room." Agnes felt this was the best way to explain things without revealing too much yet. It was better that the truth came from Carl, if he survived.

"I can go by myself if that's all it is," Jackie said.

"I don't want either of you to go through this alone," she replied with a smile.

"Thank you." Jackie hugged her friend. A nagging thought still lingered in Jackie's mind. She felt that Agnes was not telling her the whole story. Nothing was adding up.

Carl had briefly discussed legal arrangements if something were to happen. He told her that he had his papers updated to reflect her as his heir and grant her power of attorney. She shuddered at the thought, but it was necessary. She hoped these papers would not have to be used before the wedding. Her worst fears were coming true.

As Jackie tossed together a bag for a couple of nights, she retrieved the documents from the safe.

Carl's stomach was pumped and the contents whisked away to the lab for analysis. Unconscious, he rested in ICU. The doctors were unsure when he would wake up.

The amount of Vicodin and alcohol he ingested should have killed him. He had the quick-acting staff of the hotel and Agnes to thank for still being alive.

Internally, his mind still raced. Visions of Alexi taunted him. She kept telling him to leave Jackie and marry her. He told Alexi over and over again that he loved Jackie and would stay with her until the end of time. His mental image of Alexi changed from one enticing outfit to another. Each time, she asked. Every time, he refused. Each time he said the word "no" it emerged from his lips stronger. He felt himself growing stronger inside.

Once an hour, a nurse entered the room and checked Carl's vital signs. His pulse was growing stronger. The EEG readings showed more vibrant brain activity. She made notes on the chart. The RN speculated to her coworkers that Carl might regain consciousness before the night was over.

Agnes and Jackie landed late in the evening in Houston. The night air was stifling. Both ladies paused to catch their breath as they stepped out to enter the taxi pickup area. Agnes paused to check her voice mail for the name of the hospital. She breathed a sigh of minute relief upon hearing that it was the one run by Rice University.

Visiting hours were well over. Agnes showed her doctor's credentials to the ICU desk nurse. She stated that Carl Costello was a patient of hers. The middle-aged African-American adjusted her glasses as she tried to make out the Czech document. She stated that she would have to check this out with the on-call doctor.

Jackie pulled out her power of attorney papers and slapped them on the counter. "Will this help? I'm his fiancée. He has no living relatives. These notarized papers give me power of attorney in case Carl is incapacitated. We want to see him now."

The woman cleared her throat and read the papers. She made no indication that she was going to tell the pair what room Carl was in.

"Dr. Agnes Novotny is Carl's psychiatrist. She also has a legal right to view her patient."

"Not here in Texas she doesn't," barked the woman, "not until I have clearance from Dr. Jimenes. As for you, miss high and mighty, visiting hours ended at 8:00. You are going to just have to wait until 8:00 tomorrow morning when they start again."

Agnes placed a hand on Jackie's mouth. She said, "We'll just go wait over there." She pointed to a few chairs in a stark waiting area. "Call Dr. Jimenes. We would like to speak to him directly."

As Agnes escorted Jackie away from the desk, the desk nurse first paged the hospital's authorized translator for Czech, a janitor. Fifteen minutes passed before the janitor arrived. He looked over Agnes' credentials. He said they appeared to be authentic. Only then did the nurse call Dr. Jimenes.

A portly fellow of Mexican descent emerged from around a corner. "Dr. Novotny and Miss Harris, I apologize for Nurse Johnson's rudeness. I'm Dr. Ron Jimenes. I did not treat Mr. Costello when he arrived earlier this afternoon, but I can fill you in. I'll take you to see him."

The ladies followed the man. They passed by the desk first, whereupon Nurse Johnson was instructed to return the documents.

They paused just outside the room. "Costello has been unconscious since he came in," began Dr. Jimenes. "He had ingested an unknown amount of Vicodin and a fifth of Jack Daniels. Never a healthy combination. He arrested just as he arrived at the hospital. The ER was able to revive him. His stomach was pumped and the contents were sent to our lab. I am still awaiting the results. We should have those in the morning. We just want to be sure there were not any other drugs in his system. Nurses on staff report that his vital signs are getting stronger each hour. We hope that he wakes up soon so we can better evaluate brain and physical function. I think having both of you here will help him recover faster. Miss Harris, you can go on in. Dr. Novotny, I would like to speak to you doctor to doctor in my office."

Jackie did not say a word and slipped inside the room. She threw herself half onto Carl's body. Her hands wrapped around his torso. She sobbed onto his chest, wetting the gown he had been changed into, soaking his soft chest hair.

Carl sensed that someone was there other than the nurse who arrived on the hour, other than the doctor. Jacqueline was here. She had come for him. It was not Alexi. Only a true love would come. His true love was Jacqueline. His mother was right. He could not give up now. He had to fight back. *I love you, Jacqueline Harris.*

Chapter LXXVIII

Sunday, July 26, 1998: Agnes seated herself across from Dr. Jimenes.

He spoke with a Texas drawl. Agnes figured he was at least a second or third generation American. She did not like the Southern accents of the United States. She found many of them hard to understand. Thankfully, the doctor's accent was not so pronounced.

"How is it you still have a Czech Republic doctor's credentials, Dr. Novotny?" He stroked his chin.

"I am still awaiting the proper documents from immigration and the Illinois board." Agnes should have guessed what this conversation was going to be about. Her powers of intuition were waning from being in a state of near exhaustion.

"And Mr. Costello is your patient?"

"I have been treating him free of charge. He's my husband's boss. I offered my services as a friend first and let him come to me."

"Do you think this was an attempted suicide?"

She shook her head and shrugged. "I hope not. All he stated when I spoke with him on the phone, at which point he told me that he only took one Vicodin and half a bottle of whisky, that he wanted to get relaxed enough to not have any sexual urges toward another woman. Either he lied to me about the amount then or he ingested a lot more after he hung up. I ordered a pot of coffee to be brought up. Staff checking up on Carl is what saved him."

"You are right about that, ma'am." He looked down at Carl's file. "Can you tell me anything else that you observed or that he told you that might help?"

"All I know is that he was a lot worse off before he met Jackie. He had been experiencing what is likely post-traumatic stress syndrome from finding his mother's murdered body. He recently had to deal with the parole board for her killer. It was not easy on him, but could have been a lot worse if it weren't for Jackie being there to support him."

"Was he on Prozac or any other anti-depressants?"

Agnes shook her head. "Not that I am aware of. I can't prescribe anything at the moment, but the team doctor Gina Hargrove would be willing to help out in that regard if necessary."

"Team doctor?"

"Oh yes, the Chicago Stampede. Carl is the owner of the Stampede and the Philadelphia Minute Men. He was in Houston for the All-Star match," Agnes explained.

"Oh right, soccer. I'm an Astros fan, sorry." Dr. Jimenes smiled. "Would Dr. Hargrove have Carl's medical files?"

"I think so. I'll give you her contact info. Please advise her to keep the reasons under wraps if you talk to her before I do. Carl would want to keep this affair private."

"Yes, ma'am."

Agnes continued, "Any media inquiries please instruct the staff to direct to myself or Jacqueline Harris." She stood. "I need to check on Jackie and would like to review the workup on Carl when he came into the emergency room."

Dr. Jimenes handed Agnes the chart. "Here you go. I'll join you."

Jackie was still lying on top of Carl. She stroked his hair. Her tears had stopped because she knew he was alive. Her ear lay against his chest. She listened to his slow steady heartbeat. Her breathing matched his.

Agnes and Dr. Jimenes entered the room. Agnes placed her hand on Jackie's hair. "Honey, we need to talk to you."

Jackie slowly raised her head and blinked. "Is he going to wake up?"

Dr. Jimenes fielded the question. "We don't know. With you here, Jacqueline, I'm positive he will wake up faster."

"Agnes?" Jackie probed.

"I'm afraid he's right. We don't know," Agnes said.

Jackie turned her attention back to her beloved. "Carl, honey, wake up for me." She kissed him. His lips were dry and cracked. "Agnes, do you have any Chapstick?"

"Yes, just a minute." Agnes dug in her purse. "Here."

The doctors watched Jackie affectionately rub lip balm on Carl. "Here you are, honey," she cooed. "I love you. I need you to wake up, Carl. Please wake up for me."

Dr. Jimenes tapped Jackie on the shoulder. "I want to check Carl's coma scale reading and his vital signs."

Jackie stood up. "Okay." She tried to pull herself together. She had not felt so strongly about anyone before, so tied to a soul as she did Carl's, not even to her own family. She was glad that Agnes was there. She hugged her friend.

Agnes escorted Jackie out of the room. "I need to go find us a hotel. Will you be okay alone? Do you want to come with me? It might be a while before Carl wakes up."

"I don't know. I suppose it would be good to go with you so I know where the hotel is. I might feel better if I wash the tears off my face." Jackie smiled weakly. "I just want to get back soon. I want to be by Carl's side when he wakes up."

Agnes laid her hand on Jackie's shoulder. "I know you do."

Carl sensed Jackie leave. His mind drifted back into a dreamlike state again.

"Jacqueline, where are you?" He checked his watch. She was late for their wedding. He looked out over the gathered family and friends and business associates. Alexi was seated on the groom's side in the last row.

The scene went black.

"Carl, wake up, it's time to go to school," his mother urged.

Carl was a young teenager again. He was buried underneath the covers. "I don't want to," he protested.

"And why not, young man?" Mother peeled back the covers exposing her son to the sunlight streaming through the window.

"The girl I like won't go to the school dance with me. She turned me down and is going out with Billy Adams. She said I was a zit-faced nerd." He tried to pull the comforter back over his head, but his mom was stronger.

"She'll regret it later," said mom. "Your zits will go away, but your nerdiness is something that makes you you. Just remember that the geeks win in the end. Look at Bill Gates."

"I know, Mom. That's exactly what I told Rina."

"And?"

"She still wants to go with Billy Adams."

"Then she doesn't deserve you." Mother yanked the covers off completely. "Now, get your geeky butt out of bed."

Carl slowly swung one foot onto the floor. "Okay, Mom, I'm getting up."

It was five a.m. Dr. Jimenes studied the printout of Carl's EEG. He made a notation in the chart. "Patient has entered a dreamlike state. Increased brain activity combined with stronger heart and breaths mean it won't be long before he regains consciousness."

Jackie returned at six. She had fallen asleep in the hotel room for a few hours. Agnes left her alone. There was little chance that Carl would come to overnight.

Agnes was dozing when Jackie left. Traffic was minimal going to the hospital. She got breakfast with a strong coffee and entered Carl's room.

Carl's olfactory nerves awoke. He smelled the java. He breathed deeper. Jackie sensed Carl's deep breath. She held the coffee closer. His facial muscles twitched.

"Good morning, darling. It's time to wake up," she cooed in a singsong voice. The short sleep helped her feel a lot better. "You can have my coffee, but first you have to wake up." She took a sip and set the cup on the nightstand.

She pulled a chair closer and opened the paper sack containing the takeout. The smell of greasy bacon and eggs wafted toward Carl. Out of the corner of her eye, she noticed Carl's tongue flick.

She took a tiny bit of egg and placed it on his lips to see if there was any reaction. They parted and he took in the food. She smiled, encouraged. He did not chew, but mashed the bit with his tongue before swallowing.

"Okay, now I know you are playing with me. You are going to have to wake up before I feed you anymore," she stated firmly. She sat down and began to eat.

Carl reached out his hand.

"Carl, honey, you have to sit up and open your eyes if you want anymore of this food," she reiterated.

She thought she saw him smile, but was not sure. She continued to eat. She needed to keep her strength up.

Carl appeared to settle back into a deeper state of sleep. Jackie found it hard to continually watch him, but she did not want to miss the moment when he opened his eyes. She could have taken a magazine from the waiting area or a book from the shelf there. Instead she thought about all the times she had been with Carl in their short few months of whirlwind romance.

Was she being crazy for giving her heart and soul over to this man? Was she just setting herself up to be hurt? And why would Carl try to kill himself? That uncertainty was what bothered her the most.

She stared at Carl, sleeping like an innocent but mischievous child. She wished that she could read his mind. On the other hand, from what little bits he had told her and what Agnes had attempted to clue her in on, she might as well be staring into the pits of hell.

Carl made her happy. Jackie had never before been so full emotionally in her life. Yes, he was handsome. Yes, he had money, but those things were just bonuses. Carl's mother had raised her son to be a gentleman, to treat women with respect, to be warm and loving. Those were the qualities she fell in love with. Those were the ones she sensed the moment he picked her out of the crowd at Axis.

He stirred. She stood and began to stroke his hair. She laid her lips on his. He responded. His eyes opened. He blinked as his eyes adjusted to the light. "You're here," he said in a cracked voice.

"Yes, honey, I'm here. I'll always be here for you."

Chapter LXXIX

Carl was dismissed later that day. Agnes insisted they all stay in Houston one more night. She wanted to talk to Carl about what happened, if, that is, he remembered much. She had Jackie go off shopping, reminding her that she probably had to find some things for the wedding. Jackie protested mildly, but left anyway.

Carl sat across from Agnes in the hotel room. He was nervous about the ensuing conversation. He knew he had gone too far this last time.

Agnes cut to the heart of the matter. "Was it because of Alexi?"

Carl nodded slightly. His shoulders slumped. Alexi was his Achilles' heel.

"Tell me what happened before you took the Vicodin." Agnes kept a professional tone.

Carl breathed out slowly. "Agnes, I can't resist her charms without fucking myself up with downers, to the point where I don't think or feel. Alexi gets what Alexi wants. She always has. She wants me. Why, I don't really know. She is well aware that I am engaged to Jacqueline. So now, Alexi has proposed a business partnership to get another team in the FLA. She thinks she has it all planned out, claiming that she has the business resources to pull it off, but needs fifty percent of the investment cash from me to do it. She thinks, I think, that if she is with me in a business partnership that she will get closer, that she'll get me in bed again—and more—that way. I don't know what to do, Agnes."

"Have you considered telling Jackie? She will be able to help you."

"How? By forbidding me from seeing her?"

Agnes nodded. "That is likely, yes. And I wouldn't blame her. I would try to do the same thing with Paul, if the situation were ever to come up. But here is what I think. Go into the partnership with Alexi, but give Jackie the reins. It will be the two women. See if Alexi still wants to deal then. If so, then it's a legitimate business offer. Plus if there is a meeting, it will be the two of them or the three of you and not just Alexi and you."

Carl stroked his chin. "Ingenious!"

"Jackie does not have to know the rest of your woes until you are ready for her to know."

"Wonderful idea, Agnes. How can I ever repay you?" Carl stood to reach over and hug his friend and confidant.

Agnes smiled. "I'll just retroactively bill you once I get my license."

Chapter LXXX

The next week was spent with a lot of quiet time at home. Carl felt wrung out and was constantly fighting the urge to pop a few painkillers. Jackie tried not to let him drink, but conceded that a pint or two of ale would not hurt anything.

Mirek wanted to honor the Stampedistas and the Barclay's Pub teams at halftime of the August 6th home match. Carl approved.

Saturday's match was an away game at Los Angeles. Carl did not feel up to traveling. Jackie was glad.

FRIDAY, JULY 31, 1998: Jackie received an early morning phone call from the French seamstress. The dress was ready for a final fitting and adjustment.

"I wish I could come to your boutique but my fiancé needs me nearby right now," Jackie mused. "He's going through a hard time."

"*Oui*, I understand. You must love him very much."

"Yes, yes, I do." Jackie thought for a moment. "How does your schedule look for the next week?"

"I have appointments I can reschedule. It should not be any trouble."

"I want to fly you to Chicago. Then I'd like to have you out in Los Angeles for the wedding weekend in October, in case there are any problems with the dress. I'll even get you tickets to the FLA Cup, if you like le football."

The request did not surprise the lady. She was used to it. She had earned a wonderful reputation for beauty and skill and rich women and men liked to have her at their beck and call.

"*Oui, mademoiselle.* That would be perfect."

"Arrange a flight into O'Hare and tack it onto my bill." Jackie could have used a week away from everything and everyone in Paris, but it was best to bring her seamstress to Chicago. Carl would object, saying that she could have gone to France, but Agnes would be on her side.

As Jackie laid down the receiver, she felt a headache coming on. She rubbed her temples. The last week had been a steady diet of Excedrin and strong coffee. She had not been sleeping well. As she reached for the medicine cabinet, she paused to stare at the dark circles forming under her eyes. Maybe she should cut back on the coffee, she thought.

Carl was not up to running full speed yet. He was not thinking clearly and was in the office in a limited capacity. Thankfully, there was not much to be done. He allowed Jackie to step in and take care of a few minor details.

A few trade opportunities were on the table, but at Mirek's request and Jackie's strong advice, the kibosh was put on them. The team was to remain in the state that it was in, at least until the off-season. Mirek had come to the conclusion that they would break themselves out of their minor slump.

Chapter LXXXI

SATURDAY, AUGUST 1, 1998: Molly complained loudly enough about her suspension from work that she was offered a front office position with the company. She took it. It was easy, often boring work, but at least it was a paycheck. She wanted to try to remain financially independent of Ian or any man for that matter.

She had to work in the morning, so that nixed any tentative plans to travel with Ian and the team to Los Angeles. She kissed him bon voyage at the airport. "I love you, Ian."

"I love you, too," he replied.

She made a lot of phone calls trying to find replacements for last minute call offs. She gained a new appreciation for the scheduling department personnel. Despite the busy work, she was bored. Renata had to work security at a rave that night. Molly sighed, guess I'll have to hit the clubs by myself tonight. Better than staying home.

The team had a light workout in the hotel exercise facilities. Ian and Carlos opted for a swim. They raced for the first few laps. They ended in a dead heat.

"Ian, you're a good swimmer."

"So are you," Ian replied in amazement.

"Do you surf?" Carlos pulled himself up out of the water.

"Yeah, I used to. Can't in Chicago."

Carlos laughed. "Sometimes, the wind makes big waves on the lake." He started to towel off. "We need to save energy for the game later."

Ian climbed out. "I agree. The Stars are a tough team at home. We'll have a hard time cracking through their defense."

They made quite a pair walking back to their room. Both had their towels draped around their necks. Ian wore only a red Speedo. Carlos wore simple elastic-banded swim trunks. Both sported chiseled physiques.

One young maid tried to avert her eyes, but could not help flirting with Carlos. He smiled back. "*Hola*," he said with a wink.

She just giggled like a schoolgirl, watching the pair round the corner.

Ian suggested, "You should invite her to the game. We have several tickets to use for friends and family."

Carlos shrugged.

"Go on; she was cute."

"Okay, I go." Carlos wrestled the door open with his arms. He scurried down the hall and peaked around the corner. He spotted the housekeeping cart. Ian is right, he thought, I should invite the chica to the game. He took a deep breath and approached the cart.

The lady did not notice him. She came out of a room to retrieve a fresh batch of linens. He watched her rear wiggle underneath the polyester uniform.

"*Con permiso*," Carlos said.

The housekeeper looked up. "*¿Sí?*"

He asked in his native tongue, "Do you like fútbol?"

"A little," she replied. "Why?"

"*Soy Carlos Cortez.* I play with Chicago Stampede." He extended his right stump. Gingerly, she gripped it for a shake. "*Soy Lupe.*"

"Would you like to come see me play tonight, Lupe?"

"Okay, but *mi hijo* needs a ticket, too."

"*No problema.*" He paused. "How old is your son?"

"He's five." She smiled.

"*Por favor,* write your name so I can leave tickets for you at will call."

"*Muchas gracias,*" she said. She wrote down her name and handed it to Carlos. He gripped it with his stumps. She kissed him lightly on the cheek.

Carlos scurried back to his room. Ian let him in. "She has a son," he said. There was a hint of disappointment in his voice. "I said I would get her two tickets."

Ian took the piece of paper from his teammate. "You did something nice and that's good." He crossed to the phone.

The Mexican nodded. "She did give me a little kiss. I know Gemma won't mind."

The match kicked off shortly before sunset. Mirek made a few lineup adjustments to accommodate for Starkov's red card suspension. The team captain, Baumgartner, stayed in Chicago. He was nursing a pulled calf muscle. Gina advised that he not make the trip. She did not want to risk a blood clot forming on the long flight. Paul Novotny wore the captain's armband that night.

DeAnya sang the national anthem. Ian stared at the lady. Her shape, her voice was familiar. She hit every note perfectly. As she finished and was escorted off the pitch by LA Stars owner Sugar Lipinski, it hit him. That was his ex-girlfriend Deanna. She had rebranded herself. Who knew she could sing, too?

He watched Sugar kiss her in a more than just a friendly manner. His heart sunk. He knew that they broke it off cleanly. She wanted to go back to Los Angeles and he let her. However, he found it strange that Deanna, DeAnya—whatever she wanted to call herself—still ended up with the Stars; she had never really expressed much interest in what Ian did on the field.

He shook himself as they took their positions on the grass for kickoff. He had to find a way to concentrate on the game at hand.

Molly settled in at Sueños early. She found a nice comfy barstool with an unobstructed view of the television. She opted for the cheap domestic on special that night, since she was short on cash—unless someone else started buying, of course.

Lawrence bellied up to the bar next to her. The broadcast cut in from commercial as DeAnya walked off the pitch. He pointed and commented to Molly. "Isn't that Ian's ex?"

Molly shrugged. "Maybe. I thought her name was Deanna. It's an awfully close resemblance. But then again a lot of the women in LA look alike."

"Same plastic surgeon," Pauline piped in.

Molly sighed on the inside as she took a long swig of Miller Lite. It's going to be an interesting night.

The spirited match sprayed lots of sand fill upward from tackles on both ends of the pitch. Captain Dan recorded his first of many saves in the match in the fifteenth minute. He screamed at his defensive line for letting them through. By the end of the game, Dan would be hoarse.

Paul smacked Ian on the back of the head several times. "Get your head out of your ass," Paul warned him. Even Mirek got fed up with Ian's level of play. Maxwell Harp came on for him in the 79th minute.

The Stampede had been down since Xuan Xavier Xoy scored for the Stars in the 21st minute off a beautiful bending corner kick. The Stars just kept beating them back. The Stars second goal came off of a direct free kick in the 65th minute, after Brendan received a yellow card for a nasty tackle on Xoy. The heavy boot of Lancelot Stevens powered the ball through the Stampede wall and past Captain Dan.

Ian slumped down on the bench. He sipped sports drink slowly as he cooled off. Why did Deanna have to be there and get back into his head?

With little comment to the folks around her, Molly watched the game. She shook her head at Ian's miscues. She could sense that something got into his head. He only messed up when he was mentally distracted. She began to think that he would be subbed out at halftime. Half the bar patrons watching the match clapped when Ian was subbed out. Molly lowered her head in disgust.

There grew hope for the Stampede in the 89th minute when Mickey Madison was shown a yellow card for dragging down Harp just inside the penalty box. Cristobal lined up to take the shot. It came off his foot wrong and went just wide of the post. Ironically, Tomlinson, the Star keeper, had leaped the other way.

Molly threw her hand in the air. "God you guys suck today," she yelled at the transmitted image.

There was a general murmur of agreement.

Pauline patted Molly on the shoulder. "There's always next week."

Molly brushed off the hand. She gave Pauline a hard look. Pauline backed off. Molly finished her beer and left the bar.

She sat behind the wheel of her car. For five minutes, she relished the silence.

The final whistle blew leaving the Stampede with a loss of 2 to 0. Mark Johnson and Ante Nastav came over and cornered Ian. "We expected a better performance from you, Tigg," Mark said.

Ian shrugged. "I just couldn't get past seeing Deanna with Sugar. How long has that been going on?"

"Probably since shortly after the two of you started going on," Ante said.

Mark nodded, "Might as well know the truth now, since your broke up."

Ian sighed. "No wonder she wanted to get back to LA."

They all stopped and began signing autographs for some kids and other fans. Ian asked, "Do you guys still go out to SambaSinTrick?"

"Yeah, they're still around. Get the whole team together and come on out. They never ID us, so don't worry about Carlos," Ante replied.

"Cool, it will be good to catch up and shake Deanna from my head." Ian headed off to the visitor's locker room. "See you over there."

Molly drove out to Smiler Coogan's. She needed a good dose of metal. It would not quite be the same without her running buddy Renata, but she could manage. None of the bands on the bill were connected to Jack, so she could likely relax and perhaps blow off some steam in the pit.

Before going in, she looked at her phone for messages from Ian. There was nothing. She thought about calling him, but hesitated. Let him come to me, she thought. She slipped her phone in her jeans pocket and paid the cover charge.

Ian talked most of the team, including Gina and Mirek, into going to SambaSinTrick.

SambaSinTrick was a Brazilian-themed club near the coast. The main dance floor was on an open-air third floor balcony. The two teams arrived at close to the same time. It was just after eleven, so the club was just beginning to pick up. Several LA fans were already bellied up to the bar and continuing to drink and savor their team's victory.

Ian bought Mirek his first vodka neat of the night. "I'm sorry. I saw Deanna and I couldn't get her out of my head."

Mirek patted him on the back. "I probably should have pulled you out sooner, but so it goes. We'll win the next one. Just relax. We have a late flight back to Chicago, tomorrow."

Ian tried a Brazilian Colônia Malzbier. He thought it was a bit strong, but sipped it just the same. He saw Carlos and Brendan at a table and joined them.

The music slowly increased in volume. Carlos saw Deanna enter with Sugar Lipinski. He nudged Ian. "She's here."

Ian took a quick glance. "Crap. I should have known better. Of course, she would come out to be with the team. Sugar always liked to hang with his players after matches."

Mark came over and straddled a backwards chair as he sat down. "Are you going to be okay with Deanna here?"

Ian shrugged. "I'll be fine. I just have to remember that the break up was mutual."

Carlos suggested, "Why don't you call Molly? She's the one who loves you now."

"Yes, yes, that's a great idea. *Muchas gracias, Carlos.*" Ian jumped up and excused himself to the men's room where it was a bit quieter. He dialed Molly. It went into voicemail. "Just wanted you to know that I am thinking of you, Molly. I love you."

Molly played a few of her favorite songs on the metal-dominated jukebox. The last band on the bill had canceled due to their drummer being arrested the night before for DUI. She joked with the regulars. The Jack and Coke she had been drinking was starting to take effect.

Jacek came in. His hair was starting to grow back. He put his hand on her back in the approximate area of the scar. Molly jumped.

"Relax," Jacek said.

Molly turned around and was relieved to see his familiar face.

"Can I freshen your drink?" he offered.

"Sure." She felt what she thought might be her cell phone vibrating. She ignored it.

Jacek signaled for the bartender and ordered drinks for the both of them. "Out by yourself?"

She nodded. "Yeah, Renata had to work late, and, of course, you know Ian is in LA."

The barstool next to her was vacated. Jacek commandeered it. "I watched the game with some of the Ultras in one of the Polish bars. No one wanted to come over here. I'm glad I ran into you. I was hoping to."

Molly raised her eyebrows. "Oh?"

The bartender set their drinks in front of them. Jacek pulled out a fat roll from his pocket and peeled off a twenty-dollar bill.

Molly watched him. She should not have been surprised at his wad of cash. She knew he worked in the underground economy that built Chicagoland. She thanked him for the drink.

He touched her back again, gently. His fingers felt her scar. He traced it through her t-shirt. "It's healing well."

Molly smiled. "Yes. I'm back to normal speed, but they won't let me work security or ushering again yet."

"How are you and Ian?"

"He's been good during all of this. He's offered to pay my rent and bills but I don't like relying on other people. I talked the company into letting me work in the office. It sucks, but at least I feel like I'm doing something." She took a long drink, leaving nothing but ice and the straw in the small plastic cup.

Jacek signaled for another drink. He sipped his vodka like a gentleman rather than swigging it like he had been earlier in the evening. "Have you heard from Jack?"

"I haven't seen any of his friends tonight. Kind of unusual, actually." She glanced at the clock. It was fast approaching 2:00 AM. "They usually show up here by now." She took a sip of the new drink. "I'm tired of running from him, of defending myself to his lackeys."

"I know."

"How? How do you know?" A flash of paranoia coursed through her.

Jacek touched her hair. "Just observation, that's all. No need to panic. I'm on your side."

Ian returned from making the phone call. "She didn't answer," he told Carlos.

"Maybe she is sleeping."

"Yeah, maybe. It's two hours later there."

Deanna approached. "Ian, it's good to see you." Her voice dripped with fake honey.

Ian stiffened. "I see you're with Sugar, now."

"He treats me well," she said. "What do you care, anyway? You have your little usher chick. You downgraded. I upgraded."

Ian guffawed. "I think you have that backwards." He went to the bar to get another beer.

Deanna placed her hands on her hips in an exaggerated pout.

Mirek came over. "Leave my player alone, *pierdolona suka*."

Tomás stood behind Mirek. "You've done enough damage today."

Deanna wandered off to the ladies room.

Ian watched his ex sashay away. One of the LA fans asked him to dance. He shrugged, might as well. He set his beer on the table with his friends and went to the dance floor.

Before long, several players from both sides had paired up with fans or other patrons on the dance floor.

Mirek found himself left with Gina. They both watched everyone having a good time. She looked at the coach. "Do you think you could polka to this beat?"

"It's a bit fast. Why? Do you want to try?"

"Might as well. Care to dance?"

Mirek and Gina went out and twirled polka steps to the rapid steady techno dance beat. Tomás looked over and laughed.

Jacek caught Molly as she swooned from too much whiskey. "I'm taking you home."

She was in no condition to protest.

Jacek reached in her pocket and got out her car keys. She giggled. "That tickles."

"Good, at least you still feel something."

It was just past 3:00 AM when he loaded her into the passenger seat of her own car. He buckled the belt. He slid the driver's seat back before he got behind the wheel. It was going to be closer to take her to his place—a lot closer. He smiled. He could hold her close for at least one night.

Bobby Lonestar got on the DJ microphone. "I see both our soccer teams have a fair amount of rhythm. What say they to an old-fashioned dance off?"

The bar patrons got behind the idea instantly. "Dance off, dance off," they chanted.

"I've got the music already picked out right here," Bobby said holding up a mix CD.

Both teams looked at each other. They were all having fun. "What's the prize, Bobby?" yelled Mark.

"I don't know. Pride?"

The bartender pulled out an unopened liter of Belvedere Vodka. Tomás and Mirek lit up. "We'll polka for that," Tomás said pointing at the bottle.

"Bobby," hollered the bartender. "SambaSinTrick will give a bottle of Belvedere to the winner."

"There ya go. What say you, Stars and Stampede?"

Both teams looked at each other with a competitive eye. Mark said, "The Stars are in."

Mirek concurred, "We'll dance circles around you."

"Okay, then, we've got ourselves a dance off." Bobby laid down the microphone and put in the CD. He cued up the first song. "Okay, here's the format. Both teams will line up on the sides of the dance floor, facing each other. Two will go down the aisle dancing against each other. SambaSinTrick's DJ Sanga will be judging the first round. Then we will move on and let the fans decide. We're going to have fun with this. Kick it!"

Gina tried to sneak away. Mirek grabbed her arm. "Oh, no you don't. My partner isn't going anywhere. You are a part of the team."

"Okay, let's go, Stampede!" She joined the line.

Magnetix's club single "Sphere of Lonliness" started the play. Tomás was the lead off man for the Stampede. He faced Xuan Xavier Xoy. One fan tossed a soccer ball at them when they were halfway down the line. Xuan chested it up and bounced and balanced it to the music. The Polack took the ball from the Star and did a few tricks of his own. At the end of the line, the ball was headed to Ian, next up for Chicago. Ian faced Mark. Ian bounced the ball on his head as he spun and shuffled down the line. Mark tried to take the ball away from him. Ian retained control until the end—keeping to the beat the entire way. He pushed the ball up to almost the ceiling; when it came back down, he laid in for a bicycle kick to get the ball back up the line to Carlos.

The next track started, DJ Montell's "This is How We Do It '98 (1998 Revolution Mix)". Ante grooved against Carlos. Ante got the ball back for the Stars. Carlos did not dance very well. He moved his feet well, but lost his balance halfway down the line. Gina and Mirek helped him to his feet. He made a move like he meant to do that. Ante rolled the ball back. The opposing goalkeepers were next. They both kept the ball low to show off their rhythm and footwork. About two thirds of the way down the line, they both laid their hands on the ball. Dan made a twisting move to try to wrest the ball away. Tomlinson followed his move. Both men did nearly simultaneous cartwheels while still holding onto the sphere!

The audience erupted in thunderous applause.

Paul Novotny versus Lancelot Stevens. The tune changed to Innertales' "Bohemian Odyssee (Plyphène Mix)". The ball did not factor into their dance. Next up were the two couples of Deanna & Sugar and Gina & Mirek. Gina was whirled and twirled by Mirek. It seemed to those watching that they had been dancing together for a long time. Sugar went to dip Deanna and lost his grip. Deanna broke her high heel in the tumble. She went running off the dance floor. Sugar chased after her.

With a rib nudge, Tomás commented to Ian, "I guess we know who won that round."

"Yeah, any of the ladies in my life right now, any of the Stampedistas, could kick Deanna's ass any day." Ian grinned.

Brendan got the pleasure of the more industrial sounding Black Sun Empire's "1138". Blonde Dieter Baum versus the bleached blonde Iceman. Dieter could not keep up with Brendan's moves. Brendan moved like he was on the stage in a Chippendale's show.

Juan Cristobal faced Toro Hilgado about halfway through the song. They play fought. They both knew the art of Brazilian capoeira. The moves were fluid, graceful. Both lines had to back to the edges of the dance floor to accommodate their fighting style.

DJ Sanga looked at Bobby. "These guys are great. Let them keep going."

Bobby got on the mike. "We're going to let these Juan & Toro mix it up for a while."

The pair continued—concentrating only on each other, through the next song, DJ Looney Tune's "Jumpin' and Pumpin'". The entire club clapped to the beat to encourage them.

Bobby faded out the song. Juan and Toro wrapped up their battle with a hand grip and manly hug. "Holy shit! That was great! Who is winning right now, Sanga?"

"Chicago has the slight edge," was the response.

Some of the rowdier fans booed.

"Okay, fans, it's your turn. You get to be the judge. Each one will have one minute down the line by themselves, alternating. Chicago will go first. No couples this time, Mirek and Gina. Fans, clubbers, you write down the top three on a cocktail napkin and turn them in at the bar. Let's kick this final round off with some Tony B." Bobby cued up "Rap de Polymarch" and the games began anew.

Brendan jumped to the front of the Stampede line when he heard the opening phrases. He recognized the song and wanted to get grooving on the opening lines, "Get up, get up, like a sex machine, man."

Molly passed out on the way to Jacek's humble abode. Using a fireman's carry, he took her into his house and laid her on the bed. She stirred and rolled over. He took her shoes off.

As she slept off the alcohol, he secured her car. He would have to go back for his motorcycle in the morning. He stripped down to a tee shirt and boxers and laid next to her.

He nuzzled her neck and kissed her lightly on the ear lobe. She moaned contentedly. His loins ached to take advantage of her.

She rolled to face him. Her eyes were half-closed. The room was lit with only a bubbling, red lava lamp. She started to kiss Jacek. He smiled under the smooches. She rubbed his head and pulled him closer. His hands followed her body to her waist. He pulled her on top of him as he shifted onto his back.

She straddled him and removed her shirt. With one hand, he unhooked her black lacy bra. She tossed it to the side. He caressed her perky breasts. Her hips rested directly over his dick. He throbbed, poking a little out of his boxers. She stood, wobbling, over him as she removed her jeans. He helped her reveal her strong legs. He touched the scar on her back, tracing it lightly with his fingertips.

He lowered her back down. His stiff dick was fully out of the boxers now. She settled onto him.

"Mmm," she murmured.

As she rode him, she tossed her brunette locks. He grinned from ear to ear. Her breasts bounced. He wanted to hold back his burst, but he had been holding back long enough. As she grew more turned on, her pussy squeezed his dick. "*Tak!*" he cried out as he came inside of her.

She fell to his side. She continued to run her hands over him, stroking him like a cat, until she passed back out.

It was a close competition. Bobby and DJ Sanga finally just had to call it a tie. The bartender reluctantly parted with a second bottle of Belvedere. Vodka neats all around.

Mirek and Gina slipped off back to the hotel. "I never knew you were so much fun," she said.

"I used to go dancing all the time with my wife." He bit his lip at her memory.

Gina touched his leathered cheek. "It's okay. Why don't you come into my room for a nightcap? We'll just talk."

"Yeah, these crazy dance clubs, you can't really talk in there."

"They call them meat markets," she told him.

In the hotel room, she ordered up a chocolate soufflé and a bottle of wine.

Mirek relaxed back on the bed. "This day has been exhausting. I wish we could have won the match. Carl will be disappointed."

"Oh, I think even he knows you win some and you lose some. It's a tough league for being so new in the world of soccer. But enough about work."

He agreed. "*Tak,* what about you, Gina. How come you have never married?"

"Oh pick a reason, no time, haven't found the right guy, you know." She sat on the edge of the other bed. "So what are you suggesting?"

He shrugged. "Me dating again would be weird. I never thought I would have to again. And really, I didn't much with my wife. We grew up on the same street. It just felt natural for us to be together forever."

"It must have been devastating to lose her."

"*Tak, tak,*" he replied quietly. He closed his eyes. They were silent for a moment. Gina felt good to him as a dance partner; they worked well together for the Stampede, but could she be more? Would she be willing to be the stepmother to two wild teenage daughters? "Gina, would you date me?" He kept his eyes closed.

"Oh, I might give it a try." She stood and kissed him on the forehead.

He smiled.

A barefoot Deanna cornered Ian just before he left the club. She pinned him to the wall and grabbed his crotch. She laid her lips on him.

He pushed her back. "You crazy bitch."

"Just seeing if you were over me." She turned and sashayed back to the bar.

Ian rearranged his underwear. He pulled out his cell phone and dialed Molly. It went straight to voice mail. He hung up without leaving a message.

Chapter LXXXII

Sunday, August 2, 1998: Molly woke up to sunlight streaming through partially closed Venetian blinds. She looked around. The room did not look familiar at all. She saw her clothes on the floor on the side of the bed. She looked at the lightly snoring figure next to her. It was certainly not Ian. Oh fuck, it's Jacek.

She jumped out of bed and grabbed her clothes. She scurried into the bathroom. There was no door to shut. She sat down on the toilet anyway. She needed to pee. After relieving herself, she looked at the tissue for telltale evidence that she had had sex. Upon seeing drying remnants of jism, she hung her head and sat there for a moment. What have I done, she thought.

What's done is done. She knew she could not change what happened last night. She decided that Ian could never know. She got dressed and went back to face Jacek.

"Good morning, sunshine. How are you feeling?" he greeted her.

"How did I get here?"

"I drove us here in your car." He got up and pulled on a pair of sweatpants. "Before you disappear in a panic, I need you to take me back to Coogan's to get my bike."

"Did we?"

He nodded.

"Don't you dare say a word about this to anyone."

"Of course not, why would I admit to sleeping with the enemy?"

She harrumphed.

"Look, Mol, you were very drunk. It just happened. I did not force you." He tried to smooth her ruffled feathers. "But you certainly left me happy."

She groaned. "Come on. Let's go get something to eat and I'll take you to your bike."

Chapter LXXXIII

Beginning in August, Soldier Field would have to be shared with the Chicago Bears. The field would not be in as good of shape as it had been during the previous months of the season, especially along the sidelines where the opposing heavy gladiators stood awaiting their turn at play. Also, gridiron paint lines would remain, albeit in faded state on the pitch. The soccer lines would be laid down in yellow. To the untrained fan's eye, this tended to be confusing. On the plus side, offside position calls became easier as was the calculation of ten yards on a freekick. Jackie saw it as a necessary trade off of evils. Carl saw it as a welcome revival of "soccer-specific stadium" talks among fans and politicos.

The Chicago Stampede went into the month with a virtual lock on a playoff spot but not home field advantage. They were second in the conference and fourth overall with 27 points. For the FLA, the playoff format was the top 8 teams, four from each conference with Chicago in the Western Conference, competing in a 2-match home and away aggregate goal series in a straight knockout tournament. The final match was the FLA Cup scheduled at the Rose Bowl in Pasadena, California. Home field advantage meant that in the quarterfinals and the semifinals the higher seeded team would play the second match at home.

THURSDAY, AUGUST 6, 1998: The sportscasters were instructed to get the goods on Carl's obvious absence from the All-Star match owners' skybox. Carl was uncomfortable to say the least. He was glad that Jackie was by his side, at least until they had to go down for halftime.

Carl closed the door to the owner's skybox and locked the door. That was unusual. Carl liked to keep everything open. He thought maybe he could escape to Section 12, but Jackie pointed out that they were close to the cameras and the sideline reporter would be looking for him there.

"Jacqueline, I don't know how much longer I can keep everything secret," Carl mused. He swirled a 15-year-old single malt scotch in a rocks glass.

"It's up to you, but I think it might hurt your bargaining power to expose your weakness. Even Agnes thinks so."

He turned from her and looked out on the pitch. The match had just kicked off. He sipped his elixir. "I know; I know."

Jackie placed her hand on his shoulder and gave it a squeeze. "Is there something else I should know?"

"No, Jacqueline, there's not." Carl shook his head. He stared at the game. Mirek had decided to use some subs instead of the usual starting eleven. The Stampede were pressing, but possession seemed to be only about fifty percent. Neither team made it very deep toward the opposing goal.

Carl's cell phone rang. He answered it without looking at the caller ID. "Hello."

"Carl, darling, it's Alexi."

He wanted to hang up, tell her she had a wrong number. A bead of sweat formed on his brow.

She continued without letting him reply, "I hope you are feeling better. I'm watching the match right now. Usually you are down on the sidelines or in Section 12, but I haven't seen you."

"I'm taking a meeting in my skybox." He smiled at Jackie. She returned the smile.

"I was wondering if you thought much about the joint venture. Lance Merton has been pressing me for a solid answer. He wants to expand by two teams next season."

"How much do you want from me?" Jackie looked at Carl quizzically.

"Cash outlay? That hasn't been finalized yet. DJ Sanchez and Lance have agreed to field a team next season in Houston. They will play at Rice University until the stadium is built. Lance told me that they have the minimum required number of season ticket deposits both in Houston and in Denver."

"Denver, eh?" Carl rubbed his chin with his free hand. It was time to put Jackie in control of something. If she could handle the last couple of weeks around the Stampede front office, she could handle Alexi and Denver. He looked at his beloved. "Alexi, let me put you on hold for a minute." He put the phone to his side. "Jacqueline, do you want a job?"

"Um, depends on what it is. That's Alexi Taman on the line?"

"Keep it on the qt, but I want you to partner with Alexi Taman to run an expansion team in Denver. I'll outlay 50% of the cash and she will put up the other half. I have my hands full with Philly and Chicago, especially Chicago. Alexi will obviously be mostly in Jersey. You'll run Denver."

Jackie's hands flew to her mouth. "Oh my god, are you serious?"

"I'm very serious. So will you do it? We need to move quickly."

"Yes, Carl, anything for you. Yes, I'll do it." Jackie squealed with glee.

Carl kissed her, and then resumed his phone conversation. "Alexi, I'll do it, but Jackie will be taking the majority of the meetings for me. She'll be either the GM or you two will decide on an outside party for the job."

Carl could just hear Alexi cringe on the other end. "Damn you, Carl. Okay, I will tell Lance. Expect to see some paperwork by Monday."

Carl snapped his phone shut. He looked at the match. Still little action outside the midfield.

"So?" Jackie said.

"I think there will be a sit down next week, so keep your schedule clear."

"Absolutely." Jackie was excited at the prospect of truly embarking on a new career. The back of her mind was telling her something. A red light was going off. There was more to this partnership than meets the eye. "Carl, how well do you know Alexi?"

Carl was not expecting that question. "She's a business associate. I've only known her as long as I've been in the FLA." It was best to leave out the schoolboy crush and pictures in the locker at this time.

"Okay. I was just wondering what she was like to work with."

"I guess we'll find out. She's a bit of a wildcat, I've been told." Carl crossed to the wet bar to pour himself another scotch.

Jackie nodded. "Hmm, this will be interesting." She made a mental note to call Magia and to do some biographical research on Alexi via the Internet. "How long do I have to keep this mum?"

"Until Lance, DJ, Alexi and I can get our ducks in a row and make an official press announcement. Could be until after the wedding. We don't want anything to overshadow that, now do we?" Carl pulled her into a tight embrace. They kissed deeply.

Doubts about Carl's relationship with Alexi seemed to melt from Jackie's mind. "No, we don't." She kissed him again.

At halftime, Carl and Alexi joined the Stampedistas and the Barclay's Pub team pitchside. The TV broadcast reporter lay in wait. Carl glanced at him and could tell he was like a salivating jackal.

The two teams were introduced and recognized. Carl walked down the line and shook everyone's hand, giving a gentleman's kiss on the back of the hand to each lady. Section 12 gave a loud roar of recognition all.

After the brief ceremony, the reporter approached. "Good evening, Carl. Jackie."

"Hello," both politely replied.

A cameraman was just behind the microphone-wielding hunter. "The guys in the booth want me to ask you a few questions during halftime."

Carl sighed. "Okay, if you must."

"John, let me know when you're ready up there." There was a reply in the earpiece. "Okay, Carl, we're just waiting for the commercial break to end. This will be brief."

"Good."

Jackie, who was holding Carl's hand, gave it a little squeeze.

"Okay, here we go, five seconds."

Carl cleared his throat.

"Thank you, John. I've got Carl Costello here, owner of the Chicago Stampede and Philadelphia Minute Men. Everyone in soccer has been wondering why you were not present at the stadium for the All-Star match a couple of weeks ago. We have not seen any official releases. Speculations are running wild. Any comments?"

"Jason, I just had an allergic reaction to something I ate for lunch. It was bad enough to go to the hospital. But I'm fine now." Carl was glad he was able to say that with a perfectly straight face.

"Okay, I guess that clears that up then. Any comments on Mirek's use of bench players in this match?"

"I trust Mirek's judgment. He thought that some of our players needed some more pitchtime than they were getting off the bench. I think they are doing well, although I would like to see a goal in the second half."

"Wouldn't we all, Carl. Thank you for your time. Back to you, John." Jason reached for Carl's hand. The two men shook. The cameraman resumed gathering crowd shots for background until the second half began. Jason added, "For the record, I thought it was something like that."

Carl nodded. "I'm just glad it didn't turn into a grilling. The past couple weeks have been a lot of paperwork and trade negotiations. It's just been harder since I've been recovering from the hives and all."

"I'm glad you're healthy now."

"Thanks, Jason."

Alexi stood in front of the mirror. Naked, she rubbed her hand over her slowing expanding womb. Her clothes were beginning to fit tighter. She dreaded the thought of having to buy a new wardrobe every month for the next six months or so. But that was the price she would have to pay. Right now, she needed to be concerned about minimizing her girth for the sit-down. She wholly intended to be at the meeting in person, rather than via conference call. She had to keep her pregnancy secret until Carl and Jackie's wedding in October, when she was sure to be showing.

When she heard Carl's voice on the television, she turned to watch. Seeing Carl gave her a rush of happiness. Hearing his answer about why he was not at the All-Star match was disconcerting. It had to be a lie.

"Oh, Carl, you stayed away because I was there. I know you did. You know you did," she said to the image.

She looked down at her belly again. "Time for me to call in my old pal Sergé for a wardrobe consultation."

Chapter LXXXIV

FRIDAY, AUGUST 7, 1998: Molly had been feeling strange all week since her slip up with Jacek. She did not feel that she could talk to anyone about it. True, Renata was a good friend from both the world of heavy metal and work, but she did not feel that she could trust her with this problem.

Ian noticed that she had been distant. He would try to cuddle with her in bed and she just rolled away. He thought she might be on the rag but saw no evidence in the bathroom to support that idea.

Over breakfast, he asked, "Is it because of the court case?"

She nodded. "Maybe I should look for a new job, just to get my mind off of it."

"What would you do?"

She shrugged. "Maybe I could bartend at Sueños or Smiler's. I do have some experience in that."

"I could talk to Carl."

She shook her head. "No, it's best that nothing I do has any connection to the team."

"You're right." He stood to clear the table. "Just do me a favor while I'm in practice today, honey. Call Agnes."

"Agnes? Why Agnes?" she countered.

"I think something is bothering you that you are not telling me. You know she's a psychologist, don't you?"

"Oh, yeah, of course. But how would I pay her?"

Ian kissed her. "Don't you worry yourself about that."

Ian left for Halas Hall for team practice. Molly stared at her computer screen. She tried to update her web zine, but nothing was coming to her. She just wanted to crawl back in bed and hide the rest of the day. Maybe Ian was right, maybe she did need to talk to Agnes. Ethics would bind her to secrecy. Clearing her conscious by telling someone would help. She picked up the phone. "Agnes, I need to talk to someone. I'm feeling a bit down."

"Come on over," the Czech doctor replied.

Molly pulled up at the Novotny bungalow in west Chicago. She sat outside in her car. She felt like she would be admitting that she was weak if she talked to a shrink.

293

Agnes pulled the drapery aside and looked out at Molly. She went outside and pulled the distraught lass from her car. "Molly, you need to talk to me. Think of me as a friend and not as a shrink, if that helps. The shrink part just is for legal secrecy."

Molly sighed heavily. Agnes led her into the house. Molly flopped down on the fainting couch. "I fucked up." There, she said it

"How do you think you screwed up?" Agnes encouraged.

"I cheated on Ian!" she burst out in tears.

Agnes handed her a box of tissues. She stroked her comfortingly, like a mother. It wasn't important whom, but Agnes was curious. If it were another member of the Stampede, it would complicate the whole situation further. "May I ask who?"

"With Jacek, the head Ultra. I've known him as an acquaintance for a while from the metal underground. It was last Saturday night. I got too drunk at Smiler Coogan's and he took care of me."

"Are you sure then that you had sex with him?"

Molly nodded with her whole body. "Yes."

"Do you think it was rape? Do you think he slipped you a drug in your drink?"

She shook her head. "No, Agnes, it was nothing like that. I just had too much hard liquor. I was feeling down about knowing that Ian's ex-girlfriend was at the LA match. I was feeling down about the whole riot incident. And Renata was working, so she couldn't be there to make sure I didn't get too wasted." Molly paused to blow her nose.

Molly ended up telling Agnes most of her life story from the past year—about Jack, about what she thought about Jacek had done, about her relationship with Ian.

"So, you think that Jack had someone stab you during the riot?"

Molly drew in a deep breath. She lifted her tee shirt. Agnes looked at the scar. It still appeared angry.

Agnes went on with her verifying, "And you also think that Jacek killed this person for you?"

"I can't prove it, but yes."

"Perhaps," Agnes offered, "you're subconscious mind was allowing you to thank your protector last weekend."

Both ladies were silent as Molly digested the thought. "Should I tell Ian?"

"Only if you want to." Agnes stood. "I'm going to make us some sandwiches for lunch. You can rest here, or join me in the kitchen, if you want."

"Thank you."

Later that evening, Ian took Molly out to Sybaris for a romantic weekend for just the two of them. Molly had left Agnes' house numb and wrung out. "Did Agnes put you up to this?" she questioned Ian's motives.

"No, I came up with this idea all by myself," he beamed.

He booked the paradise pool suite. Molly's jaw dropped. She had seen the ads on television, but never expected the room to be this nice. Ian requested rose petals be laid out on the bed in a heart. Champagne chilled in a bucket on a table. There was a waterfall over a private swimming pool. Molly felt like she had stepped into a tropical heaven.

She looked into Ian's eyes. "Thank you."

He scooped her into his arms and threw her back on the bed. "I love you, Molly." He covered her with kisses.

"I love you, too."

Chapter LXXXV

WEDNESDAY, AUGUST 12, 1998: The expansion meeting was scheduled to be in Chicago at 10 AM. DJ and Lance were eager to get two teams fielded as early as the 1999 season. Carl and Alexi were vital to that process.

Jackie was present when they all sat down in the conference room in the Stampede front office. Lance sat at the head of the table with Carl and Jackie on one side and Alexi and DJ on the other.

Alexi's stylist had done wonders at concealing her small belly for the meeting, without making her feel uncomfortable in her outfit. Carl never suspected a thing was wrong. She decided to be on her best behavior and keep her flirting to a minimum or at least redirected at DJ instead, who was a smartly dressed *el guapo*.

Lance started the meeting. "I'm so glad we could all sit down and get the shows in Houston and Denver on the road. Let's start with an update on things in Houston from DJ."

DJ cleared his throat. He spoke English without much affectation. "Thank you, Lance. I've been working with supporters of soccer in the Houston area for quite a while. Once Lance told me about the minimum season ticket holder deposit requirement, I was pleased as I already had at least twice that number tell me they had the money ready. Within days of making the announcement, the coffers filled. For 1999, we plan to use Rice University stadium. They have excellent practice facilities and are happy to have the extra infusion of dollars during the summer months. They already have a women's soccer team and talks are underway to establish a men's soccer team, which may be used as a farm team, so to speak, for young talent. It is understood that this location at Rice is temporary—unless of course we fill the entire 70,000-seat stadium on a weekly basis. I have talked with a few collar suburban areas about building a 30,000 to 40,000-seat stadium designed to meet the soccer fans and players needs. I feel that we can easily consistently fill a stadium of that size. Lance and I are in agreement that the league needs to expand in pairs to keep the tables and divisions balanced. That is where you two come in." He gestured at Alexi and Carl.

Alexi spoke next, "I wanted to field another team since I enjoy the process of building so much. But I needed the extra cash from a partner, ideally Carl."

Carl thought to himself, of course, it would have to be me.

"Carl had already looked into the Denver market prior to the 1998 expansion. The discussion lists were outraged from the area that Philadelphia was selected instead.

They put together a network at the time of 500 strong to lobby for a team and even established a season ticket deposit account. Those in the initial group ponied up their deposits and worked to get more. When the 1999 expansion rumors hit the boards and lists, that number began to grow. Denver has waited long enough. Their season ticket deposit count is now up to 1756, as of this morning."

Carl interjected, "I'm glad to hear that. Makes me feel better about the whole deal. We would be losing money by playing initially in Mile High."

"Carl," Alexi said, "I've already had a few discussions with the mayor of Golden about building a stadium there. Plus Coors could easily be brought aboard as a sponsor."

"That's good news," Lance said. "But how does Jackie fit into this equation?"

Jackie started to speak for herself, but Carl replied faster. "I've selected Jackie to be my day-to-day go to person for the Denver operation once the initial deal is finalized. She is also a CPA and can help us work out the financial logistics, thus taking some of that burden off of you, Lance."

Lance scowled.

Jackie added, "My true ambition is to be a coach. I've recently been working hard to achieve the necessary knowledge of the intricacies of the game. However, given my accounting background, I might be better in a front office."

"What do you think, Alexi?" Lance turned to her.

"If that is what it takes to get Carl on board, then I'll have to cope with it. So how much cash outlay did we discuss earlier, Lance? I don't remember off the top of my head."

They discussed the dollar amounts. Jackie was not surprised by the figures. She had also done some recent reading on league finances. The whole single entity aspect of the FLA did bother her, but perhaps after a decade or so that would dissolve into a structure more like the ones in Europe, especially England.

Lance pulled out papers for DJ, Carl and Alexi to sign. It was official. 1999 would bring Houston and Denver into the Fútbol League America.

The last order of business with Lance was scheduling a press conference. They decided not to wait. The fans wanted to know for certain if their ticket deposit monies were well spent or not. Lance wanted to wait until the next day, but the others insisted on that afternoon.

Jackie went out and asked Carrie to work the media Rolodex for a 4:00 PM meeting. "Call the locals, especially the Fox Sports Chicago guys so they can get a feed to the Denver and Houston markets."

"Will do. What should I say?"

"Just say that there is a major league announcement from Lance Merton, Carl Costello, Alexi Taman and DJ Sanchez. That should be enough of a teaser."

"Will this be a conference call as well? I can set one up. Might be a good idea for the papers in Texas and Denver."

"Good idea. I'll let the others know." With that Jackie went back into the room.

DJ and Lance were talking off to the side. Carl and Alexi were discussing Jackie's position. Jackie slowly went to the table.

"I'm still not so sure about Jackie being your go-to for this deal, Carl. I would much rather deal with you directly," Alexi said somewhat heatedly. She tried to keep her voice lowered, because Lance and DJ were still in the room.

"I know you would. But let's be honest, I've got my hands full with two teams already. I know we could probably find a more qualified GM for Denver, but Jackie is here right now. She wants this type of career change." Carl fought hard. He did not want to have to deal with Alexi everyday. It would put too much of a strain on his relationship with Jackie.

"You are aware that she will have to be in Denver much of the year," Alexi threw back.

"It is something we will both have to live with. If things get uncomfortable in that regard, we will hire an outside GM. But look, we have to move quickly. April 1999 is just around the corner. We have less than a year to pick a team, negotiate stadium and vendor deals, media, et cetera. Jackie can get this done. I have full confidence in her. And, no, that is not blinded by my love for her. If we were just friends, I would still recommend her. She's a strong woman, just like you."

"Damn, you're stubborn, Carl."

"Hey, I thought my ears were burning." Jackie smiled as she sat back down next to Carl. "By the way, Carrie suggested that a conference call be part of this afternoon's dog and pony show."

"Excellent," said Lance. "Carl, you got some wonderful folks in your office."

"Thank you," said Carl. "Jackie, how would you like to be general manager?"

"If that's what's needed to get going, sure. I'll get started on making a list of things that need to be done." Jackie pulled a legal pad closer to her and pulled a pen from behind her ear. She began to brainstorm with the help of her new bosses.

Alexi for the first time really watched Carl with Jackie. There was definitely love between them. All she had with Carl was a strong sexual yen. She wished she could be like that with Carl.

Jackie caught Alexi coquettishly looking at Carl. Jackie gave her a hard territorial challenge eye. Jackie was not threatened by Alexi's looks or standing. She was the one who had Carl, not her. Carl loved her and not Alexi and Jackie sensed it with every fiber of her being.

Carl dared not make too much eye contact with Alexi. He was more confident about dealing with the vixen when Jackie was at his side. Perhaps all these feelings of attraction would lessen over time. He sure hoped so.

All five parties worked through lunch. Lance had Chicago-style deep-dish pizza ordered from Pizzeria Uno. Carrie was even invited to eat. She declined and continued working the press contacts while grazing on a salad she had brought from home.

The press conference started promptly at 4:00.

"Good afternoon, ladies and gentlemen of the media," began Lance. "The Fútbol League America now has 12 teams. We have been very pleased with the response in the 12 cities of the fans and have been exploring options to bring the fun and excitement of FLA to two new markets and bring in one new owner, Diego Juan "DJ" Sanchez.

"As most of you may know we have been placing our recent All-Star matches in test markets like San Diego and Houston. DJ will be the new owner of the Houston 1999 expansion team.

"Our second expansion team will be co-owned by Alexi Taman and Carl Costello. Carl and Alexi have both been working with the wonderful fan group in Denver.

"Right now I'll let DJ Sanchez have the podium, then Carl and Alexi. After that, we will open up the floor for questions." Lance stepped aside.

"Gracias, Lance," said DJ. "I do wish I could have made this announcement in Houston, but Chicago is a great city as well. I look forward to Houston beating Chicago in the 1999 season."

"We'll see about that," Carl jousted back.

There was some laughter among the media present, including those on the conference call.

"Houston is eager for a professional soccer team. As of this morning, we have 2372 season ticket seat deposits. We will be fielding a team at Rice University until a new stadium deal is worked out. I cannot speak much further about the stadium, at this time, for fear of blowing any deals. I have already begun to look at players from other teams. We look forward to the off-season wheeling and dealing." DJ winked at Carl and Alexi. "I'll turn over the podium to Carl and Alexi to talk about Denver."

Alexi spoke first. "Thank you, DJ. Carl and I are pleased to have Jackie Harris on board as the general manager of the Denver squad. We are all eager to make this a successful and winning team for the Rocky Mountain region. Right now, we have 1756 season ticket seat deposits. We anticipate this number growing as word spreads. We will be playing in Mile High Stadium in 1999 and anticipate a stadium deal closing this winter."

"And DJ," Carl had to put in, leaning into the microphone, "I think Philly, Chicago and Denver will all give you a run for your money."

Lance then said, "Now we'll open up the floor for any questions." A few raised their hands. "Yes, you there in the back row."

"My question is for Jackie Harris. Jackie, how do you anticipate balancing your newlywed status with your new position?"

Jackie smiled. "I'll probably rack up the frequent flyer miles." She paused to let a few laugh. "Seriously, though, if either Carl or I find the separation too stressful, I will look for a replacement."

"DJ, why the United States? You have previously stated that soccer will never succeed here. Why the sudden interest?"

"I have been watching Lance's league grow since its inception in 1996. Attendance numbers are up, but I know it could be better. I intend to set an example of marketing to build a strong fan base in Houston. It's a challenge and I intend to aim for turning a profit."

"So this isn't just going to be a tax write off for you?"

"Absolutely not."

Lance stepped in. "It's getting hostile in here," he said with a grin. "Let's see if anyone on the conference call has a question."

"*Rocky Mountain News* here, Lance. I have a question. Has there been a team nickname selected yet?"

"I'll field this one," Jackie said. "I plan to arrange for a contest for the nickname and logo design to be staged in Denver and the surrounding area. If your organization would like to be involved, it would be greatly appreciated."

"I'll mention it to my editor," said the reporter.

"*Houston Sports* for DJ," piped in another voice from the call device resting on the table. "DJ, same question to you. Have you selected a team nickname and logo yet?"

"No. Some ideas have been tossed around, but nothing yet. I do like Jackie's contest idea."

Carl and Alexi looked at each other. They had not even thought that far ahead. Already Jackie was acting like a general manager. Despite Alexi's doubts, she knew they had made a wise choice.

Lance said, "As you can see, we have a lot of work to do in both cities, but we will be expanded to 14 teams in 1999. Division structure and season length is yet to be determined. It is likely that we will again have 2 divisions, of 7 teams each, of which the top 4 in each division qualify for playoffs. At this time, we will end the press conference. All of us will be available for individual interviews at future dates. Please contact our secretaries for scheduling. Thank you all for coming or joining us via phone on such short notice."

The conference call ended.

Internally, Jackie had been shaking the entire time. She surprised herself by her calm delivery and quick thinking. She had wanted to wait until next week to announce a naming contest, but since the *Rocky Mountain News* had brought it up, it couldn't hurt to throw out a teaser. And hopefully, the *RMN* will be a co-promoter. She made a mental note to call the reporter who dialed in and asked the question.

Carl hugged her. "I shouldn't do this with the cameras still around," he teased. "I'm so glad I met you." As they kissed a few reporters snapped some shots.

Alexi tried not to show any emotion as she watched the spectacle. She felt a quickening. She smiled. It seemed as if she was smiling at Jackie and Carl, but really she was smiling at the life stirring inside.

Lance shook Jackie's hand. "It will be a pleasure to work with you. You just proved that you can think fast on your feet. That's important when doing press conferences."

"Thanks, Lance. I agree. The contest was something I was thinking about anyway. It's the easiest way to generate ideas and get the fans and community involved."

"Putting the paper on the spot was brilliant," he continued to praise.

"Hey, I was going to have to spend some advertising dollars anyway. Why not get them to be a sponsor? Makes perfect sense."

"Right you are." Lance turned to Carl. "You've got a good woman here, Carl. Don't let her go."

"I won't. Not for anyone or anything." Carl beamed with love and pride.

Chapter LXXXVI

THURSDAY, AUGUST 13, 1998: Jackie awoke earlier than usual to begin her first full day as general manager of the Denver soccer club, at least in her mind that is what she was referring to it as. She logged onto the *Rocky Mountain News* web site to read the article, and then checked a few other news sites to see what their spin was.

She contacted the reporter, Jason Fallon, to talk to him about the contest and arrange to have a classified ad in the help wanted section of the Sunday paper. Jason brought in his editor and they worked out a contest:

Submissions would be taken by the newspaper website until the organization website was up and running. A team of judges consisting of Jason Fallon, Jackie, Alexi, Carl, Lance, and three season ticket deposit holders, who would be exempt from submitting names, but would be compensated by the team in other means would select the winning name. If multiple persons submitted the same name, the grand prizewinner would be drawn from those submissions. The winner would receive a year's subscription to the *RMN*, two seasons worth of tickets and a trip to the first road match—location and date to be determined. All those submitting the winning name would receive an invitation to a party in a skybox during the inaugural home match. Jason, Jackie and the editor felt that many folks would submit the winning name. As an added bonus, if there was a winning name submission with a logo, those would be entered into a separate contest and the winner would receive the grand prize plus a lifetime season ticket. Jackie, Carl and Alexi would determine the winning logo design.

Alexi was still in town. Her flight back would not be until the evening. Jackie decided to meet with her without Carl. A late lunch was decided on. Carl had a full day at the office.

The women met at Café Luciano's on Rush Street. Both were craving pasta.

Alexi arrived first and secured a quiet table by the window. Jackie spotted her. Alexi was on her cell phone with Magia straightening out a minicrisis. She held up one finger. "Magia, don't worry about it. I'm coming back tonight. If things are not worked out in the morning, I'll deal with it myself. You tell the boys that."

Alexi snapped her Motorola closed. "Sorry about that. Just wait until you have staff to deal with."

"Thanks for the warning," said Jackie as she sat down. "I'm glad we could have this sit down before you head back to New York."

"So am I." Alexi set her phone down on the table. "Hopefully, it won't ring while we chat and eat. I was famished so I went ahead and ordered for the both of us. I hope fettuccine alfredo is okay with you."

"That's fine. Thanks." Jackie pulled a breadstick out of the basket. "I was on the phone a lot setting things up with the *Rocky Mountain News*. The contest is in place and help wanted ads are set to run. Besides a coach, we need to hire a webmaster very quickly."

"I agree. I have some ideas for coaching staff."

"Good. Plus I need you to give me the contacts you've cultivated among the Denver deposit holders."

"I'll have Magia email you the list and any other info I have. When do you plan on going to Denver?"

"Sunday night. We need to lease office space."

The two went back and forth. The lunch was all about business, until they got to dessert.

Alexi was the one who decided to swing the subject to the personal. "So, how did you meet Carl?"

"A group of us went to Axis, a club where the team hangs out after the matches. Carl had negotiated a nice promotion with the owner. Anyway, it was the night they were all celebrating Carlos' debut. I was just leaning and watching Maddie and Tomás dance. Carl came down from the private party room and picked me out of everyone else in the club. I don't know. I didn't go after him or anything. I had talked to him before at the match in Section 12, but the club was really where it started."

"It's pretty quick to get married, don't you think?"

"Not if you know that he's the right one. Carl and I are like two puzzle pieces that each of us had been searching for that fit together. You know what I mean?"

"I guess so. I have not ever been in a relationship remotely close to that."

Jackie turned the tables. "Had you know Carl before his buying into the FLA?"

"No, but every man in America and many in the world at least know who I am, supermodel cum self-made businesswoman."

"Ah, I remember seeing some of your ads when I was a teenager."

"Exactly. That was toward the end of my career as a model, though." Alexi thought for a moment. "Why do you think Carl insisted on putting you in charge of Denver?"

"I'm not sure. He is busy with things around Chicago and with the coaching chance in Philadelphia earlier this season. I'm surprised, really, that he wanted me to do it instead of promoting one of his assistants in the front office. They certainly would have more experience and contacts in the league and the sport." Jackie wondered about the nature of the question. So far, she had only gotten the impression from Alexi that she generally liked her.

"I'm just wondering because Carl was so adamant about it," Alexi said. Jackie must not know about the tryst, Alexi thought to herself. Good, a wedding crushing announcement would be so much fun. "After this afternoon's discussion and yesterday's press conference, I have no doubt that you'll be more than fine. You have a wonderful business savvy that comes naturally. But are you sure that you will be able to be away from Carl during long stretches of time?"

"That one I'm not so sure about." Jackie hesitated. A red flag started to wave inside her head. There had to be something more to this questioning. She wanted to talk to Alexi about Carl's problems with substance abuse in the past, but quickly decided that was best left a secret only a few in the inner circle knew. "I'll be okay with it. And if Carl wasn't, he would have said something and insisted that I have a different title or find a GM first."

Alexi nodded. There was a weakness in the relationship. Separate Jackie from him and Carl becomes vulnerable to me. Perfect. This is the perfect arrangement, she internally mused. "I'm sure everything will be fine. A little separation is good for the soul sometimes."

"And lovemaking will likely be sweeter when we see each other again."

"Oh, girl, stop with the reworked clichés." Alexi laughed.

They fussed over who paid the bill. They decided it wouldn't really matter since it was an expense-accountable lunch, so Alexi used her American Express card.

Jackie decided to walk back to the condominium. It was a mild day for August and she needed the downtime to process the meeting. Alexi returned to her hotel to collect her bags and be on the way to the airport.

The end of the lunch portion of the conversation was what weighed on her the most. It was not just girl talk. Some of the phrasings seemed like Alexi was probing to see if she could make a move on Carl. Nah. Carl would be too young for her, or would he? There was no way. Sure it was possible that Carl admired her for how she looked. But would he cheat? He loved her too much to do that. At least she hoped so.

During her walk, the gravity of the situation began to sink in. She would have to spend a lot of time in Denver. She would certainly miss Chicago. She might even have to learn how to snow ski for business meetings. That would not be so bad. It would certainly help to keep her in shape. Alexi did mention that she had a villa in Vail. Jackie was sure that she would be able to use it for retreats.

The possibility that Alexi would try to take Carl's heart away from her crept back into her mind. She had to steel herself for the event, just in case.

Jackie reached the lake. She sat on the concrete and looked out over the fresh blue waters caressing the city's edge. Sailboats dotted the horizon. Seagulls battled pigeons for bits of discarded tourist food crumbs. She hoped that she would not have to leave Chicago permanently. It would not be easy, but she was ready for the journey and the challenge.

Chapter LXXXVII

FRIDAY, AUGUST 14, 1998: It was a match day evening at Sueños. Joe found himself short handed by a bartender and a waitress. They had both called in sick, but he suspected they were lying.

Shortly after 5:00 PM, his *salvadora* walked in the door. "Molly," he called out. "I hear you have been applying for bartending jobs."

"I didn't think you had any openings."

Joe handed her a navy Sueños tee shirt, the color wore on Stampede game days. "Go change; you're hired."

She gave Joe an odd look.

"Go, change, you start right now. I hope you wore comfortable shoes."

"I always do." She smiled and scurried to the restroom to swap her white jersey with Ian's name on it for the navy work wear.

Joe ran her quickly through the pricing and how the antique register worked. She only had two hours to get the lay of the bar. She helped the usual after work crowd. She just did drink orders. Joe took care of relaying the food orders to the kitchen.

Molly was not surprised that Joe had a strict policy of his staff not drinking on the job. He showed her his special staff 'whisky' that was just amber colored water for doing shots with patrons. It was a trade secret. Also, it was a bottle to use when certain patrons had a few too many and still insisted on drinking. Molly nodded understandingly.

Ordering slowed down somewhat during the first minutes of the match

Lawrence and Matt were both startled to see Molly behind the bar. "Quit security?"

"It's still up in the air. The case isn't resolved yet." She shrugged. "I just needed something to do so I didn't feel like I was relying on Ian so much."

Sean came in and sat down at the bar. He started to order a beer, then saw that it was Molly. He quickly switched his order to a Coke. Księżnicka was at his side. She ordered a Shirley Temple.

Many of the Stampede fans arrived straight from work and had dinner before the match. Joe was glad that his kitchen staff had all shown up for work. He paused to watch Molly. She picked up everything quickly. She was going to make a good bar wife.

The match was in Philadelphia. The Stampede needed a win to stay in the top portion of the table. The match was nothing to write home about. Tomás received a yellow card caution in the 39th minute. Novotny took revenge for the team five minutes later by scoring off of a corner kick. Paul took the kick at the flag and bent it beautifully with nary a deflection into the net.

Molly was so busy she did not notice that the Stampede had scored until the bar erupted with whoops of joy.

Their excitement was dulled slightly when Jon Eagle, Jr. scored just before the halftime whistle.

Everyone in the bar needed refreshment on his or her drinks during the brief ten-minute break. Molly worked up a sweat jerking ales and pouring drinks. By this time, she had developed a rhythm. Her tip jar was growing quite stuffed.

Late in the match, Chicago took the lead when Ian scored off a nice feed from the fresh-legged Tarpey. Molly just happened to glance up at the right time to see her boyfriend score. She was the first one with a loud "GOOOOOOOOOOOOAAAAAA AAAAAALLLLLLLLLL!" out of her mouth.

Matt flagged Molly over. "Prepare the victory lemon drop shots. I'm ordering a dozen on my tab."

"Don't jinx it," Lawrence chided.

At just that moment, Minute Man forward Thrasher was called offside. A collective sigh of relief was heard in the pub.

Brendan scored the coffin nail in the 89th minute on a direct free kick. "That's my man," Lawrence bellowed.

"Bring on those shots, Mols," Matt hollered.

She slid the tray of chilled vodka shots with a dozen sugared lemon wedges toward him.

"I hope you poured yourself one," Matt said.

Molly pointed to a shot of cold water sitting to her right on the mat. Vodka, boda. The words are so close in Polish because they look so much alike. At least that what she figured. It fooled Matt anyway. At the final whistle, Matt, Lawrence, Molly and ten others lifted their shot glasses and drank to victory. Philadelphia 1—Stampede 3.

Chapter LXXXVIII

Sunday, August 16, 1998: "Are you ready for this?" Carl asked from the back of the parked limousine. He touched his fiancée's face lightly with his fingertips. He gazed softly into her eyes.

"I'm nervous, but yes, I'm ready, Carl," she stated with some confidence.

"I'm glad. I know you'll do well, my love." He kissed her gently.

The driver was busy pulling out her luggage. Carl had purchased a couple more pieces of the Hartmann Wings collection for her. She wanted to have plenty of clothes to leave in the corporate apartment she would be renting until suitable property for purchase could be located.

Jackie felt weird traveling with that much luggage. She was usually the one bag carry-on type of person. She traveled more like a man in that respect.

The driver opened the door. "Are you ready, Miss Harris?"

She took the driver's hand as she climbed out of the car. "Yes, thank you. As ready as I'll ever be."

Truthfully, she felt like she was on automatic pilot. Everything was happening too fast. She kissed Carl goodbye one last time and turned to have her bags checked in by the skycap.

"I love you, Jacqueline," Carl shouted as she disappeared inside the terminal.

On the jet, Jackie pulled out a notepad and began to jot down a dream FLA list based on current rosters. She had not had a chance to look at much college or even high school talent for the draft, but those would be to fill in on the bench and if they broke out as stars on the pitch, then so be it. She could not help thinking like a coach. That is truly what she wanted to do. She was in a position of power to be a behind the scenes coach, but she knew that she could simply not do that to whomever she hired. She was hired to be a general manager and that was it. Perhaps the ideal situation to appease her yen for strategy was to pick a coach who was stronger on conditioning and mediocre on strategy.

From the Stampede, she wrote down Brendan Glazier and Maxwell Harp. Harp would be easier to get than Glazier. San Francisco had expressed a strong interest in Brendan so there might be a postseason trade. From Philadelphia, she wanted Andre LeCock minding the net. She liked his style during her week there, and she thought that he deserved a chance to be a starter.

She scratched her head with the end of her pen. It was not easy. Not many of the bench players had seen much playing time. That may change once the playoff positions are locked in. Then, perhaps, the coaches may decide to rest some of the key starters in favor of giving the second stringers a chance to prove their mettle on the lush green pitch of dreams.

She wrote down, "Luis Natal, Tallahassee, forward mid." Maybe. He had seen some time for Tallahassee, especially since old Socrates Kosmos was out with a nagging groin injury a lot this summer. Tallahassee may be more willing to part with Kosmos, if he did not retire on his own. If at all possible, Jackie was not about to let herself get talked into contracting an old player who was past his prime. The main problem of that would be the drain on the precious salary cap. Besides, older players, while smarter, tended to be injury prone.

Jackie laid her head back on the well-cushioned leather headrest. She closed her eyes. She needed to relax and think about nothing soccer-related for a while.

After the plane landed at Denver International, Jackie collected her baggage. She met a prearranged hired car that took her to the Embassy Suites on 19th and Curtis. The driver helped her with her luggage. "You have a lot of bags, ma'am," he commented with a smile.

"I know. I'm going to be here a while. Could I have your number to call you directly in case I need anything?" Jackie wanted to be prepared.

"Yes, ma'am. If I'm on another run, I can always let one of my friends have the fare." The driver pulled out a business card containing his name and cell phone. "My name is Jimmy. Call me anytime."

"Thank you." Jackie tucked the card inside her brief. She tipped Jimmy generously. A bellboy took the loaded cart the rest of the way into the hotel.

It was still early in the evening. Jackie checked in and freshened up. She opened up her daily planner and looked up Tavie Natchez's number. Tavie was to be her main contact in Denver with the fan group. Tavie's husband was a high level banker where the ticket deposit monies were being held in an interest bearing account. Tavie herself owned an employment agency.

"Tavie, it's Jackie. I'm in town. Are you two up for some dinner?"

"Sounds great, Jackie. It will be good to finally meet you in person," Tavie replied.

They met at the Wynkoop Brewing Company brewpub in the LoDo area. It was an easy walk for Jackie from her hotel. The Rockies baseball game was on all the television when they entered. Tavie and her husband, Ricky, brought along another couple. Tavie was a hyper petite woman with long black hair. She was dressed in a smart weekend outfit of fashionable blue jeans and Ralph Lauren polo. Ricky looked like a young Vicente Fox with some salt in his black pepper hair.

"Jackie, this is Han and Sonia Carling. The Carlings are in real estate. Han, Sonia, this is Jackie Harris, manager of the Denver FLA soccer club," Tavie introduced. There were handshakes and niceties. Han was a tall man of Germanic decent. Blonde receding locks, wire-rimmed glasses and a rough beard set off deep blue eyes. His wife, Sonia, was an athletic lady of Jackie's height. Soft curls were pushed back off her heart-shaped face by Donna Karan sunglasses.

They were seated, and Ricky immediately ordered a pitcher of the dark house brew for the table. When it was served, Ricky stood and offered up a toast, "To the success of soccer in Denver and the United States, and to Jackie Harris for taking on the duties of general manager."

"Cheers!" all joined in.

"Thank you, Ricky," said Jackie humbly.

"How much business should we talk about tonight?" Tavie asked.

"At least enough to get the tax write-off," joked Han.

"Jackie," began Sonia, "Han and I have some nice office spaces lined up. I thought you might like to take a look at them first thing in the morning. The trick is finding a floor with enough square footage to handle all the day-to-day personnel you will have, plus a nice office with a view for you."

"Of course, that sounds like a plan. I also want to look at some condos. I don't plan on being at the Embassy for long."

Sonia nodded.

Tavie said, "I've got some résumés that might work for a few key positions. I've also contacted a sports headhunter to get some more good candidates."

"Sounds great." Jackie took a long swig of her ale. "You all are helping to make this easier on me than I expected. Carl was right about the Denver fans."

"All we need is a team name," Sonia said.

The five chatted for a few hours after dinner. Jackie left with a good feeling about her new career and home away from home. Success was to be had here.

Chapter LXXXIX

The next week was very exhausting for Jackie. Han and Sonia divided Jackie's real estate needs between them. Han handled looking for the right office space. Sonia worked with her to find a perfect condominium. Jackie also had Jimmy running. The two decided that she really needed her own car in Denver. Jackie thought about renting one, but concluded that owning one would be the best course of action.

Tavie arranged to have the man running the fan website become the official webmaster and turn the website into the official website of the team. Harley was more than pleased to have a steady gig. He did not even give proper notice at the Taco Bell where he was a shift supervisor. "Finally," he posted up on the site, "my hobby is paying off."

Jackie named Tavie and her company head of human resources. It would be easier to have the screening outsourced.

On Tuesday, the *Rocky Mountain News* ran a full-page ad in the sports section announcing the naming contest.

On Wednesday, Jackie signed a lease for a floor in the financial district. A web company had just gone under and had left all their equipment and furniture. Jackie agreed to purchase a lot of it from them. It was a nice deal. She sent some of the newly unemployed IT folks to Tavie to check out for employment. Jackie suggested that it might be wise to have someone who already knew how the computers were networked together to be on staff.

FRIDAY, AUGUST 21, 1998: Jackie had Carl wire money to the seller of a building in Larimer Square. There was a bar downstairs and a couple of rental units above. Jackie moved into one and extended the leases of the other occupied units. She set up the bar on a lease deal as well, assuring that they would not be kicked out as long as the sports-themed place agreed to air future FLA matches. The bar owner shrugged and signed the lease.

"You seriously did not write that into his lease, did you, Jackie?" Sonia asked.

"See for yourself."

Sonia scanned the document. "Oh my god, you are insane, woman. This area is all baseball in the summer and all Broncos in the fall."

"I know." Jackie grinned.

"You are so evil." Sonia laughed. "Want to go furniture shopping?"

"Sure, I'll need a place to lay my head next week."

Jackie hopped a plane back to Chicago later that evening. She had missed Carl, but frankly, she was so busy that she did not notice much.

It was clear when she crawled into the back of Carl's limousine that he had missed her more. He covered her with kisses as the driver took them back to the Lake Point condo.

"I've missed you so much, Jacqueline," he cooed repeatedly. He buried his face in her hair and drank in her scent. He eased his lips up her neck, jaw line, chin to her soft mouth. They kissed long and deep. He held her in a tight embrace. "I love you, my bride."

"I love you, too, Carl, my groom."

In the morning, Carl crawled on top of her. He could not wait any longer. She appeared too tired the night before, so he remained a gentleman and merely cuddled.

Carl ran his fingers along her naked flesh under the silken sheets. She responded by twisting toward him. He touched her curly bush. She arched her back and lifted her hips. His fingers caressed her clit. "Oh, Carl," she encouraged. He moved his body closer to her. His flesh was already well engorged. He ran the tip of his along her thigh. She moaned. She was wet and ready.

Carl rammed his dick into her. She met his hungry thrust with equal desire. Absence does make the heart and the flesh grow fonder. They made love long and sweaty, making up for the weekdays of sleeping alone. He pounded her with the precision of a metronome. She clenched her legs around him and dug her nails into his back. Carl felt a trickle of blood from one scratch and the sting of the perspiration. He flipped them over. She rode him like a bucking bull. Carl cupped his hands under her firm bouncing breasts. She reared her head back as she reached a climactic plateau. "Come for me!" she screamed.

He unloaded in her. She shivered on his pole and collapsed onto his furred chest. Wet, sticky, shaking from the pleasures of each other, they both lie there, breathing heavily, hearts racing. "I love you, Carl. I'm sorry I didn't realize how much I missed coming home to you this past week."

He smiled. It was her first true admittance of her feelings. He knew in his heart that she could not live without him, nor could he without her. "I sensed it, Jacqueline. I knew you missed me as much as I missed you."

She slid off him and splayed herself on the mattress.

He looked over at her. He wondered if the power he had bestowed upon her was an aphrodisiac, like it was for many men in power, himself not excluded. He remembered her emails from the past week. Many were very businesslike, reporting on progress and people hired. He saw solid business acumen in her, not unlike Alexi's. Jackie was a strong woman; it was best not to put too many restrictions on her, especially after they were married, lest he lose her. In a lot of ways, Jackie was like Alexi, only better.

Jackie heard a rummaging in the kitchen. "Who's here?"

"I called in a personal chef for the morning. He's getting breakfast ready for us." She pulled the sheet over their naked bodies. "Why didn't you tell me?"

"I wanted it to be a surprise." Carl smiled. He kissed her gently.

"Sounds good. I think we've worked up an appetite." She grinned from ear to ear.

"Indeed."

Sunday's parting at the airport was harder this time. They knew that the weekends spent together over the next several months would be intense ones, and the longing in between would be greater. They each resolved to handle it like adults.

CHAPTER XC

MONDAY, AUGUST 24, 1998: Alexi flew in to check up on progress in Denver. Jackie was not sure why Alexi felt that she had to check things out so early in the process. She met the woman in the new office.

"Nice loft space you picked out," Alexi voiced her approval.

"We got lucky with a dotcom going out of business. We were able to get a great deal on the equipment and furnishings, too," Jackie beamed. She looked Alexi up and down. It looked like she was putting on a little weight around the lower abdomen. The word pregnancy crossed her mind, but she decided not to mention it. Alexi was probably self-conscious of it. Models tended to be when it came to their appearances.

"Good job. Did you find a place to live while you're down here?"

"Yeah, a nice investment property."

"Excellent. I see you are making some wonderful decisions without much interference from Carl or me." Alexi seated herself behind a desk. She flipped on a computer workstation. The home page was set to the Denver team home page. "This is nice."

"Oh, yeah, Harley was running the fan website. I hired him and bought the rights to the web name and site contents. He's very pleased to be an insider now. You'll probably meet him later today. He had been working on the system all weekend. I've also been trying to retain one or two of the IT guys from the dotcom that was in here. One is on a consulting contract now, but he may decide to go perm. It depends on how he looks to Tavie, who runs our outsourced employment agency."

"You've been very productive your first week, dear. You've done more than I could have. How in the world?"

"A good network in place with the ticket deposit drive helped a bunch. That's where Tavie and her husband, Ricky, came from. Also, the real estate agents who helped me find the properties."

"Wonderful." Alexi ran her fingers along the stainless steel of the desktop. The décor was stark, modern, efficient. "We do need to sport this place up a bit, though."

"I agree. I was hoping to pick out a team nick and logo first."

"Good idea. When is the deadline for the contest by the way?" Alexi blinked when she looked at Jackie. My god, Carl picked out a good one.

"Sunday, August 30th. We will meet on Labor Day to go over the submissions and pick out the best one and announce the winner the next day."

"Sounds good. Are we meeting here or in Chicago?"

"It's up to Carl."

"Okay."

Back in Chicago, Mirek was not happy with the goose egg performance of his team last Friday. He allowed the team to stay over Saturday night to relax in Boston and take in the sights. The flight back on Sunday afternoon was tense. Mirek, Gina and the rest of the coaching staff sat well apart from the players. Baumgartner was the only one who sat relatively close. He had suffered a nasty deep knee contusion and was scheduled for an MRI today to assure that there was no ligament damage.

Late in the match, Vladimir Starkov and Paddy Kirkhoven got into a scuffle. Somehow, Paddy's shorts were torn. Telephoto lenses focused on the exposed tattoo of the Kirkhoven family crest on Paddy's left butt cheek. It was a relatively funny topper to an otherwise awful match.

Mirek kept his emotions in check and did not really give much of a post match talk like he usually did. This made the team collectively nervous.

Baumgartner was the only one excused from the prepractice meeting at 7:00 AM. Gina and the German captain went to Northwestern. Mirek hoped for a good report.

"I could barely stand to watch you play Friday evening," Mirek began. "Ian, where were you passing to most of the time? When did I trade you to the Bulldogs?"

Ian lowered his head.

"Answer me," Mirek barked. He bent over and grabbed Ian's chin and forced him to look up. Mirek's military past was starting to boil back to the surface.

"No one was running patterns like they were supposed to be," Ian replied.

Carlos shot back, "*Pinche pendejo,* we were so. Los perros were just intercepting and covering us too tight."

Mirek turned to Carlos. "Then it's your responsibility to create the open space." He looked at the rest of the team. "It's your responsibility to create space. The Bulldogs have studied our game tapes. All of you have started to fall into a rut. We can't go into the playoffs with this attitude. What do I have to do to break you of your bad habits?"

"I don't understand," Brendan said.

"*Kudowa,* Glazier, you are one of the worst. Why do you think you can't get anything done on the pitch? Today we are going to work on opposites. If you normally pass or shoot with your left, you will be shooting or passing with your right. Understand?"

A group shrug.

"Understand? Opposite day. Now get up and get warmed up."

The trainers and assistants began to run the team through warm ups and drills. Mirek's cell phone rang.

"It's Gina. The news is not so good."

Mirek drew a deep breath. "Go on."

"Baumgartner has a minor tear in his left meniscus. I'm going to advise rest and that he not play the next match."

"*Kudowa*, Heinrich is the one who makes the pitch stable. This is not what I want to hear this late in the season."

"I know, honey, but it's best. We are in the playoffs. The next couple of matches will be fine without Heinrich. He'll be needed more in the playoffs. In the meantime, you can find out who is a candidate for that captain's armband on a regular basis when Heinrich is gone."

"This was not on my list of things to figure out this season."

"It will be okay. With some rest, he'll be as good as new come the playoffs."

"Okay, doc." He snapped his phone shut. At least they did not have another match until August 30th, match day 21 out of 22. The playoffs started on September 12th, not too far off. Mirek hoped he could whip his team into shape for two more W's in order to secure home field advantage.

Chapter XCI

TUESDAY, AUGUST 25, 1998: Carl woke up in a cold sweat. He had one of his nightmares again. This time, Jackie was not there to comfort him. Jackie was in the dream. It was the same visions he had when he found his mother and father murdered, except that instead of his mother, it was Jackie.

He padded to the bathroom and flung open the medicine cabinet. He needed something to calm his nerves. He twisted bottles around until he found the one marked Vicodin. He popped one, washing it down with a generous amount of water.

As he closed his eyes to splash water on his face, a vision of Alexi with a pistol danced in his mind. Was Alexi capable of shooting Jackie? He sure as hell hoped not. She did want him for way more than a business partnership, but he was pretty sure, at least on a conscious level, that she would not sink to murder to get rid of her competition.

He went back into the bedroom and reached for the phone. He dialed Agnes.

"I'm sorry to call you so early, Agnes. But I really need to talk."

Agnes cleared her throat. "It's okay, Carl. I'm here for you. What's wrong?"

"I'm really worried about Jackie being with Alexi down in Denver without me around."

"They are fine. Nothing will go wrong."

"I'm worried that Alexi will do something to Jackie, something to hurt her."

"Like what? Tell her about your tryst? I don't think Alexi is up to that. She seems to me to be above that. But I've only met her once. Most of what I know about her is from your sessions." Agnes waved at Paul so that he would leave the room. Her husband nodded. He was used to it.

Carl let out a long deep breath. "I don't know. That dream just really scared me. I don't know what I would do if I lost Jackie."

"You would be strong. Like you were when you mother died. You were strong then and you are strong now. You just don't realize it."

"I'm not, Agnes," he countered. "I took a Vicodin this morning."

"That's it, Carl. I'm coming over." Agnes stood and reached for her sweatpants. "You are not to move until I get there."

"Let's not be hasty, doc. I'm fine. I'm still going to work. I just needed to vent a little." He tried to stave her off.

"Okay, go to the office. But I'm coming by later to see how you are doing."

Carl sighed, "Okay."

At the office, Carrie sent him to work on signing some letters that needed to go out right away. That kept his mind occupied for a while. Until a phone call from Alexi rattled him:

"Carl, darling," Alexi cooed from the Rockies. "I'm going to stop by tomorrow on my way back to New York, so clear your schedule."

"I can't," he lied. "I have a phone conference and a meeting with Quigley regarding some player movements."

"Can't be, Quigley is going to be meeting with Jackie in Denver tomorrow. I'm stopping by first thing in the morning. I'll come by your condo."

Damn it all to hell, he thought to himself. Just tell her no. "Okay."

Alexi smirked as she clicked the 'end' button on her cellular phone. She fingered the set of keys and the key card that she had temporarily stolen from Jackie. She took them just long enough to get copies made. Getting the keycard duplicated was not easy, but you pay any forgery geek enough money and anything is possible.

Alexi always gets what she wants.

Carl sat stunned. He could not tell Alexi no. He wanted to call Jackie, but he had promised her that he would not bother her on the phone unless it was business related during the daytime working hours. Carl needed something to cling to.

He buzzed Carrie. "Hold all my calls."

"No problem, Carl," Carrie replied.

Carl stood, closed the door, and crossed to his office bar. He poured himself a stiff Jack Daniels in a rocks glass. He tossed back about half of it. He set down the drink. "Why do I let her do this to me?" he mused. He sat down on the couch and buried his head in his hands.

Chapter XCII

Wednesday, August 26, 1998: Alexi slipped into Lake Point Towers at 3:20 AM. The doorman on duty was snoring loud enough to rattle the door glass. Alexi was glad. She could not recall Carl's unit number. She carefully reached around the desk and grabbed the man's information binder. Alexi flipped the pages until she found Carl's name. Her fingernail followed the line over, "Unit 5502."

She quietly replaced the book.

Once on the floor, she instinctively turned toward Carl's unit. The first key she tried did not fit. It belonged to Jackie's loft. The second one was the right one.

She crept in and closed the door. Her keen ears heard her lover's soft breathing. She followed the sound, shedding clothes as she approached. Pausing, she stared at Carl's sleeping form. He twitched ever so slightly. Alexi speculated he must have been dreaming. She eased back the covers. He slept naked. His lanky form sprawled out in all its glory gave her a rush. Alexi needed to be next to him, her baby's daddy.

She slid in next to him. He stirred, mumbling, "Jackie."

Alexi ran her hands over his body. She gripped his half-hard penis. He responded to her touch. She pressed her breasts against his hairy back. Her legs rubbed against his. Her growing belly nestled in the small of his back. Everything felt perfect. Nothing was hurried. Neither one was drunk.

She kissed the back of his neck. His scent intoxicated her. "I need you, Carl," she breathed.

He slowly turned his body. He was fully engorged. Alexi could not be sure if he opened his eyes or not. The room was dark, with only faint ambient light from the city skyline coming through the window.

He mounted her from the side. It was gentle. With her legs, she pulled him into syncopation. For the first time in months, she felt the rush of sexual satisfaction.

Carl slowly came to. He responded more with his entire body. His lips found her nipples. She moaned softly, "Yes, Carl, that's it."

Carl heard the voice, but did not connect it with being in bed with him. He was still in a dreamlike state of mind. He responded to her vocalizations. He gently turned her so she was on her back. "Make love to me, Carl."

His stroking inside of her was steady, tender. Her juices flowed lubing his piston. She approached a plateau of orgasmic pleasure and raised her loins as she dug her nails into his back. "Come with me, honey."

He shuddered inside of her, filling her. His lips fell on hers. "Mmm, thank you." Sticky, he rolled over. She spooned him and fell asleep.

Carl found himself on the beach. The waves lapped at his bare feet. A cool breeze tousled his hair. The sun was setting on the watery horizon. He looked around. It was quiet. Sunbathers were packing up their towels and bottles of sunscreen.

A finger tapped his shoulder from behind. Carl turned slowly. Jackie cried tears of blood. "I can't take it, Carl. I'm leaving you." Her wedding dress was ripped.

She turned and walked away, fading quickly as she went.

Carl fell to his knees. "Don't leave me," he sobbed. "I'm sorry, Jackie, I'm so sorry."

Carl awoke with a start. He found an arm draped over his chest. He studied its painted nails. Jackie never paints her nails. He turned and looked at Alexi.

"What the fuck are you doing here?" he exclaimed as he sat up quickly.

Alexi rubbed her eyes, smearing the last remaining bits of azure eye shadow. "Good morning, darling."

"Oh god, not again, we didn't—"

"We did," she interjected with a smile.

"Fuck." Carl let his torso fall back. He rubbed his temples.

"It was more like making love." Alexi finger-combed her hair.

"Dammit, I just can't resist you, can I? I try downers and alcohol, but that failed in Houston. I've tried avoidance, but that made me more vulnerable with Jackie in Denver. Damn, damn, damn." He removed his arm so he could stare at her. "How in the fuck did you get in here anyway?"

"I have my ways." She blinked.

"Look, you know I'm going to marry Jackie. Why do you insist on trying to screw it up? You can have any man you want. Please, go screw around with someone else." This was the most ballsy that Carl had ever been talking to Alexi.

"Because I want you." Her voice softened. She reached out and took his hand in hers. She cocked her head. "Please, at least be my lover, be close to me, even if you cannot marry me."

Carl did not know what to say. She sounded desperate. His expression softened. He pulled her closer. Her proposal sounded like a perfectly workable solution, especially with Jackie having to be in Denver most of the time now. "Okay." He pulled her into a kiss.

I am my father's son, he said to himself.

Chapter XCIII

WEDNESDAY, AUGUST 26, 1998: Denver, CO: The opening date has been set for the 1999 Fútbol League America season. Saturday, April 3, 1999 is set as the inaugural match for the to be yet nicknamed Denver team. The match will take place at Mile High Stadium against an opponent to be announced later. It is rumored to be Houston, the other expansion team.

General Manager Jacqueline Harris stated that progress is being made in the search for a coach. She refused to speculate on candidates.

THURSDAY, AUGUST 27, 1998: Denver, CO: Arturo Rodriguez has been awarded the head coaching position in the Denver FLA organization. General Manager, Jacqueline Harris, made the announcement yesterday during a quick press conference.

"We are pleased to have Arturo on board so quickly. He brings a flair to every team he has coached."

Rodriguez was let go from his coaching position earlier this year from a Guatemalan first division team. He refused to comment on the terms of the departure, only stating, "I'm sorry things did not work out for the 1998-1999 campaign, but it gives me an opportunity to help build fútbol in the United States."

Terms of the contract were not disclosed.

The *RMN* reported to her on Friday that they had received more than 1500 entries. Tavie found some key folks for marketing and a wonderful administrative assistant.

Saturday, Jackie returned to Chicago. She had a productive week again. She was satisfied with the way everything was coming together. The next major step would be in player negotiations. Money was flowing in for season tickets.

Still it felt good to be back home in Carl's arms.

Chapter XCIV

Sunday, August 30, 1998: The Chicago Stampede had a road match in Columbus. Jackie and Carl decided to hit Sueños to watch the match instead of traveling.

Molly tended bar. She developed quite a knack for inventing new and delicious mixed shots.

Lawrence and Sheila traveled to Columbus with a group of 12-Steppers. Columbus was only an easy six to seven hour drive depending on what side of Chicago you started out on. A bus full had left that morning at 6:00 AM. The match was in the afternoon. If there were no problems, they should get there in time to do a little tailgating. Lawrence and Sheila drove on their own. They had plans to meet up with Brendan and the rest of the team later.

Vladimir who was serving his red card suspension decided to make an appearance at Sueños. His wife and three small kids joined him. They sat in a booth in the back room. Standing on chairs, the kids took over the foosball table.

Sean and Matt, of course, could not resist bothering the defender about the last match. The Koneki girls kept trying to pull their boyfriends away, but eventually gave up. They knew that players did not like to be bothered when they were out as regular people. Księżnicka told Molly, who told Jose and Joe. Joe went over just before kickoff and dragged the two men away from Vladimir. "Dammit, Joe," complained Sean, "we were just getting to some good questions."

"Oh, piss off. You two will stay in this room for the rest of the day until Vladimir leaves."

"What if we need to visit the john, Joe?" asked Matt in a smart-alecky way.

"Of course, you can piss in the john, but not when Vladimir is in there."

"One drink on the house?" asked Sean.

"No. You only get cokes anyway."

"But-"

"No buts," Joe spat back. "If I catch you with alcohol in your hands or mouth of any kind, you will be banned from this bar. I can't risk my license on some smart ass punk like you."

Matt found a single empty barstool. Róża sidled up next to him. He pulled her up on his lap. They kissed briefly.

Jackie saw them kiss. "I'm surprised they are still together," she commented to Molly.

Molly shrugged. "As long as they're both happy and she doesn't drink alcohol in here. Newcastles?"

"Yes, please."

"How are things going in Denver?" Molly made conversation as she drew the brews.

"Surprisingly well. A lot of deals are starting to come together. But I can't talk too much about it yet."

Molly nodded. "I understand." She set the pints in front of Jackie. "I'll put them on your tab."

"Thanks." Jackie turned to go back to the table with Carl and Agnes. She wanted to get back to her notebook. Watching the matches now was like scouting for players to try to trade for in the off season.

The teams took the field before a respectable turnout in Columbus. The Stampede's passing was crisper than the last match. Virgil Amat started in goal instead of Dan. He played a solid game and recorded a shut out in the end. Carlos suffered a strained calf muscle late in the first half. He was subbed out for Randall Silva at the beginning of the second half. The three goals were scored by Maxwell Harp in the 36th minute on a penalty kick, Brendan Glazier off a direct free kick in the 57th minute and the coffin nail by Ian with an assist going to Taylor MacLeod who came on for Tomás in the 80th minute.

Mirek was pleased with the way the team looked. He chalked the prior match up to an off day—at least that is what he hoped.

He did pull Tomás aside, as the rest of the team went into the showers. Speaking in Polish, he said, "Do I need to schedule anger management classes for you?"

Tomás laughed. "You're joking, right?"

"No, I'm not. This is not Europe where things are used to being a bit rougher. The fourth official said he would have called your yellow card a straight red."

"On the pitch, I apologize for nothing. I get into the match. I take every game seriously. That's what you want out of me, right?"

"*Tak, tak*, but that's the point, I need you IN the match and not sitting in Sueños serving league detention."

"I hear Molly mixes a mean cocktail," Tomás jested.

"Shut up! Go take a shower." Mirek swatted his defender on the ass so hard his palm stung.

Chapter XCV

TUESDAY, SEPTEMBER 1, 1998: The *Rocky Mountain News* expressed a package containing all the mail in entries and printouts from the web entries to the Stampede office. Alexi would meet them to help make a decision on the Denver team name. Carl suggested that an outside accounting firm be hired for the day to assist in sorting out the duplicate entries. The ladies agreed.

The firm filed into the office like an army of geeks. The mixed sex group divided the task and spread out piles on the large conference table. One compiled a tally spreadsheet on a laptop. It was a noisy affair. They laughed at some of the more absurd suggestions.

Winnie and Carrie kept the group plied with coffee and snacks.

Carl, Jackie and Alexi sat down in Carl's office. Alexi and Carl displayed no signs that anything illicit had taken place earlier in the week. It was a tacit agreement. They chatted about player availability at the end of the year. A few New York players would be free agents. Alexi expressed her desire to keep Akeem Williams, one of the star forwards. Jackie brought up her desire for getting Andre LeCock from Philadelphia.

"But he's just a backup with little field time. Don't you want to try to get a real keeper like Brady?" Carl suggested.

"Don't screw with Brady," Alexi warned. "He's mine."

"Which is exactly why I think Andre would be happy to make the move. Depending on who else Arturo and I pick up in the upcoming drafts, I might be able to guarantee him a starting position."

"Have you seen LeCock play?"

Jackie glared at Carl as she cleared her throat. "Have you forgotten so quickly my week's stint in Philly?"

"Oh, right, I'm sorry." Carl shook his head. He now had to deal with two bull-headed women on a daily basis. "Alexi, how many upcoming free agents does Quigley represent?"

"Probably about 75 percent of them."

"That man is going to live comfortably off of FLA money," Carl commented.

"I always hated my agent, but he was too good to ever let go," Alexi put in.

Jackie raised her eyebrows. "Really? Tell us about it."

Alexi told them about the harassment she took from Rasheem Conyers. She had met Rasheem during a model search shoot early in her career. Rasheem was hanging out in the lobby, scouting for new talent. He took one look at a sixteen-year-old Alexi, and his jaw hit the floor. Rasheem took her under his wing and got her on the covers of many magazines and on Paris and Milan runways. The first contract gave him a forty percent cut plus expenses. Alexi's saving grace was that the contract was only until Alexi turned 18. After that, she renegotiated. Alexi was the hottest model on his roster. He could not afford to lose her, so he agreed to fifteen percent plus expenses. However, Rasheem wanted more. Frequently, he would pressure her into having sex with him in his office. To Alexi, even that young, she knew that something was not right. She knew that sometimes, female singers married their agents, but she felt that such a relationship was wrong, a conflict of interest. For twenty years, she put up with him, until, financially, she could leave him and represent herself. After she dumped Rasheem, she flourished by being her own woman. She would not have it any other way. "To this day," she added at the end, "I refuse to deal with Conyers. If a player I want is represented by Conyers, I take the player aside and tell him he's got a deal if he dumps Conyers."

"That's quite a story, Alexi," Jackie said.

"I did learn a lot from him."

Jackie nodded. "Indeed."

Carl was speechless. Alexi had not told him that story. Few people knew, he speculated, otherwise he might have known about that big part of her past.

Winnie knocked on the door. "It's time," she announced.

The trio went to the conference room. There were six large stacks in the center and several smaller ones surrounding them. The computer data enterer explained, "The six stacks in the center are the most popular requests. The others are anywhere from one to a dozen or so in duplication. The rest are going to break for lunch, but I'll stay here to answer any questions. We must say that some of the suggestions are bloody awful."

Jackie picked up a single sheet. "Denver Dingbats," she read aloud.

"See what I mean?" the enterer said.

Nods all the way around.

Jackie set the submission in an empty paper box. "Here's how I would like to do this. We will quickly go through all the small requests and toss rejects into the box. If even one of us likes one, it will be set aside for further consideration. All the entries will be added to a database when I get back to Denver. Agreed?"

Alexi and Carl both verbally agreed to the process.

Carl picked up one. "I'll start. Colorado Sheepshaggers." It was immediately rejected. They went around the table. Not a single small stack survived the cut.

"Okay, let's see what we have. Jackie, read me the list of the top six." Jackie sat down for the first time since leaving Carl's office.

"Number six, Denver Gunslingers." She tried hard to sound like David Letterman.

"No."

"No."

"Box it."

Carl picked up the stack and placed it in the receptacle.

"Number five, Denver Pumas."

Alexi had to repeat that one to herself a few times before final rejection. The cats were placed with the Gunslingers.

"Number four, Colorado Miners."

This time it was Carl. "Let's put that one aside. There may be some good artwork in that stack."

"Number three, Colorado Rush."

"Oh wow, I like that one," Alexi gushed.

"Number two, Colorado Mountaineers."

Three thumbs down.

"And the number one suggestion, Denver Dynamo."

Carl said, "I've changed my mind about Miners. I'll put that one away."

The ladies agreed.

Jackie said, "What is the difference in suggestions between Dynamo and Rush?"

"Two percentage points," replied Jack.

Alexi suggested, "Let's look through the stacks for artwork submissions. That might help us."

"We could put it to an Internet vote," suggested Carl.

"No," said Jackie, "I want this decision made today. We need to start the branding, jersey design, and so on. The fans want something to latch onto besides just 'the Denver soccer team'."

"Why did I ever agree to put you in charge?" Carl sighed, rolling his eyes.

Alexi smiled and chuckled. Her baby stirred. She tried not to wince. She placed her hand on her belly.

Jackie was already sorting through the Rush stack. She weeded out only five logo submissions. Carl and Alexi split the Dynamo stack and found 10 logo submissions. They put their heads together and found two good ones. Most of the rest contained clichéd starbursts or nuclear blast clouds. Jackie pulled out two of the five Rush logos. Jack took them and taped them to the wall.

Jackie pointed at one Dynamo logo. "I'll bet he's a Kiev fan. It's too close. That one's got to go."

Alexi closed her eyes to try to recall what the Dynamo Kiev logo looked like. "You're right. It does. Too much of a trademark risk." She removed the candidate.

Carl studied the remaining three. "I really like the color use in this one." He tapped a Rush logo with forest green, blue, gold, and silver tones. "Three jersey possibilities there."

"Rush. Colorado Rush." Alexi repeated over and over.

"Okay, it's between these two. We need to get that web conference up with Lance, Jason Fallon at the Rocky Mountain News, and those three ticket holders we talked about," Jackie said.

"Should we give them three choices?" Carl asked.

"Only if they can't come up with a winner between these two," Alexi said.

Carl stepped out to get Carrie. The four in the room broke for a quick lunch while the web conference was set up.

At two, they all met back in the conference room. The other accountants were in the room monitoring the process.

Lance spoke first, "It's good to see everyone. So we are trying to decide on a name for the Denver team, right?"

"That's correct, Lance. The choices are between Colorado Rush and Denver Dynamo," said Jackie.

"Jason Fallon here with the three season ticket holders. We are split between the two names. Two votes for Dynamo and two votes for Rush."

Jackie looked at Lance. He was stroking his chin in contemplation. Jackie looked over at Carl, "What's your final vote?"

"Colorado Rush."

"Alexi?"

"Colorado Rush."

"Lance?"

"I must say I like Rush better. Too many Eastern European teams are nicknamed Dynamo."

"I agree; my vote is for Colorado Rush. So it's decided. The team will be named the Colorado Rush." The team of accountants set to work folding all the Rush submissions individually and putting them into a tumbler cage they had brought in. Meanwhile, Jackie held up the two logo possibilities. There was a unanimous vote for the green, blue, gold & silver one. Jackie folded the loser and tossed it in with the rest of the winning names. "We have a winner in the logo contest portion. The winner will receive lifetime season tickets at the midfield line for the Colorado Rush. His name is Gerry Buchanan. We also want to announce that all the winning name submitters will receive an invitation to a skybox party at Mile High Stadium for the kickoff of the 1999 inaugural season. How are we coming over there?"

"Almost all folded and tumbled," said one worker bee.

Lance spoke, "It looks like you had a great response to the contest."

Jason replied, "We received just over 3000 entries."

"Wonderful. I'm glad to have the *Rocky Mountain News* on board as one of the FLA sponsors."

"It's been a pleasure covering the FLA and will be fun reporting on the Colorado Rush. Wow, that does have a nice ring to it. I was a vote for the other. Comes right off the tongue nice and easy."

"I told you," said one of the fans in the *RMN* office. He playfully punched Jason in the arm.

"Carl," addressed Lance, "I'm glad we were able to talk you into taking on half of another team."

"Aw shucks, dad, thanks," Carl joked.

There was an announcement from the tumbler. "We're ready."

The tumbler rolled over ten turns. The cage was opened. Jack stood up and drew the winning name. "Darin McAuley."

Jackie said, "Darin McAuley wins a year's subscription to the *RMN*, two seasons worth of Colorado Rush tickets and a trip to the first road match—location and date to be determined. Thank you Darin, Gerry and all those who submitted names in this contest. Go Colorado Rush!"

Chapter XCVI

THURSDAY, SEPTEMBER 3, 1998: After a brief few days in Denver, Jackie packed a weekend bag to go to Los Angeles. Bobby Lonestar had called her about some signatures he needed to finalize the contracts for the beach party.

Bobby met Jackie at the airport. He drove an old Cadillac convertible with wide longhorns on the hood. He was a lanky man who dressed in full rockabilly regalia. Jackie whistled at the condition of the classic automobile. She tossed her bag in the trunk and hopped in without opening the door.

They did not say much as he drove her to her hotel near the Rose Bowl in Pasadena. The sun was fading over the ocean and neon and glitz began to light up the hazy balmy evening air. The air felt heavy to Jackie's lungs. She had started to get used to breathing the thinner oxygen in the Mile High City.

Bobby mentioned that the plan was to drop Jackie's bags off at the hotel, then head to the wedding site. He wanted to be sure that Jackie saw it at nightfall, since the ceremony was to take place shortly after sunset. Friday, they would meet with the folks who needed at least a bride or groom's signature.

"Are you getting nervous, Jackie?" he asked as they cruised to the beach.

"With the new position, I haven't had much time to even think about it." She pulled a strand of hair out of her mouth and tried to tuck it back in her ponytail. "Everything has gone smoothly, I hope, with the plans?"

"To be perfectly honest," Bobby replied with a quick glance at her, "I thought I would be in over my head. I've planned a lot of parties before, but never a wedding. Hell, I don't even have a steady girlfriend."

Jackie smiled. "It can't be that much different."

"No, it really isn't." He pulled into a parking space. "We have a little walking to do."

Bobby had picked out his favorite location on Redondo Beach. Jackie paused at the end of the sand to take her sandals off. She enjoyed the feel of sand on bare feet. "I want to get married with my toes wriggling in the sand," she commented.

"You will." She followed his lead. He stopped, mid beach. "Right here is where the party will be. I've arranged to have a canopy. We can arrange it where either you face the ocean or the land. To make setting up chairs easier, there will be Astroturf laid out. I can arrange it so the aisle is not covered. It's up to you. We will keep the artificial lighting to a minimum, opting for romantic long taper candles. Outside the tent, depending on winds, we will have either a barbeque pit or an open bonfire. I'm still waiting on permits for that."

"Sounds lovely. What about the menu?"

"We are hiring a pair of sushi chefs for a cash sushi bar. Unless you want to foot the bill for the night."

"I don't think Carl will have a problem with that. Wines?"

"Only the best from California will do. We don't take to kindly to foreign wines around here." Bobby chuckled. "Also, I'm working with a local brewer to produce a special batch of ale with collector's labels stating the date of the wedding. I got permission from Lance to put the FLA Cup logo on it and would like to do the opposing team logos, but there may not be enough production time for that."

"I would just stick with the FLA logo."

Bobby nodded. "I'll let Lance and the brew master know."

"The bottles would make a nice souvenir for those attending the party. How many are we talking about?"

"How many ever comes out of a batch at the brewery. I'm really not sure. I'll have to see about that." Bobby studied her while she looked around the spot. "What do you think?"

"I love it." She sat down on the cool sand. "Everything is so perfect." She closed her eyes. "I can see myself walking down the aisle in my red dress. Carl waiting at the end for me, handsome, smiling. All our friends gathered around to celebrate."

Bobby sat down next to her. "You really are totally in love with Carl, aren't you?"

"Why do you ask?"

"There were some rumors going around that you were in it just for his money."

"Oh, no, not at all. It does feel like a fairy tale, but if it were he would not have dreamed of putting me to work running the Colorado Rush."

"I thought so."

Neither said anything for a while. Relaxing, they listened to the waves licking the shore. Jackie enjoyed the sound of the surf. She liked the beauty of the mountains, too, but she loved to be near water. It always seemed so much more refreshing to her. This was the absolute ideal spot to get married. She was glad that Carl suggested a beach wedding.

Chapter XCVII

FRIDAY, SEPTEMBER 4, 1998: Carl flew into LAX early the next morning. Bobby had arranged a meeting in their hotel in Pasadena with the various contractors so that the bride and groom could make the required down payments and sign contracts.

A breakfast bar was in the conference room. Jackie discussed flowers with the florist over espresso and pastries. Carl sat next to her. His hand rested on her thigh.

While the other contractors waited their turn, they exchanged client leads over coffee.

By lunchtime, Carl and Jackie were finally alone. Bobby said that he had to get back to work. They thanked him for all his hard work. Carl slipped him a check to pay for his time and effort on everything. Bobby looked at him puzzled, but said, "Thank you."

Jackie was curious as to how much Carl had paid Bobby. From the expression on Bobby's face, it was obvious that Bobby intended to do this out of the goodness of his heart. Jackie decided not to ask.

Carl's cell phone rang. "Excuse me," he said as he turned away from her. "Carl Costello," he answered. He did not look at the caller ID.

"It's Alexi."

"I'm busy with Jackie right now in LA. What do you need?"

"Carl, I need you to make sure you are at the meeting in Denver on Tuesday with Quigley and a few players he's representing."

"I thought you were going to be there."

"I can't make it." Alexi lied. She did not want to expose anyone to her widening girth. The baby inside of her belly decided to have a growth spurt. There was not much she could do short of wearing muumuus to hide it anymore. Thankfully, the wedding was in six weeks. Then, everyone would know. The whole pregnancy and who the father was would come out in the open. She just had to keep coming up with believable excuses to avoid creating any suspicion. "I had a crisis come up here that I need to be here to deal with."

"Okay, I'm sure Jackie won't mind me spending an extra day with her." Smiling, he turned to look at her.

"Thanks a bunch, darling," Alexi cooed.

"No problem, I'll just have Carrie push back a few appointments to Wednesday."

"Sounds good. We'll talk next week."

Carl hung up and faced Jackie. "You'll have to deal with me on Tuesday."

"Oh goody!" Jackie squealed with glee. She threw her arms around her groom and planted a long kiss on his lips.

Chapter XCVIII

Monday, September 7, 1998: Today was the final day of the regular season: Monday night fútbol for Los Angeles and the Chicago Stampede. The standings going into the match for the playoffs were:

EASTERN CONFERENCE

DC Eagles	54
NY Mad Cabbies	36
Sol de Miami	36
Philadelphia Minute Men	30

WESTERN CONFERENCE

Los Angeles Stars	38
Chicago Stampede	35
San Francisco Fogdogs	35
Dallas Lone Stars	25

Chicago was second with goal differential and a game in hand. New York earned second in the Eastern Conference on goal differential. In the East, the standard tournament bracket was set up so that DC played Philadelphia and New York would play Miami. Playoffs during the quarterfinals and semifinals were a home and away series, aggregate goals, all goals counted the same—there was no extra point for away goals. The higher seeded team would host the second match.

The Western conference bracket was yet to be determined. Tonight's match would decide it. A loss or tie by the Stampede and the standings would remain as they were. But a win, that would guarantee home field advantage through the playoffs for Chicago.

The discussion boards were full of scenarios and speculations. Baumgartner was still listed as probable, but everyone felt that Mirek would not play him. Starkov was back from his suspension. Sin Brazos was also probable, but everyone felt that was just a ploy to deceive the other team into thinking he was injured. Calf strains usually healed with rest. The team had a whole week off, except for practices.

Molly was nervous for another reason. She intercepted a phone call to Ian's apartment from Deanna. She was coming to town as Sugar Lipinski's escort.

The night before, Molly mentioned it over dinner. "Deanna called. She'll be in town with Sugar."

Ian shrugged his indifference. "I'm over her." He looked her in the eyes. "I'm over her."

"How can I be sure?" She extended her hand.

He grabbed it gently. "Because I love you, Molly." He kissed the back of her hand.

She smiled. "I love you too."

Molly found herself at the pregame party in the owner's box. She was face to face with Ian's ex. Deanna was gorgeous, but that's about all she had going for her. From the moment that Deanna introduced herself to Molly, she decided that the woman was nothing to be worried about. Only then, could she relax and be confident in Ian's proclamations of love.

After an hour, Molly pulled Carl aside and excused herself to go join the 12-Steppers out in the parking lot. Carl waved her off. On the way, she stopped by and chatted with Renata who was coming to work her old beat, the yellow seats. The two had seen very little of each other since Molly was suspended from working security.

Renata excused herself to start the briefing. Molly headed out of the stadium. The 12-Steppers were easy to spot. They had a large group of revelers gathered around the edge of the east parking lot. A red flag with a horned bull holding a beer bottle with the number 12 on it—the group's adopted logo—flew high and proud above a smoldering charcoal grill covered with bratwursts and burgers.

Jacek spotted her. "Molly, have a piwo." He plunged his hand deep in an ice-filled cooler and pulled out a Zywiec from the bottom. He removed the cap before handing it to her.

"*Dziękuję*," she replied. "How have you been? I thought you might be at the watch parties at Sueños. You know I've been bartending there."

The shorn Pole shook his head. "No, the Ultras usually gather at different bars in our neighborhood. I've been looking for you at Smiler's after hours, though."

"I'm usually exhausted after getting off work and sick of cigarette smoke."

Jacek nodded. "I understand."

The two were silent for a bit, each drinking their brews and watching the rest of the fans milling about. He broke the quiet, "I thought you might want to know that I've heard that Jack is trying to plan another hit on you."

She drew a deep breath.

He placed his hand on her shoulder. "I've got your back, Molly," he whispered in her ear. He left her before she could reply. Molly noticed that he always seemed to keep one eye on her. She did not know what to think. It felt a little bit creepy and comforting at the same time.

She made her way toward the food and grabbed herself a brat and another beer. Madeline cornered her and they began to chat. Molly started to relax again.

Mirek did not release his starting lineup until the last minute. He did not want to face any public scrutiny from the 12-Steppers or otherwise for choosing to start Randall Silva over Carlos. He wanted to make sure that Carlos did not get injured in this match headed into the playoffs. Otherwise, his starting lineup was fairly regular. He wanted to finish strong and apparently so did LA, since their lineup was mostly their first string as well.

The action was end to end with good defense on both sides. The Stars' Toro Hilgado struck first in the 27th minute. It came off of a cracker of a bending corner kick. Toro curled the ball directly into the net. Dan yelled at his teammates. "You can't block my view! Shit like this happens when you block my view!"

Tomás pulled his defensive line together before the next kickoff. "We can't let this happen again."

"Agreed," said Starkov, Patrick Mathison & Manny Larsen in unison.

Midfield action mostly for the next several minutes. In the 39th minute, Harris found the ball at his feet and a clean run toward the goal. He took the opportunity and started going straight at Tomlinson. Mickey Madison shook the cobwebs from his head and caught Ian. He drug Ian down forcibly just outside the box. The referee whipped out the yellow card.

John O'Connor lined up for the ensuing direct free kick. Randall took a nice run toward the box when the ball was booted and put in a nice downward redirective header just out of reach of Tomlinson. Goal, 41st minute, 1:1.

The score remained tied going into the halftime break.

Carl, Sugar and Deanna went down to the locker rooms. "I still can't believe you get this involved in your team," Sugar commented during the ride down.

"It's what I like to do. I like to show that I'm not just an owner who only cares about the bottom dollar. I care about the performance of my team."

"And Koneki doesn't mind?"

"I don't interfere. I just give a quick pep talk."

Sugar shook his head.

As they got off the elevator, Deanna asked, "Can I go in and say hi to Ian?"

"Absolutely not," replied Sugar like a stern father. "I will not have my number one Starlet consorting with the enemy."

Carl laughed.

She pouted in an exaggerated manner.

"Come on, Dee, let's go pump up our boys," Sugar said tugging on her arm lightly.

Carl popped into the Stampede homeroom. "Good show so far out there."

Tomás looked up. "Does it look as ugly from up there as it feels on the pitch?"

The owner nodded. "Unfortunately. I'm not pleased with this assigned head ref, but we just have to play through it. Don't lose your temper, Tomás."

The aging player nodded.

Mirek chimed in, in their native tongue, "We cannot afford to lose you for the playoffs." He then turned to Carlos. "Start warming up. I want you to be ready to go for late in the match, just in case. Diaz, you, too." The two went out to the field to begin a kick around with Virgil Amat.

Carl ducked out. Ian followed him. In the hall, Ian said, "Hey, did Molly behave herself around Deanna?"

He nodded. "She was fine. They chatted a little. Then, she excused herself to go to the 12-Steppers' tailgate." He paused. He saw concern in his face. "For what it's worth, I think she's a bit of a bubblehead. I could see that Molly sensed that she had nothing to worry about."

Ian smiled. "Good."

"Do me a favor; just focus on the match."

"Will do, sir."

The Stampede came out on the attack forcing Tomlinson to make a spectacular save. He placed the ball perfectly at Xoy's feet, dashing toward goal. Dan played off his line. Ante Nastav made a run with Xoy and received a well-placed leading cross. Ante one-timed the ball past a lunging Dan into the net for the lead in the 47th minute.

The game got choppier as the minutes wore on. The referee let a lot of it go uncalled. The fans in the stands got restless and started to call for his head. In the front row of section 12, Sean pulled out a noose. Matt held up a sign with a tree on it. "We got a rope; we got a tree; all we need is a referee," came the chant.

The man in black did not pull out his book again until the 73rd minute. Who for? Who else, Tomás. The Polack took out the Stars' beloved Mark 'Knothead' Johnson by grabbing his trailing dreadlocks and dragging him to the turf. Even to the Stampede fans, the call could have easily been a straight red.

Mark twisted his knee on the way down and was subbed out a few minutes later. Mickey retaliated for his teammate, but the victim was not Tomás, but on Paul Novotny. Mickey received his second yellow for the studs up tackle in midfield. Paul was spun half over the sideline in front of his bench. He eased himself off the playing area so that play could go on. Gina took a look and shook her head. Mirek signaled for Carlos to take Paul's place. The stadium erupted when the board lit up with Carlos' number 7 in green in the 81st minute.

Three minutes later, Carlos took a nice pass from Juan Cristobal and pulled the Stampede level.

Lance Stevens decked Ian with a malicious elbow to the head. Stevens received a yellow card. Ian came off. He was bleeding. Mirek, rather than wait for Gina to patch him up, called for Leo Diaz to go on.

In stoppage time, fresh-legged Leo hooked up with Brendan to score his first goal and the game winner. The Stampede would go into the playoffs as the first place Western conference team. Their next victim would be the Lone Stars of Dallas.

Chapter XCIX

TUESDAY, SEPTEMBER 8, 1998: Quigley paced nervously near the baggage claim. He already had claimed his luggage. He was waiting on his three charges to arrive.

The first to deplane was 19-year-old Mark Torres. He was a forward from UCLA. He was willing to sacrifice a lucrative college scholarship in order to make the jump early. Mark played 90 percent of the total minutes of his freshman season. He scored or assisted in almost all the matches he played. The youth national team coaches had him in camp a few times, but he failed to make the cut. This was one of the main reasons he felt that he needed to get out of the college game. He needed the challenge of the higher level of play that the FLA would give him.

It was Mark who approached Quigley to represent him. Mark was aware that the retention of an agent might disqualify him from ever playing in the NCAA again. Quigley counseled him to stay in the academic part. UCLA did not want to lose a student so they found a way for him to complete distance-learning classes when the schedule necessitated. Mark's major was prelaw.

Hector Lanza was an old schoolmate of Carlos Cortez. Hector played defense in front of Carlos until the accident, then helped Carlos come back as a forward. Lanza was disappointed that he would be signing initially with Colorado, but he might be able to be traded so that he could play with Carlos instead of against.

Darylton Fortner currently lived in New York. He had been cut from an A-League team in the off season after he went down with an injury to his knee. He spent the entire summer rehabbing the rebuilt cartilage. He worked out with the New York Mad Cabbies. He retained Michael Quigley as an agent after talking to Jerzy and Magia. Alexi had seen him in practice and talked to him about the opportunity in the expansion team. Darylton hoped to get back on the pitch as a starting midfielder. The Colorado Rush was going to be a great fit and restart to his playing career.

The four piled their bags into the back of a limo and they were whisked to the Rush front office.

Carl and Jackie waited in the conference room. Jackie had copies of the contract offers in front of her. Carl wanted her to run the show. He told her earlier that he wanted to see her negotiation skills in action. Also present was coach Arturo Rodriguez. Jackie and he had reviewed the game tapes of the three. Arturo was pleased with the suggestions and felt they would provide a good foundation for the Rush to build on and around.

The players and Michael arrived. Introductions were made around the table.

Jackie sat at the head of the table. Carl was to her left, Arturo to her right. Michael pulled up a chair next to Carl; Hector sat across from him. The other two filled in balancing the horseshoe.

"Let's get this meeting started." Jackie looked down at her notes. "The first file that I have is for Darylton Fortner. Based on your experience and reviews of game tapes and practice footage with the Cabbies, Carl, Alexi and I are prepared to offer you a nice deal. Arturo informs me that he expects you to be a leader on the field."

"Yes, ma'am," Darylton said respectfully, "I would like to be able to be a strong foundation to a new and winning team." The player spoke with a polite Southern drawl.

Arturo smiled at him.

"I'm glad to hear that. Quigley, did you get the initial offers in advance from Alexi?"

"Yes, they arrived a couple of days ago. The four of us haven't had much time to think about the offers." Michael shuffled through his paperwork for the Darylton file and offer.

"Darylton, may I call you Daryl for simplicity's sake?"

"Yes, ma'am, you may. Most folks do."

"Daryl, the Colorado Rush would like you to join us for a salary of $70,000 with bonuses."

"Mr. Quigley and I have talked this offer over and feel that it is reasonable. What are the bonuses? That was not clarified in earlier discussions."

"The bonuses that Carl and Alexi usually offer are housing allowances and transportation, if required."

Daryl looked over at Quigley who nodded. "I think that sounds fine. Show me where to sign."

"Welcome aboard, Darylton Fortner." Carl shook his hand.

Carl mostly watched Jackie in action. The negotiations with the other two were a bit tougher. Daryl knew his way around contract deal; the other two did not.

Mark and Hector were untested in the professional realm. All parties knew this. Carl gave no indications to Jackie on how high to go. Alexi did provide some guidelines, but not much of a framework to be useful. Jackie and Arturo knew they would both excel in their positions, but did not want to commit large portions of the salary cap to just a few players.

Both players finally settled at $50,000, comfortably above league minimum. There were housing allowances, of course. Hector got his trade clause included in case a deal to play on the same team as Carlos Cortez came up. Arturo at that point whispered that he would enjoy having Carlos come to Colorado to play. Jackie grinned in agreement. Carl raised his eyebrow at the discreet exchange.

Dotted lines were signed. Everyone was happy.

Carl sat in the visitor's chair across from Jackie who was behind her desk. It felt like a bit of a role reversal, to both of them.

"I was really impressed with you today, Jacqueline," he praised his employee.

"Thank you, darling. You didn't think I had it in me, did you?"

He shook his head. "No, I didn't. Suspected, yes, confirmed? Well, that you did for me today."

"Yeah, it felt strange dealing with Quigley on a business level. He's always just been a pub drinking buddy."

Carl nodded. "I know. But he is good at what he does. He really looks out for his clients, but understands the realistic needs of salary cap situations and so on."

"What do you think of the three that we signed today?"

"A good combination to build on. I think they will play well together."

"I think so, too. Arturo has an eye for on pitch chemistry."

"You do, too, Jacqueline. Don't underestimate yourself."

Her cheeks pinked slightly. "Thank you."

Carl stood and kissed her across the desk. "I'm so glad I found you."

She blushed even more. "Stop it. You're embarrassing me."

"There's no one else in here." He gestured sweepingly. He then pulled her into a fuller embrace. Kissing her deeply, he swung her back onto the top of the desk. He pulled her long skirt up. She smiled, giving no resistance. Carl whipped open his pants and pulled out his engorged member.

He placed his fingers inside of her. She was ready. The negotiations had turned her on.

He entered her forcefully. A pen cup tumbled to the floor as she moaned her pleasure. Carl fucked her hard and fast. "I love you," he kept repeating in her ear. "I love everything about you, you tough boardroom broad."

"Oh, Carl," she sighed in heavy panting breaths.

"Jacqueline." He pounded her until she could not help but scream in an extreme pleasurable orgasm. That triggered a huge release from Carl.

He draped himself over her. Kissing her softly on the neck, he said, "I love you, Jacqueline Harris."

"I love you, too, Carl Costello," she replied.

They separated and smoothed their appearances. He did not feel embarrassed, but she did a little, especially about the noisy outburst she had emitted. "I hope no one heard me," she said.

"Don't worry. Everyone knows we are together," Carl said. "What is so wrong about two people who love each other making a little noise?"

"Um, nothing." She smiled sheepishly. Jackie was not normally that way. She normally did not care, but being the boss in Denver gave her a different feel about the situation overall. She would just have to learn to adjust to the oddness of the whole situation.

CHAPTER C

WEDNESDAY, SEPTEMBER 9, 1998: Ian was prescribed rest. Gina found a hairline fracture in his right cheekbone. Molly played nursemaid during the day. Joe had her working the evening shift. The tips were good from the regulars.

Ian lie in bed and patted for Molly to join him. She snuggled up in his arms. "I'd make love to you right now, but isn't this the wrong week for that?"

"I haven't started yet."

"Well then." He rolled on top of her and began kissing her neck. They made tender sweet love.

Later that evening, the bar was slow and Molly found her mind wandering. What if I'm pregnant? She counted back the weeks, just be sure. She should have had her period two weeks ago! I'm on the Pill. I take it religiously. It's got to just be stress, she tried to conclude.

But her body wouldn't let her.

During a break, she walked down the block to Walgreens and bought a pregnancy test. She shoved it deep in her purse so that no one would see it at work.

The next morning, she called Agnes. "I'm booked solid today, honey, but I can see you tomorrow afternoon. Paul and the team will be flying out to Dallas in the morning, so anytime in the afternoon would be good."

"Okay," Molly said weakly. She just wanted some confidential support. She loved her best friend Renata, but felt that she could not be trusted to keep the secret of that accidental night with Jacek.

Friday afternoon, Molly went to Agnes' home office.

"I think I might be pregnant. I brought the tests with me, but I haven't taken them yet. I'm scared."

Agnes hugged her. "You don't think it might be Ian's?"

"I counted back. It could be either Jacek or Ian."

"Well, the first thing we need to do is to piss on those sticks." The doctor took Molly's hand and led her to the guest bathroom. "I'll be right here."

"Okay."

Molly's hands shook as she opened the package. She handed Agnes the box and the instructions. She could barely hold the stick steady enough to get it wet with her urine stream. Agnes watched her. She took the stick from her hand and capped the wet end.

The test popped up positive before it hit the counter.

"You must be several weeks along," Agnes said. "It's usually supposed to take a while."

Normally strong Molly began to cry.

Chapter CI

SATURDAY, SEPTEMBER 12, 1998: PLAYOFFS: Ian and Paul made the trip with the rest of the team, but Gina advised Mirek that neither should be in the starting lineup. Ian wore a FIFA-approved clear facemask to protect his cheekbone from further damage. It would be more likely, Mirek said, that Paul would go in late in the match rather than Ian. If they were behind, Ian would probably be put in. Randall was excited to have his first FLA start in a playoff match.

Carlos and Randall had been working out a lot running patterns during the past week. Mirek had complete confidence in the chemistry between the two strikers.

Heinrich insisted on starting. Mirek agreed and said they would evaluate his knee at the half. Gina shook her finger at the stubborn German. "If you blow it out completely tonight, you won't get to play in the Cup Final."

The match started out fairly cleanly. The Lone Stars' Holtz went up with Baumgartner in an aerial battle. Holtz came down with an elbow to Heinrich's temple. Gina jumped up and waited for the signal to be waved out to her player's side. Mirek screamed for a card. The referee just awarded the Stampede a direct free kick and gave Holtz a stern verbal warning.

Heinrich got up without Gina's assistance, shook himself off, and went on to play. He grinned at the doc as if to say, I'm fine.

The Stampede controlled the midfield most of the first half. Dallas got a few chances on counter attacks, but nothing went in until a stunning strike from Tuffatore from thirty yards out. Dan hardly saw it coming. The TV broadcasters calculated that the ball traveled 81 miles per hour!

A stunned hush fell over the packed crowd at Sueños. The Cotton Bowl erupted and threw confetti and streamers all over the stadium.

Halftime, Dallas 1—Stampede 0.

Gina attended to Heinrich in the locker room. He winced whenever she touched his knee. "You've got to be subbed out."

Silently, he nodded his agreement. "It's better for the team," he said when Mirek came in.

MacLeod was his replacement when the second half kicked off.

Dallas came out from their break with guns ablazing and attitudes to match. Defender Lieb viciously drug Brendan down after Brendan had passed off the ball.

341

For that, the referee issued Lieb the match's first yellow card. Brendan got up and screamed at Lieb. "You fucking asshole, you're going to pay for that"

"Oh yeah, faggot?"

"You're going down for that," Brendan spat back.

Just a few minutes later, Holtz annihilated Tomás with a tackle from behind. As the Chicago defender crumpled, his foot got caught in the rough turf and twisted his knee the wrong way. "*Kudowa!*" he screamed.

"Just a taste of your own medicine, polack," Holtz yelled.

Tomás pushed Holtz off of him. He clutched his knee and writhed in pain, not all of it exaggerated.

Mirek cringed as he witnessed the event. Gina signaled the trainers to grab the litter. The referee waved the Stampede support staff to Tomás' side.

"How bad is it?" Gina asked Tomás.

"I think I've really torn something," he replied.

"Shit! Get him on the litter so we can continue the match," Gina barked.

Mirek had his entire bench begin warming up. He knew he would have to make another sub soon.

In the 58th minute, Maxwell Harp came on for Tomás. The ten field players shifted their positioning a little. Larsen moved back to left back. Starkov took over the central defender's role that Tomás usually played. Harp floated in the midfield.

The Stampede's first goal of the match came in the 66th minute. Dan placed the ball on John O'Connor's head. John tapped it to Randall's feet. Slippery Silva found a path around two defenders and through the five hole of a lunging Mallen.

A collective sigh of relief could be heard roiling out of Sueños.

The next goal was a combination between Silva and Carlos. A textbook back and forth between the two, drawing Mallen off his line for an easy goal by Sin Brazos.

Mallen tore into his defensive line, accusing them of leaving him exposed. The next time Carlos was close, Mallen spat, "You fucking freak, you shouldn't be playing."

Carlos was used to that type of abuse from opposing teams. He had heard plenty of it in Mexico before coming to the FLA.

In the 81st minute, there was a mad scramble in the box on a Stampede corner kick. John got decked. He did not see who or what body part hit him before he blacked out. Ah, thankfully, the sideline judge and the referee did. Mallen's fist connected with John's head.

"I was playing the ball," protested Mallen as he faced the wrath of the red card.

John was loaded onto the stretcher and carried over the end line where the Chicago staff worked on reviving him.

Dallas pulled off a forward as a sub for the keeper position sending in Terrazas. Carlos blasted the awarded PK into the net.

Three minutes after the red card was issued, ten on ten, MacLeod assisted Brendan's punishing strike for a 4 to 1 lead.

And that would be the final score after one more issuance of a yellow card to Dallas' Cassanova in the 89th minute.

After the match, Mirek shook his head at the damages. He got his W but at what cost.

Chapter CII

MONDAY, SEPTEMBER 14, 1998: Gina delivered the bad news to Mirek personally. "Tomás is out. This may be a career ending injury for the old man."

"If he wants to stick around next season, he can. He won't retire until he can't play an entire match. Patch him up, doc." Mirek returned to watching the game tape.

"For what it's worth, I'm going to advise him to retire officially after the Cup."

"Noted," said the grizzled coach, not looking up from the screen.

Gina left. She knew that Tomás was stubborn enough to make it through another knee reconstruction and rehab, but his age would make it harder. The scans showed that he had the knees of a sixty-five year old, not one in his late thirties. Soccer players did put their lower joints through a lot of stress, but twice the living time? That did not make sense to her scientific mind.

WEDNESDAY, SEPTEMBER 16, 1998: Ian took a day off from practice to accompany Molly to the doctor. He grew nervous when he saw that it was an obstetrician she had an appointment with.

"Are you pregnant?" he asked quietly in the waiting room.

"That's what I'm here to find out. I just want you by my side."

"I'm here for you no matter what, Molly. You know that." He kissed her on the cheek.

Heavy with child, a woman sitting across from them smiled. "It's good he's here with you. My husband is with the Army fighting drug trafficking in Columbia," she said to her.

"I hope he makes it back safely," replied Ian.

In the examining room, Molly received confirmation that she was pregnant. The doctor performed an ultrasound and predicted the due date was in early May. Molly could not shake concern from her face and voice. Ian was elated. She thought to herself, I hope it's yours; please, let it be yours.

"But I was on the Pill," Molly tried to protest the facts.

The doctor said, "If you were not on antibiotics around the time of conception and if you were taking it as prescribed, then there is still a half percent chance that you will get pregnant. You must be in the hyper fertile lucky half percent."

Molly mumbled incoherently.

The doctor added, "You still have a few weeks left in the legal window for abortion."

Ian looked at Molly and bit his lip. "No, sweetie, don't let your mind go there." He touched her still flat belly. "I want both of you."

Molly shed a small tear. "Okay, honey, but your child had better not kick the shit out of me in my womb."

The doctor cocked her head and studied Ian's face. "Oh, I get it; you're one of the Chicago Stampede."

"Yes, ma'am," Ian replied.

"Then I hate to break it to you, Miss Karver, but the kid probably will. Both of my boys did, and now they are stars on the Chicago Magic youth team."

"Wonderful," Molly said sarcastically. And if the kid is using his fists on my uterine wall, she thought, I know it will probably be Jacek's.

Chapter CIII

Playoffs, Match Two: Thursday, September 17, 1998: John O'Connor was listed as out due to a concussion. He had tried to practice on Monday, but when he took his first header, he complained to Gina of a massive headache.

"I told you to take this week off, Johnny," Gina had scolded.

Tomás was out also, due to his blown knee.

At least, this would be a home match.

The core group of 12-Steppers who threw the tailgate party skipped out of work early that day. Matt commented that he had the threat of a pink slip hanging over his head if he came to work the next day with a hangover. He laughed it off and drank anyway. The Koneki girls came straight to the parking lot as soon as Księżnicka was out of school.

Matt gave Róża a peck on the cheek. "How did you get your dad to approve?"

"He's over it. I'm eighteen now and as long as Księżnicka doesn't turn up pregnant or drunk, he's okay with it."

"He must be mellowing."

"The Ultras here are nothing compared to how they are in Poland."

Matt nodded. "True. Did you bring more ice?"

"Yeah, we'll fill the chests. The piwo will be ice cold by the time everyone starts coming."

Brendan pulled up and dropped Lawrence off. "Have a good match, honey." The two men embraced warmly and kissed long.

Lawrence got out; Brendan drove around into the north lot inside the stadium.

By five, the charcoals were perfect. The official 12-Stepper tailgate flag was hoisted to mark the location. Matt & Lawrence flipped burgers and rolled brats. Sean handled the coolers. Fans were starting to roll in.

The excitement flowed into the stadium. Section 12 was loud and proud from the time the opening lineup was announced.

The only other difference in the lineup was the insertion of Harp in the central midfield for Baumgartner who still said he did not feel 100 percent. Paul wore the captain's armband in his stead.

Dallas was in the hole by three goals going into the match. Mirek advised his players that they would attack hard and leave themselves vulnerable in the back, especially with their second string keeper, Terrazas.

Carlos and Brendan looked at each other with knowing ear-to-ear greedy grins.

The match was destined to be ugly right from kickoff. The Lone Stars aggressively challenged every ball. There were a lot of stoppages and restarts due to hard tackles, but the referee chose to keep his wallet in his pocket.

In the 39th minute, Harp fed a square ball to Brendan who took it forward a few steps. He dumped a leading cross off to Carlos. Carlos was alone. He had help coming, but the Dallas D was back on their heels. Mahruder came flying in studs up and swept Carlos off his feet in a spectacular fashion. The Mexican spun through the air and landed hard on the pitch.

A collective gasp could be heard throughout Soldier Field, temporarily dropping the air pressure. The referee had seen enough. Time to try to get a handle on the match. He pulled out a straight red.

The crowd breathed a sigh of relief and erupted with applause and chanting, "CARLOS CORTEZ" clap, clap, clap, clap, clap, "CARLOS CORTEZ."

Carlos still lay in a heap. The referee bent over to check on the player. "*¿Esta bien?*"

Carlos just moaned. Doc Gina was motioned into action. She had the litter brought out. The litter was always faster for getting an injured player off the field. She was not going to take any chances with their star striker during the playoffs.

The Chicago trainers rolled Carlos onto the stretcher and carried him off the field via the shortest route.

Chicago restarted on a direct free kick. Dallas did not back the line up fast enough for the referee's liking so he issued a yellow card for dissent to Smythe. Both Ian and Brendan lined up to take the kick. At the whistle, Ian ran past the ball; Brendan took the kick. Jameson leaped and redirected the orb in a hard downward motion with his head. It bounced past the keeper and into the net for a goal. Chicago 1 Dallas 0.

The score remained that way going into the locker room. Mirek was happy, but he did have something critical to say. "Your passing is looking like shit again. You all had better straighten it up in the second half or we are going to suffer through passing drills all next week."

Mirek went to chat with Gina about Carlos. "What's going on with Carlos?"

"It's not too bad," Doc advised.

"How do you feel?" he asked the lad directly.

Carlos shrugged. He had ice packs taped to his calf and ankle where the full force of the Mahruder's boots had hit him. "You can sub me out."

Gina nodded in agreement. "It's better. We're likely to win the game and series given the way things have gone so far. Better to rest Carlito rather than risk further injury to his ankle. Right now, I think it's just bruising."

Mirek looked over at his subs. "Randall!"

He jumped up. "Yes, coach."

"Go warm up. You're going in for Carlos at the start of the second half."

Dallas made no changes coming out. Tuffatore and Magione were their strongest strikers. Coach Dunkirk was not going to risk anything if he thought he had a chance to dig out of the deep hole in the next forty-five minutes.

The ugliness continued. Chicago tried their best to stay out of the fray, but Dallas kept baiting them. Harp finally bit in the 58th minute with a yellow-cardable offense as he pushed Magione hard over the line and into his own bench.

Paul pulled Harp aside and calmed him down. Harp had his revenge though with an assist two minutes later. He fed Ian a nice pass who nutmegged Ferguson on his way to an easy chip over the keeper.

Ferguson was not pleased with Ian's ball skills. A few minutes later, Ian found himself drug down in the box by Ferguson. Mathison volunteered to take the penalty shot. Paul gave his blessing. After all, defenders did not get too many chances at the glory of a goal. Mathison shot straight down the center; Terrazas dove to the left. Goal, 64th minute. Chicago 3—Dallas 0.

The final goal for Chicago came on an 88th minute corner kick taken by Paul. He floated the ball into the box. Starkov climbed his man and redirected the ball into the net. Terrazas screamed at the referee for a card. Terrazas eventually got a yellow for dissent. It didn't matter. The match was nearly over. The referee opted to not add any stoppage time. He failed to see the point; he was sick of getting screamed at by the sore Lone Stars; he just wanted a hot shower and a cold beer.

Final score, Chicago 4—Dallas 0, aggregate Chicago 8—Dallas 1.

In the other match in the Western Conference side of the bracket, Los Angeles bowed out to San Francisco, 6-3 on aggregate. In the east, DC knocked out Philadelphia 4-2 aggregate and the Mad Cabbies overcame goose eggs in the away match to win the right to advance over el Sol de Miami 3-0 on aggregate. Chicago's next match was Thursday in San Francisco.

Chapter CIV

Friday, September 18, 1998: Despite not having been a victim of a yellow-cardable offense the evening before, Brendan woke up rather stiff. Lawrence had spent the night. He rubbed his lover's aching muscles.

"Oh, that feels good," Brendan moaned. "You should look into getting a massage therapist license."

Lawrence quietly worked over his body. Brendan continued to moan his pleasure. Sheila set out breakfast and then left for work, leaving the two guys alone.

"I'm surprised you're this sore," Lawrence commented.

"You watched the game. I got knocked around quite a bit last night."

"Yeah, the referee was awful. He didn't get a handle on the match soon enough."

"So how many cards would you have issued?"

"A helluva lot more."

"Well, all of us are pretty banged up. I think we have a light practice today."

"Why don't you stay home and relax? I've got a day off."

"Good idea." Brendan reached for the phone. "I'll call Mirek."

Lawrence helped his boyfriend do some light stretches, but mostly they lounged all day. They ordered pizza and had movies delivered by Kozmo.com. Brendan napped; Lawrence straightened the apartment quietly. Neither Sheila nor Brendan was a neat freak, but they were not exactly slobs either. Lawrence liked an orderly house. Perhaps he was more cut out to be a housewife than a husband.

Brendan awoke. He noticed the magazines were arranged neatly on the coffee table, the normal layer of dust was gone from the entertainment center and especially the television screen, the breakfast table was cleared and everything put away. Lawrence was sitting by the window immersed in the latest issue of *Four Four Two*. Brendan stared at him wrapped in soft sunlight filtered by the sheer curtains. "Marry me," said Brendan.

Lawrence looked up from the page. He took off his reading glasses. "Are you serious?"

Brendan got up and crossed to him. He bent down on one knee. "Marry me."

Lawrence dropped the magazine. "Oh my god, you are serious. Yes, but, what about Sheila."

"You know we can't legally marry yet. But whenever we will be able to, Sheila will grant me a divorce. She'll probably have a fiancée by then, too."

Lawrence took Brendan outstretched hand. "Yes, yes, I'll marry you." Tears of joy started to stream down his face. "I love you, Brendan Glazier."

"I love you, too, Lawrence Jones."

Chapter CV

MONDAY, SEPTEMBER 21, 1998: Molly awoke in the morning to a phone call from the security and ushering company. Groggily, she hollered for Ian to get it, and then realized what time it was. Ian had already left for practice. She picked it up on the fifth ring. On six, it was set to go to voice mail.

"Molly, you are free to go back to work as a guard."

"Huh?" She rubbed the sleep out of her eyes.

"The lawsuit was dropped by the family. You are cleared to work games and concerts again."

"Oh, right, security. I'm bartending now."

"Could you work the next soccer game?"

"Yeah, I can do that. But then that's it. I might call in for a concert or whatever, if available, but I'm making a lot more money bartending."

"I understand. I've got you down for the home match on Saturday, October 3rd. We don't know what time kickoff is yet."

"I think Ian wrote down 3pm, but I know to be there three hours before."

"Yep, good memory, Mols. We'll see you there."

WEDNESDAY, SEPTEMBER 23, 1998: Practice was light before the team boarded the team bus to go to the airport for the charter flight to San Francisco. Brendan dressed for the workout, but could not keep up. He had laid off the previous two days, per a mutual agreement between Gina and him.

Mirek shook his head as the Iceman moved gingerly around the pitch. He called him over. "You look tight."

Brendan nodded. "If you want me to stay here, I can. That way I'll be fully rested for the home match."

"Sounds good." Mirek added, "And given the last time we took a trip to San Francisco, it's probably best anyway."

Brendan looked at his feet. "I understand, but I am engaged now." It was the first he had told anyone, including Sheila.

"To Lawrence?"

The bleached blonde bobbed his head with a smile.

"Congratulations." Mirek patted Brendan on the back. "Go shower. In the morning have a light work out with weights and enjoy the match at Sueños."

"Sounds good. I'll see you on Saturday for the next practice." Brendan walked off, chugging a bottle of Gatorade. Lawrence will be pleased to have me with him at the bar tomorrow evening, he thought.

FRIDAY, SEPTEMBER 25, 1998:

SAN FRANCISO, CA: No Tomás Lozowski and no Brendan Glazier did not hurt the Chicago Stampede. It did not help them either. Last night, Chicago dropped the first leg of the semifinals 3 to 2 to the San Francisco Fog Dogs.

Ian Harris struck early in the 4th minute for Chicago, scoring off a set piece from Paul Novotny. San Francisco's first goal came in the 26th minute with a spectacular header from Billy Rosado. Dima Lovchev earned the ball back in the midfield and serviced his teammate perfectly. Seven minutes later, the Fog Dogs took the lead when Dima's brother Maxim fed Cherokee Fox for a textbook strike.

The second half would prove to be equally exciting. San Francisco extended their lead in the 65th minute when the Lovchev siblings hooked up. Maxim had the goal while Dima had the assist, as had been usual during their childhood on the streets of Moscow.

Jack McDuffy received a straight red card for his takedown of Juan Cristobal in the 73rd minute. Cristobal was carried off the field and did not return. Coach Mirek Koneki chose to use his first substitution, sending in Maxwell Harp in the 76th minute. There was no word as of press time as to extent of Cristobal's injuries, if any.

Late in the match, the Stampede captain signaled to the sidelines for a substitution. He indicated that he was cramping up. Koneki sent in midfielder Timothy Myerson in the 83rd minute. At the same time, the Fog Dogs used their first substitution, pulling Maxim Lovchev for defensive midfielder Scott O'Brian.

Chicago pushed hard to get two goals to tie up the match. Byron Jameson was called for a yellow cardable challenge on Jackson Marumo. Marumo was subbed out for defender Miguel Lopez in the 89th minute. Chicago was able to take advantage of the back line juggling of the Fog Dogs for a goal by Maxwell Harp with an assist from Carlos Cortez in the first minute of stoppage time.

The next match will take place at Soldier Field on Saturday, October 3rd. Both coaches believe the eight days between the matches will help. Steve Mercado said, "I hate to see McDuffy get a red card, but if we win the series we'll have him back for the Final."

As to going home with a deficit, Koneki said, "We are up for the challenge. We are only a goal down on aggregate. Glazier will be back which will strengthen our striking ability. We beat them twice early in the season. We can do it again."

During the post-match press conference, McDuffy was asked about his red card. As usual, none of his comments are printable in this family publication.

Chapter CVI

Saturday, October 3, 1998: The last home match of the year was set to take place. Ian expressed his disappointment that Molly would be working the match rather than enjoying the game and cheering him on. The report came in that over 15,000 tickets had been presold. There was strong possibility of a large walkup crowd. It was a weekend; a lot of folks did not plan that far in advance, especially the Mexican contingency.

Renata and Molly embraced and kissed each other on the cheeks, as if they were European. "I'm so glad you're back," gushed Renata.

"Just for this game. I'm not going to work security much after this."

"Well, a lot of the staff we get from the Bears games training are crap."

"Why do you think I'm hanging up my stair running boots?"

"No kidding. If it weren't for the differential they are giving me for working Sections 16 & 18 during the Bears matches, I would tell the company to piss off as well."

Renata and Molly were assigned to work the yellow seats. Molly decided to split it up. She would take section 16 and up toward the north end. Renata would take section 14 and down toward the blue seats, including the always boisterous section 12. Everyone agreed that this was a wise decision given the previous circumstances during Molly's work.

The stands filled quickly as kickoff approached. There was a steady walkup through the first twenty minutes as well. Section 12 was in full voice, getting the rest of the stadium to respond to and participate in their singing and chanting.

Molly was glad when things settled with the seating. She witnessed the first goal of the match. In the 24th minute in the midfield, Ian battled for the ball, whisking it cleanly off Ron Hunter's feet. After a few controlling touches, he passed it forward to Brendan. The Iceman dribbled straight for goal, drawing goalkeeper Baby Lepao off his line. Brendan chipped it over the lunging portero. It dribbled into the net.

Molly forgot she was working and jumped for joy with the rest of the stadium. She fed the need for high fives with several of the wheelchair-bound fans in the lowest row of Section 16.

Section 12 unfurled their huge logoed flag and hoisted it above their heads. It waved proudly, moved by the hundreds of arms and hands underneath it. Shortly after the action started again, the flag moved ceremoniously with even speed down to the first row, where it would lie in wait until the next Stampede goal.

In the 40th minute, Maxim Lovchev broke away from the back line and received a nice forward cross from his brother Dima. Paul Novotny was the closest Stampede player. He flew as fast as he could and tried to reach Maxim cleanly. He ended up dragging Maxim down by the shoulder. The foul was called just inside the box. A yellow card was issued; Marumo scored on the ensuing penalty kick—1:1. Chicago would have to score two more goals while allowing none if they wanted to get into the final.

The Fog Dog goal did not squelch Section 12. They roared and chanted louder than ever. Carl went down and joined the 12-Steppers' drum line. Tonight, he was not going to watch his team from the skybox anymore.

At halftime, everyone took a breather. The concourses were flooded with thirsty folks. Lines spilled out of the bathroom doors of both the men's and the women's rooms. Molly wanted to sneak down to the locker room, but she could not while she was working. It was forbidden.

Carl went to give his team his usual pep talk. He opened the door and heard Mirek. "Everyone is playing great. We just have to get better. Patrick, Vlad, you two have to shut down Maxim. Manny, you cannot let your eyes off of Fox. He's wily and will sneak past you. We still have to score three more. That is everyone's job. You cannot let those damn dogs score any more goals. That is everyone's job. Do I make myself clear?"

The team barked back in unison as if they were in a barracks, "Sir, yes, sir."

Carl closed the door with a smile. He knew he did not have to say anything.

The second half kicked off with a both teams battling hard. The Dogs were not content to just sit back and defend. They wanted to increase their lead on aggregate to assure a trip to the Cup Final. Chicago did not want to get scored on either. They pushed forward as much as they could.

In the 52nd minute, crafty Cherokee Fox fielded a nice long ball from his teammate Kyle Pierce. He nutmegged Paul then got past Starkov. He chipped it over Captain Dan's shoulder as Dan dove to where he thought the ball might be.

Dan sprang to his feet and started yelling at Starkov and Paul. "You've got to watch your fucking man!"

Vlad and Paul managed to redeem themselves in the 76th minute. Paul took a free kick. The ball floated into the box. Vlad went up, climbing a Dog back, and redirected the orb down for a bounce into the goal.

An aura of hope settled on the fans and the team.

In the 84th minute, Baby Lepao coldcocked Ian as they both went for the ball.

Molly's breath momentarily left her as she saw the incident. Motionless, Ian lie on the cleat-torn turf.

The referee immediately called for Doc Gina and her crew to come out. Instinctively, the litter was carried with the first aid kit bags.

The referee issued Baby Lepao a yellow card caution and awarded a penalty kick.

Ian was lifted onto the stretcher. He was moved the few yards off the pitch over the end line. Molly made her way as close as she could. She peered over the chain link fence at her lover.

Meanwhile, Carlos lined up the penalty shot. As he buried it hard in the back of the net, the stadium erupted. Ian started to come around to the smelling salts. Carlos ran over to Ian. "I scored for you."

Ian attempted to raise his hand.

"I'll score for you again," Carlos said before jogging back onto the pitch.

Prophetically, Carlos scored in stoppage time on an unassisted romp through the Dog defense. Chicago 4—San Francisco 2. Chicago was going to the Cup Final in Pasadena, California on a 6 to 5 aggregate score.

Fireworks erupted in the north end of the stadium. An announced crowd of fewer than 26,000 fans applauded. Molly wished she could run straight out to Ian. She was so glad that this was the last match that she would be working. Being a player's girlfriend was so much more fun.

Ian had recovered enough to jog around the pitch with his team. They applauded the crowd for their support in their inaugural year. They paused in front of Section 12 and entered the first few rows of the stands. Sweaty jerseys were tossed at the adoring.

The autograph session after the match was longer than usual. Ian kissed Molly. She looked at his black eye and kissed his boo-boo. He smiled tenderly and returned to signing stubs, jerseys and other objects lowered over the concrete barrier.

DC Eagles would be their opponent for the Cup. They beat the Mad Cabbies on a 5 to 4 aggregate to earn their repeat trip to the Final.

Chapter CVII

MONDAY, OCTOBER 12, 1998: This was it. This was the final few days of being a single woman. Jackie bit her lip as she boarded the plane from Denver to Los Angeles. Carl would be meeting her out there in a few days. He wanted to fly in with the team as a show of unity for the Cup.

Jackie was going to meet with her gown designer who was coming in direct to Los Angeles from Paris with the dress. She would also be bringing a dress for Agnes who agreed to be her matron of honor. Mirek would be Carl's best man. The couple agreed to keep the wedding party to a bare minimum for simplicity's sake.

Agnes' flight from Chicago was scheduled to land within an hour of Jackie's. The Parisian seamstress would arrive later in the day with the dresses. They were scheduled for a final fitting on Tuesday. That would provide Veronique ample time to make any last minute adjustments.

Jackie met Agnes at baggage claim. The two ladies embraced.

"Are you nervous?" Agnes asked.

Jackie shook her head. "No, not yet. Ask me again before I walk down the aisle." She smiled.

As they waited for their luggage, they chatted about Jackie's job in Denver.

"Carl can't stop talking about how well you've been handling everything, especially player negotiations," Agnes commented. "I guess you really impressed him."

Jackie shrugged. "Just doing my job. He should have toned it down by now."

"I think he keeps it up because he misses you during the week."

"Well, at least we have a two-week honeymoon after the game."

"Has he told you where you two are going?"

"He keeps saying it's a surprise."

"Did he at least tell you what to pack?" Agnes inquired.

Jackie shook her head. "He said to take nothing."

Loud clanging and sirens signaled the activation of the baggage claim carousel. They just needed to get Agnes' bags. Jackie had already collected her set prior to meeting Agnes.

"Nothing?"

"Yep, nothing. Guess he figured any wardrobe clues might give it away."

"Sounds like it, unless it's a nudist colony." Both ladies giggled. Agnes watched the rotating menagerie of luggage. She was glad that she did not have a black set.

A hired car took them to the hotel. The driver complained vehemently that the pair had too much luggage. Jackie laughed and slipped him a fifty-dollar bill to shut him up.

As soon as Jackie was settled into her suite, she called Bobby Lonestar. He had left her an urgent but cryptic message on her cell phone.

"Good news, Jackie," he began. "The labels for the beer will be able to have both the Eagles logo and the Stampede logo."

"Wonderful, how in the world did you manage to have that pulled off?"

"Jon and Betty Eagle wanted to make sure DC was not forgotten this weekend. So they threw in the extra monies for a rush printing order."

Jackie laughed. "You're kidding, right?"

"No, I'm serious. That's what they said. But after all, we did discuss having opposing team logos on the bottles."

"Yes, yes, we did."

Jackie and Bobby agreed to meet on Wednesday one final time with the caterer. It was going to be a busy week.

Chapter CVIII

Tuesday, October 13, 1998: "Oh my god, Jackie," Agnes gushed, "your gown is gorgeous."

Jackie slipped into the Stampede red and silver fabric. The *couturiere* assisted with the hidden side zipper. Agnes helped Cinderella into her shoes. Veronique went to work on the hem as Jackie stood on a chair.

The basic pattern was alternating red and silver V-shaped strips. Starting with red, plunging at the neckline and ending with the seventh and widest strip draping to the ankles. From the top of that V-strip on the sides of the skirt, lace panels tatted by Veronique in primarily navy with silver accents hinged the front to the back. A hexagonal soccer ball pattern was subtle in the lace but there. Between the red strip and the lace were silver panels. The back nearly mirrored the front, but was more revealing, dropping to the bride's waistline. The V's accentuated her full buttocks.

Jackie chose to wear lower princess heels. She would be walking on an Astroturf carpet but sand would be surrounding the canopied area. She had a spa date to work her legs over and get a good wax job. She would not be wearing stockings, but would have a garter on her thigh.

Veronique worked quickly, whipping stitches instead of just pinning. Agnes sat on the edge of the bed and watched in awe.

"What was your wedding dress like, Agnes?" Jackie asked to break the silence.

"Oh, very traditional. My dress has been passed down from mother to daughter for three generations now. Someday you will have to come over so I can show you photos from our wedding."

"Sounds lovely," replied Jackie. "So when are Paul and you going to have kids?"

"When it happens it happens." Agnes shrugged. "We would like to have one of each. What about you? Have you discussed anything like that with Carl?"

Jackie shook her head. She took great care that the rest of her body remained like a mannequin. "Actually, we haven't. I think we need to be a couple for a few years."

"You're right. Plus, it's going to be tough with you in Denver most of the time right now."

"Yeah. You know, even though this week is going to be stressful in terms of pulling together the wedding, I actually feel like I can relax."

"I'm glad to hear that. You seem to be taking the stress rather well." Agnes smiled her friendly and psychiatric approval.

Veronique stood. "Finished," she announced.

Jackie spun in front of the mirror atop the chair. "Perfect." She slipped out of her shoes before stepping down.

"It is your turn, Agnes," said Veronique as she assisted the bride out of the gown.

"I think I'm more nervous than you are, Jackie," Agnes commented. "I have no idea what you two decided for me to wear."

The matron of honor's gown was navy with silver lace and trim.

"*Zut, zut!*" fussed Veronique. "Mademoiselle Jacqueline did not know your measurements very well."

Jackie frowned. "At least I overestimated."

"*Oui, oui,* better than too little. It will be not be so bad to make the dress smaller. You have a lovely figure, Agnes."

"*Merci beaucoup,*" replied Agnes.

"Ah, you speak French?"

"Probably more than Jackie knows," Agnes laughed.

Jackie joined with a chuckle. "You are probably right. I know very little."

Veronique started pinning and conversing in French about the adjustments with Agnes. Jackie rolled her eyes at them.

After the fitting session, Jackie and Agnes went to dinner at a sushi bar. After stuffing themselves with maki and sake, Agnes shoved the bride into a cab and handed the driver an address.

The cabbie drove to a small bar. Agnes with the help of Lonestar had rented out the place for the evening. The Stampedistas had flown in early. So had the female employees from Denver. It was time for the bachelorette party.

The bartender was shirtless except for a tuxedo bowtie collar, like what the Chippendales dancers pose in. Jackie took a closer look. It was Darylton.

Hector Lanza was there as a waiter. He was dressed in the same fashion. Black jeans were skintight. Mark Torres was also part of the wait staff.

Jackie turned to Agnes. Laughing, she said, "I did a pretty good job, didn't I?"

Agnes giggled. "Yes, you did."

Jackie leaned over the bar. Darylton gave her a quick kiss on the lips. "What will it be milady?" he asked.

"I didn't know you had bartending experience."

"Actually, I bartended through college since the soccer scholarships didn't pay for all my fun."

"Well, then, let's see what you can do with a martini. I'll have a cherry chocolate martini." She smacked her lips.

"Right away, Jackie."

As Jackie watched him work, she bobbed her head to the dance music playing in the background. It was not loud. Agnes made sure that it was kept at a level conducive to conversation.

Mark walked over. He placed his large hands around Jackie's waist and lifted her up onto the bar. Jackie was startled at the movement. "The lady of the evening needs to be at the center of attention."

"Thank you, Mark."

Darylton handed her the requested martini. Jackie sipped it. "Oh, Darylton, if you are ever injured, you are so working in the owner's box mixing drinks."

"I'm glad you like it." He turned and set to work preparing other cocktails for the ladies in attendance.

Molly came over. "Agnes put me in charge of festivities tonight. I hope you enjoy the silly party games we came up with."

Jackie rolled her eyes. "I'd rather just get soused and enjoy touching some fine male flesh before I can't enjoy it like a single woman anymore."

"Ah, that's the spirit," said Leah who stood behind Molly. She took a bottle of beer from Darylton's outstretched hand.

Magia came over. "I'm glad, because I've got some fine ass strippers coming in later."

Jackie raised an eyebrow. "And what would you know about strippers, Magia?"

"You'd be surprised, Jackie."

"It's good to see you. It's been too long." Jackie patted a spot next to her on the bar. "Hop up here and let's get caught up. You can give me the dirt on Alexi."

"Oh, I don't know about that." Magia jumped up. "She keeps me too busy for me to hang out with her much. Actually, lately, Alexi has not been in the office much. She looks like she's been putting on weight. I'm sure it's just stress."

"She had been coming out to Denver a lot until recently. I hope she's okay," put in Jackie. "How have Jerzy and you been?"

"Wonderful. We may be getting married next Spring, before the '99 season starts. We are trying to fix a date that his family can work with coming over here. We've decided to get married in the States."

"Wonderful. I'll be there," said the bride.

After about an hour of catching up, Molly announced, "It's time for gifts."

One by one, a gift was brought to the bride.

"A vibrator?" Jackie held up a twelve-inch long penis-shaped latex unit.

"Squeeze its balls," yelled Natasha.

Jackie did so and the object began thrashing with a loud twisting. "Oh my god," she exclaimed.

Natasha added, "It's for those long weeks without Carl when you are in Denver."

"Okay." Jackie squeezed it off and laid it aside. "Next please."

The next few gifts were of lingerie. She was glad. They would get used on the honeymoon, since he had told her not to pack too much. Then the fun began again.

She unwrapped an unusually large box. It was from Sheila. "A swing?"

"Oh, darling, not just any swing. Look closer." Sheila pointed at the box.

Jackie read the cover. "Oh," she said slowly. "Oh, I don't know. Our sex is pretty good as it is."

"Wait a few years and you'll need it for sure," chimed in Leah.

"How long have you been married?"

"Dan and I got hitched when we were 18, so, uh, about ten years. Trust me, you'll need it to keep things interesting."

"Got it." She found herself picturing Leah in a swing hanging from the crossbar of a goal framework.

The next gift was from Molly. Jackie pulled out a pair of police quality handcuffs. "How did you get these?"

"Never you mind that. Just think of the possibilities," quipped Molly.

The ladies laughed.

"Hmm," Jackie began, "I might just want to handcuff Darylton to me tonight."

Darylton sidled to the opposite end of the bar. He shook his head. "I don't like the sound of that."

Jackie gave him a come hither look, emphasizing with her right index finger. Slowly, he made his way closer. She grabbed his shoulders and pulled him closer. Playfully, she kissed his nose and let him go. "Fix me another martini."

"Yes, your highness." He bowed playfully.

The collection of sex toys and lingerie grew. The best one was a partner set of wireless remote controlled butterfly electric pulse stimulators. That one was from the Koneki girls.

"They let you into a sex shop?" Jackie said.

"We had Matt go get it. We told him kind of what we wanted to get you and gave him the money. That's what he came up with," said Księżnicka.

Matt. Wow. Jackie had not given him much thought for a while. The poem he wrote and performed for her at a springtime tailgate popped into her head. How did he know that I wanted to try one of these? She thought to herself. "He did well. Thank you, girls."

After the gifts, they all resumed dancing and drinking and talking. Jackie continued to think about Matt. He knew that he was still dating Róża. She wondered what her life this past summer might have been like if she had not had met Carl.

She hopped down from the bar and grabbed Agnes by the wrist. "Come with me." Jackie led her confidant to the ladies' room. She closed and locked the door.

"What's wrong?" Agnes looked at her friend.

"I think I'm getting cold feet."

"That answer isn't good enough. What's going on in your head right now?" Agnes voice was concerned yet demanding.

"I'm wondering if things would have been different with Matt instead of Carl."

"Of course they would be. From what I've seen of Matt's behavior, he would have dumped you by now. I'm concerned about how close Róża has grown to him. So is Mirek. Matt is bad news. He's too neurotic for you."

"And Carl isn't? With all his painkillers and almost killing himself?"

Agnes wanted to tell Jackie about Carl's indiscretion with Alexi, but she was ethically sworn not to. She thought for a minute before responding. "Carl has his problems, but he is working through them. They were experiential. Matt's, I fear, may be more of a chemical imbalance. That's just based on observation from a distance. The best thing that has happened to Carl was you, Jackie. You can't back out now. You love him and he loves you. If the love wasn't there, the whole Denver thing would have torn you both apart within a matter of weeks."

A tear squirted from the corner of Jackie's right eye. She sniffed and wiped at it. "I know. I do love him."

"You have to continue to be strong. It's been hard on Carl with you being in Denver. But he's handled it quite well. That's how I know that you two are ready for marriage."

"Really?"

"Yes, really. Carl and you are destined to be the strongest, most powerful couple in soccer. You have a partnership that was meant to be. Carl said that he knew you were the one the minute he spotted you in Section 12 and confirmed it when he saw you and invited you to the team party in Axis. He fell in love with you instantly and wholly. This much I can assure you."

Jackie blinked. She felt a little woozy from the martinis and the confusion in her head. She extended her hand to steady herself and caught Agnes' shoulder.

"Sit down for a minute on the toilet there," Agnes advised. Jackie complied. "Jackie, dear, I've seen the way you two look at each other. The electricity and the love between you is the stuff that romance novels are made of. You can't back out. It will destroy you both."

Jackie nodded. "Okay," she said meekly. "I think I'm going to throw up." She got up and turned around. Agnes flipped up the seat and then held her friend's hair back. Jackie tossed up everything sitting on her stomach. "I'm so sorry," she sputtered.

"Oh, stop, you just knocked back four martinis. I'm glad you are throwing up. Keeps the alcohol poisoning away."

"Yeah, whatever."

Ten minutes later, the two ladies emerged from the restroom. Agnes signaled for Mark to get her a tall glass of ice water. Jackie shook herself. "No, I'm cool. No water, get me a beer."

Agnes threw her hands up. Molly came over and patted her on the back. "You're a woman after my own heart," she said.

"Yeesh," Agnes sighed, like a true American.

"The dancers are here," Molly said.

Jackie was led to the center of the bar where a lone chair was placed. She gave a sideways nod of acknowledgment. "Let's get it on."

The music was cued. The lights were dimmed. A spotlight was trained on Jackie in the chair. A red spot was aimed toward the door to the back room. Jackie peered at the end of the red beam with interest. A tall slender man in a business suit emerged. His face was chiseled. He carried an attaché. Under the suit coat was a white button-down shirt was a pocket protector. Jackie cocked her head to the right and focused her left eye with brow raised at the spectacle. What were her friends thinking?

The man strutted and pulled a calculator out of his pocket.

An accountant as a stripper? She thought.

He removed his suit coat and tossed it aside. He strutted around Jackie's chair. Pacing to the beat of the music. He toyed with her hair. Jackie was still not sure what to make of it all.

The red spotlight blinked eleven times, one for each new body emerging from the back room. The disco ball started to turn above Jackie's head. The eleven new bodies were all wearing Stampede uniforms, in full gear. Jackie's curiosity raced. They surrounded the accountant character and ripped his clothes off. "Get away from our woman!" the eleven shouted in unison.

The Stampedistas whooped in delight. Jackie laughed. It all clicked. This was a performance show more than a basic strip tease. The whole show was symbolic of her major life change.

The players signaled for two of the Stampedistas to drag the accountant character to the back. Sturdy Sheila and Molly jumped at the chance.

The eleven players shimmied to the music around the bride. Each one took turns kicking a ball between the chair legs for goals, and then promptly removing their jerseys in celebration. The men were chiseled like the players she knew. Jackie watched their footwork. She knew these guys were not average strippers, but certainly had mad soccer skills. Jackie cursed herself for thinking like a businesswoman at a time when she should be enjoying herself fully.

The eleven disrobed down to nothing but g-strings and their socks and shoes. They gyrated suggestively. One even gave her a lap dance. It was all Jackie could do to keep from taking her own clothes off and fucking the man right there. She may be getting married, but she was not dead.

The show ended. The men put their shorts back on, but kept their shirts off at the request of the ladies.

"Where in the hell did you find these guys?"

"The Starlets, LA's reserve team," replied Magia with a grin larger than life. "What do you think?"

"I liked the show. Not at all what I expected. Thank you."

Mark brought Jackie another beer and Agnes' still insisted upon glass of water. Jackie knew that Agnes was right and she sipped the water before chugging back the beer. The next day would bring on her last hangover as a single woman for sure.

Agnes managed to get Jackie back to the hotel before she passed out. The psychologist tucked her friend into bed. Jackie grabbed the Czech's hand. "Tell me I'm doing the right thing. Tell me Carl will never hurt me."

Agnes swallowed hard. "You are doing the right thing. Carl would never hurt you, not in a million years."

Chapter CIX

FRIDAY, OCTOBER 16, 1998: Lance Merton called an owner's meeting. He wanted to go over the structure of the FLA for the 1999 season, especially with the expansion teams. Every owner was present except for Alexi.

Lance explained her absence, "Alexi was detained in New York. She will be here tomorrow for the wedding and Supporters' Beach Ball."

There was some grumbling about special privileges among the other owners.

Lance pounded the oak conference table with his fist. "Attention, I just want to say a few words to get us started."

A hush fell over the moneyed group of investors.

"We've had a wonderful third year of the FLA. The two new teams have had successful seasons. Philadelphia survived the sudden loss of Coach Bierkov. Chicago is continuing their storied season. Thank you, Carl, for believing in the league enough to invest halfway into a third team."

Carl nodded with a smile.

Lance continued, "We will continue to grow for the 1999 season. The Denver team is up and running with Jackie Harris as the GM. The Houston group is coming along as well. They do not have a coach in place, but we expect to hear news of that as well.

"The expansion from twelve to fourteen teams will dilute the talent pool of each team slightly. We will be having an expansion draft before the regular draft in January. Each team will be able to protect 14 players. The remaining are fair game. A coin flip will decide whether Houston or Denver will have the first pick. Each new team will be able to select up to ten players each. However, they are not required to use all ten.

"The order of picks of the January draft will be determined by a random fishbowl drawing one week before. This is different from last year's off season when we used end of season ranking in reverse order. We're going to try the NBA's style this time and see how things shake out. So yes, Chicago or DC might get a first pick, but equally so might Kansas City or Columbus or the expansion teams.

"A team of schedulers from everyone's teams has been working with the NFL and the NCAA for the shared stadiums, so we can get a lot of dates nailed down as soon as possible. We have learned in the past three seasons that it is easier for our season ticket sales crews to sell the packages when dates are known as soon as possible. Folks have weddings to schedule around fixture lists, we keep being told. We need to have the calendars out to our fans and the press earlier than we have been."

Lots of murmurs of agreement rumbled through the room.

"That being said," Lance went on, "as a group, we need to get more of our own stadiums online sooner. This meeting will go around the room with progress reports on governmental negotiations for stadiums. We'll start with Sugar."

"This coming year, we will be out of Pasadena and into the LA Coliseum. They are offering us a better deal with regards to concessions and control of operations. We are still working on possibilities for a stadium of our own, but for now at least we will not have to share with UCLA in the fall of '99."

Sugar turned his head to Teddy Schakelford. With his trademark Southern drawl, Teddy reported, "I've been going to a lot of town meetings, but our best bet might be the area north of Dallas. The tollway is growing that way and word has it that there will be a city springing out of thin air practically in the next ten years or so. We've got our hopes in this area. With the tollway, it won't be too bad for folks to travel to this area."

The FLA president nodded. "Good work. Let me know how I can help."

"Will do."

"Evan, how are things in Tallahassee?"

"Things are looking good. We've completed an environmental impact study for a site we've acquired. I have an architect working on a rendering of the stadium and surrounding complex. It will be part of an outlet mall development. It's kind of hard for folks to envision what my partners and I have come up with. We will release the rendering as soon as we approve it.

"Miami will continue to play at Lockhart for now. I wish we could do something there. I've floated the idea of putting a stadium on a ship that sails into international waters so we can all gamble, but Lance doesn't seem to like that idea."

Lance clapped. "Wonderful. Clark, how goes it in Columbus and Kansas City?"

Clark Logan cleared his throat. "The stadium on the Ohio state fairgrounds will be ready next season. Barring any weather delays in construction, we won't have to have more than half of the season's home matches at OSU. As for KC, we've extended our lease agreement with Arrowhead. We were able to negotiate better terms, but our hopes are dismal for the immediate future. We are going to have to wait until the local political climate shifts a bit after the next municipal election cycle."

"Wish KC was a more positive report, but we are all glad that your Columbus stadium will be opening next year. Paddy?"

Paddy Kirkhoven, Sr. said, "Foxborough is constructing a new NFL stadium next to the old one. We've tried to get the community to agree to convert the old stadium to a soccer specific stadium—downsizing it by building nice skyboxes and a press box, but they wouldn't hear of it. When the new one is open, the old will be torn down for parking. So we are looking at other options. Land is scarce in New England, as you all know. And when we can get our hands on a good site, it's either cost or environmentally prohibitive."

"Jon, Betty, congratulations on making the final again. How are things with stadium prospects?"

Jon touched his wife's arm. "You go ahead, honey. You are the one who goes to all the city meetings."

Betty smiled. "RFK looks like they will be our home for several seasons to come. We have the same land shortage problem that Paddy has. But the Redskins will be in their new home soon, leaving us with RFK all to ourselves. We've looked at some sites in the Arlington area, but nothing is really in the works right now."

"Thank you, Betty." Lance shuffled through some papers. "Alexi faxed over a report on New York's search. They are in negotiations with several communities, but no solid progress yet. Carl?"

"In Chicago, we are looking for an urban type of locale a la Wrigley Field. Soldier Field will be our 1999 home. Philadelphia," he paused. "We are looking on both the New Jersey and the Penn side of the river. Some developers in Atlantic City have expressed interest in working something out with a hotel and casino complex. In Denver, things are rolling along nicely."

Lance turned to Frank Steele. "Sorry to leave you last. How are things in San Fran?"

"No worries. At least we didn't finish last." He smiled and looked directly at Carl. "You put up a great match last weekend."

Carl chuckled lightly.

Frank continued, "We don't have anything good yet. California is a damn bitch to work with on the environmental requirements, fucking hippies."

"I hear ya," Sugar agreed.

After the reports, Lance just let the owners chat casually. Some paired off to begin player trade negotiations. Sugar pulled Carl aside. "You've got a bachelor party coming to you tonight. We're going to pick you up at your hotel at seven."

Chapter CX

S̲ATURDAY, OCTOBER 17, 1998, WEDDING DAY: Alexi landed her chartered jet at the airport in Long Beach. She did not want to risk any part of the big surprise she was planning. She was alone except for her maid, who was the only one besides her doctor and stylist who knew the truth behind Alexi's recent "weight gain".

She used a limousine service she trusted for their utmost discretion in matters of celebrity privacy. That was a rare trait indeed in Los Angeles. The hotel she booked was nowhere near any of the hoopla of the FLA Cup. She chose a bed-and-breakfast near Venice Beach, where she paid to have all the rooms vacant besides hers. The owners did not mind. They were getting paid to keep the place empty for the weekend. Less work for them, they shrugged, acting like it happened all the time.

The driver was paid for the entire weekend. Alexi provided him a room at the bed and breakfast. The maid also stayed there as well. Three rooms occupied out of the fifteen the couple usually had to clean made for a relaxing few days for a change.

The wedding ceremony was scheduled to start at seven in the evening. Alexi wanted to time her day so that she was arrive just in time to seat herself in the back. She consulted the driver on traffic and routing issues. She was informed not to worry and that if they were early she could hide behind the dark glass until the time was right. They would leave at six-thirty.

Carl was shaking when he woke. He had been with Mirek in a hotel separate from all the Stampedistas, including his own Jacqueline. It made for a rough week. Jackie insisted on keeping 'the not seeing the bride before the ceremony on the wedding day being bad luck' tradition.

Mirek had promised to try and keep Carl clean for the week, excluding the massive amounts of alcohol to be imbibed at the bachelor party of course. He noticed Carl's tremors. "Are you okay?"

"It's not DT's, if that's what you are implying. I'm just nervous about tonight," Carl said defensively.

"Ah, that's natural." Mirek sat next to Carl on the edge of the bed. He placed his hand firmly on his shoulder. "I felt that way the day I married my wife. I think most grooms do."

Carl nodded. "You're probably right, but can I have one little drink to calm my nerves?"

"No, you can't. You need to enter into your new life with Jackie sober and full of raw emotions. Not ones colored by alcohol."

"You're right. Keep me away from the liquor cabinet, Mirek." Carl cracked a smile.

"That's the spirit." Mirek playfully punched his boss in the arm.

Jackie and Agnes awoke early. Veronique wanted to make sure the dresses fit exactly. They would dress at the hotel before getting into the limousine. A makeup artist and hairdresser were scheduled to arrive at 2:00 PM. It was going to be a full day. Jackie was glad that she had Lonestar handling all the ceremonial and reception details.

THE CEREMONY: Guests arrived and were seated. The setting was simple and beautiful. A light breeze blew off the ocean. The waves lapped gently. Gulls circled overhead, squawking.

The bar was off to the side. Every guest was given a complimentary first beer as a souvenir. The bottles' labels commemorated the event and the meeting of the Chicago Stampede and the DC Eagles.

Promptly at seven, the groom and Mirek took their places. The traditional wedding march was played. Agnes walked down the aisle. Paul smiled as he watched his wife perform as matron of honor.

Alexi waited in her hired car. She watched with opera glasses. She wanted to go in when she could slip into a back row undetected. The perfect moment was about to begin.

Jackie began to approach the altar. She felt someone touch her arm. She looked up. It was her father. "Oh my god, I didn't think you'd come. I just sent the invitation out of courtesy."

"I wouldn't miss my daughter's wedding for the world," he replied. "May I give you away?"

"Yes."

Father and daughter continued the procession. Carl beamed. It was his idea to fly out her parents, even though he had not met them. He felt that they would want to be there.

When Alexi slipped quietly into a rear row seat on the groom's side, Jackie was about halfway to the altar. Carl noted the late arrival, but at that distance did not see exactly who it was. It was hard to tell with everyone standing.

Reverend Taylor MacLeod, the Stampede second-string defender, stood in a formal Scottish kilt. He held a Bible and his notes for the ceremony. Jackie was puzzled for a moment. She did not know that any of the Chicago players were ordained. "Who gives this woman's hand in marriage?"

"Her father, Jackson Harris," replied the gray haired man at her side. He looked straight at Carl. "Take good care of her." He patted the groom on the arm, gave Jackie a peck on the cheek and sat down in the first row next to his wife.

"We are gathered here today before God," began Taylor, "to join this man and this woman in holy matrimony."

"Marriage is a sacred institution which should not be entered into lightly," began Taylor. He gave a short platitude regarding the social and religious expectations of marriage. Then he looked out at the congregation and asked, "If there is anyone present who has just cause why these two should not be united in matrimony, speak now or forever hold your peace."

Alexi rose up, revealing her full pregnant form. "I do."

Everyone spun around to face her. She stepped out into the aisle and approached the altar. "Carl Costello is my baby's father." Flashbulbs popped.

Jackie did not know how to react. Her mouth fell agape. Her lips quivered as she spoke, blinking at Carl in disbelief, "You wouldn't; you couldn't."

Carl remained silent.

"The baby was conceived during the Chicago—New York match in May. He did not stay at his hotel that night, Jackie. He was with me."

Jackie felt a jealous rage overtake her. She thrust her bouquet into Agnes' hands. She marched right up to Alexi and slapped her across the face. "How could you?"

Alexi just smiled and patted her tummy. "We'll always have a bond. Carl is the father. He never was and never will be faithful to you."

Jackie spun on her heels to face her groom. "Is this true?" Tears began to form, stinging her eyes.

"I'm sorry." Carl reached out to her. "Can we go talk this out?"

"Fine," spat Jackie. "Agnes, Taylor, please come with us."

Taylor nodded. "Folks, we will have a delay while we work this out. In the meantime, please, feel free to visit the bar to refresh your drinks, but don't touch the cake."

The four followed by Alexi walked about 100 yards from the edge of the canopy. Carl took his bride's hands in his. "Jacqueline, I love you with all my heart. My attraction to Alexi was only a physical indiscretion. It happened only once—"

Alexi interrupted, "No, it didn't. I visited him when you were in Denver."

"Why didn't you tell me you were pregnant?" Carl put in accusatorily.

Alexi smirked. "This was so much more fun."

"What? What do you want from me?" Carl pleaded. "We are already business partners."

"I want all of you."

"You can't have him," Jackie seethed. "You don't know what kind of hell he has been through."

"Oh? And you do?" Alexi countered.

"I do."

"You are like a bad drug that I can't kick, Alexi. Do you know why I got drunk and didn't make the All-Star match?"

She shook her head.

"It was because I was trying to avoid you, you conniving little bitch."

Taylor raised his hands and stepped into the middle of the love triangle. "Let's not resort to name calling." He looked to the sky, asking God silently for guidance. "Jacqueline, the decision is ultimately yours. You will have to deal with Alexi in business, socially and as an extended family member if you marry Carl. Carl has not denied that he is indeed the baby's father. We will assume that to be true." In the background, Agnes nodded. She was glad that Taylor was taking the lead. Taylor continued, "Alexi, it is clear to me that you may never have the special bond that Carl has with Jacqueline. However, you two are to be forever bonded through the child you carry."

Carl added, "Jacqueline, I feel that all is right with the world when I am with you. Every time I have been with Alexi, I have agonized from both guilt and with flashbacks. The physical felt right, but nothing else did. It just confirmed how much more I wanted to be with you."

Agnes spoke, "It's true, Jackie."

"You knew?"

"I wish I didn't have to keep the secret, but I was ethically bound to."

Alexi flinched at the baby kicked. She rubbed the spot.

Jackie bit her lip.

Taylor asked, "Do you still want to marry Carl today?"

She looked Carl in the eyes. There remained the connection that she felt the first night they met at Axis. Slowly, a smile crossed her lips. "I do."

"Good," Taylor clapped his hands once. "Let's go back and finish the ceremony."

Alexi was not sure how the big reveal would turn out. She did not totally expect to have Carl run to her just because she was pregnant. She did see now how much Jackie and he were meant for each other.

She reseated herself. An usher brought her a glass of ginger ale. She wanted to have a sip some wine to take the edge off her despair, but she could not risk her baby's health.

The ceremony continued. Taylor apologized for the delay. Agnes read a short epigram of Martial (Book IV, XIII): "A blessing, O Hymenaeus, be upon this torches! So well does rare cinnamon blend with its own nard; so well Massic wine with Attic combs. Not closer are elms linked to tender vines, nor greater love hath the lotos for the waters, the myrtle for the shore. Fair Concord, rest thou unbroken on that bed, and may Venus be ever kindly to a bond so equal knit! May the wife love her husband when anon he is grey, and she herself, even when she is old, seem not so to her spouse!"

Taylor read a couplet from Robert Burns, in a wonderful Scottish brogue, "'But to see her was to love her. Love but her, and love for ever!'"

"Do you Jacqueline Harris, take Carl Costello, to be your lawfully wedding husband? Do you promise to love, honor, cherish and protect him, forsaking all others and holding only unto him?"

"I do," Jackie said loudly.

Alexi started to cry. Eyeliner and mascara streaking, she ducked out and made her way quickly to the waiting limousine.

Agnes noticed and shook her head.

"Do you, Carl Costello, take Jacqueline Harris to be your lawfully wedded wife? Do you promise to love, honor, cherish and protect her, forsaking all others and holding only unto her?"

"I do," replied Carl.

"Now for the rings."

Agnes handed Jackie the husband's gold band. Mirek handed Carl Jackie's ring.

"Repeat after me, With this ring, I thee wed; all my love, I do thee give."

They repeated the ring vows and exchanged rings.

"By the power vested in me by God and the State of California, I, Reverend Taylor MacLeod, now pronounce you husband and wife. Carl, you may kiss the bride."

Carl's lips fell on Jackie's. The kiss was long and deep. Jackie felt relieved, loved, and happy despite the earlier event. Carl pulled her tight. He never wanted to let her go.

The kiss lasted over two minutes. When they finally separated, Taylor announced, "Ladies and gentlemen, it is my great pleasure to present to you Mr. & Mrs. Carl Costello."

The recessional was played. Before everyone scattered to the bar, Taylor reported, "If you are playing or are otherwise with the teams tomorrow, our curfew is 10:00 PM. The cake will be cut shortly. Everyone is encouraged to eat, drink and be merry, for tomorrow we go to war." Taylor thrust his fist in the air.

"Oh, put a sock in it," yelled an Eagle supporter.

With that, the rest of the evening was a strange combination of fans trash-talking and congratulatory hugs to the Costellos. The booze flowed freely. All of the souvenir bottles of beer were snatched up and quickly drained. Bobby Lonestar exhausted himself coordinating everything. No one seemed to miss Alexi or even notice, except the psychologist, that she had slipped out during the reading of the vows.

Chapter CXI

Sunday, October 18, 1998: FLA CUP: The Rose Bowl is situated in the middle of a golf course and city park. It seems strange to someone not used to it to be parking on a golf course. Usually, the turf is treated like sacred ground that no rubber except that of a lawn mower can touch.

The teams arrived about three hours prior to kickoff. The fans were allowed to begin setting up their tailgate parties at approximately the same time.

All the groups of Section 12 united to form one big party. Carl had a 16' x 20' Chicago city flag that he donated to the cause. It was hoisted up with great pride. The newlyweds eschewed the owner's box party to be with the supporters.

It was a beautiful day. The game was expected to kick off at 2:00 PM local time, plenty of time for a cookout lunch and a good liquoring up before invading the stadium.

Sean recruited a crew to go in early and hang banners. The Koneki girls pitched in, as did some other fans. Carl gave the group sticker passes so they could go in and prepare and then come back out without any consequences.

Jackie showed off her ring to Lawrence. They both admired how it glinted and fractured the sunlight into a lovely rainbow prism. Lawrence told Jackie about his engagement. They had shared the event with no one but Sheila until now. "I'm happy for you," Jackie praised. They hugged. "I'll be at your wedding."

Tomás came in. Maddie set up a folding chaise lounge for him. Tomás had knee surgery and was confined to crutches. He eased himself into webbed aluminum framework. Maddie handed him a Zywiec ale and opened one for herself. Jackie watched the scene. Maddie was tender to the man fifteen years her senior. As she pecked him on the cheek, Jackie saw his expression soften. It was a strange relationship. She never thought Maddie would choose someone like Tomás, especially since the Pole was married. Maybe she didn't care.

Matt and Róża had grown closer. Jackie sensed that he had stopped pining for her, openly at least. She was glad.

Magia and Jerzy announced that they would wed over the winter break. They would tie the knot in Poland so that his family could attend, as well as all the friends and extended family that she had grown up with.

Rumors abounded that Mirek and Gina were getting closer than just coworkers. No one on the team or Mirek's daughters could confirm or deny it.

As game time approached and the alcohol buzz settled over the fan groups, the chanting wars began. The rumble grew and carried into the stadium as they marched en masse. The echoes inside the access tunnels were deafening.

There was a huge inflatable soccer ball in the middle of the pitch. Logoed banners from all the teams in the FLA streamed out from the ball across the grass. Soccer related songs blared over the PA system. The video screen at the end of the bowl played highlights from the season.

The atmosphere grew in color as the fans filed in.

Carlos doubled over. "I think I'm going to be sick."

"It's just nerves," Ian said, trying to calm the lad. "I felt that way last year when I played for LA in the final. They pass once we get the game started."

"I sure hope so," Carlos replied choking back the taste of bile. He shook himself.

The teams entered the battlefield to the FIFA anthem. Side by side, they paraded between two columns of cheering youth teams lined up single file. DeAnya sang the national anthem. Then the lineups were announced.

"Here's your starting lineup for the Western Conference Champions Chicago Stampede: In goal, number 18, Daniel Danzig; defender, number 6, Patrick Mathison; defender, number 3, Vladimir Starkov; defender, number 17, Manny Larsen; midfielder, number 5, Paul Novotny; midfielder, number 10, team captain, Heinrich Baumgartner; midfielder, number 21, Maxwell Harp; midfielder, number 8, Juan Cristobal; midfielder, number 9, Brendan Glazier; forward, number 14, Ian Harris; forward, number 7, Carlos Cortez; and the coach, Mirek Koneki."

Cheers throughout the stadium. The 12-Steppers and Chicago Ultras screamed their appreciation at the top of their collective lungs.

"And now, let's welcome the defending Cup champions and this year's Eastern Conference champions DC Eagles. Goalkeeper, number 1, Brett Hathaway; defender, number 2, Rock Martino; defender, number 3, Michael Parlow; defender, number 4, Fabian; defender, number 5, Isaac Udi; midfielder, number 8, Adam Bakersfield; midfielder, number 10, team captain, Juan Tellum; midfielder, number 13, Thomas Lagerblom; midfielder, number 16, Dion Jackson; forward, number 11, Darin Milano; forward, number 9, Dylan Avila; and coach Marvin Terrelton."

The DC supporters yelled just as loud as the Chicago fans. All the neutral attendees clapped equally for both teams.

DC as the defending champions were the home team. They wore their black uniforms. Chicago was supposed to wear the white, but Carl insisted to Lance and the media broadcasters that they had to wear their red kits. Both shrugged and let it happen. There was no issue of color similarity to worry about.

The whistle for kickoff sounded. "HERE WE GO! HERE WE GO! HERE WE GO!" both sides chanted in near unison. Drums pounded loudly. Flags waved. And the teams battled on the pitch for the ball in the midfield.

Tomás stood up on his crutch next to Mirek. If he was not going to be involved in the game on the grass, he was certainly going to be involved on the sidelines. Meanwhile, his mistress was in the stands with the 12-Steppers.

The first scoring chance came in the 12th minute. Tellum beat Harp to the ball in the air off of Danzig's distribution. The Eagle made a short run cutting to the right slightly then dumped it back to Lagerblom. Novotny intercepted and slowed the Finn down. Lagerblom fed it forward and to the left to Milano who streaked inside the box. Starkov slid in for the tackle just as Milano got a shot off. Danzig was forced to make the save.

Both sides cheered their teams.

As the teams reset, Tomás yelled at Vladimir, "Be careful or you'll get carded."

Vlad nodded. "Ha, you're one to talk," he spat back.

Chicago had a good opportunity a few minutes later. Brendan fed the ball to Carlos who headed it into the crossbar. Hathaway bobbled the rebound. It squirted loose. Ian got to it before Fabian did. Ian took two controlling dribbles then left-footed it past a lunging Hathaway into the back of the net. 17th minute, DC 0—Chicago 1.

Chicago's cheering section unfurled the large banner over their heads.

DC equalized in the 26th minute. Lagerblom took a corner kick and sailed it directly to a leaping Dion Jackson's head. Jackson knocked it downward forcefully under Danzig's armpit for the score.

Starkov swept Avila off his feet just inside the box in the 37th minute. It was a clear yellow card. Avila fell hard and made a meal of it until he saw the card coming out of the referee's pocket. Unfortunately for Chicago, it meant a penalty kick for DC. Juan Tellum lined up for the kick. Danzig committed one way, Juan knocked the ball the other. 38th minute, DC 2—Chicago 1.

The halftime concert was not all that entertaining. The hardcore soccer fans simply headed out through the tunnels to get refills of Budweiser and other drinks. Those who got sodas drank the top off then emptied small airplane bottles of whiskey or rum into the drinks.

As a couple, Carl and Jackie went to the locker room, as was customary for him. Mirek stood outside the door. He was trying to collect his thoughts into something of comprehensible English. He did not like how the course of the match was going. Baumgartner's distribution in the midfield was atrocious. He needed to sub him out, but did not want to waste an early sub. Manny was letting Milano and Jackson too close to goal. He was usually better. But all in all was doing well filling Tomás' shoes.

"Carl, you go yell at them. I can't think straight right now."

Carl placed his hand on his best man's shoulder. "Calm down. It will all come together. Jackie's here." He opened the door and shooed her in.

Crap, out of the frying pan and into the fire, she thought. She drew in a deep breath and stood tall, striding confidently in front of the men.

"Gentlemen," she began with a booming voice, "Mirek is so disappointed in your performance he sent me in first."

Carlos cracked, "*Sí, mamacita.*"

"I'll take that as a compliment," she retorted. "Let's start in the back. Dan, you're distribution is fine. It's up to the midfield to get into the space. Vlad, you did what you had to do when you got the yellow. It was just unfortunate that it was over the line for the PK. Patrick and Manny, you can't let your man get that close. Stick tight, but not to the exclusion of the others who may be attacking. You've got to cover both sides. Moving on, Paul? Where have you been? Get in the game. Heinrich, are you not feeling 100 percent today?"

The German shrugged. "I'm cramping up a little."

Jackie looked around the room. "Byron, go warm up."

Number 15 jumped up and began stretching.

"Maxwell, Juan, don't be afraid to challenge. I know you are usually not. Brendan, Ian, Carlos, keep up the good work. But you've got to get creative. Create space. Marvin had them watch a lot of game tape. That's how they win championships. Let's not let them win a third. Who's going to stop them?"

"We are!" the team yelled.

"Who's going to win?"

"We are!"

Both men had their ears to the door, trying to hear, but it was drowned out by the ruckus from the pop band.

The door opened slowly. Carl and Mirek poked their heads in. Jackie gave her hair a little toss, pushing it back over her shoulders. "Gentlemen," she acknowledged. "Mirek, sub in Jameson for Baumgartner at the start of the second half. Heinrich's just not giving it his all. I'll let you decide who gets the armband."

Mirek nodded. He had no room to argue with her assessment. Jameson was a good sub. He still had two left, just in case. He just hoped the new team "mom" helped.

Mirek confirmed that Bryon was going on. Heinrich pulled off his boots and began to undress for a shower. "I expect you back on the sidelines to cheer on your teammates."

"*Da*," he said gruffly. He removed his jersey.

"When that damn band shuts up, everyone will be ready to go back on the pitch for warm ups," Carl said. "Just get out there and win us a championship, guys."

Carl and Mirek slipped out. Jackie was right behind them. "What did you tell them?" Carl asked.

She shrugged. "Nothing special."

"I don't care what you said; I just hope it works."

"Have faith in your players. They just need a little encouragement. Harris is the only one who has been in this Cup situation before."

"Yeah, and he was on the losing side last season."

"He'll be on the winning one today," Jackie asserted.

The second half kicked off. Most of the fans were back in the stands. Only a few dawdlers were left in line at the beer stands around the stadium.

Jameson officially came on for Baumgartner and immediately made a difference. In the 48th minute, Byron ripped the ball away from Tellum. Harp made the run with him. They passed the ball back and forth between them, weaving through the Eagle blacks. Brendan made space for Ian and Carlos to run into. Still barely in the onside position, Ian took a pass at his feet. He one-timed the orb into the back of the net.

Hathaway screamed at his teammates to wake up. Ian just laughed as he ran in to retrieve the ball. He poked it under his jersey like he was pregnant and jogged toward centerfield. The referee shook his finger at him. Ian tossed him the ball.

Jameson proved to be a major pest for Tellum. Juan got pissed off enough to deliberately deliver a hard elbow to Byron's face during an aerial battle. Byron crumpled clutching his face. The whistle was immediately blown. Blood gushed between Byron's fingers. The referee waved to Chicago's bench for Gina to come on with her crew. Byron was led off the pitch. Tellum received a yellow card in the 69th minute.

Gina set to work with an alum stick and butterfly bandages trying to get the bleeding stopped. Tomás hovered nearby for Mirek, who was keeping his eye on the play.

A man down, Chicago took the direct free kick. The Stampede were determined to take the lead. They pushed DC back. Tellum tackled Maxwell from behind. Max flopped down face first. He came up spitting out a mouthful of sand. "You fucking idiot," he yelled and ran at his tackler.

Tellum stood firm and took the two handed shove from Max. Paul grabbed his teammate and pulled him back. "You don't want to do this. He's out of the game. He's not worth it."

"Damn it." Max continued to try to clear the grit from his mouth. "I feel like I've been eating dirty clams."

The referee issued Tellum his second yellow card caution—thus DC was to play a man down for the remainder of the match. Max for his outburst received a booking for unsportsmanlike conduct.

Gina managed to get Byron patched up enough to stop the bleeding. Bandaged, he was allowed back on the field in the 76th minute. Now, Chicago was up a man.

Carlos scored on a corner kick that Brendan earned. Paul served it perfectly to Sin Brazos' cabeza. 81st minute, DC 2—Chicago 3.

The 12-Steppers went crazy! In contrast, the DC fans were momentarily silenced. They picked up their loud support again when Milano and Avila took the restart kick.

In the 87th minute, Marvin made a decision to pull a defender in favor of a forward. Udi came off; Raul Cardenas replaced him. A three-man attack with one set of fresh legs was served up. DC was not going to roll over. Paul settled back to help the Stampede back line, pushing the lineup to look more like a 4-4-2. DC shifted to a 2-4-3, throwing all their might forward to at least tie the match to send it into golden goal overtime.

In the 90th minute, just before it clicked over to stoppage time, Cardenas scored an unassisted goal. Marvin's move worked. Unless, Chicago could move the ball into the net in the four minutes of ensuing stoppage time, they were looking at overtime.

The whistle tweeted three times, signaling the end of regulation. The game was tied 3-3. But in this match, there had to be a winner. There was no such thing as co-champions. There was to be two fifteen minutes periods of extra time. The team who scored first during this time was the winner—thus the term golden goal. If the score remained tied after the thirty minutes, the game would be decided on penalty kicks.

Mirek bit his lip and looked over his team. They played much better in the second half. He wanted to sub out Starkov, just because he was sitting on a yellow card, but did not want to risk tinkering with the back line. He made no changes. Marvin subbed in Peter Go for Bakersfield at the start of the first overtime period.

On the pitch, Paul gathered his teammates into a huddle. "Let's make this a short overtime. I'm ready for a lager."

"CHI—CA—GO!" the hollered in unison as they broke out into their positions.

The receipt of the first kick was determined by a coin toss. DC won the toss and elected to receive the ball. Cardenas kicked it forward to Avila. The Eagles came at the Stampede forcefully. Danzig was forced to make a spectacular diving catch for a save in the 92nd minute.

He motioned his men downfield. He served the ball with a forceful placement twenty yards past the midfield line. Juan Cristobal won the jump for it. He controlled it before right-footing it to Brendan. The Iceman nutmegged Martino then slipped the ball through two Eagles to Carlos. Carlos faked left and went center, with two steps and a hard left-footed strike. Hathaway got a fingertip on the ball but it was not enough to redirect the ball. *¡GOLAZO DE ORO!*

Carlos did a front flip in celebration. His teammates hoisted him onto their shoulders. They made their way toward their hometown fans. Several Polish fans grabbed Carlos and lifted him into the celebration. Colored smoke bombs swirled around their heads. Silver, red and navy confetti spewed through the air throughout the stadium—shot from league-supplied cannons, loaded at the last moment with paper bits in the correct winning colors.

Carlos bodysurfed through the crowd. He was their hero. He helped win their first piece of hardware. Carlos Cortez would go down in history.

As the DC fans quickly exited to drown their sorrows, Chicago fans stuck around to see the trophy presentation. Jackie accompanied her husband on the stage. She felt a thrill, like the cup was partially hers as well—and not just by marriage. She placed her hands on the gold-plated surface. Next year it would be in Denver. She smiled at the thought. Yes, next year it would be Denver's.

ACKNOWLEDGEMENTS

Thank you, Tim Schulz, for enduring the readings of the early drafts.

Thank you, Peter Wilt, for the early encouragement.

Thank you, Dan Loney, for prodding me to finish every time we chatted online when I should have been writing.

Thank you, Paul & Victor, for letting me have weekends to myself, so I could finish the first volume.

Thank you to all the colorful soccer folks I have met in the past nine years, who have provided me with a plethora of inspiration.

And to you, dear reader, thank you, for buying and reading *Red Tales*.